THE SIX Night TRUCE

HANNAH SHIELD

Copyright © 2023 by Hannah Shield

The Six Night Truce (West Oaks Heroes series)

All rights reserved.

No part of this book may be reproduced in any form or by any electronic or mechanical means, including information storage and retrieval systems, without written permission from the author, except for the use of brief quotations in a book review.

Cover Photography: Michelle Lancaster @lanefotograf

Cover Model: Mitchell Wick

Cover Design: Okay Creations

Published by Diana Road Books

THE SIX Night TRUCE

1

Janie

I stare through my windshield at the courthouse, a monolith of glass and concrete against a steel-blue sky. Wind lashes the fronds of the palm trees on the horizon. My fingers are pink as they squeeze the steering wheel, my knuckles white.

"I am fierce. I am fearless. I am a warrior."

I am sitting alone in my car and muttering to myself.

Yep, it's one of *those* kinds of mornings.

For the hearing I'm about to walk into, I need to be Jane the Panther. The top defense attorney in West Oaks. One of the "Forty Under Forty to Watch" in the last issue of the Southern California Legal Bulletin. That's who my client needs me to be.

I *am* her, most days.

But today, I feel more like Janie the Kitty Cat. I want to curl up against something warm and comforting and lick my wounds.

"I am a damned *warrior*."

I meet my red-rimmed eyes in the rearview mirror and try for a growl, but it comes out more like a dejected meow.

Raindrops begin to splatter on the glass, blurring out my view of the West Oaks County Courthouse.

It's just the rain. I am not wiping my eyes right now.

Please don't call bullshit.

I sigh and grab my travel mug of coffee. I'm just making myself feel more pathetic with this half-assed pep talk.

There are at least a dozen people in that courthouse who want my head, who'll sneer the moment they see me. They probably assume I'm to blame for today's hearing. Perhaps for the dreary weather too.

And I can't wait, because that's exactly what I need. A battle to wage. That's when I'm at my best.

David, my client, is in serious trouble. I'm not the cause, but I'm probably the only person with a chance of fixing it. That's why I returned to West Oaks instead of staying back home in Tucson with Gran. Cherishing our last few days together before...

"Okay," I breathe. "I can do this."

A sip of hot black coffee, a fresh swipe of red lipstick, and ready or not, here I come.

I push open the driver's side door. Moisture dots my legs as I step out. The strap of my leather case drapes over my shoulder, and I move my coffee to my left hand so I can open my umbrella with my right.

This weather is a small blessing, though, because it's keeping the media at bay. I hide my face under the cover of my umbrella and try to blend in with the other people trudging into the courthouse.

But one of the vultures spots me.

"Jane Simon?" a reporter asks as I pass, microphone aiming in my direction. "Did you advise your client to change his plea? Have you been in secret talks with the former governor?"

I dash up the slick steps. Which is a really dumb idea,

because my pencil skirt is so tailored I can't maneuver well, and my sky-high stilettos have zero traction.

Did I mention that I'm off my game today?

I have a split second to curse my lack of foresight as my foot shoots forward and my shoulders tip back.

A hundred bucks says this ends up on the ten o'clock news. The prosecutors will turn it into a GIF and send it around their team chat. An endless loop of Jane Simon pratfalls.

But at the last moment before my seams rip and I'm showing the world my heart-print panties, a thick arm wraps around my waist. I land against a solid, warm wall of muscle. My umbrella goes flying, but nary a drop of coffee escapes the travel lid.

"Careful," a gruff voice says.

Hot breath caresses my cheek. I turn my head and look up into deep brown eyes. Eyes that narrow with a gleam that says, *You're lucky I didn't let you fall*.

And honestly? I'm a little surprised he didn't.

"Morning, detective," I say.

"Morning, counselor." The tightness of his voice keeps me at arm's length, even though his actual arm still cradles me, my back to his chest. My ass is pressed against his thigh. And what a firm, thick thigh it is.

Sean Holt pushes me upright, then bends to grab my umbrella from where it's skittered down a few steps. The reporter has lost interest and is touching up her face powder. The wind has changed, and the marble facade of the building shelters us from the storm.

"Thanks for the help," I say.

Sean collapses my umbrella, spattering us both with tiny droplets.

And then he just *glares*.

A smile traces across my lips. I can feel my claws extending, my sorrow retreating, and *damn* it's a relief. "I said thank you. You could say you're welcome."

"I could."

"Then why don't you?"

He hasn't responded. He's still holding my small umbrella in his fist. His unrelenting gaze moves down my body to my red heels, then back up again to my face.

"Do you have something to say to me, detective?" I see him debating whether or not to answer. And I just can't resist pushing. "Is there a reason you don't like me, apart from my job? Or is that enough on its own."

He inhales slowly before responding. "It's not your job title. It's because you're always making messes for other people to swoop in and clean up."

I bark a laugh. Clearly, Sean has a bee up his butt. And it's not about having to use his muscles just now.

It's about the hearing that starts soon. Where I'll be sitting at the defense table, and Sean will be sitting on the opposite side with the prosecution. Not as a lawyer, but as an advisory witness.

But sure, I'll play along. "Are you implying I slipped on purpose?"

He holds out his hands in a questioning gesture. We're standing in front of the revolving doors, and a stream of people breaks against us and goes around, casting dirty looks.

"I don't understand the things you do. I just know you like attention."

"And whose attention did I want? *Yours*? I saw you behind me—with the eyes in the back of my head—and decided to wipe out on the courthouse steps so you could catch me at the perfect moment?"

"You do have a sense for timing."

"What are you *really* trying to say, detective?"

The Six Night Truce

He shifts his weight as he eyes me. His suit jacket is folded over his arm, his biceps straining the seams of his button-down. Sean's tie hangs loosely from his unbuttoned collar, his hair unruly, like he combed it with his fingers right after he showered and didn't bother to do more.

He steps in closer.

Then he pokes my hip with my umbrella, and I can't help but imagine he's poking me with something else.

Alpha males are not exactly subtle.

"You might have some people fooled," Sean says, all growly and low, "but not me. You love nothing more than chaos."

"You don't even know me."

"I know you have a bigger set of balls than most of the Marines I used to serve with."

My smile grows. Was that a compliment? For little old me? "But are mine bigger than yours?"

"You hoping to inspect for yourself?"

I shrug one padded shoulder of my blazer. "Whip 'em out. Then we'll see who's desperate for attention."

His deadpan expression hasn't budged, but I'd swear there's a tiny flicker of amusement in those dark eyes.

He holds out my umbrella. My hand closes around it, and he tugs back just briefly before letting go.

The guy seems to think I'm some evil super-villain. I have a bit of a reputation, but I would've thought an experienced detective would investigate for himself. Instead, he's hated me on principle since the moment we met a few months ago.

I don't dislike Sean Holt because he's a cop. I can't stand him because he's a raging dick.

I nod toward the entrance and gesture for him to go first. "After you, Detective Holt. Unless you're afraid to turn your back on me?"

He dips one hand into his pocket and walks past me into

the revolving doors. I take the opportunity to ogle his butt in those suit pants. The wool can barely contain him. Too bad those fine, toned cheeks are surrounded by a gigantic asshole.

I smirk at his back.

But then the fizziness of the moment, the joy of the argument, fades. I'm left feeling small and alone, like I did in the car. Like I have since last night when my sister called with the news about Gran.

I'd known that the day would come, but knowing in the abstract is easier than living it, you know? Hearing the words and feeling that gaping emptiness in my heart.

But I have a reputation to uphold. Super-lawyer or super-villain, depending on your perspective.

I straighten my spine and follow Sean into the lobby, where I join the line passing through security. Sean works for the government, so he just flashes his badge and walks through a special entrance, skirting the metal detectors. I assume he doesn't have his gun, but nobody's checking.

As for me? I'm a private attorney, so I have to wait in line with the public and everyone who got called for jury duty today. Arg.

On the other side of security, I see Sean's profile from the corner of my eye and hear his dress shoes pounding the granite beside me. I wonder if he waited for me. But I don't look over.

I won't give him the satisfaction. I have bigger things to worry about today than Sean Holt and his monster-sized ego.

2

Sean

I've never met anyone as heartless as Jane Simon. And trust me—I've met some cold-blooded women in my time.

It's Jane's fault that I'm standing here in the courthouse today. Jane and her machinations, her dirty tactics and games.

I never use the "b" word because my momma raised me up to be a gentleman. But damn, I'm tempted.

My eyes follow her down the hallway. Jane's suit is practically painted on. Her jacket hugs her tiny waist, just like my arm was doing on the courthouse steps. Her skirt cups her round ass like it's taunting me.

Jane's treacherous. And she looks so good while she's being bad.

Nicolas Dominguez strides over to me, taking mincing steps, looking shell-shocked. He's a deputy district attorney, the prosecutor assigned to the hearing today.

"What the hell are we going to do?" Nicolas hisses.

"Can you not lose your shit in a public hallway half an

hour before the courtroom opens?" I mutter. "Take a breath. Stay calm."

Journalists are probably lurking around because this case is getting tons of media coverage. And who knows? Jane Simon probably has spies hanging around, too. Wouldn't put it past her.

Those mile-long legs, made even longer by her five-inch stilettos. All the better to stab me with. She's got dark chestnut hair. Large eyes that might look innocent if she wasn't always glaring.

When she was nestled against me earlier, I got a good whiff of her scent. Like some exotic flower that's poisonous, or maybe carnivorous. Her skin was dewy, not marred by a trace of makeup except that slash of vivid red across her lips.

Red from the blood of whatever innocent creature she last feasted upon.

Okay, I'm not usually so full of dramatic metaphors and comparisons. I was a college boy at the University of Texas for a year before I joined up with the Marines, and I was mostly there for the football, not the English Lit classes.

But that woman burns me the fuck up. And not in the good way.

To answer Nic's question from earlier, I don't have a clue what we can do about it.

Nicolas closes his eyes and starts counting down from ten. While he goes to his Zen place, I check my phone. My mom is taking Henry to the beach today. I wanted to go with them, of course, because today was supposed to be my day off. Until this damned hearing got called.

I text Mom, reminding her not to forget Henry's hat. Or his extra swim diapers. And snacks.

She sends me back an eye-roll emoji.

I know I'm a helicopter dad. But I didn't even meet Henry until about six months ago. I didn't even know he existed.

Before. That's how I think of my old life. The life I lived before everything turned upside down. Before I became a father.

No—I was a father already, even though I had no idea. My "after" started the moment I found out I was Henry's dad. From that first inhale in my new world, I knew I had to get out of LA. Away from my shithole apartment, my sky-high rent, away from the cynicism that had grown over my heart like a toughened skin.

Before I joined West Oaks PD's major crimes unit, I was with the LAPD Gang and Narcotics Division. I saw the worst sides of humanity. And I had to get down in the pit with them.

I wanted my kid to have more. I wanted to *be* more.

West Oaks seemed like a natural choice. Not so far by distance that I had to start over, but without the smog and crowds and relentless push of LA.

West Oaks combines the breathtaking hills of Malibu, the small-town feel of Santa Barbara, and the hip boutiques and restaurants of Santa Monica. Not to mention kickass surfing and soft-sand beaches. People complain about rising crime here, but to me, this place is pretty damn close to paradise. When I moved here, I felt like I could breathe. Like my kid would have the kind of childhood he deserves as he grows.

Or so I thought.

It was supposed to be a quieter, calmer pace of life. Weekend barbecues with my close friends who already live here. Walks to the playground in the clean, salt-scented air. I hadn't planned to be a dad, but once it happened, I was all in. I knew my priorities. Family, not an endless crusade against bad guys.

That was before Jane Simon hit me like a hurricane.

Shitty people are everywhere, I guess. There's no escape. But even in LA, I never met anyone quite like Jane. Makes me wonder what she's got planned next. Wish I could say I'm ready for it. But if anyone's off balance this morning, between the two of us, it's me.

3

Janie

Outside the courtroom, my assistant Tracey is already waiting with her rolling crate of documents and files. She scurries over, forehead etched with concern.

Which means she's heard.

"Your sister texted. Why didn't you tell me, Janie?"

I take another sip of coffee. "I just wanted to get through the hearing."

"But should you? I could call the clerk. See if the judge will postpone."

"That's impossible, Trace. There's no postponing this one."

Tracey frowns. She knows I'm right. "But how are you holding up?" She grabs my free hand in both of hers, and I feel something unclench inside of me. Which is bad, because the tears are threatening again.

Then Sean Holt saunters by, his skeptical eyes snagging on mine, and that makes the well dry right up.

No way in hell will I ever cry in front of that arrogant, uptight prick. I am better than that.

I take a gulp of bitter coffee and squeeze Tracey's hands. "I'm okay. Sad, but I'll get through it." Gran would tell me to buck up. *Lift that chin, girl, and show the world what you're made of.* She never put up with pouting or whining. Not when there was work to be done, and in her book, there was always work to be done.

"Well, I brought you a little something." Tracey picks up a brown paper bag from her crate and holds it out. "Your favorite."

"No way. You didn't."

"I did."

I open the sack. It's a bright pink cookie covered in rainbow frosting and glitter sprinkles. I'm not even sure it can be classified as food, but I don't care. It's delicious and the colors make me smile. Only this one bakery way on the south side of town makes them.

"You are the best," I say.

"No, *you* are. Always taking care of everyone else, including me. You need someone to take care of you."

"Nope, pretty sure I just needed a cookie." I take a bite. The treat is so sugary it makes my teeth ache. I tip my head back and moan. My inner kitty cat is purring.

"I don't know how you can eat that," Tracey says.

"It tastes like blue and pink and purple. And sparkle."

"Those are not flavors."

"But they're good."

Tracey laughs at me fondly. She's around my mother's age, though that one fact is the only thing Tracey has in common with Mom. "It makes you happy, and that's what matters. You deserve it."

"Thank you."

"And you are welcome."

My eyes mist over once more, and then I blink the moisture away. I'm done with that.

There's work to do, Gran's voice says in my memory.

The Six Night Truce

"Have you seen David yet?" I ask, taking another bite of glitter cookie.

My client is out on bail. I tried to get him to come to my office yesterday to meet and discuss what's happening, but he refused. He would barely even speak to me on the phone. I hope he's ready to talk.

"He went straight to an attorney meeting room. He's waiting for you."

We head down the hall, and Tracey pulls her crate behind her.

In the attorney meeting room, David Daily sits at the table, staring down at his hands. He doesn't even raise his eyes when I come in. The guy looks despondent, broken down, and I feel bad about being so caught up in my own sorrow. Before, I was upset about leaving Arizona early because of this crisis in David's case. It meant losing precious moments with Gran that I'll never get back.

But my client needs me. I have to step up.

Tracey closes the door behind us. I slide into the chair across from him, laying my case on the table. "How are you, David?"

"Did you get the check I dropped off? At your office?"

"Um, I assume so. Paying your bill is nowhere near urgent right now." Most of my clients aren't so concerned about my invoices. Maybe it just shows how freaked out David's feeling. He's not thinking straight.

I wish I knew *what* he was thinking. Seems like the media and the prosecution want to blame me for David's sudden change of heart, but I'm as lost as they are.

"Could Tracey grab you a drink? I have half a cookie here. A really good cookie."

"That won't help." He props his elbows on the table, head in his hands.

"David, are you ready to tell me why you're backing out of your plea deal? Why you're refusing to testify?"

No answer. Not the best start.

"The prosecution has filed a motion to withdraw your plea and set an immediate trial date," I explain. "That's why the judge dragged us in today. You're facing decades in prison if the jury finds you guilty, which they probably will. All the documentary evidence is against you. But it's not too late to fix this. We can go tell the judge you still want to testify before the special grand jury. We can salvage your deal."

But David shakes his head. "I can't."

He's charged with the biggest financial fraud scheme West Oaks has ever seen. Thousands of people were cheated out of a combined billion dollars. That's right, billion with a *b*. They all thought they were investing in a revolutionary, offshore tidal-power plant that could supply the electricity for the entire Los Angeles metro.

David handled the accounting books, but a man named Asher Temple was the mastermind. The charming smile behind the entire scheme. When the money vanished, Asher hid behind his family pedigree and blamed the losses on… you guessed it…the accountant.

David. My client.

The West Oaks DA's Office offered David a deal. He'd broken some rules and had known that Asher was misleading investors, and he pled guilty to those lesser offenses. But David never embezzled a cent. The DA needed David's testimony against Asher Temple to prove what really happened. I thought we were set.

But while I was in Arizona with Gran over the weekend, I got the call that David had suddenly changed his mind.

"Did someone threaten you?" I ask. "Was it Nixon Temple or somebody working for him?"

Finally, his eyes raise. "They said they'd kill me."

Behind me, Tracey gasps. Cold races across my skin. *"Who*? Who said that? The Temple family?"

"If I stay quiet, everyone will be safe."

"Tell me who threatened you."

"I've got an insurance policy, okay?" He shakes his head. "I'm hoping you never have to know anything about it."

I can't stand vague hints and riddles. "We need specifics to tell the judge." But David has clammed up again.

I sigh. Damn it. I shove my hands into my hair and grip the roots in frustration.

I'll need to ask the judge for an *ex parte* hearing. That means without the prosecution, without the public. I'll explain about the death threat and that this isn't David's fault. He's only refusing to testify because he's under duress.

Will the judge believe me if David won't open up? I don't know. But I haven't got any other choice.

This day just keeps on getting worse.

4

Sean

I lean against the cold granite wall of the hallway. Mom just texted a picture of Henry wearing adult-sized sunglasses, and I snort. Why is the image of a kid in big glasses so universally funny? I know it's not just me.

"What is it?" Nicolas asks, his voice all panicked.

"Nothing." Jeez, didn't mean to rile the slumbering beast. "It's not long until the hearing. Have you come up with any ideas?"

Nicolas winces, like I'm not helping.

The prosecutors have moved to withdraw David Daily's plea deal, but that's the last thing they want to do. They need Daily to testify. But how to make that happen? Wish I knew.

I handle investigations. Catching bad guys. This negotiation and court filing stuff is supposed to be Nicolas's forte, not mine. I sigh and shift my weight.

Meanwhile, I text my mom to give Henry a hug and a kiss for me. She messages back the "peace" hand sign, the two fingers sticking up. Did she really mean to use the "OK" symbol? I don't know.

I hate emojis. And my mom doesn't fully understand

them. She sends the "mind blown" one far too often. Me being on my way home from work does not blow one's mind.

Once, she randomly sent a peach emoji, and it turned out that Henry was having canned peaches for a snack. She had no idea she was making a butt reference.

I send a heart to her because I'm a good son. My mom moved here to West Oaks to help take care of Henry, so I'd be a real peach if I wasn't grateful, if you know what I mean. My mom's the best.

Texting finished, I tuck my phone into my jacket pocket. "So what's your plan?"

Nicolas's eyes pop open. "Plan?"

"For this hearing." *You fuckwit*, I hold back. I'm pissy today, aren't I? "You need to put pressure on Daily to testify. Put the fear of God into him."

"I...well, I looked at other charges we could add against him if Daily forces us to trial, but—"

"But?"

"I'm not sure yet. Lana's out of town."

Lana Marchetti, the assistant district attorney. By far the smartest person in the office, and she's on her honeymoon right now. The actual DA is too busy politicking to handle sudden hearings. But this shit wasn't supposed to happen.

It was supposed to be Asher Temple in our sights right now, not his fall guy.

I've still got my eye on the closed door where Jane is talking to her client. The door opens, and they both step out, along with Jane's assistant.

Jane doesn't look happy, though. She looks shaken. I wonder what that's about.

"I'm not the lawyer here," I say to Nicolas. In the courtroom today, I'm not even supposed to speak. I'll be there to whisper info about the case to Nicolas. But I can't stick my hand in his back and puppeteer him. "So you'd better think fast and do some research. Call somebody. *Something*. Because in a few minutes, those courtroom doors will unlock, and we'll have to walk inside. You need to have a plan to get the case against Temple back on track. We have one week. Or did you forget that part?"

Nicolas looks green. He's nodding. But I'm all out of trust.

Shit.

Somebody needs to fix this, and it looks like I'm up.

I walk toward Jane. I'm going to corner her and demand some answers.

Then I see who's just arrived wearing a shit-eating grin. Asher Temple himself, flanked by an entourage of lawyers, political hacks, and advisors. No doubt he's here to gloat. There's no other reason for him to show for this hearing.

Only thing that could make it worse? If Asher's father Nixon, the beloved ex-governor, were here.

I scowl at Asher, but he's not looking my way. Instead, the guy is staring at Jane Simon. He nods at her, like it's some kind of signal.

What does that mean?

I storm down the hallway toward her. Jane looks up as I approach, and the indecision in her eyes evaporates as she stares me down.

"We need to talk," I bark.

Her sculpted eyebrow lifts. "Why is that?"

"Because I say so." Not my best response, but I'm frustrated. I was supposed to be at the beach with my kid wearing big sunglasses, dammit. "*Please*," I grind out.

"Fine." Jane's eyes dart to her assistant, who's watching us from the other side of the hallway. David Daily slumps against the wall. Weirdly, he's eating a pink cookie with neon icing like he's the saddest birthday boy in existence.

I can feel Asher Temple's gaze on us. Jane quipped about

having eyes on the back of her head, but I kinda do. It's intuition built up over years in the military and then on the streets of LA. More than one kind of war zone.

There's a tension to this moment that I can't put my finger on. We're players waiting backstage for the curtain to go up. But what's about to happen?

I nod my head at the less-crowded area down the hall. "This way."

I hear Jane's heels click as she follows me. We reach the bend in the hallway, where there's another courtroom and potential jurors are milling around. But here, at the junction between one hall and the next, we have some space. A buffer so we won't be overheard.

I turn around to face her. "If Daily backs out of his deal, the DA's office will come down hard. They'll add more charges. Racketeering, tax evasion. They'll make an example of him, and I'll be the key witness in the prosecution's case. Daily won't see the outside until his hair's gone gray."

Jane tilts her head like she knows I'm bullshitting those new charges. "Anything else?"

"Did you talk Daily into changing his mind, or did you always know Daily would back out?" I fold my arms over my chest. "I guess it doesn't matter. But you know what's clear? Your *real* client is Asher Temple."

It's what we're all thinking. Somebody needs to say it out loud, and it seems nobody else is willing to do it but me. There's nothing I despise more than people who give their word and go back on it. Who lie and steal and *cheat*.

Jane's careful composure slips, and her eyes darken. "You're way off base."

"I saw Temple nod at you."

"And I have control over the motions of his head?" Her lower lip shakes. Some of the red has worn off. "You don't have a clue what's going on."

"Then enlighten me."

"I can't. It's confidential."

"Big fucking surprise."

Over Jane's shoulders, two dozen people stare at us from down the hall. The journalists and the lawyers. Asher Temple, Daily, Jane's assistant and Nicolas.

I'm still focused on Jane, but I'm also monitoring the area. I like to know who's around. Who might pose a threat. Most of the time, it's more caution than necessary. Bordering on paranoia.

But right now, right this second, I sense something's wrong just before it appears in the open. It's like I can see three seconds into the future.

And I don't like where this is going.

There are two guys in suits standing against a wall. They're yards apart from one another. Yet I see a wordless signal pass between them.

Their hands dip into their coats.

"Gun!" I shout.

I grab hold of Jane and bend her over, steering her toward cover.

There's a loud pop. Another. Another.

Screams.

I feel my heartbeat, throbbing in slow motion in my head.

Two active shooters. My morning just went straight to hell.

5

Janie

At first, I have no idea what's happening. Only that Sean Holt is manhandling me. I wonder if his hatred for me has finally boiled over. If he's lost his mind and gone feral.

Then I feel something punch into my shoulder. A strange sting.

I hear the gunshots.

It's like my brain can't process everything at once. Each moment catches up to me like another domino falling.

Sean's arms pushing me forward, his body against my back.

A darkened doorway.

The thunder of feet as people flee.

Screams. So many screams.

A door slams closed, and Sean's warm weight is gone. We're in a dark room. No lights except the long, narrow window in the steel door.

I'm still bent over, and I watch him drag something heavy and slam it against the wall.

My mind catches up.

We're in an attorney meeting room. Not the one I used earlier, but another. Sean has turned the table on its side to barricade the door.

There are no locks on these types of rooms. Anyone could follow us inside. And we can't go out there. We're trapped.

Screams and gunshots echo outside.

"Get down!" Sean falls to his knees, pulling me with him. We're pressed against the wall to one side of the door. I can barely see with the light off, but I feel Sean's heart beating against me. I hear my stuttering gasps as I try to breathe.

Where's Tracey? David? Are they okay?

There's a loud pop, much louder than the others, and something thuds into the opposite wall of the room. Glass smashes. I scream. A roar of static fills my ears.

Sean rolls on top of me, pressing me into the floor. My vertebrae grind into the hard surface.

There's pain in my arm, but it seems detached from me. Like it's happening somewhere else.

I'm not sure how much time passes, but eventually Sean lifts off of me. The white noise in my ears has dulled. He crawls away from me, and I hear a smack. It's still hard to see, but it looks like Sean is smashing his heel into a chair. He breaks off a metal chair leg. Holds it in his fist as he returns to my side.

Light filters through the broken window in the door. I haven't heard any more gunshots. The screams have scattered. But who knows what's going on and what could come next.

"I need to find my assistant Tracey," I say haltingly. My arm throbs. The skin feels hot and cold at the same time. "And David."

"Did you see them? Were they hit?" Sean's voice is a hoarse growl.

"I don't know." It all happened so fast, and Sean was

facing their direction when it started. I wasn't. I didn't see what happened.

Panic seeps into my skin, followed by nausea and dizziness. There's something really wrong with my arm, but I don't want to think about it. I'm struggling to keep my mind focused as it is.

Sean's fist clenches around the chair leg. He gets up and cranes his head as he peers through the window.

"See anything?" I ask.

"Not yet."

"What does that mean?"

"Probably that the shooters are either neutralized or have fled. Maybe West Oaks PD or the sheriff's office is in pursuit. But if the shooters were still here, I'd expect the police or sheriff would've rolled in already."

"They wouldn't wait for SWAT?"

"No, that would cost precious minutes. They wouldn't wait. I'm going to check outside. Stay here."

"Wait." If Sean's going, so am I. "I'm coming with you."

He frowns, but he holds out his hand to help me up. When I reach for it, searing white-hot pain knifes up and down my arm. I bite down on a scream.

"You're bleeding." He kneels, and the chair leg clatters to the floor. "You've been shot."

I look down at my jacket. The black fabric is somehow even blacker. There's a stripe of deep red peeking through just below my shoulder. It looks wet and ragged. I gag as I look at it. I guess that explains what I've been feeling. Or rather, trying to ignore.

Pain and nausea explode again, clawing at my insides. Sean's fingers prod, and I choke back another scream. "How bad is it?"

"The bullet just grazed you. You were lucky." He tugs off his necktie and cinches it around my arm.

Another explosion of pain. I swallow it down. I'm better with something to fight against, and right now, that's the pain. I will *not* let it control me.

"Did you see who it was? The shooter?" I ask.

He nods, still fiddling with the tie. "Two of them. No clue who they were." Sean sits back on his heels, then stands again. "I'm going to call in. Should've done it already." He paces the tiny room and holds his phone to his ear. "Murphy? It's Holt. I'm inside the courthouse. There's—yeah. Two of them. Jane Simon's hurt."

While he speaks, I look for my bag, but I can't find it. I must've dropped it in the hall. My phone and my other belongings are inside. I hardly care about my stuff. But how can I check on Tracey? I know she must be worried about me, and I can't process the thought of her being anything other than safe.

Please, please let her be okay.

My mind continues to play catch up, spinning through possibilities.

Did the shooting have something to do with the hearing? With *me*?

David said someone threatened to kill him.

Was David shot? Could he be *dead*?

Sean drops his phone to his side, cursing under his breath. "I reported our location. West Oaks PD and the sheriff's department are responding. They're going to clear the building one room at a time."

"Can we still go out there? I have to find Tracey and David."

"I've been ordered not to leave this position."

"Can't you break the rules?"

Sean paces. "You're hurt, and I can't leave you here wounded."

I slump against the wall. "Guess we're stuck with each other for the moment."

"Fuck," he barks. "*Fuck.*"

"It's really that bad to spend a few minutes with me?" I'm just giving him a hard time. Trying to lighten the mood. It's not easy to wrap my head around what's happened.

Holy crap. Sean really might have saved my life. I'm about to put on my big-girl panties and thank him—for the second time today—but then he gets back to his usual asshole routine.

"Not everything is about you, *Jane*."

My name has four letters, but he says it like it's a different kind of four-letter word.

Sean punches his thumb into his phone. I hear it ringing. "Mom? It's me. Where are you?" He listens. "There's been an emergency at the courthouse. Yeah, that's probably why you hear the sirens. I'm okay, but I want you to stay off the roads. All right? I have no idea what's going on. Can you get to a restaurant or a store? Away from any windows?"

I can't hear exactly what his mom is saying, but her tone is enough to convey her worry.

"I'm probably being overly cautious," he says, in a softer voice than I thought him capable of. "But I'll feel better if I know you're in a safe place. Can you do that for me? Thanks, Mom. Give Henry—yeah. Love you both."

Sean ends the call, and I avert my eyes like I wasn't listening. As if I could help it. "Where's your mom?"

"North Beach."

Which explains his concern. That's less than a mile away. "Who's Henry?"

His mouth twists like he doesn't want to answer. "My son."

"I didn't know you have a son."

"Why would you?"

Why would you? I repeat in a mocking tone in my head. But I hold my tongue.

Sean and I have several mutual friends. West Oaks is a small town in many ways. No one's mentioned if he has a spouse or kids. But they *have* claimed he's a nice guy. *So* easy to get along with. I've never seen any evidence of that.

Even when he's saving my life, he has to be obnoxious about it.

I've already lost my shoes. I try to find a more comfortable sitting position. No simple feat in this skirt. I wore this suit today because it makes me feel like a million bucks, and I needed the boost. Some fashion statements are worth suffering for. But my suit is ruined, and I'm suffering in too many other ways already.

Like the wound in my arm. And being stuck with Sean Holt.

I've got control of very few things right now. But this skirt? This problem, I can remedy. I struggle up to standing and grasp my side zipper with my good hand.

"What are you doing?" he asks.

The zipper slides down, and I wiggle my hips, trying to get out of the tight garment. But my arm is screaming, and every movement of my body makes the pain worse.

"Help me take this off."

"What? *Why*?"

"Because this skirt wasn't meant for sitting. It was designed for standing at a podium and making my ass look perky."

"Are you wearing anything underneath?"

I cast a sneer over my shoulder. "What do you think?" Does Sean think I'm about to moon him?

Or does he think I'm coming on to him? Seriously? He needs to get over himself.

"Could you just do it? Please?"

Grumbling, he grasps the edges of my skirt in his fists and yanks. The tube of fabric falls to the floor, and I step out of it. I'm wearing stretchy black bike shorts underneath. Technically, these are meant more for sculpting and smoothing than wearing on their own. But they look enough like exercise shorts that I can get away with it.

And I'm wearing a blood-soaked jacket with Sean's tie around my arm like a tourniquet. Fashion has dropped to the bottom of my list of priorities.

I sink back to the ground as another wave of pain spreads from my arm to the rest of me. My eyes water. I don't want to cry, but damn it, I'm not sure how long I can hold out.

I start to shake.

"Are you okay?" he asks.

I look up at him. His light-brown hair is sticking up, and sweat beads at his temples. Blood dots his white shirt. *My* blood. "I'll live."

Sean takes off his suit jacket and lays it over my legs. I feel his body heat lingering in the fabric.

He's standing over me. Staring down. Minutes pass.

Is he going to interrogate me about Asher Temple again? I have no idea why Asher nodded at me. Probably some sort of head game. Asher and I have a history—barely—but I'm not going to discuss that with Sean Holt.

But I continue sitting there, huddled beneath the warmth of his jacket.

"Could you try calling Tracey for me?" I ask.

"You know her number?"

I have it memorized. She's one of the few people I call on an almost daily basis. I rattle off the digits, and Sean hands me the device.

It rings and rings. Her voicemail picks up.

"She's not there." I hold out his phone, trying not to freak out about why she's not answering. She might've dropped her phone as she fled the shooters, like I did.

"Is there anyone else you need to call?" he asks.

"There's no one." I clear my throat. "No one else." I could call my sister, but what's the point? She's in Arizona. This incident could make the national news, but she's not likely to pay attention to headlines. I'll mention it next week when I'm there for Gran's memorial service. Or not at all.

Most of my life is taken up by my clients. But our relationships are transactional. I work for them. A few have become friends, but not close ones. Not the kinds who'd be worrying over me right now, anxiously awaiting my call.

Sean takes the phone and slips it into his pocket. He doesn't call anyone else either. No wives or girlfriends.

He paces a little longer. We start to hear noises coming from the hallway, but nobody has approached our room yet.

I tip my head against the wall and look at the ceiling. I don't want to think about the pain. My arm, Gran, Tracey... None of it.

"You were with LAPD before, right?" I ask.

"Yeah." His response is short. Clipped.

"I was surprised when you moved here. Going from Gang and Narcotics to this sleepy seaside town? Isn't that a step down?"

His jaw tightens. "This is hardly a sleepy town. You just got shot."

Yeah, don't remind me. I'm trying to distract myself.

"And it wasn't a step down. It was...a lateral move."

"Why?" I ask.

"Why what?"

"Why leave LA?"

"Do I need a reason?"

It seems I've struck a nerve. "Fine. Don't tell me."

"I won't."

We both go silent.

"I'm not from West Oaks either, but, whatever. I doubt you care." I'm not even sure why I said that.

He sighs, like he's placating me. "Where are you from?"

I don't want to tell him anymore. Why would I want to give Sean Holt a single real piece of me? "Forget it. It's not important."

"You're right. It's not. What's important is what just happened. Why we're here. Who those shooters were, and why they acted."

My throat goes tight as I wonder who's been shot. Not just grazed, like me.

Then Sean turns around and fixes me with a hard glare. His expression is more ruthless, more hateful, than any he's ever thrown at me. "Did you have any knowledge of this? Any at all?"

"Are you kidding me?" I point at my injured arm. "I got shot!"

"Maybe that gunman wasn't aiming for you. But then I pushed you into a different place, and you got hit accidentally."

"If you suspect me of being in on it, why were you trying to save me at all? Maybe you shouldn't have bothered."

"I'll remember that for next time."

I stand up, dropping his jacket onto the ground. "You know what? I'm done here. You were ordered to stay, but I wasn't." I'd rather have sheriff's deputies shouting at me, guns raised, than listen to these accusations.

But Sean blocks the door. "Do you work for Asher Temple?"

"*Fuck. You.* Let me out."

"Not until you answer me."

"Why should I? You won't believe me anyway." The man won't move, and I'm so pissed off, I can't hold this in. "You want to know what's going on? David told me someone threatened to kill him. *That's* why he backed out of testifying. But I didn't think they'd do it *now*. Today. I didn't think people would be shooting at me and my client and Tracey! After yesterday—after Gran—"

My heart is a runaway horse in my chest. I'm gasping, and I can't get enough air. My body trembles, which only intensifies the pain in my arm.

My knees start to go weak. I stumble backward.

Sean reaches for me.

"Don't you *dare* touch me." I lean against the wall, determined to hold myself up. I force my lips into a smirk. "Wouldn't want you to strain something."

His scowl returns. "Don't worry. I could spend the rest of my life not touching you, and I'd be doing just fine."

Sean turns his back on me, and we both glare at the door. Waiting to be rescued from each other.

6

Sean

Well, now I feel like a real asshole.

She's hurt, and I was yelling at her. Accusing her, once again, of a diabolical plan to force me to save her. As if I didn't swoop in of my own accord.

My mom wouldn't be too impressed. I've earned myself that peach emoji. And maybe the monkey slapping his face with his palm.

But was I wrong about Jane? Is she not the ruthless rhymes-with-witch that I thought?

It's hard to imagine she's faking her distress. If that guy had been working with Jane, it's insane to think he would've recklessly shot in her direction just for show. Bullets from a handgun aren't that precise.

And I didn't see random aggression in that man's eyes when he aimed at us. It was more careful. Deliberate.

So, yeah. I suck. I was upset and keyed up and I spoke too soon. "I'm sorry. I shouldn't have accused you."

Jane's smirk only grows. Her jaw works like she's chewing up my apology and plans to spit it back out.

I hold up my hands in surrender and step away from the door. "You can go if you want. I'm not stopping you."

"I'm not your prisoner?"

"My *prisoner*? Hardly."

Her eye-roll says she was just trying to get a rise out of me.

But she makes no move toward the door. It's possible she isn't feeling well enough to storm out of here at the moment. All the color has drained from Jane's skin. She looks smaller without her shoes and with her suit in ruins. Sadder.

I'm worried that scratch on her arm is worse than I thought. I didn't want to make her lose more blood by inspecting the wound, but it's been years since I had any training in field medicine. Not since I was on patrol. I consider stepping out into the hall and waving down the EMTs. But there could be critically injured people out there. I'm hoping Nicolas, the deputy district attorney I was talking to earlier, isn't one of them.

I have to wait. Follow orders. And fuck, I kinda hate being a good boy and doing what I'm told.

Outside the door, I hear heavy footsteps approaching. Louder voices. Thank goodness. They're clearing our part of the building.

Jane pushes off the wall. Her good arm hugs her middle, and her shoulders are bowed, but her legs are steadier. Maybe she's not the chaos-hungry force of nature I thought she was. But Jane's tough.

I gotta give her respect for that.

∼

THE SHOOTERS GOT AWAY. THAT'S THE FIRST THING I hear when a sheriff's officer escorts Jane and me from the building.

They fucking got away.

But that means the immediate threat has passed, and the investigation has already begun.

Outside, the rain has stopped. Jane doesn't give me a single glance as I walk away, heading for the mobile command center.

I wave to the sergeant on my way. Detective Angela Murphy is outside mobile command, speaking into her phone. I wait a moment, gathering my thoughts. In the background, the sergeant is giving orders to our patrol officers and coordinating our response to the aftermath of the shooting.

A hundred people have been evacuated from the courthouse, and they're huddling in small, scared groups. More are still streaming outside. Judges, jurors, lawyers, court staff. Patrol officers will need to speak with each person, record their ID and info, and separate out key witnesses for a formal statement.

Paramedics are here giving medical attention to whoever needs it. I've already heard an ambulance roaring away.

Meanwhile, our forensics team has shown up to examine the crime scene for evidence. Fingerprints, bullet casings, DNA. Our investigators need to pull video footage and hopefully trace the shooters on their way in and out. I imagine we'll request help from the state authorities to provide extra manpower and lab work.

The security inside the courthouse failed. Big time. A lot of people are going to want answers, and they deserve to get them.

It's a mess out here, and it'll take hours before we know what we're dealing with.

My eye strays to where I last saw Jane. An EMT is bandaging her arm, and her assistant—Tracey—is hugging her.

Glad to see Tracey's okay. I don't know the woman except by sight, but Jane was so worried about her.

I haven't spotted David Daily, though. Or anyone else who was right outside the courtroom where the shooting began. I wonder if there's more I could've done. If I could've disarmed the gunmen somehow. But in my gut, I know I did my best. Jane was right there next to me, and I protected her. I would've done the same for anyone else in my vicinity.

I need to talk to Detective Murphy and find out what's going on.

She gets off the phone, and I pounce. "Murphy? Are you taking lead on this?"

She puts her phone away. "I am. Glad to see you in one piece." She nods her head at the mobile command center. "Let's chat."

We go inside the trailer. It's like a small office, with TV screens on the walls and a conference table. Murphy doesn't bother to sit down.

She's been with West Oaks PD far longer than me, though we have about the same amount of overall experience. Given my work with LAPD, most people might expect me to have seniority here. But the sergeant decides who's in charge for any particular case. Right now, I'm a witness, so I expect that my position in this investigation is already precarious.

If I have to roll over and show my belly, I will. Just so long as I can be involved in this. Whoever those shooters were, whoever put them in place, I want to nail the fuckers.

"Are we in pursuit of the suspects?" I ask.

"They had a getaway car ready. They slipped through our attempts to set up roadblocks. But we're using traffic cameras and tracking the plates."

I curse under my breath.

"You saw it go down?" Murphy asks.

I repeat what I already told her briefly on the phone, but in more detail. The two shooters. The sense I had beforehand that they didn't belong.

She nods as I speak. "How do you think they got the guns inside?"

"Probably had fake government IDs to let them around the metal detectors. Media's going to be all over this." A lot of courthouses use similar protocols.

"No doubt. David Daily was shot in the head and chest."

I close my eyes, clenching my jaw. I wonder if Jane's heard.

"He was rushed to the hospital. I sent an officer along just in case Daily can give a statement, but it's not looking good. Do you think it was Asher Temple behind this? Making sure Daily couldn't testify?"

"That's my guess."

"We have to consider other options, too. What if it wasn't Temple? Who'd want to shoot up the crowd waiting to go into that courtroom?"

My mind draws a blank. "One of the shooters aimed at either Jane or me. It seemed intentional, not random."

"Maybe a disgruntled client?" Murphy suggests. "I'm sure the dragon lady has plenty of those."

I hide my cringe at that description of Jane. It feels over the top now. Maybe even unfair. She got shot—well, grazed—so she's having a bad enough day without the name calling. "Possible. But I've got enemies, too."

"Enemies who'd want to kill both you *and* David Daily?"

I shrug. "I don't know at this point. We need more to go on. When can we question Temple?"

Murphy's expression brightens. "Right away. The asshole is being *very* cooperative. He only wants to help, according to him. I sent him ahead to the station to await a formal interview."

"So he's there waiting for us?"

Murphy nods. "Let me finish up a few things here and check in with the sergeant, and then we can go. I want to get a full interview from Jane Simon as well. I want to see what part she really played in this."

"She's being treated by the paramedics."

"Right, you mentioned she was hurt. How bad?"

"Grazed by a bullet."

"Sounds like karma to me. I'll tell an officer to find her and bring her to the station. Let's get to the bottom of this mess, shall we?"

I couldn't agree more.

∼

I RIDE ALONG WITH MURPHY BACK TO THE station. We each have partners who are junior to us, and they've got tasks to handle. But Murphy and I are the most senior detectives in major crimes. If it's not me leading a case, it's usually her. Which means we don't work together often.

But a shooting at the courthouse is big enough to bring everyone in.

Including the chief of police, who's been peppering us both with pithy text messages. Like, *I want answers*. And, *Why the hell aren't you here yet?*

Oh, so much to look forward to.

While I sit in the passenger seat for the short drive, I text my mom.

Me: I've left the courthouse. You staying put?

Mom: Yes, son. [Smiley face emoji.] We're relaxing at a quiet coffee shop off Ocean Lane. Henry is napping in his stroller. He

The Six Night Truce

got worn out building sandcastles this morning. While wearing his hat and his swim diaper, I promise.

I smile, imagining him playing in the sand. He's just over a year old, so I'm sure my mom was doing most of the sandcastle building. But it's still fun, and I wish I'd been there.

We live close to the station and close to the beach, which means my mom walked his stroller there. I didn't want her walking all the way back when there were active shooters on the loose. Now, it seems the immediate danger has passed, but I still don't like the idea of them hoofing it home.

Me: I'm heading to the station. Need to question some witnesses. But when I can sneak away, I'll get the car and pick you up. Okay?

Mom: No problem. I've got an extra large toffee latte and a brand new novel on my e-reader. Hours of enjoyment ahead of me.

I stifle a groan. My mom likes those romance novels about Navy SEALs and shit. The kind with half-naked men on the covers. Two of my best friends in West Oaks are former Navy SEALS, and I've always been hesitant to introduce them to Mom for that reason. She doesn't have a filter when she speaks. I'm frightened of what she might say. My friends would probably be good sports about being objectified by a grandma, but she's my mom. No thanks.

Me: Good. Thank you for placating me. Text me the address of the coffee shop, and I'll let you know when I'm on my way. Enjoy your novel. [Heart emoji.]

Mom: Oh, I will. [Eggplant emoji.]

Me: That had better be about your dinner plans and nothing else!

Mom: Of course, son. You know I'm clueless about this texting stuff. [Side-eye emoji.]

Ugh. So gross. I put my phone away before my mother can text anything else horrifying.

7

Janie

I'm so relieved when I see Tracey that I almost cry. I ignore the pain in my arm, the questions in my head, and I just hug her.

"Janie, they shot David. They shot him."

I pull back to look at her. Tracey's hazel eyes are usually a bastion of calm. She's the cool waters to my fire. That's why we work so well together. I can be a little intense, and some of my clients need that nurturing hand. Hell, sometimes I do.

Tracey raised two sons to adulthood. She's been married for thirty years. The woman can handle big personalities and soothe even the most hysterical clients.

So seeing the terror in her eyes scares me more than anything I've been through yet this morning.

"You saw David get hit?" I ask.

Tracey nods. "There was blood everywhere." Her gaze has gone distant, hollow. "I saw it all happen. Right in front of me. That guy shot David, and he could've gone after me too. But he didn't. He ran."

Sean said there were two gunmen. Now our suspicions are confirmed. One targeted David, while the other probably went after me. But why? Was it some kind of revenge? Just because I represent David?

"I'm so sorry," I say. "This is awful."

"I'm sorry, too. Just wish I could've done something."

There are people everywhere, and a fearful energy surrounds us. EMTs are moving through the crowd, treating injuries. Patrol officers are trying to manage everyone and write down contact info.

Tracey finally notices the state I'm in. "Oh, Lord. Janie. Are you hurt?"

"I'm okay."

She points at Sean's tie, which is still wrapped around my arm and spotted with dried blood. "You *are* hurt!"

"Just grazed. I'll deal with it later."

Tracey and I are both witnesses, which means we'll need to make a statement. But my first concern is my client and his family. "My phone and bag are still inside. Can I use yours? I need to start making calls." Most of David's loved ones distanced themselves from him after his arrest, including his fiancée Gabriela. But now, he needs them more than ever.

A bit of steadiness returns to Tracey's expression. "No way. First you're getting treated. You can't help David if you haven't seen to yourself."

"Yes, Mom." I roll my eyes, but she's right.

While Tracey hugs my side, a paramedic checks my arm, cleans it, and bandages it up. "You sure you don't want to be transported to the hospital?" the EMT asks me. "I'd recommend that you get checked out and get that gash stitched."

"No, thanks. I'm good for now." I need to get to the hospital to check on David, but I can drive myself. I don't have extra money to blow on ambulance rides. Whoever says criminal defense will get you rich is either lying or representing only the Asher Temples of the world.

Tracey finally lets me use her phone, and I try David's fiancée's number, which Tracey noted in our digital client file. Gabriela doesn't answer, so I leave a voicemail telling her David's been injured and asking her to head to the hospital. I assume the police or the nurses will get in touch with Gabriela as well, since she's probably his emergency contact. But I want to make sure she knows I'm here for whatever she and David need.

Never in my career have I had a client targeted this way. On my watch, when I should've been responsible for him. The moment he told me he'd been threatened this morning, I should've made sure he was protected.

But I just didn't expect it. In the middle of the courthouse, surrounded by detectives and lawyers? With sheriff's officers steps away in the vestibule? The courthouse is my turf. A place I always feel comfortable and in control. But that sense of safety was an illusion.

I want to know how those assholes got guns inside, but I already have some ideas. The sheriff's department is supposed to keep the courthouse secure, but if they'd been doing their jobs this could never have happened.

My eyes scan the sea of faces for Detective Holt, and of course, he's disappeared. But someone else is approaching. A friendly face, despite her patrol uniform.

"Jane! You doing all right?"

Officer Madison Shelborne is jogging toward me with a smile. Believe it or not, I have a few allies at West Oaks PD. Several months back, one of my clients was falsely accused of murder, and Officer Shelborne helped stop the real killer. She's taller than me, willowy, with pale blond hair and striking green eyes. I haven't spent much time with her, but she seems like a woman who doesn't take shit from anyone. Always a quality that I admire.

"I'm hanging in," I say. "This is Tracey, my assistant.

Tracey, this is—you know, I've always heard people call you Shelby, but I've never asked what you prefer."

"Most people on the force call me Shelby, yeah. But at home, I'm Madison."

"Then I'll go with Madison. Because I'm no cop."

She grins and holds out a leather bag. I realize it's mine. "Detective Holt asked me to return this to you. We finished the *in situ* pictures inside the building. I'm sure you're eager to have your stuff back." She glances down at my bare feet. "Holt didn't say you were missing your shoes. I would've grabbed them."

I already got rid of my ruined jacket, which has left me in just my blouse and my black bike shorts. I'd barely even noticed as I walked out that I was barefoot. "I'm sure I'll get them later."

"I left some files in the building, too," Tracey says. I glance at her, and she adds, "Nothing too sensitive."

Madison gets out her phone. "I'll make a note. Somebody will grab them for you. I'm also supposed to bring you both down to the station for a formal interview."

"Holt's request?" My shoulders tighten.

"Murphy's, actually. She's leading the investigation."

I debate internally. Head to the hospital, or the station? Witness interviews are always voluntary. West Oaks PD doesn't determine my priorities or my schedule. I don't jump just because they tell me.

But getting into a pissing match with Detective Murphy over my witness statement is a waste of my time. More importantly? While I'm at the station, I can start demanding answers. Somebody's head is going to roll. I just need to find out whose.

"Fine," I say. "Are you driving?" I assume that all the roads around the courthouse have been blocked off to non-emergency vehicles.

Madison nods. "I bet I've got some sneakers in my gym bag. Size eight and half?"

"Close enough. I'd appreciate it." Maybe she has a spare sweatshirt, too. I'm practically in my underwear.

The three of us weave through the crowd toward the parking lot.

"And maybe we can grab some food?" Tracey suggests. "Jane's injured, and all she's eaten today is half a cookie that was more artificial coloring than anything else."

I roll my eyes, even though she's right. I am a bit woozy.

We reach Madison's squad car, and she digs out a worn pair of Nikes for me. I sigh as my feet sink into them. "These feel amazing." The stilettos make me taller and boost my confidence when I need it. But comfortable? Ha.

Madison laughs. "They're all yours."

She offers me a hoodie with *West Oaks Police* emblazoned on the front. I decline. I'll just have to let my attitude make up for my lack of wardrobe at the moment.

We stop at a drive-through, and I get chicken nuggets. Tracey complains that I should eat something resembling real food, but I'll think about vitamins and minerals on a less stressful day. Tracey's eating a granola bar she had stashed in her purse, in typical mom fashion.

I've come a long way from my lackluster mood this morning, though. I can almost feel Gran at my shoulder, cheering me on. *Go get 'em, Janie. Give 'em hell.*

By the time we cover the short distance to the West Oaks PD headquarters—no more than a mile—my batteries are recharged and I'm ready for battle. The parking lot for the station is overrun, and news vans line the curb in front of the building. Madison's given me a hair tie, which I've used to wind my hair into a neat bun.

"We should have a couple witness interview rooms open,"

Madison says. "I'll check in with Detective Murphy. She texted me that she and Holt are already here."

Inside, the hallways are surprisingly subdued. I guess most of the available patrol officers and detectives are still at the scene. But there's a hum in the air here. Intense focus, adrenaline. The murmur of voices.

Then there's a familiar voice. Not a welcome one.

Asher Temple is standing outside Chief of Police Alex Liu's office. The two of them look serious as they converse, but there's a level of informality between them that I don't like.

Asher is around my age—mid-thirties. He's the kind of handsome that only the truly wealthy can achieve. Every inch of him is polished to a sheen, like he's never seen a day of hard work in his life. Shiny cufflinks. Patek Philippe watch. Impeccable white teeth. From everything David told me, I assume Asher didn't even work all that hard at cheating his investors. He just grinned and did whatever he wanted and the world bent to his will.

The guy couldn't be more different from his father. Nixon Temple was governor of California until he'd served all the terms he could. Before that, he was a military hero and self-made multi-millionaire. Nixon is just as handsome as his son, but far more rugged. He's a man who's lived life. Who's overcome obstacles and won. Who wouldn't admire that? Hell, I voted for him more than once. The citizens of California still clamor for Nixon Temple to run for President—despite the unfortunate first name—but he's an Independent, and he claims to have fulfilled any and all political ambitions. Now he's a winemaker up in Sonoma.

And he's also been pulling a lot of strings in his son's defense. Even so far as pressuring the West Oaks District Attorney not to prosecute, which is why the DA tasked a special grand jury with considering the charges. Chief Liu hasn't caved to Nixon's influence, but I have to wonder if he's more sympathetic to the Temples than I realized.

The chief is savvy. He's trying to play both sides in the name of "fairness." Funny how Chief Liu is only concerned about fairness when the defendant is mega-connected and rich.

"Asher Temple," I say, striding toward him and the police chief. "It was you, wasn't it? Do you honestly think you can try to murder the key witness against you and get away with it?"

"Jane. Feisty as ever, I see. So relieved you're all right." He looks me up and down, smirking at my sneakers and the remains of my outfit. "But you sound like a prosecutor. Did you switch sides on me?"

I turn my glare on the chief. "Liu, why isn't he in cuffs?"

The chief frowns and stays quiet. He's usually the strong, silent type unless he's in a press conference with the mayor.

"You're accusing me of hiring thugs to shoot David?" Asher glances at my bandaged arm. "Did you forget I was standing right there outside the courtroom? I could've been hit. I was running for my life just like you were."

A door opens down the hall, and Sean Holt leans out, watching the exchange with curiosity. I try to ignore him.

"Perfect alibi," I say.

Asher's smile is patronizing. "David's made a lot of enemies. He stole money from innocent people, without my knowledge, and I guess some of them decided to take matters into their own hands. I'm sorry you got caught up in it."

I tilt my head. "Did you know you clench your butt cheeks when you lie? It's one of your tells. Your hips do this little popping thing. It's cute."

Down the hall, Sean snickers silently. He's enjoying the show.

"That's enough, Ms. Simon," Chief Liu says. "If you're

here to provide a witness interview, get on with it. If not, I don't believe your presence is needed."

Madison and Tracey are both lingering a few steps back. Madison clears her throat. "This way, Ms. Simon." She's trying not to smile.

"Thank you, officer," I say primly.

Sean doesn't say a word as I pass by on my way to the witness room. But when our eyes lock, he *winks*.

I flip him off behind my back, and this time, his laughter fills the hall.

8

Sean

Today is turning out to be unexpected in all sorts of ways. And I'm not even talking about the active shooter situation.

Jane actually has a decent sense of humor. I enjoy her snark a lot more when I'm not the one she's pissed at. From Chief Liu's expression, though, he doesn't appreciate my burst of laughter as Jane passes by.

I get back to work.

Detective Murphy handles Asher Temple's interview, and I hover, playing the grumpy cop in the corner. Meanwhile, Shelby and another patrol officer handle Jane and Tracey's witness interviews. I text Shelby, asking her to offer them a ride home or wherever. Given the mess at the courthouse, it might not be easy to get their cars out until later.

I also check in with the officers at the hospital, who are eagerly awaiting a statement from David Daily. But he's apparently in surgery and not doing well. I hope the guy pulls through. Partly because I'm not a complete ass, and partly because we could really use some info about that death threat Daily got. And, you know, his testimony against Asher Temple.

I'm with Jane. I think Asher is our most likely culprit for arranging the shooting. It's also possible his father Nixon played a role. It won't be easy to prove. Men like the Temples know how to cover their tracks.

Priority number one for this investigation is tracking down the shooters. Once we find them, the rest of the answers will follow.

We work through the lunch hour. But my angelically patient mother is still chilling at that coffee shop, and she's getting antsy.

Mom: Henry woke up from his nap, has eaten all his snacks, done fifty laps around the table, and looks five minutes shy of a meltdown. And the Navy SEAL in my romance novel got his HEA. If you don't pick us up soon, I'm walking home.

I almost ask what an "HEA" is, but instead I tell Murphy I'm taking a break. "Bring back tacos," she says, barely glancing up from her desk.

"Fish or carne asada?"

Her nose wrinkles. "Al pastor."

I grumble. I don't think pineapple belongs in savory food, but I realize that debate has already been lost. Doesn't mean I'm eating it, though.

I've already changed out of my court shoes. My tie was last seen wrapped around Jane's bloody arm, and my suit jacket needs to visit the dry cleaner. The storm clouds from earlier have all cleared and the sun's out, so I strip off my button-down and go out in my undershirt.

I usually walk to work because I live so close. But I need to get my car to pick up Mom and Henry—with shooters still on the loose, I want them encased in steel before going in the open—so I jog toward home.

My mom and I went in together on a tiny, Mid-century house that's a twenty-minute walk from the beach. It's just outside that ring of ultra-pricey real estate that borders Ocean Lane, but it's not quite to the freeway.

Some people might scoff at a man in his thirties needing his mom's help to buy a house. But Mom's widowed and I'm single, and we both wanted a nice place for Henry.

In many ways, my mom is my best friend. I think she gets me. She knows I can be sociable and easy-going a lot of the time, but I can get testy and short-tempered when the world pisses me off. Mom knows when to push me, and when to back away and leave me alone. And I know when to do the same for her.

All in all, it's working for us so far.

I can't exactly bring women home. My mom has assured me she wouldn't mind, but I can't think of anything that would kill a boner faster than knowing my mom's in the next room with her romance novels and their naked-torso covers. The excitement of sneaking a girl into my room under my parents' noses diminished once I graduated high school.

Besides, sex that doesn't test the structural quality of the bed and get the dogs of the neighborhood howling? Sounds kinda boring to me. I don't like holding back.

I could spend a night out here and there if I wanted. But the truth is, I don't want. I got burned enough by Henry's mom. LA dating is the tenth circle of hell, and if the West Oaks singles scene is half that bad, count me out. I'm taking a breather and focusing on my son. When I start dating again, I'd like to spend my time and energy on a woman who values me enough to be honest.

I reach my street and walk down the block. The rain

earlier has left a sheen over the world, and the asphalt is a darker gray.

Most of my neighbors are professionals, so things are quiet here during the day. That's one of the things that attracted me and Mom to this house. Speed bumps to slow down cars. Porches where people sit out in the evenings to have a margarita or mojito.

Sunlight glitters off of the roof of my truck. I jog up the sidewalk toward my driveway, bouncing my keys in my palm.

Then that intuition hits me again. My senses are already heightened from the shooting earlier. And this is my home. I've only lived here a few months, but I've come to know everything about this place. The way the curtains fall in the windows. Even how our shoeprints disturb the dust on the sidewalk.

Something's off. I slow as I approach my driveway and run my eyes over the scene.

There it is. A shadow moving across one of the windows.

Someone's inside my house.

I run and crouch behind a bougainvillea bush. My hand dips to my lower back, pulling my Glock from its holster.

The shadow inside moves from the kitchen to the back of the building.

Fury burns in my throat. I send a quick text to Murphy. *Intruders at my home address. Send backup.*

Keeping low, I dash toward the house and press myself against the white siding. Through a crack in Henry's curtains, I see a man tearing through the room. Pulling baby bottles out of the dresser, scattering lotion and powder from the changing table.

What. The. Fuck.

He doesn't stay there long. Instead he moves on. I think he must've gone into my room or my mother's, both of which are at the rear part of the house off a long hallway.

I creep toward the backyard, hiding behind the fence that borders the driveway. The hinges on the back door squeak as someone steps out. I've been meaning to fix that, but I just haven't gotten around to it. Keeping my gun ready, I watch the man through the thin cracks in the fence. Then I hear voices.

"Did you find it?"

"No, man. Nothing."

Shit. There are two of them. Another two-man team. Like the shooters at the courthouse. Different faces, though.

And these guys aren't wearing suits. Instead, they're dressed in the typical uniform of LA gangbangers of all shapes, sizes, and colors. Oversized T-shirts, low-slung pants. Ideal for concealing weapons.

And then I see the tattoos that run along the insides of their arms.

Cold sweat inches down my back. I know exactly who these people are. Not their individual names, but their loyalty.

The Serpents.

They're a motorcycle club from the edge of the LA suburbs, wannabe gangsters who pretend to be as tough as the hardened men of LA's roughest neighborhoods.

But even pretenders can do a hell of a lot of damage when they're waving guns around. What are they doing here in West Oaks? At *my house*?

They're whispering to each other, heads bent. They sound frustrated. Tense. They were hoping to find something here. Could explain why they'd toss a baby's room, aside from just being psychopaths.

Soundlessly, I moved toward the gate. I lift the latch. The gate is new, just installed before we bought the place. So this metal doesn't creak. It doesn't give me away.

I throw open the gate and burst through, my gun raised. "West Oaks PD. On the ground!"

The one on the left goes instantly for the gun in his waistband. Dumb idea, but hey, he's choosing his own adventure. I fire. The round hits his lower leg, and he goes down, losing his grip on his weapon.

The other decides he's better off running.

I have to spend a few seconds taking the gun from the asshole bleeding and crying on the grass. Then, I take off after the runner. He's already over the fence.

I shove my gun into its holster, the spare into my pocket, and vault over behind him.

This guy has the more elaborate tattoos, snakes crawling around both wrists, which indicates he's the senior member. Could explain why he chose to run, which I'd say is the smarter choice. But more work for me.

I chase him through a neighbor's yard. I hear screams and shout at the residents to get back inside. The asshole spins and fires off two rounds at me. There's far more chance of him hitting some innocent person inside a house than me, the intended target. Or who knows, maybe he's just trying to slow me down. But the reckless cruelty, the casual indifference, fires up my blood.

With a burst of speed, I leap at the guy just as his legs tangle up in a lawn chair. I slam into his back. We both come down hard on a concrete patio. Pool toys and a kid's collection of plastic ponies surround us. He's struggling and bucking beneath me, but I wrench the gun away from him and pin his arms behind his back.

I grab my cuffs and snap them onto the asshole's wrists, right where the snakes are sticking out their forked tongues.

His nose must've slammed hard into the concrete, because there's blood spraying as he bellows, "Police brutality!"

I struggle up to standing, catching my breath. I'm going to be sore tomorrow, but I probably could skip my workout this evening. I'm trying to look on the bright side.

"You fucking pig! You're gonna be sorry for this!"

"You have the right to remain silent, and I suggest you use it. Because I'm sick of hearing your voice."

9

Janie

Madison drives Tracey and me to the hospital. I'm coming down from the adrenaline rush of this morning. Exhaustion creeps in. I rest my forehead against my hand and look out the window as palm trees and brightly painted buildings crawl past.

When we reach the hospital, I try to get info on David's condition. But I'm not family, and the place is already flooded with people. No one else was shot at the courthouse, but several people were injured in the panic. The nurses shut me out. David's fiancée Gabriela isn't here, and when I try calling her again, she still doesn't answer.

But I'm pleased to find two more West Oaks PD officers here who're going to keep an eye on David and make sure he's safe. Apparently, it was Detective Holt who made that request, just like he asked Madison to drive me around. This must be a twisted new tactic of his. Sean's being nice because he can tell it annoys me.

While I'm at the hospital, I figure I might as well get my arm stitched. It takes a couple of hours, but eventually, I'm sewn up and freshly bandaged. The wound looks ugly and it hurts, but they throw antibiotics and Ibuprofen at me and say I'll be fine.

I've done all I can here, and Tracey's husband has already made the drive across town to pick her up. I accept Madison's offer to drive me to my office. I'm just going to let my car stay at the courthouse until tomorrow. Right now, I feel an adrenaline crash looming, and I need something else to focus on. Either David's case, or another one of my clients.

There's work to do, Gran would say. There's always work to do.

Madison's upbeat on the way. I don't think I've ever seen her in a bad mood.

"What happened with the detective exams?" I ask. "Last I heard, you were gearing up for them."

Madison's smile slips. "They went okay. But not well enough. It was my first try, so now I know what to expect."

"You'll get there. We need more detectives like you."

She side-eyes me. "You mean, detectives who don't hate you?"

"It is one of your more endearing characteristics."

She chuckles. "Unfortunately, you got Detective Holt instead. I know you're not a fan."

"What do you think of him?" I'm fishing for gossip, but most of my job is negotiation and strategy. I'm always angling for info.

That's my only interest in Sean, of course. Strategy. Nothing else.

"Detective Holt is a great guy."

I groan. "Don't get diplomatic on me now."

"It's true. I like him. He's easy to work with. Professional. Conscientious. And funny, too."

"I don't know why people keep saying that. Around me he's the grumpiest grump who ever grumped."

"That's just around you. Ask Chase, and he'll tell you the same thing. Everybody at the station likes Holt."

Chase Collins is my other ally within West Oaks PD. His wife is my former client who was wrongly charged with murder, and Chase is one of those people who's nice to just about everyone. Even me. Madison's cheerful, but she's also more sarcastic.

I can tell I'm not going to get anything juicier from her. Madison might like me, but she's loyal. And she probably sees through my thinly veiled attempt to dig for info.

"The problem," Madison goes on, "is that you love antagonizing your opponents. Which is fine. You do you. Obviously, it makes you a great advocate, and if I'm ever on the wrong side of the law, you're the first person I'd call. Well, after the union rep anyway. But you can't exactly get mad when Holt takes the bait you're dangling."

I smirk. But my humor vanishes when I think about David. Nothing about this is funny.

My clients' struggles become mine while I represent them. Their worries burrow beneath my skin. When I add that to my grief over losing Gran yesterday, it's enough to make me lightheaded.

Sometimes, I wish I had someone waiting for me at home, someone I could share these moments of doubt with. My past boyfriends couldn't handle how intense I can be. I have a softer side too, but I guess those guys wanted a girl who's easier, and I was more than happy to cut them loose before they beat me to it. My friends know and love who I really am, and that's enough for me.

Madison pulls into the parking lot of my office. It's in the more commercial and industrial part of West Oaks, where strip malls and auto body shops dominate. But my office is in a cute, converted home, with a welcoming porch and flowers planted in window boxes. I like for my clients to feel relaxed here.

That's how I feel too, the moment Madison puts the gear into park. A full-body exhale.

I pick up my bag, which is nestled between my feet. "Thanks again," I say, "for everything. You made this day a lot easier."

"Happy I could help. I know you'd do the same for me."

"Anytime. Just ask."

"Let me know if anything else comes up. I'll try to find out what's going on with David from the officers at the hospital. If there are updates, I'll pass them on."

I thank her once again, then push out of the passenger door. The knotted tension in my shoulders unwinds the closer I get to my office.

But that sense of relief doesn't last long.

As I'm about to put my key in the lock, I notice scratches on the metal that weren't there before. And the latch isn't lining up quite right.

The door's open.

I spin and run, waving my arms as Madison's cruiser drives toward the exit. I see red as her brake lights flare. She stops the car and gets out.

"What is it?"

"Someone broke in. I saw scratches on the lock plate. I didn't go inside."

Madison's hand rests on the butt of her gun as she eyes the building.

As far as I can tell, there's nothing else out of place. I can't see any lights on inside, but it's daytime and the curtains are drawn across the front windows.

"Do you have an alarm?" Madison asks.

"No. Margins are tight enough already." And it's not like I keep many valuables inside. Most of my client files are kept digitally. I can't imagine who would want to get into my office.

Madison uses the radio attached to her uniform to request back up. She jogs toward the entrance of the building. "I'll take a look. Back up should be here in just a few minutes."

She tries to wave me off, but I stay at her heels. This office is *mine*. I worked my ass off to build this practice, even as I'm still paying off my law school loans. This building is more a home to me than my apartment, which is less than a mile away and bare bones compared to the care I've put into my office space. Sometimes I even sleep on the couch in the back here. The bathroom has a shower and all my favorite toiletries, and I can't count the number of times I've freshened up for court after an all-nighter of trial prep.

While Madison checks the perimeter of the building, I mount the porch steps again and try to see through the cracks in the curtains.

The view makes my chest seize.

Chairs are toppled over in the waiting area, picture frames smashed on the floor. Tracey's desk at the front has been ransacked. Office supplies and papers are scattered.

What on earth happened here? Why would someone do this?

Did they take our hard drives? Our computers? Everything's password protected, but there's a ton of client info on the cloud and my backup drives. Most passwords can be circumvented with enough effort.

Does Asher Temple have something to do with this? Did he want my files on David?

Then my blood heats as my imagination runs. I can think of someone else who might stoop to this. Without David's testimony, their case against Asher is falling apart as it is.

West Oaks PD and the DA's office might've gotten

desperate enough to cross the line. But that would mean Madison…

No. She's my friend. I need to slow down and figure out what's going on. I'm not like Sean Holt, jumping to the worst conclusions without seeing the evidence first.

"See anything?" Madison asks.

"Someone trashed my office."

"That sucks. I'm sorry. Backup will be here soon, and we'll investigate this, I promise."

I know Madison means it, but she's not in charge. I don't expect West Oaks PD to take this seriously. Either because they hate me or because of darker reasons. I don't know what to think.

"I need to find out what's missing." I head for the door again. I don't want to disrupt fingerprints or other evidence, so I use my elbow to gently push on the door. Slowly, it swings inward.

The mess inside is more upsetting, more real without the window glass in between. More visceral. Whoever did this violated my space, my clients' privacy. Violated *me*.

The door is only open partway when it meets resistance. "There's something behind it. It's stuck." I push harder, and then a bunch of things happen in quick succession.

Madison shouts. Her arms close around me.

The door swings.

Madison launches us backward away from the door.

And an explosion, even louder than the gunshots at the courthouse, rends the air.

10

Sean

"Hey, Holt?" Officer Chase Collins says. "You should take a look at this."

I'm in my backyard. My partner and another detective are photographing the scene. The paramedics have just left with the Serpent I shot in the leg. The other perp is in the back of a squad car, cooling his heels before we take him to the station for interrogation and booking. He's got gauze stuffed up his bleeding nose.

My house is a disaster. I poked my head inside after my backup arrived and they issued the all-clear. Nearly lost my breakfast seeing the full extent of the mess inside.

My mom's a tough woman. She was in the Navy and wrangled three hell-raising sons, including me. But in her retirement, she moved out here to California to help me, and this is how I thank her? Bringing this shit home from work?

I want to know what two LA gangbangers were doing at my house. No way is this random. It has something to do with *me*.

But first, I need to see what Collins has for me.

Holding my breath, I go in the back door and walk down

the hallway toward the front of the house. Collins is studying something with tension in his posture.

"Over here," he says.

My eyes bounce over the living room. At the stuffing torn from the couch. Food from my fridge splattered on the walls. My mom's collection of porcelain figurines, smashed into the carpet. I hated those little figures, but it breaks my heart to see them destroyed.

"Where am I supposed to be looking?" I ask.

"Front door." But Collins bars an arm in front of me before I can walk forward. "It's a bomb, Holt. Don't go any closer."

"The *fuck*?" Finally, I see what should've been obvious, if I wasn't so distracted by the wreckage of my home.

There's a small explosive device duct-taped to the door. Wires run along the top of the jam.

I've seen things like this plenty of times. It's a rudimentary pipe bomb. Who knows what's inside of it. Maybe homemade plastic explosive, with some screws and bolts tucked in like a nightmarish piñata.

If I'd gone in the house that way, the wires would've pulled and the friction would've triggered a fuse, in turn setting off the device. It wouldn't have enough punch to do a fraction of the damage already wrought to my home's interior. But if I'd been standing right there? It probably would've shredded me.

Or Mom. Or Henry.

If Mom had decided to head home before me… If she'd been holding him in her arms as she opened the door…

I suppress a wave of nausea. Blinding rage follows.

What. The fuck. Is going on.

"Do you think this is related to what went down at the courthouse?" Until this statement, Collins has been quiet, letting my mind take in what could've happened.

"No clue. But I'm going to find out. Have you called the bomb squad?"

"Yep. They're on the way."

We turn around and retreat to the back of the house. "You've had more than your share of excitement today," Collins says.

"And now you're here. Didn't want to keep all the fun to myself."

"And you thought West Oaks was going to be a change of pace." He shakes his head.

"Guess I brought some LA along with me when I moved."

And I mean that literally. The Serpents aren't supposed to be active this far west of Los Angeles.

We step outside, avoiding the tape that's blocked off certain parts of the yard. One of my colleagues is kneeling to snap a pic of the bloodstained grass. I squint into the sun.

"Want me to head back to the station?" Collins asks. "I could get started on paperwork for you."

I exhale. "Jeez, would you? I'll owe you."

"I know you want to see your mom and Henry. That's the priority right now, not writing up the discharge of your weapon. Anybody's going to see that was a clean shoot."

Chase Collins is a good guy, a family man. He's a fellow Marine. He's on patrol with major crimes, but I met him before I joined West Oaks PD, too. I got involved in a case where Chase and his wife were witnesses.

I know Chase would do anything for his wife and daughter, and his sympathetic expression tells me he understands what I'm feeling.

Earlier, when Collins and the rest of my backup arrived, I arranged for a squad car to pick up Mom and Henry at the coffee shop. They're back at the station waiting for me. I didn't take a full inhale until I had word they were safe.

Now, I need to go see to them.

"Yeah," I say. "I need to break the news to Mom about her Precious Moments collection."

Chase looks confused. I don't explain. He's a Californian, so maybe he doesn't have a frame of reference. Nobody can fit more little knick-knacks and priceless "collectibles" into their home than a Texan momma. At least, not in my experience.

He claps a hand on my shoulder. "You need anything else, like a place to stay, I've got you. We have plenty of baby stuff for Henry. Haley has so many toys she won't notice if a few go missing."

The offer warms me with gratitude. "I need to see what's going on before I decide anything. But thanks."

My phone rings. It's Detective Murphy calling. She's back at headquarters, busy with the courthouse shooting. I wonder what she needs.

I answer the call, praying that some other disaster hasn't struck. "Hey, Murphy. Sorry lunch is delayed. Funny thing happened on the way to the taco truck."

She already knows about the attack at my house. But she doesn't laugh at my joke or throw one back.

"Holt, there was an incident at Jane Simon's law office. I need you back here. Now."

˜

Whenever a case gets really hairy, I like to sit down at my desk and make lists.

Things I know.

Things I need to follow up on.

Witnesses I've talked to, and what they've said.

People I still need to reach.

Physical evidence and leads to explore.

All the stuff that's happened today? It's coming at me so

fast, I don't have time to sit down in a bathroom stall, much less visit my desk and put pen to paper.

When I reach the station, I can't even spare a moment to find Mom and Henry before Jane Simon's demanding voice booms from down the hall.

"I want to know what you're going to do about this!"

I stride toward the sound. Jane is facing off against Detective Murphy. Jane's shirt and her arm bandage are covered in dirt. Her hair's an unruly halo. And she has a wild fury in her eyes I've never seen before. Like all her smoothness and polish have been worn away, revealing the unguarded woman beneath.

Maybe yesterday, I would've smirked at seeing her so fazed. But right now, I don't feel an ounce of satisfaction.

For one, I don't look much better. My undershirt has my sweat and another man's blood on it. There's a rip in the knee of my pants, the nice ones I save for court.

Two? This is the second time today I've seen the hints that Jane is human. Maybe I'm a soft touch, but I don't want to see anyone scared and hurting. Especially a woman. Guess I'm old-fashioned like that.

Murphy, at least, is as cool as ever. "Any theories about who went after you?"

"*Theories*? Oh, I have theories. Either it was Asher Temple—who you've already let go on his merry way, I hear—or it was someone from this department."

"That's a serious accusation."

"I know it's serious. Believe me. As serious as having a bomb go off at my office and nearly kill me!"

I heard about the explosion. Who else is betting it was a pipe bomb affixed to the building's front door?

A dozen officers are watching Jane's meltdown. I heard Madison Shelborne was with her when the explosion happened, but I don't see Shelby anywhere. Instead, it's guys from patrol who seem to be enjoying this. And some people wearing CHP uniforms. California Highway Patrol. Murphy requested reinforcements from the state to help us handle the crisis at the courthouse.

Jane finally notices me. Her eyes narrow, taking in the new stains and tears in my clothes. "And here's Holt. Where have *you* been?"

"Getting shot at. Again."

Her mouth is already open to fling more anger at me, but I see the moment my words reach her brain. Jane's eyes widen. Her long eyelashes flare. "What?"

I walk toward her, grab her elbow, and steer her toward a witness room. "We need to talk."

Jane stumbles after me. She doesn't have much choice with me holding onto her. "Weren't we talking already?"

"In private."

We go inside the room. I shut the door. The witness interview spaces aren't like interrogation rooms. There are comfy leather chairs, a coffee table. Gentle lighting.

Jane frowns at my hand, which is still on her arm. "Could you let me go, please?"

Her voice simmers with a warning. I release her. We start speaking at the same time.

"What happened at your office?"

"Who shot at you?"

We both pause. Her scowl commands me to answer first.

"I got home and two assholes were there. They'd broken in. Pulled guns when they saw me." I'm paraphrasing, but close enough.

Jane's hand flies to her mouth. "Is your son okay? Your mom?"

I'm surprised for a moment. Then I remember I mentioned them at the courthouse. It's...nice of her to ask. "They weren't at the house. I was going home for my car so I could pick them up." I shake my head, trying to focus. She doesn't need every small detail.

"Where are they now?" she asks.

"Here. The station."

"And they're all right?"

"I assume so. I haven't had the chance to check on them."

"Then you should…" She waves a hand at the door. I see concern in her face, but her eyes shutter and her mouth presses together. "Go ahead and do what you need to do. You're the one who insisted we talk."

"Because we need to. My mom and Henry can wait a little longer. Your door was wired with an explosive?"

"I assume so. All I know is that Officer Shelborne drove me to my office, and when I got there, I thought someone had broken in."

"Why?"

"Marks on the lock plate. I could see through the curtain that the lobby had been trashed."

Like my house. Shit. "And then?"

"I tried to open the door. There was resistance, and I pushed. Somehow, Officer Shelborne realized what was going on. She said something about seeing a wire hanging down? She pulled me away just before the bomb exploded." Jane shrugs, holding her arms around her middle. "I think she saved my life. Second cop to do that today."

Her eyes flick over to mine, then away.

"Shelby's a good officer," I say. "I'm glad she was there."

Jane's mouth twists. "She had more injuries than me. Some deep scratches from pieces of the bomb. She's at the hospital. I didn't know if I should stay with her, or come here and demand some answers."

It's clear which one she chose. "What about your residence? Did it get tossed as well?"

"No. The officers who responded to Officer Shelborne's

call checked on that. My apartment's just a few blocks from my office, but it was untouched. Like they knew I didn't spend that much time there. Which I don't."

Figures that Jane is a workaholic who lives at the office. Before Henry, that was me.

But I wonder if the assholes behind this plot have been watching us. If they figured out Jane would be easier to target at her office than at home. Or if they had another reason.

She blows out a heavy sigh. "I just want to know why this is happening. The courthouse, my office. The bombs. What's this about?"

"That's what I want to know, too. My house was turned inside out. All my stuff, my family's stuff, trashed. And there was a pipe bomb attached to my door. Just like at your office."

Her eyebrows arch.

"Whoever set those bombs, they didn't care who else might get hurt. It could've been my mom who was killed. Or your assistant Tracey or even your office cleaning crew. These people don't care about collateral damage. They're desperate, and they're not going to stop."

"What do they want? Is it tied to the courthouse?"

"Has to be. I think someone's trying to kill us."

She snorts. "Yeah. No shit, detective." Jane turns away from me, starting to pace. I rest a hand on her arm to stop her.

"No. Think about this. Someone's trying to kill *us*. You and me. Why?"

"If it's Asher Temple, he has reason enough to hate us both. And don't forget, David got shot too. The key potential witness against Asher."

"Sure, but a guy like Asher doesn't arrange brazen hits against all the people who annoy him. There's got to be a deeper reason."

Jane's gaze turns inward. She's thinking. Damn, she's intense when she thinks. Like a four-star general planning an offensive campaign. I can see why most of the prosecutors piss their pants having to go against her. I've never seen someone with such a single-minded focus.

I need her on my side. The two of us, working together instead of constantly battling. I'll bet she's got info I need locked inside her head, and there's no way we can figure this out otherwise.

But I don't know if she'll agree to a ceasefire. I guess that depends on how much she hates me. And whether she hates the people targeting us more.

"They ripped apart my house and your office. I overheard them say they were looking for something. But they didn't find it."

She nods, tapping her chin with a finger. "Was it something that we'd both have? Or different things?"

"Any ideas?"

"A few, but I need to puzzle it out more. What about you? Don't *you* have ideas? Aren't you the investigator?"

"That's what I'm doing. Investigating."

"My mistake." Jane rolls her eyes.

"We could work together. Share what we know."

"A truce? Is that what you're proposing?"

"Sure. A truce. An alliance. Whatever you want to call it. People are trying to kill us. If we band together, we have a better shot at figuring out why."

She studies me, arms crossed. "I don't know yet if I can trust you."

"What a coincidence. Not sure I can trust you, either."

"Then how will this possibly work?"

I chew the inside of my lip. One of us has to back off first, and I guess it's gonna be me. Best way to cut through the bullshit. "Let's start with an exchange of information. I share something, then you share."

"Okay. I'll bite. What other clues have you found, detective? Anything that'll help us figure out who's doing this, and why?"

I know a little more about the who. Those two gangbangers at my house were members of the Serpents. I need to wait on the forensics report, but I'm guessing their fingerprints will turn up at Jane's office as well.

Does Jane have any connections to the LA Serpents?

I'm about to ask, but Murphy barges in. There's a couple of guys in suits behind her. The first is older, with dark slicked-back hair and an arrogant expression.

"Holt, this is Agent Nathan Winfrey. And—"

The second is younger, blond, more subdued, but equally polished. I already know his name. "Agent Josh Hartford," I finish for her.

Hartford is a CBI agent. I've worked with him in the past when I was with LAPD Gang and Narcotics. He seemed all right, but I'm reserving judgment. I want to see what he and this other agent are doing here.

Murphy's eyes flick to Jane. "Agents Winfrey and Hartford need to speak with Ms. Simon."

Jane and I exchange a glance. Neither of us is happy about this development, though maybe for different reasons. "Why is that?" I ask. "Did we request CBI's help with this matter?"

Winfrey visibly puffs up, taking up space like this is his station, not ours. "You've made it clear you can't handle this yourselves. And I hear a connection to LA organized crime has come up?"

"Organized crime?" Jane asks. "What are you talking about?"

No one answers her. Winfrey stares me down. Hartford is

less aggressive in his stance, but lifts his chin like he's sending me a message. *Back down, Holt. You can't win this one.*

CBI, the California Bureau of Investigation, can step in to support local law enforcement on certain complex cases. But this doesn't feel like the typical friendly offer of help. Winfrey's pulling rank like some puffed-up Fed in a cheesy crime thriller.

Hartford is a solid agent, and I've had drinks with him more than once. He's younger than me, ambitious. From a family of political donors, probably angling to run for a state senate seat in not too long. He wasn't partnered with Winfrey before, and I wonder if this is a promotion for Hartford.

Why's CBI so interested in taking over this investigation?

I put myself between Winfrey and Jane. "I think Detective Murphy will agree with me when I say we *can* handle it. That's what we've been doing all day. And what we'll continue to do. If we need extra help, we can let you know."

Winfrey's smile is apologetic, but his eyes glitter with something sharper. "That's not possible, Detective Holt. CBI is in charge of this investigation now. You and Ms. Simon are going into protective custody. I'm afraid it's out of your hands."

11

Janie

This CBI suit can't just order us into protective custody. I know my rights.

So why am I marching into a suburban hotel halfway to Los Angeles right now?

Well...some extra protection seems like a good idea at the moment. Considering the day I'm having. The day that's still not over. I swear it's been twenty hours at least, yet there's still blue in the sky.

I think there's some kind of time warp going on. A strange bending of space-time that's keeping the sun from setting. Maybe the gods are playing a joke on me.

Which would explain why I'm checking into a hotel with Sean Holt beside me.

I'm wearing fresh clothes, provided by Madison from her locker at the station. Sweats with *West Oaks PD* stamped all over them. Yes, folks, this is what I've been reduced to. A walking advertisement for the police. The pants pool at my ankles.

Sean has changed into jeans and a windbreaker, which is zipped up to his neck. He has no right to look that effortlessly handsome when his day's been as bad as mine. He's all long legs, towering over me. Earlier this morning, I stood eye-to-eye with him in my stilettos. I don't like the fact that I have to look up to him now.

The front desk attendant is ready with our keys. "You're on the third floor," the guy says to Sean, who has already passed over his badge and some paperwork. "You'll be in rooms 304 and 305. They're adjoining, as requested."

I lean my elbow on the counter. "I'm sorry, what? Why do we have adjoining rooms?" I frown at Sean, wondering if he's behind it.

Is this part of his "truce" idea? Forcing me to work with him?

But Sean mirrors my posture, leaning forward. "That seems unnecessary."

"Just doing what I'm told."

We both grumble. "I guess it's more defensible," Sean says under his breath. "They can get us together in one room under guard without going into the hall."

Sean drove his mom and baby son here in his personal vehicle, while I had to ride along with California Highway Patrol. I was all by my lonesome behind the grate, texting with Tracey. But I couldn't tell her any specifics about where I was going.

On my way here, the charm of West Oaks disappeared quickly, replaced by rolling suburban concrete and big box stores. This hotel is corporate, nondescript. New enough that it's still nice. But don't worry, taxpayers, there's no trace of luxury. Not that I mind. I saw a diner beside the hotel that looked inviting, and my stomach is complaining about my lack of dinner.

I glance around the lobby, holding my bag to my side. A CHP officer frowns at me from the sliding entrance doors. Sean's mother and baby are playing on a couch over by the breakfast area. She looks over and smiles wearily at me. I wave.

Does Mrs. Holt know who I am? Has Sean told her about my evil, defense-attorney ways?

I'm about to go introduce myself when Sean pushes back from the counter with a sigh. He grabs his duffle from the floor. "Let's head up." He's announced it loudly, like that statement equally applies to me and his mom.

Um, who put him in charge?

But I don't argue. Instead, I join the small crowd converging on the elevators. Sean, his family, plus two police officers with big bellies and even larger mustaches. They belong to the suburban jurisdiction we're in right now. The CHP handed me off.

"I'll take the stairs," I say quietly.

One of the officers groans and throws an annoyed glance at the others. I head for the doorway to the stairwell. His footsteps thud into the carpet as he follows me. I jog up to the third floor, and the man is huffing and puffing.

I beat everyone to my room, wave the keycard, and slip inside.

The door shuts. My back hits it, and I slide down to the floor, my bag resting in my lap.

What a mess. What an utter, complete mess.

I don't even know how long I'm supposed to stay here. How will I keep up with my other clients' cases? I don't have my laptop. I'm not sure if my laptop is currently in one piece.

I could crawl under the covers of the bed, turn on the Hallmark Channel, and binge watch some feel-good movies. I could pretend my life hasn't capsized within the space of a single twenty-four-hour period.

It's tempting.

Instead, I force myself up to standing, carry my bag to the

bathroom, and undress. The small room soon fills with the patter of water against tile. Steam clings to the mirror.

Ten minutes later, I switch off the faucet, feeling slightly more like myself. At least I'm clean.

Earlier, a West Oaks PD officer—I missed her name—went by my apartment and packed some things for me. I open my bag and find athleisure, jeans, tops, even a suit. And several pairs of shoes and all my toiletries from my bathroom drawer. She even packed fresh bandages and antibiotic ointment for me, too. I'll have to find out her name and thank her.

First, I see to the stitched-up wound in my arm, replacing the sodden bandage with a fresh one. I pop some Ibuprofen and swallow the pills, chasing them with tap water from the sink.

I dress in stonewash jeans, a tank top, and an oversized sweater that immediately slips down my uninjured shoulder. My fingers twist my damp hair into a clip.

Now that I'm cleaned up, I dump my bag on the floor and sit on the bed with my phone.

Tracey picks up on the first ring. "Are you at the hotel?"

I settle against the pillows and close my eyes. "Yeah. What about you?"

"Arrived at my cousin's. She's already complaining about how hard it is to cook for us in her tiny kitchen. Which is code for, *Order Chinese takeout, Trace, and don't skimp on the dumplings*. Ralph is hiding in the guestroom watching classic football games on cable."

A smile sneaks across my face, brightening my mood even more than the shower. Tracey's husband doesn't get along with her cousin. But I was worried someone would come after Tracey like they did me. I asked her to stay away from her house for a few days until we could be sure the threat was over.

The Six Night Truce

"Order all the dumplings you want. Put it on your business card, because it's on me. I'm so sorry about this."

"Janie, this is not your fault. You're the one who's in real danger."

"I'll be fine."

"Are you sure? Maybe you should head back to Arizona. You're due there in a week anyway, right? For the memorial service? Wouldn't it be safer to get out of town?"

Maybe. But running back to Arizona isn't going to solve any of my problems. That'll just mean wallowing in my sorrow over Gran's death even more.

And David is here in Southern California. Madison's last text said he's out of surgery and under heavy sedation. He's still in critical condition. As far as I know, none of his family has shown at the hospital. I'm not going to abandon him.

"There are officers guarding the hallway, more outside the hotel. And I've got Detective Holt right next door. I'm surrounded."

"Surrounded in enemy territory, you mean." Tracey laughs, and I laugh with her.

"Insert quote about the enemy of my enemy, or strange bedfellows..." I wave my hand at the empty room. "Take your pick. I'll be able to practice my witty comebacks to their verbal jabs."

"Like you need practice." She exhales, and her joking tone softens. "Janie, you've been through a lot between yesterday and today. I just hate to think of you alone there. Call me if you need to talk? Or call your sister?"

"I promise, Tracey, I'm okay. Order your takeout. I need you fed and energized tomorrow, because you'll be running my office from your cousin's guestroom." I'll need her to inform my clients that I'm away, reschedule upcoming filing deadlines—ugh, it's a mess.

"Don't worry, I'll handle things. Take care of yourself."

"I always do." I end the call and stare at the ceiling.

The truth is, I've been alone for a long time. Alone is safer. It's what I'm used to.

∽

My mind drifts for a while, grasping for answers to so many questions.

Then I hear a bubbly baby-laugh coming from next door. Followed by a knock. I jump up to answer the door connecting my room to Sean's.

The moment I open it, a bowling ball on wobbly legs charges through.

Sean's mother smiles at me from the doorway. "We've got too much energy to be contained in one hotel room, I'm afraid."

"I don't mind." I glance over her shoulder, but I don't see Sean.

"My son is taking a phone call in the hallway. I'm Liza Holt."

I take her offered hand. "Jane Simon."

"Of course. I've heard of you."

"Don't believe everything you hear."

She laughs. "I've heard you're whip-smart, formidable in the courtroom, and you keep my son and the rest of West Oaks PD on their toes. I'm inclined to believe all that."

Liza has a soft Texan drawl. Her curly gray hair falls around her shoulders, and she has Sean's brown eyes. Only, hers are warm and disarming instead of flinty.

Then she rushes past me, heading for the nightstand, where the baby is pulling at the cord for the lamp. "No, Henry. None of that, little man. That's not for you." Liza lifts the baby into her arms and taps his nose with her fingertip. "All my boys were little hellions, just like this one.

And his daddy was the worst of the lot. The youngest and wildest."

"You mean Sean?"

"Who else? A thorn in my side, that one. I worried more over him than the rest of them combined." She's speaking to me, but she hasn't taken her eyes from her grandson, who is smiling and laughing at the silly faces she's making. "But my youngest grew up to make me proud."

I'm not sure what to make of this new information about Sean. But everybody's mother has nice things to say about them. Except mine, maybe, but she hardly counts.

The baby squirms until Liza sets him down. Then he's off again, running through the room. He finds my bag and starts yanking clothes out.

"Oh, I'm sorry," Liza says, rushing over.

"It's okay, let him. I don't care. If it keeps him occupied, right?"

She sighs. "This one's going to be a handful, bless his heart."

Sean said his mom and son weren't at the house when it was invaded, but I still feel I should ask. "Were you all right today? I know Sean was concerned."

Liza shrugged. "Oh, we were fine. I was trying to avoid that subject for the time being. Wasn't sure if you'd had enough of it." She nods at my bandage, though it's not visible beneath my sweater except as a bump under the fabric. "Sean told me you were injured."

"It wasn't too bad. Probably would've been much worse if Sean didn't pull me out of the way."

"As he should, given all the government training he's had. I'd hope it was good for something. But I was in the Navy myself, and I know good intentions don't always lead to results."

Henry is now playing with the buttons on the air conditioner, which I can't imagine will cause too much damage. Liza seems to be keeping one eye on him, even as she strides over to me. "But would you mind if I take a look? I was a nurse in Vietnam. Some skills never get rusty. I'd feel better if I knew they patched you up right."

I take off my sweater and show her my bandaged arm. She checks it carefully and prods the skin around the wound. "Any pain?"

"Not much."

She eyes me skeptically.

"I'm taking over-the-counter painkillers. I can handle it. A little pain never stopped me."

She nods, an approving smile inching up the corners of her mouth.

Henry's getting aggressive with the air conditioner, so we head into the other room, where she sets him down in front of a pile of toys. "The other officers and detectives brought things for Henry, since our home is currently a crime scene. He loves all these new things to play with. Which, of course, keeps him busy for about five minutes at a time."

I sit on the edge of one of the queen beds. We both watch Henry play. It's like meditation. Hearing his laugh and seeing his smiles keeps me in this moment, away from the mazes that my brain was running through earlier.

But Liza doesn't stay quiet for long. "Tell me about yourself, Jane Simon. We're neighbors, at least temporarily, and that's one step away from friends. Might as well make it official."

"Call me Janie." I don't even know I'm going to say it until I do. "That's what my friends call me." My closest friends, which aren't that many in number. "I'm from Tucson originally. I went to law school in LA, moved to West Oaks to join the public defender's office, and then branched out on my own so I could choose my own clients and set my own caseload. That's pretty much it."

"Significant other? Children? Family?"

I clear my throat. "I have an older sister. She's married, one kiddo." *I had Gran,* I say silently, *but she's gone. Mom might as well be.*

Liza is watching me like she heard the parts I left out.

"What about you?" I ask. "How long have you lived in West Oaks?"

"Not long at all. California's not my cup of joe, to be honest. I did my time in Oakland in the Navy—Treasure Island—then went home to Texas and married my high school sweetheart. Raised three boys with him in West Houston. He passed a few years ago. Heart attack."

"I'm sorry."

"Me too. But I was enjoying my retirement and my older grandkids until I was called to duty once again." Liza nods at Henry, who is dragging a toy train by a string across the floor. "Moved here to help out with Henry. And I'm loving every second of it."

I'm curious about Henry's mother. Is she around? Was she Sean's wife? A one-night stand?

But I don't ask. Those seem like questions for Sean, not his mother. And I can't imagine Sean would have any interest in telling me. I might be fast friends with Liza, but her son? Not so much.

"I try to visit everyone back in Houston as often as possible," Liza adds, "but I suppose I'm a Californian now. What we do for our children."

"Sean's lucky to have you."

"And we're *all* lucky to have Henry." Liza reaches down to tickle him. Their smiles and giggles are contagious.

12

Sean

As soon as mom and Henry are settled in the room, I go out into the hall to call Murphy.

The local officers are stationed at each end of the third floor. We're the only rooms occupied. Whoever set this up probably spent a while calling around to find a hotel that could accommodate us. But this place isn't exactly the Beverly Hilton.

I get some small satisfaction when I find Murphy is just as pissed off as I am about CBI's takeover of our case.

"How did they find out so fast about the Serpents connection?" I ask.

"I informed the joint task force on organized crime the moment you told me. I had no idea CBI would react the way they did."

I curse, but this makes sense. The joint task force has representatives from multiple jurisdictions. People from the local, state, and federal levels. It's meant to facilitate investigations that impact more than just one area. But we haven't seen anything like this from CBI before, including when I was with LAPD.

"Do you think they have some ulterior motive here?" I ask Murphy.

"That's hard for me to imagine. They haven't shut me out of the investigation. Just you, because you're a witness and in danger. But I'll keep you updated on everything I learn. As long as you do the same for me?"

I'm glad she knows I won't stay out of it. Saves me the trouble of informing her. "Of course. Did Agents Winfrey or Hartford mention if they got anything else useful from Jane when they spoke?"

"During their interview? Winfrey bitched and moaned about how uncooperative Jane was. Hartford agreed, but he wasn't the one asking the questions. Privately, Hartford said it might've gone better if Winfrey had tried a different tactic."

That doesn't surprise me. I fight back a smile. "Winfrey should've known better than to come in with so much attitude."

"Almost sounds like you're defending her."

"I'm just starting to know her better, that's all. I think maybe Jane's easier to work with if you show her some honey instead of just vinegar. Sounds like Agent Hartford might agree."

Murphy snorts. "I'll leave that strategy to you. I'm pretty sure Jane is ornery no matter what. She's got only one mode, and that's attack."

"I guess we'll see." I promise to let Murphy know if I learn anything useful from Jane while we're stuck in close proximity. After getting a few more updates, we hang up.

I see a voicemail from Nicolas, the prosecutor assigned to the Daily case, and I return his call.

Where Murphy's anger was low and steady, Nicolas is panicked. "Did you hear? They're taking over the case. I mean, what the hell?"

"Yeah, CBI is throwing their weight around."

"Not just them. The attorney general's office sent state prosecutors to demand our files. Not just the Daily case, but the special grand jury for Asher Temple. They're taking *all* of it."

"That stings," I say, "considering all the work our offices have already put in. But without Daily's testimony, I don't see where we can go as far as the special grand jury is concerned. Not with so little time left."

Nicolas groans. "One week." He says it like a lament. And I know exactly how he feels.

"Yeah. One week. And the key witness is still unconscious at the hospital. Murphy said he might never wake up."

A miracle could happen. David might come to, having changed his mind about testifying. Or we might find some new piece of evidence against Asher at the last minute.

Barring that? When it comes to holding Asher Temple accountable for the money he's stolen, it's hard to see how there's any hope left.

∽

PICTURE THIS.

West Oaks PD and the district attorney's office work their asses off investigating the massive fraud that Asher Temple carried out. Our people interview dozens of distraught citizens. We spend months of late nights poring over documents.

This goes on for a year and a half.

Then the lead detective in charge leaves West Oaks, and I transfer from LA. Now, I'm the head of the investigation.

We finally corner David Daily, the accountant, and we get him to flip on his boss. Because Temple was always the big fish we wanted to fry. We file a complaint against Daily, and he agrees to plead guilty and testify against Temple in exchange for a lighter sentence.

Meanwhile, the West Oaks DA convenes a special grand jury to consider the charges against Temple. Grand jury indictments aren't required in California, but the Temple family is political royalty here, so we need to get this done exactly right. If there are no formal charges? There can be no trial. No conviction.

Now, here's where it all goes wrong.

I'd rather not give a shit about the procedural stuff. Rule of law, statutes, the Constitution... Wake me when we get to the exciting part. But it's important. Otherwise the case will get overturned on appeal. Jane knows all about that.

Basically, all we needed was for Daily to get his ass in front of the special grand jury and testify so we could continue on with the case against Asher Temple.

Sounds so easy. Right?

But here's what actually went down.

Every time the date came for Daily to testify before the grand jury, Jane called with apologies. *David is sick. He doesn't feel up to it. What about next week?*

I started getting antsy. The prosecutors shushed me. Don't worry Detective Holt, leave it to us. Not your problem.

This is one of those times that I hate to be right.

Because all our time has bled away. We have one week left until the special grand jury expires. After that, they can no longer consider the charges. But without Daily's testimony to tie everything together, the grand jury won't charge Asher Temple with shit. There's just not enough. Asher covered his tracks too well.

It's likely that Asher Temple will skate with the many millions he's got tucked away somewhere. We can probably throw the book at Daily—assuming he regains consciousness —but everybody knows the accountant was just the patsy.

It's Temple who's responsible. Temple who should pay. And Temple who's going to get away with it.

No charges. No trial. No conviction.

This morning, I blamed our problems on Jane. I would've bet my left nut that she'd planned from the beginning to pull Daily's testimony out from under us.

But then I saw Jane get shot at. Her office was pipe-bombed. I saw the shock and outrage on her face. She claimed she had nothing to do with any of this, and I think I believe her.

Somewhere, there are answers to what's really going on. I think Jane can help me find them.

~

AFTER MY PHONE CALL WITH NICOLAS, I GO BACK into our hotel room. I find Jane and my mom on the carpet, rolling a ball back and forth to Henry, who's loving the attention.

Jane turns, and our eyes meet.

I stick my phone in the back pocket of my jeans. "Hi."

"Hello." She rolls the ball to Henry again, then stands. "Sorry. I didn't mean to intrude."

Before I can respond, my mom puts a hand on Jane's wrist. "Nonsense, you're not intruding. Sean was about to get us all some dinner. Weren't you, son?"

Out comes my phone again. "Of course. What would you like?"

"Janie," my mom says, "do you like pizza?"

Janie? We haven't been at the hotel for more than an hour, and these two are already on a nickname-basis?

That's my mother. Show her a line at the grocery store, and she'll show you her latest crew of BFFs.

"Who doesn't like pizza?" Jane asks. "As long as it's not Hawaiian."

I shake my head. "Uh oh. Now you've gone and done it."

My mother heaves a sigh. "And I thought you were one of the good ones, Janie."

"I don't like pineapple on pizza either," I say. "Or in tacos."

Jane makes a face. "Exactly. Sweet stuff belongs in desserts."

I point at her. "That's what I always say! See, Mom? When are you going to admit you're wrong?"

My mother waves a dismissive hand. "Just order the dang pizza, and know you're breaking your mother's heart."

I smile at Jane, and she smiles tentatively back.

Less than an hour later, the pizzas have arrived. I got one with pepperoni and sausage for the local officers, 'cause I'm thoughtful like that, and a bell pepper and barbecue chicken combo for us. Mom loves bell peppers.

My eyes keep drifting to Jane. Usually, her hair is a dark sheet of shampoo-commercial perfection. But now, it's messy, pulled back, with tiny wisps of hair curling over her forehead. I've never witnessed her so quiet and subdued. But my mom fills in the gaps in the conversation, as she usually does.

I recognize the look on Jane's face. She's turned inward. But this isn't the expression she wears when she's analyzing the hell out of a case, or dreaming up a new argument to flay a prosecutor alive.

This look, I recognize from my own mirror. It's uncertainty. The deepest kind of doubt. When I'm questioning every decision I've ever made, and wondering how I can possibly be enough for all the people who are counting on me.

I must be wrong. Fear is one thing, but I can't imagine

Jane's ever experienced that kind of insecurity. She's the most confident person I've ever met. And I was in the military.

After dinner, Henry's rubbing his eyes. He wanders over to Jane and puts his chubby starfish hand on her knee, trying to climb up. Jane instantly scoops him into her lap. I'll bet he's going to go for her ear, which for some reason is one of his favorite things.

And—there he goes. Using the spit-soaked hand that was just in his mouth.

But instead of cringing, she guffaws. A genuine belly laugh. A sound I didn't imagine could come out of her. Jane lets him tug on her ear, but she tickles the underside of Henry's chin until he's giggling.

My mom gives me some kind of look. Probably a *Jane's-nice-so-be-nice-to-her* look. But my mother gets along with everyone. She got a clerk at the downtown LA DMV to smile. Swear to God. I saw it.

And I don't think I've been *mean* to Jane. Have I? Just… skeptical. Prickly. The same way she is with me.

But I told Murphy we should try honey with Jane instead of vinegar, so I should probably take my own advice.

Mom stands up. "Bed time for Henry. It's been a lot of excitement today."

Jane hands Henry to my mom, who grabs his diaper bag and heads for the bathroom. The hotel wheeled in a crib when we arrived, and I'm praying the kid sleeps.

"Need help?" I ask.

"Nope. I know you've probably got more work to do." Mom's voice is tinny against the tile. She turns on the bath faucet. Water hits the tub. Henry babbles and laughs. Mom takes off his shirt and shorts, and Henry ditches the diaper, streaking across the small bathroom.

I go in and give him a kiss on the cheek. "Night, buddy. Your daddy loves you. Da-dee. Daddy."

Henry grabs my ear.

Sometimes, I can't believe I've only known him a few months. Funny how love can take hold of you and change everything so fast. He doesn't say anything resembling "Daddy" yet. Doesn't have many words at all. But he seems to like me, thank God.

"Night, Mom." I give her a kiss on the head. "Thank you."

"Go on. Get out of here. Henry needs to calm down."

When I emerge, Jane has retreated to the doorway between our rooms. She's hovering there, hesitating.

"Up for a chat?" I ask. "If you're not too tired."

"I could be persuaded."

"How about dessert at that diner next door?"

She stares at me. *Into* me. "Why are you buttering me up?"

"I'm not."

"You're hoping I'll get drunk on hot fudge and spill my secrets?"

"Maybe *I'll* get drunk on hot fudge. Sounds like more fun than I've had so far today." Except for my moments with Henry. Those are usually fun, and always special.

"Good point." Jane smirks. "Fine. It's a date." I know she's baiting me. But I'm not going to give her the reaction she expects.

I hold out my arm like I'm inviting her to take it.

Jane rolls her eyes and heads for the door to the hall. I follow her, dropping my arm. But I can't help it. I'm smiling.

13

Janie

We sit in a booth near the back, with our police escort taking a seat at the counter. The other officers remain at the hotel, keeping an eye out in the lobby and on the third floor.

I order a hot fudge sundae, extra whipped cream, while Sean gets a basket of fries.

"That's not a dessert," I say after the server takes our order. She's wearing an old-fashioned waitress uniform. This whole place has a fifties vibe, down to the chrome accents and jukebox. I think it's a chain, but it's still cute. I love oldies music. A Buddy Holly song is playing, and I tap my feet beneath the table.

"Fries are always an excellent idea," he responds.

I guess I can't disagree.

It's surreal to be sitting with him like we're friends. This morning, I'd have thought Sean Holt would sooner curse me out than be seen eating with me.

But the weirdest part?

I don't mind his presence that much. Maybe it's because

we've spent all this time together today. Like exposure therapy.

Sean takes off his windbreaker. Underneath, he's wearing a faded red T-shirt that says *Semper Fi.*

My eyes catch on his forearms. They're covered in tattoos. I've only seen him in long sleeves before.

The intricate designs pull me in. I feel myself leaning forward. The patterns look Celtic and seem to fit together like a Mobius strip, no beginning and no end.

My pulse kicks, and I force my eyes away from him.

"Thanks for tolerating Henry," Sean says. "He's always excited about a new friend."

Does he think I hate babies? Is that the vibe I'm giving off? Not everyone is a baby person, but that's not the same as being rude to one. "I wasn't *tolerating* him. He's adorable. If you ever need a babysitter, let me know."

"Not sure I can afford your hourly rates."

I can't tell if that was a harmless joke or a subtle dig at my profession. "You said you wanted to chat. What about?"

"I'd think it's obvious." He spreads his hands. "Everything."

"Everything? Including the inflation rate and the latest Kendrick Lamar album?"

Sean is sprawled in his side of the booth, one inked arm resting casually on the table. His light-brown hair is long enough on top to run fingers through, and it's messy like that's what he's been doing.

"You know what I mean, Jane. I'm talking about the shit storm that hit West Oaks today. That hit *us*. We have to figure out what we're going to do."

I'm not sure if this is an interrogation or a strategy session.

Probably both.

Sometimes I work with co-counsel on my cases, and I often use contract attorneys so I can delegate some of the burden. But mostly, it's just me. My brain, my plans. My ideas. It might be nice to have someone else to brainstorm with. Someone who has a totally different skill set and different assumptions.

He wanted to declare a truce.

But can Sean and I actually work together?

He still annoys me. If I think too much about all the things he's said to me in the past, it'll piss me off. Sean has made it clear, from the moment we met, that he doesn't like me.

But today, he probably saved my life. There were a few moments that we actually agreed on things.

And seeing him with Henry? It was sweet, okay? Sue me. Sean seems like a good dad. A loyal son to his mom. So he can't be all that terrible.

But I'm not going to make this easy for him.

"'We'?" I ask. "Who says there's a 'we'?"

He sighs, folding his hands together on the table. "My offer stands. We should declare a truce. If we're constantly at each other's throats, we're just making it easier for the assholes who are targeting us."

I tilt my head. "You want to combine resources? Share information? That's convenient, now that CBI has taken over your investigation and pushed West Oaks PD aside. You're looking for a new angle. A way to come out ahead, so you're turning to the enemy to gain the edge."

"It's not just because of CBI stepping in. If you remember, I suggested this *before* Winfrey and Hartford stormed into that witness room. Someone's trying to kill us both. They've endangered people we care about. You're going to let petty differences stand in the way of working together?"

Petty? *I'm* the one being petty?

"I want to hear more about CBI," I say. "Is it possible

they're working for Nixon Temple? The former governor has allies all over the state government. He has a lot of pull. Maybe even with CBI."

"I don't know Winfrey, but I know Agent Hartford. I can't imagine he'd stake his entire career on getting Asher Temple out of trouble. Besides, CBI could've gotten involved in our case against Asher earlier. They didn't."

"Sure, because that would've been too obvious. Now they've got the courthouse shooting to distract everyone. And whatever 'organized crime' connection Winfrey was talking about."

"You're suggesting a conspiracy theory. I'm not ready to assume the whole State of California is against us. Not unless we have evidence."

I snort. "Right. Because you love waiting on evidence before making judgments."

"What's that supposed to mean?"

We're glaring at one another. The waitress walks up, and her step slows like she's afraid to enter the line of fire. "Um, hot fudge sundae." She sets the glass dish in front of me. "And fries. Anything else for you both?"

"No, thanks," we both say.

She leaves the check on the table and scampers away.

I dig a spoon into my sundae. Sean bites into a french fry like it insulted his mom. We eat, still glaring. I focus on the creamy heat of the fudge, the contrasting cold of the vanilla ice cream. And the clouds of fresh whipped cream bringing it all together.

I close my mouth on a moan. It's hard to stay angry when there's something this delicious in my mouth.

He breaks first.

"You know, I'm not that bad a guy. Why do I bug you so much?"

"You're asking why I don't like you? That's rich. You're

the one who decided, before we'd even met, that you hated me. And you made that abundantly clear from the first moment you saw me."

"What are you talking about?"

"The day of the proffer. When I brought David to meet with you. Three months ago."

He pauses, a fry halfway to his mouth. "Oh."

"Yeah. *Oh*."

I remember when I first heard about the newest detective at West Oaks PD. I was curious, and I asked some of our mutual friends—like Chase Collins—about him. They assured me Sean was tough, experienced, but open-minded.

When I heard Sean was taking over the investigation into Asher and David, I was optimistic. David wanted to testify against his former boss, and I knew I'd need a good working relationship with the prosecutor and detective on the other side.

Whenever a criminal defendant enters a plea deal in exchange for giving evidence, they have to make a proffer. It's a put-up-or-shut-up moment. The prosecution wants to know if this evidence is good enough to justify the deal. Anything the defendant says at the proffer is confidential and inadmissible as evidence on its own.

Three months ago, the day of David's proffer, we showed up at the West Oaks DA's Office. Sean and the prosecutor were already waiting in a conference room. I was all politeness, keeping my claws in.

But Sean would barely look at me. He was short with David. Even with Nicolas, the prosecutor, who stammered through some of his questions.

Sean was like a simmering pot of rage, sucking up all the energy in the room. He could hardly tolerate being there.

So I called him out on being rude. I may have been a little rude back.

Sean's eyes met mine, and he boiled over. His fury was like a physical force, as if he'd wanted to leap at me from the other side of the conference table.

I don't need your input, counselor. I don't have the time or patience today. So sit down and shut your mouth so we can get this over with.

My skin flushes as I remember it.

"You were a complete dick to me that day. Like I'd personally offended you just by existing."

Sean wipes his hands on a napkin. "That was a very bad day for me. I shouldn't have taken it out on you. I apologize."

That's more than I expected. But not sure it's enough. "I would believe that apology more if you'd make eye contact."

He sits up straighter, and the regret in his brown eyes slams into me. I push out a breath.

"I'm sorry, Jane. Truly. I meant to apologize a while ago, but by then?" His lips tug upward at the corner, though his eyes remain contrite. "You'd made me your verbal punching bag every chance you got, so I didn't think an apology would be welcome."

"Or you didn't think I deserved one."

He shrugs. "That's possible. I have no excuse for my behavior. Honestly, I didn't imagine that it bothered you so much."

"You didn't think I had human feelings?"

He spreads his hands. "What can I say?"

I snort. I guess he's not the first to assume I'm a block of ice inside. "So, that was a bad day for you. Why? What happened?"

Because there must be more to that look in his eyes. The hints of defeat and sorrow.

He plays with his napkin. "That morning, Henry's mom dropped him off at my doorstep. I'd just moved to West Oaks, just joined the force, all so I could set up a decent life for him. But Alexis and I were supposed to be sharing custody. That morning, she claimed an emergency had come up, and she needed me to take him. She'd given me no notice, and that was difficult enough. But then, as soon as she drove away, Alexis texted me that she wasn't coming back for him. Henry was too much to deal with, and she wanted out. He was my responsibility. My *problem*. Her words, not mine."

Not sure what I expected Sean to say, but it wasn't this. "She abandoned Henry?"

He nods. "And she couldn't even tell me to my face. I panicked. I had about an hour to get Henry settled with a sitter before I had to meet you and David for the proffer. But it wasn't the inconvenience that really got to me, or the realization that I'd just become a full-time single parent. It was the thought that she'd left our kid like he wasn't worth the effort. After she'd already lied to me about…a lot of things. Henry and I *both* weren't worth the effort."

He glances away, looking at the wall, and his expression closes off again. Discomfort rolls off of him in waves. He clearly doesn't like talking about this. "It doesn't excuse my behavior toward you, though. That's on me."

I run my spoon through the melting ice cream. "Maybe, but it does explain it. Thank you for telling me. Apology accepted."

He's right. He shouldn't have taken out his anger on me. But he's human. So am I. I assumed his rudeness was about me, instead of about a really shitty thing someone else had done. Ever since, I've escalated the tension instead of defusing it.

"Can we start over?" Sean asks.

"It's possible."

He pushes his basket of fries toward me. "Peace offering?"

I take one. They're still hot, perfectly salted and just the right amount of greasy.

We eat a few fries in silence, fingers almost brushing each other as we reach into the basket. What is it about eating with someone that smooths over disagreements? Blunts the edges of what's been said. Not completely, of course—tense Thanksgiving dinners with family are a perfect counterpoint —but I feel the difference.

We ate pizza in his hotel room earlier, but we had Liza and Henry as a buffer. Now, it's just us. Facing one another. With a bit more honesty between us.

I think, maybe, that we're okay now. Not friends, but okay.

A mischievous grin appears on Sean's face. He takes a fry and swipes it through my hot fudge.

"Hey!"

He pops the chocolate-covered fry into his mouth. "What? It's tasty."

"I thought you didn't like to mix sweet and savory."

"There are always exceptions. Sweet and salt is good. Or sweet and spice." Sean dips another fry in my sundae. He blinks his long lashes as his mouth closes on the fry.

"Fine. I'll see for myself."

I'm about to reach for a fry, but Sean gets there first. He dips the fry. Holds it out to me.

His eyes issue a challenge. He's daring me to eat it from his hand.

Nope.

I'll never back down from a challenge, but I also refuse to let him set the parameters. If you let the other side place the pieces, you're instantly at a disadvantage in the game.

I pluck the fry from his fingers. I bite into it, but not the part he was touching. The rest of the fry I leave on a napkin.

Then I hold out my spoon to him. "The sundae's better if you get all the components at once. I'm happy to share."

His closed-lip smile deepens. Sean takes my spoon,

drags my dish closer, and scoops out a huge bite. His lips close around it, cheeks hollowing. His eyes shut and he moans, much like I did after my first bite. But he's not trying to stay quiet. Another patron glances over from a nearby table.

He licks the whipped cream from his lip. "That's a quality dessert."

He holds the spoon out.

Challenge accepted. And re-issued.

Shit. I didn't plan for this move, even though I should've seen it coming. The moment I think I've got an edge on this man, he turns things around on me.

But what the hell.

I accept the spoon and scoop up a bite. Not as big as his, but close. His eyes are on my lips.

I swear I taste something different now that his mouth has been on the spoon. A touch of mint or cinnamon. I'm absolutely imagining it. But there's a tug behind my belly button, followed by a warmth that spreads through my center.

I have no idea what we're doing right now. Joking with each other? Teasing?

Maybe even *flirting*?

Whatever this is, it's kinda fun. And better than outright fighting.

I still feel that tension between us. It hasn't vanished. I'm still a defense attorney, and he's a senior detective. There's a one-hundred percent chance we'll clash again. But as we share that spoon, I realize something.

Sean Holt and I have already forged an alliance. It happened at some point today, after he pulled me from the line of fire in the courthouse and before we arrived at the hotel. Even before I met Henry and Liza.

I stopped hating Sean and started feeling...something

else. Respect, perhaps. Gratitude. I might even…gah…like him a little?

Deep down, I think I already knew it. That we'd have no choice but to work together.

I'm just grumpy that Sean realized it first.

He offers me the last bite of ice cream, but I shake my head. "This truce idea of yours. How long would it last?"

This is a broader question. How long will we be in protective custody? How long until we're sure the danger is over? Neither of us knows. But I want to hear his thoughts.

He chases the remnants of hot fudge around the dish. "Well, the special grand jury that's considering charges against Asher expires in a week."

I nod. I'm well aware of that issue. For the last couple of months, David has been delaying his testimony before the grand jury. I didn't understand why. At first, I thought he was ashamed to admit how thoroughly Asher had played him. Now I wonder how long he's been getting death threats.

There's something else that happens in a week. Gran's memorial service in Arizona. My Gran is constantly beneath the surface of my thoughts. But I let that ever-present sadness drift back downward again. I need to focus on this conversation.

"The timing can't be a coincidence," I say. "I'm sure Asher will be breathing easier after the special grand jury is off his back. That won't guarantee he's never charged. But with CBI taking over the case?"

"And the state prosecutors, too. Nicolas told me the West Oaks DA's Office is out."

It's sounding a lot like a conspiracy to me. I hold back my commentary on that. "But Asher could've chosen to run out the clock without all these fireworks. Why shoot up the courthouse? Why try to kill David and us? He'd already gotten David to pull his testimony."

"There must be something else that could come out."

"Whatever it is," I say, "we have to find out what Asher Temple is so afraid of. What he's hiding." My gaze locks with Sean's.

Finally, I understand exactly what he wants.

It's not just a cessation of hostilities. Sean wants me at his side. The two of us, investigating.

And we have one week to do it. While Asher Temple—and whoever else—is doing everything to stop us.

Can I switch from defense to offense?

Shit. I'm already doing it.

So I'd better catch up before Sean gets the jump on me, once again.

14

Sean

Jane and I are talking about Asher Temple, but my mind's on the rest of our conversation. She had every right to be pissed off about how I acted the day we met.

That day... God, it still makes my chest squeeze so hard I can barely breathe. I had thought Alexis couldn't stoop any lower than cheating on me, but she did.

How could anyone look at that little guy and think, *Nope, I have better things to do*?

But Henry's loved and cherished, and so much better off without my ex in his life. I just hate to think I'll have to explain it to him someday. Why his mom left. Why she didn't love him enough to stay.

No matter how much I try to soften it, he'll feel the hurt. I won't be able to protect him from that. But I hope I'll have given him the confidence he needs to get past it. Just as my parents did for me. I've never had a mother leave me in the cold, but Alexis screwed me over too. I know that's not the same as what she did to Henry. But it still stings.

So, yeah. The day I met Jane, I wasn't at my best.

But I think I've been making up for it. She might even be warming to me.

And I got a little too much satisfaction from seeing Jane's lips wrapped around that spoon. The same spoon I'd just had in my mouth.

I know this isn't the moment to be smug. Jane will hit back if she notices. She won't let me get away with anything, and I appreciate that about her.

I take a gulp of ice water, pushing these thoughts away before I screw it all up again.

"Are you in?" I ask.

Jane's been sitting quietly, considering what I've said about how we should team up. "I'm in."

I exhale with relief. I expected she'd see reason, but Jane can be unpredictable. At least I *know* to keep on my toes around her. She's not acting all innocent and sweet while holding a knife behind her back. If she's coming after me, she won't be subtle about it.

"If you're tired, you should rest," I say. "We can start first thing in the morning."

"Or? If I'm not tired?"

"We can order coffee and start now." This diner is open twenty-four hours. The place is almost empty this late, so we don't need to worry about being overheard. Our suburban police escort is keeping his post at the counter, with his roving eye on the room and the exit. I nod at him, and he nods back.

Jane waves at our waitress. "Two coffees please."

"Cream and sugar, hon?"

"None for me." Jane looks over. "You?"

"I like it black. And see if our friend at the counter wants anything else. We're staying for a while."

The waitress nods and walks away. I take out my phone and pull up my notes app.

Jane reaches across the table to rest a hand on my wrist. Her fingers are long and cool. My skin tingles under her touch.

"Before we start, I need to make one thing clear. I still owe a duty to my clients. That includes confidentiality. There are exceptions. But I might not be able to tell you everything you want to know."

"I understand. I'm not going to reveal anything that could compromise West Oaks PD investigations, either."

Jane nods and pulls her hand away. The tingles spread up my arm, like ripples left in her wake.

The coffee arrives. We take sips. Jane crosses her legs on the bench, getting comfortable.

But I have my own preliminary issue to get out of the way. Something that's been bugging me.

"I know you're not working for Asher Temple," I say. "But why did he nod at you before the shooting started? Seriously."

She taps her fingertips on the table. "I can't imagine it's relevant. Asher was just...messing with me."

"You don't think that's relevant?"

Jane rolls her eyes. "We went on a couple of dates, okay? It was years ago. West Oaks is small. When I became David's lawyer, I disclosed everything to him. It wasn't an issue."

She went out with *Temple*? Really? Her taste is that questionable?

"Stop judging me," Jane snaps. "He asked me out, I said yes. I realized very quickly that Temple wasn't my type."

"But you said a couple of dates. That's more than one." I'm not even sure of my point. I'm in no position to scoff at her dating history, considering my own.

Jane is glaring. Probably best to move on from this topic. "All right. Let's go back to the beginning."

My thumbs move over my phone screen, jotting down

notes as we talk. Jane and I both know the Temple case backwards and forwards, but we've never discussed it like this. As allies.

We dig into our memories of this morning for every possible detail of the shooting. Anything that could be a clue.

At some point, we each put a hand on the table, and our fingers brush. Like we're seeking out comfort. Jane shivers, and she pulls her hand away.

"You all right?" I mean this in the broadest way possible. We've both been awake and hopped up on adrenaline for too long.

"Yep. Fine." She's blinking fast. Takes another sip of coffee. "You said you recognized the men who broke into your house this afternoon?"

"I recognized their tattoos. Snakes on their arms, circling their wrists."

Jane's gaze sharpens, and her pupils dilate.

"Sound familiar?" I ask.

She doesn't answer. Instead, she asks a different question. "Did you know those specific guys? Or just the snake tats?"

"Just the tats. I assume they're members of the Serpents motorcycle gang. They needed medical attention after I was done with them, but someone will interrogate them. Agent Winfrey or Hartford, I guess. We'll find out more."

Jane folds her arms on the table. "The Serpents. That explains why Agent Winfrey mentioned organized crime. Did someone hire them to go after us?"

"Certainly possible. But the Serpents have a separate motive to go after me. When I was with LAPD Gang and Narcotics, I led the investigation against several members that sent them to prison. They were selling black tar heroin, got caught up in a turf war. Shot up some rival gang members. But they were on their motorcycles with their snake tattoos visible. Security cameras at a convenience store caught them on video. This isn't the smartest bunch."

Jane closes her mouth on a laugh. "That, I can agree with," she mutters.

"So you *do* know them?"

"I'm trying to figure out how to answer without violating my ethical duties." She sighs. "It's…it's like this. I met with a member of the Serpents about a year ago. He was in trouble in West Oaks."

"Another date of yours?"

It's a joke, but it falls flat. Her mouth drops open. "No, you asshole. A potential client. I met with him at the jail, but I declined to take his case. He wasn't happy about it."

I wait for her to elaborate, but she's staring at the surface of the table.

"Not happy?" I ask. "How so?"

She hesitates a few more seconds. "He kept calling me. He was…aggressive. Left messages about all the ways he wanted to punish me for not taking the case. Which was the reason I declined to take him on in the first place. I didn't like…" Her lips clamp shut.

My stomach churns, but I don't think it's the food or the coffee. "He was disrespectful?"

Jane smiles slowly. "That's a polite way of putting it."

"Did the guy get convicted? Is he in prison?"

"Not sure. I didn't follow his case."

"What kind of trouble did he get into in West Oaks?"

"I'd rather not say."

"But he was never actually your client."

"Consultations are still confidential."

I clench my jaw. I can't believe Jane would protect the information of some cretin who harassed her. I don't understand her priorities.

But in her mind, she's doing the right thing. The "ethical"

thing, according to some lawyers or judges or whatever who wrote their professional rules.

We all have our rules. Our reasons. Mine probably don't make sense to her, either.

"So the Serpents have a reason to dislike you," I say. "And me. I'm waiting for word from Murphy on the forensics at your office, but it's a good bet the same guys went after us both. The matching pipe bombs make that clear."

If we can find out why the Serpents are targeting us *now*, that'll be a big piece of this puzzle.

Did someone hire them? Or just point them in our direction and give them a shove?

"Our first lead?" Jane asks.

I nod. "It's a beginning. Gotta start somewhere." Tomorrow, I'll see what else I can dig up.

We've been here for hours. Even with the coffee, Jane's yawning, and it's contagious.

"We should get to bed," I say. "It'll be another long one tomorrow." I dig out bills from my wallet, and Jane frowns.

"I can pay. You got the pizza earlier."

I scoot out of the booth, leaving the money behind. My windbreaker goes back on to cover the holster at my lower back. "You can buy breakfast and lunch. We're stuck together for a while."

She makes a disgruntled sound. "Five more nights."

"Five?"

"Well, you said a week. But technically, it's six more full days. Five nights in between. This one's pretty much over."

"I guess you're right."

I tap the shoulder of the officer at the counter. The guy looks ready to pass out. The shift change will probably be soon.

We walk across the parking lot to the hotel. Up to the third floor.

Everything's quiet except the buzz of the elevator as it descends, returning to the lobby.

Jane unlocks her door with her key card. "Do you want to come in?"

My eyebrows raise. "What?"

Is she... She couldn't be. Right?

"The connecting door's unlocked, I assume," she says. "It might be quieter than going through the main door. Is Henry a light sleeper?"

Heat spreads over my chest and up my neck. "Um, no. But my mom is. Sure, that's a good idea."

I follow her inside. Jane switches on the light. She's got double queen beds, identical to my room. Her clothes are scattered on the floor.

"Sorry." She grabs a handful and stuffs them into her bag.

"Was that Henry? If something's put away, he loves taking it out. Just-folded laundry is a top choice. But his favorite is trash from a can."

I smile at the memory of his hijinks, and when I look over, Jane's smiling back.

And then we're just...looking at each other. And smiling. And I forget for a moment that she's Jane Simon, the lawyer who hates me. If she ever actually hated me at all.

She's just a pretty woman in the hotel room next door who was kind to my son. Who likes hot fudge sundaes and pizza without pineapple. Who's friends, it seems, with my mom.

Janie.

That's what Mom called her.

Janie. That really fits.

"Goodnight, Sean," she says.

That pulls me out of my reverie.

"Night. Uh, Jane." I'm exhausted and over-sugared and

caffeinated. My brain's going to strange places. I'm sure I'll feel more normal after some sleep.

15

Sean

I wake to Henry's babble and his laughter. On the other bed, Mom rolls over and sticks her head under the pillow.

Henry's standing up in the rollaway crib. His smile broadens when he spots me, and he makes sounds like he's trying for words. I listen for a "D" but can't make one out.

He used to make sounds like "mama" a lot, but then it switched to something like "gama," which must mean my mom. He's only fourteen months—yeah, I do the month thing—and the pediatrician said that once he really starts talking, it'll happen fast, and then he won't shut up.

I feel like I've already missed so much. Now that he's with me, it's going by too quickly.

I get up and set Henry free from his prison. I hug him, but his little legs are eager to run. "Okay, buddy. Hold on. One more." Another squeeze, a kiss on his forehead, and I lower him to the floor. He's off.

With me and my brothers, my dad was always a little uncomfortable with showing affection. He gave us side-hugs only, and kisses were nonexistent. He showed love in lots of other ways.

But I'm a different kind of man. A different kind of father. I like to be close to the people I care about, and touch is connection. When it comes to those I love, I never want to look back and regret that I didn't show it in every way I could. And with Henry, I have a lot to make up for. Even if that's not entirely my fault.

Henry runs straight to the door connecting our room to Jane's.

And he starts pounding.

"Hey!" I dash over and grab his hands. "That's not nice. She's sleeping."

"Don't think anyone's sleeping anymore," Mom says blearily. She's given up trying to snooze. It's no use with this kid around.

Then there's a knock back from the other side of the connecting door. Henry steps back in surprise, landing on his diapered butt.

I cross the room and open the door. Jane's already unlocked her side. She's in pajama pants and a T-shirt, her hair loose and messy around her shoulders.

"Morning," I say.

"Morning."

Her eyes flick downward, and I remember I'm not wearing a shirt. Just a pair of shorts. I feel her gaze like a caress, but I'm not sure if there's interest.

Do I *want* her to be interested?

I must, because I'm puffing up my chest like a thirsty Insta post. Guess I can't resist showing off in front of any attractive female. Sometimes, I'm just an animal walking upright.

I think I look decent. I take care of myself. I haven't had much luck with relationships, but I never have trouble getting women to pay attention.

Jane's a tough one though. She went out with Asher

Temple, a rich douchebag if there ever was one. But she also said he wasn't her type.

I'm only curious in a general sense. Not like I'm trying to figure out what Jane's looking for in a guy.

Before Jane or I say anything else, Henry plows past me and through the doorway. He collides with Jane's legs, wrapping his arms around her.

She smiles down at him. "Morning to you too, Henry."

He babbles something and slobbers on her pajama pants. Jane picks him up, bouncing him on her hip. Henry's smile is a mile wide. "Anyone else ready for breakfast?"

Food sounds good. And coffee. Lots of coffee.

∼

A LITTLE WHILE LATER, JANE AND I ARE DRESSED and heading downstairs for food. The local officer on duty comes with us. I shoot the shit with him, while Jane walks in front.

She looks casual again in her jeans and sweater, the same thing she wore last night. And good. She always looks good. I mean, I've checked her out before, but she seems different now. Softer and inviting. My eye keeps landing on the curves of her ass.

"So you were involved in that shooting at the courthouse?" the officer asks. "In West Oaks?"

I tear my eyes away from Jane's shapely behind. "We were there. Yeah."

"Any word on the guy who was shot? The one who stole all that money."

Jane looks over her shoulder at us.

"He was hurt pretty badly," I say. "Needed surgery. I'm not sure beyond that."

The officer grunts. "Seems like the guy got what he deserved."

We reach the free breakfast spread. I clap him on the shoulder. "I'm dying for some coffee. Thanks for keeping an eye on us."

"Happy to do it, detective. Glad your family's safe."

I grab some muffins, bananas, and a carton of whole milk for Henry. I pile it all onto a tray, then add two cups of coffee.

I find Jane waiting by the elevator. She's got a coffee of her own, plus a small yogurt. We head back up.

"Not very hungry?" I ask.

"Not really," she says stiffly. "No."

"You good?"

"Actually, I'm in a crappy mood." Jane disappears into her room, carrying her yogurt. Her door slams closed.

Oh-kay then.

In my room, I find my mom eying the now-closed connecting door. "What happened to Janie? Why's she eating alone?"

I set down Mom's plate. "I don't know. She wanted to, I guess."

"Did you do something?"

"*No.*" I don't think.

But it's one thing to agree, in theory, to work together. Actually making it happen is another.

Finally, after Mom and Henry go out into the hallway to expend some of his energy, I knock on Jane's door. "Come in," she says brusquely. Like we're in the middle of an office building.

I open the door and go inside. "What're you upset about this time? Didn't I apologize enough last night?"

She scowls. "One apology for one incident doesn't give you permission to be a perpetual ass."

"What did I do?"

Her lips twist. I can tell she doesn't want to have this conversation, but then she opens her mouth. "That cop said David deserved to be shot. He deserves a firing squad? The death penalty? When he hasn't even had a trial?"

I roll my eyes. You've gotta be kidding me. "Why do you care what some cop said? I can't even remember the man's name."

"But you didn't disagree."

"I didn't say I agreed, either. I believe in fair trials."

"Do you?"

"Yeah. But I also don't need my integrity questioned every five minutes. This is supposed to be a truce. Doesn't that include giving each other the benefit of the doubt?"

Her mouth puckers like she's biting a lemon. "I'm just not sure this is going to work." She gestures between us. "You and me."

Fuck. Is she right? Are we too different? Or maybe, so equally stubborn that we'll never be in sync?

But my gut says this alliance is our best shot at living through the next week. And nailing whoever's responsible for targeting us.

"You haven't even given it a chance."

"Look," she says, "I'm trying to calm down and be reasonable here. That would be easier if you weren't in my face. Could you go back to your room, please? I'm going to call Tracey." She stands up and turns her back on me, crossing to the far side of the space.

I stalk over to the chair she just vacated and plop myself down. "Well, that's too damn bad. I'm not going anywhere."

She spins to face me. "You're refusing to leave my room?"

"Yep. You can try to move me. I don't think it'll be successful." I plant my legs and drop my arms to my sides.

Then I wiggle my pointer finger. Beckoning.

Come at me. See what happens.

Light dances in her eyes. Indignation. Then competitiveness.

Jane marches over to me, grabs my hands, and tries to haul me out of the chair.

She's strong, I'll give her that. She's putting her back and legs into it. But I've got—what, eighty pounds on her?

She's standing in between my spread thighs. I pull my hands free of hers, then close my fingers around her biceps, pinning her arms. She has slender, firm muscles, but there's softness too.

Her skin burns hot beneath my palms.

"What the hell is wrong with you?" she demands.

"If you want to tap out, I'll let you go. But that means I won."

She actually *growls*, and that light sparks again in her gaze. And it's *on*.

Jane wriggles in my grasp. She digs her knee into my thigh, trying to push off and get free. I just tug her closer, even though I shouldn't. I should stop this. Right now.

Except she's laughing. Her hands find my shoulders, and her thumbs poke into my armpits through my T-shirt, and I howl.

"Ticklish, huh?" she asks. "Do you surrender?"

"Never." I switch my grip so I can hold her wrists behind her back.

Then she flinches like she's in pain.

Fuck me, I forgot about that gunshot graze on her upper arm. I release her, and she sags into my lap, balancing on my thighs. I catch her against my chest.

For that moment, she's close enough that my lungs fill with her scent. Soapy and flowery and feminine. Her dark eyes are like windows at night. Part reflection, but with hints of what's beyond. What's underneath.

I wonder what she's seeing in mine.

Jane springs up, backing away from me. She's cradling her arm. I get up from the chair and follow her. "I'm sorry. Is your arm okay? Did I hurt you?"

Then an evil grin spreads across her face. "I got you out of the chair. That means I win."

My mouth forms an *O* of shock. I slow-clap. "Well played. The Oscar goes to…"

"Oh, it really does hurt. My arm's been bugging me constantly. I don't always show what I'm feeling." She tilts her head at me, in that way she does a lot. "But I never fake it."

"Good to know." I'm not sure why I'm breathing so hard. Not like it took that much effort to pin her down, and I'm a pretty fit guy. But my heart is racing and my lungs are straining.

I don't even know why I grabbed hold of her the way I did. I can usually control myself better than that. But I've felt the urge to lay my hands on her before, just out of sheer frustration.

She still makes me want to pin her down. Shut her up.

But now, I imagine doing that with a kiss.

Did somebody crank the heat in here?

"I'm glad I didn't make it worse," I say. "Do you need pain meds?"

"Don't try to take care of me. You're making it weird."

I sputter. "Okay, next time bullets are flying, I'll let you fend for yourself." I go back to her table and sit down. Clearly she *didn't* win because I'm still here. "Can we get started on finding the actual threats? Instead of battling each other?"

"Fine." She takes the seat beside me. "Bossy much?"

This truce isn't going to be easy. But as I pull up our notes from last night on my phone, I feel like I'm smiling all the way through my insides. Way down into the hidden parts of me.

16

Janie

Something must've gone haywire in my brain yesterday. I'm not supposed to be having this much fun with Sean.

When he grabbed my arms just now, jolts of electricity flooded my veins. And when we wrestled around, my skin felt tight and flushed, and my blood pounded.

I felt almost...turned on.

Sean's an attractive guy. I got an eyeful this morning when he opened the door wearing no shirt and those under-sized shorts. With that dark hair across his pecs, trailing down his flat stomach... The Celtic tattoos on his forearms...

And I got vibes like he was admiring *me* as much as I was him. Which is weird. And distracting.

Then, a few minutes ago, I was raring to argue with him. To fight. Which is the reaction I've usually had to Sean. But I don't even know why I was so annoyed. Obviously, it's not Sean's fault that a random cop made an asinine comment.

Yet I picked that argument. Why?

It's like I'm fighting *myself* more than him at this point. Fighting this interest. This attraction.

In the past, I've noticed that Sean had a hot body. Didn't mean I liked him. But he keeps being so nice, and funny, and cute with his son.

He's making me want him, and I don't appreciate it.

Sean calls Detective Murphy. From the seat beside him, I listen in, trying to slow my runaway pulse. He doesn't mention to Murphy that I'm here, and it feels like a secret shared between us. Like he's trusting me with a confidence.

I really don't know *what* to think about Sean Holt. So I'm going to focus on our investigation. Not on him.

"I have news about Daily," Murphy says after a few other quick updates.

"Yeah?" Sean's eyes dart to mine. "Did he wake up?"

I scoot closer. My arm brushes his sleeve, and I quickly readjust so we're not touching.

"No, he's still unconscious at the hospital. We haven't been able to talk to him yet. But after the attack on your house and Jane's office, Agent Hartford agreed to send units to check on Daily's home. It had been broken into, ransacked."

My heart rate accelerates. I use my phone to type Sean a message and hold it up. *Fiancée? Gabriela Torres.*

"What about his fiancée, Gabriela Torres?" Sean asks. "Has anyone spoken to her?"

"No. She wasn't at the house, and it didn't look like anyone but Daily had been living there recently. But get this. We found a camera in one of Daily's light fixtures."

"A camera?"

"Surveillance set-up with a Wi-Fi connection. It wasn't us, and Hartford said it wasn't CBI or anyone else he knows of. We have the wiretap warrant, but nothing that would allow a camera."

Sean's squirming. I'm not supposed to be hearing this stuff. It's touching on their prior investigation of Daily and their case against him. Yet he doesn't say anything to Murphy. "So someone else was watching him."

"That's what it looks like. Maybe the people who shot him at the courthouse yesterday."

What would they have seen David doing on the camera? Something that prompted the attack?

"What about the Serpents connection?" Sean asks. "Have you questioned the guys I caught at my house?"

"Agent Hartford's going to bring them in this morning and see what he can get. I don't mind him. He's being thorough. But I'm not a fan of his partner. Agent Winfrey shared his opinion on the Serpents connection—that there isn't one. Not to the courthouse shooting, anyway."

"*What?* And what's the basis for that conclusion?"

"That you and Jane Simon have both had prior dealings with the gang, and there's no reason to believe the courthouse shooting was connected."

I want to speak up and argue, but then Murphy will know I'm on the call. I'm surprised Agent Winfrey even knew about my tie to the Serpents. But I visited that potential client in jail, which is something the police would've known, or easily learned.

The guy's name was Jacob Ritter, aka "Cobra." A shot-caller, so he claimed, for the Serpents. He'd been arrested in West Oaks on an aggravated battery charge. When I met with him, the jerk kept staring at my tits and licking his lips. I'll put up with some mild grossness and innuendo, but he was just too much.

I believe everyone is entitled to a defense, and that you can't assume a person's guilty just because he's done other bad things. In fact, it's not my place to decide on guilt. It's the jury's.

But I don't have to represent every asshole who calls me up. No thanks.

Ritter left me some disgusting voicemails afterward, probably just out of boredom and frustration. It's hard to imagine he'd come after me when so many months have passed. Aside from him, I don't have any connection to the Serpents.

Could there be a tie between Asher Temple and a bunch of snake-tattooed motorcycle gangsters from LA?

How do these pieces fit together?

I send Tracey a text, asking her to look up Jacob Ritter on the Inmate Locator website. That'll tell me whether he's currently in prison or not.

Tracey gets back to me quickly, saying Ritter is currently serving a four-year sentence at California City Correctional. Which means Ritter wasn't one of the guys who targeted us yesterday.

After the call with Detective Murphy, Sean turns his phone facedown on the table. "I'm going to make some calls to my old informants. Maybe I can find out what the Serpents have been up to lately."

Sounds like my cue to leave. Except for the fact that this is *my* room.

"Are you going to make your calls in the hallway?" I ask.

"Mom and Henry are out there. And they might want to use the other room."

I huff. "This entire floor is empty! Get a key from downstairs to a different room if you want to set up an office." I'm sure the government is paying for all of this anyway. Law enforcement budgets are in the stratosphere.

Sean is leaning back in the chair. "But I'm comfortable here."

"This is because I won earlier. Isn't it?"

He's trying to hide his smirk. "You think I'm that childish? Besides, you didn't win. I did."

I rest a hand on my hip. Arch my eyebrow.

"I have the feeling that if I leave, you'll lock me out and

pretend I don't exist. I'm making sure that doesn't happen. I'm not letting you out of this truce."

I still don't see how this will work. Even an hour of peace between Sean and me feels like a big ask. Though our arguments seem just as likely to make me laugh now as make angry.

Or make my blood rush and my breath catch.

He puts his hands behind his head, tipping back on the chair's rear legs. "I'll get my calls out of the way, and then we'll talk about options for our next steps. I'm hoping you'll have some ideas of your own by then."

"Oh, I will. I have lots of ideas." Like where I'm tempted to shove my foot.

He grins at me and picks up his phone.

∼

I GO INTO THE HALL. LIZA AND HENRY ARE LOOKING out a window at the far end. It's a view of the diner and the parking lot, but Henry's tiny starfish hands splay on the glass like he's captivated by what he sees.

It's so cute. I snap a quick photo with my phone. It just seems like something Sean would want to see. And he's busy trying to help me right now. Well, help us both. But still.

Liza and Henry smile when they see me, though Liza's shoulders are heavy.

"Not fun being cooped up, huh?" I ask.

"Any idea how long this protective custody thing will last? I've asked my son, but he keeps deflecting."

"That's something we're trying to figure out."

Liza looks down at her grandson. "Henry's used to going on long walks, playing at the beach. Burning off his energy in the sun before his nap. I doubt he'll nap today at this rate, even though last night we were both up."

"I could play with him. If you want to rest some more."

I see her lips forming the word *no*. She's like me, hesitant to accept help. Used to being the one other people rely on. I put a hand on Liza's elbow. "You'd be doing me a favor. I almost never get to hang out with babies. Trust me, he'll be far less demanding than my typical client. And so much sweeter."

Henry shows his little teeth as he smiles, as if emphasizing the point.

Then he tears down the hall. We both follow.

She's deliberating. "You sure it's not too much trouble? If anyone should look after him, it's Sean."

"I want to. We'll be right out here."

"All right. Let me grab his diaper bag and snacks, just in case. But if he gets fussy, come knocking."

Liza goes to lie down, and Henry and I play for a while. Mostly it's running from one end of the hallway to the other. The cop keeping watch tries to give Henry a high-five every time he passes.

I work out to keep in shape, but I've never been a runner. I can't remember the last time I've been going this long. No wonder Liza is exhausted.

When Henry finally wears down, we play with chunky plastic toys on the hall carpet. There are cars, trains, colorful round people. That's where Sean finds us when he comes out.

Henry pops up immediately, holding out his arms. But instead of picking him up, Sean sits beside me. Henry climbs on him, getting hugs and kisses.

"It's almost nap time," Sean says. Henry whines. He knows that word and doesn't like it. "Aren't you tired, buddy? I think you are."

Henry scoots a toy truck on the carpet. Sean lets him keep playing. Then the baby crawls onto his dad again, eyes finally drooping, and he falls asleep in his dad's arms. Sean and I have our backs against the wall, and everything's quiet.

I'm trying not to be completely bowled over by the adorableness happening beside me. But I can only do so much.

Ugh. I do like Sean. There, I said it.

"I spoke to an informant in LA," he whispers. "Says he has info about the Serpents that could be useful, but he'll only share it in person."

"Who's the informant?"

His smirk says, *Nice try*. "You know better than that, Jane. I'm not going to share the identity of a CI with a defense attorney."

I huff. But he's right, I wouldn't expect Sean to reveal a confidential informant. His friends at the LAPD would have his head.

"But how do we know we can believe what he says?" I ask.

"We don't. All I can do is listen, and maybe it'll get us one link closer to the answer."

I nod. "Okay, but you shouldn't go alone. I'm coming with you."

Sean glances at me. Henry's lips pout as he sleeps, cradled in Sean's arms. "I was thinking you'd stay here with Mom and Henry while I'm gone." He nods his head, subtly gesturing at the cop down the hall. "I'd feel better if they weren't alone with strangers. Given everything that's going on."

"I'm not a stranger?"

"Not anymore. You're a friend."

For a moment, I can't say anything. Is Sean just trying to keep me away from his CI?

Or is this a show of trust?

But he's already trusting me. Letting me spend time with

his family, working with me, sharing information. Sean's choosing to bring me into his circle, even though we hardly know one another.

And I guess I'm trusting him too.

As I sit beside him, I feel it. A gunman could charge into this hallway, and I'd stick with Sean. Plus fight like hell on my own. But, yeah. I'd stick with Sean.

"I don't want them on their own, either," I say. "But the same goes for you. If you croak, I won't have anyone to partner with on this rogue investigation of ours."

He laughs silently.

I have another thought. "Are you sure Liza and Henry should stay here at all? They're already going stir crazy. And being around us is probably the most dangerous place for them to be."

His jaw sets.

"You want them close. I get it. But—"

"You think I'm being selfish."

"No! Not at all. But I think this will be easier if you send them elsewhere until the danger's passed."

His stern silence tells me I've said too much.

I dispense advice to my clients every day. I tell them things they don't want to hear. But that's what they pay me for. Sean doesn't want my opinions on how he deals with his family.

"Forget it. I shouldn't have—"

"No, you're right. I wanted to believe the safest place for them was with me, and it's hard to admit that it's not." He shifts Henry to one arm and wipes a hand over his face. "Chase Collins offered a place to stay. You know him, right? He's on patrol in West Oaks."

I nod. "Chase and Ruby will take good care of your family."

"They will. I'm still not going to reveal my CI's name, though."

I bump my foot against his. "Fine, keep your precious informant's identity. I don't have to know it. Let me come along with you to LA when you meet him, and we can keep names out of it."

Sean purses his lips, and he looks so much like the little boy in his arms. "I'll consider it. First I'm going to text Chase." Sean moves Henry a little so he can use both hands.

While he's messaging Chase, I get out my own device. I pull up the photo I took of Henry by the window earlier. "Hey, could I have your cell number?" I ask.

"You don't have it?" He rattles off the digits, and I add them to his contact. I only had his email and office phone. I hear the noise when he gets the text I just sent.

"What's this?"

"A picture I took a bit ago of Henry. I thought it was sweet and that you'd want to see it."

Sean looks down at the photo. Then back to me. "Thank you."

"No problem."

But he's studying me like he's trying to see into my head. Frowning. Thinking. He's gone into detective mode.

I stare back. "What?"

"Who are you, Jane Simon?"

"What do you mean? I'm just…me."

"You told my mom to call you Janie."

"I…" I wasn't sure if he'd noticed that. "Yeah. I guess I did."

We've been talking quietly so we don't wake Henry. But Sean's voice has dipped even lower than before.

"Can I call you Janie?"

Flutters spread through my chest and into my stomach. "You want to?"

He doesn't answer right away. Just keeps looking at me.

I don't know what this is. What he's trying to do. Knock me off balance? Score points in our endless battles?

If so, it's working.

I can handle Sean arguing with me. I'm getting used to Sean the hero, the family man, even Sean the flirt. But Sean being genuinely sweet to *me*? I don't know how to interpret it.

Those sparks of attraction I was feeling are starting to catch. To ignite. Which is extremely inconvenient.

We're barely even friends. We're both stressed and isolated, and that's a perfect recipe to wind up doing something we'd regret.

"I'm just trying to figure you out," he finally says. "You seem like different people sometimes."

"That's not fair. I'm always being myself. But nobody is just one thing. You're not."

There's another shift in how he's watching me. Like I've surprised him yet again.

He gets another text, and he glances down at it. "It's Chase. He's happy to have them."

"Good."

Sean's attention returns to me. His casual smile is back. "You know what this means, don't you? You and I will be stuck here with each other. Just us. No buffer."

Shit. Five more nights. With killers probably trying, this very moment, to find us. Just me and Detective Holt and this maybe-flirtation between us. This chemistry that already has my body heating up.

Whenever Sean and I are together, we clash. There's always some kind of fireworks. If we're alone in a hotel for days and nights on end?

Anticipation zips through me. But I don't know if it's the

good kind or the bad. Excitement or dread. Maybe a little of both.

17

Sean

Chase offers to come pick up Mom and Henry. When I tell Mom, I see the relief on her face. She kisses me on the cheek. "We'd rather stay with you, but this hotel sucks."

I chuckle. "I know. I'm sorry. Sorry about all of this."

She brushes that off. "Shit happens, son. I'm just glad you won't be here alone. You and Janie need to find the sons of bitches who're causing all this trouble and shut them down."

"We intend to." If it weren't for Henry, I have no doubt Mom would be sticking to my side and giving the Serpents hell. And I can't imagine what she'd do to a pissant like Asher Temple.

Jane grabs to-go sandwiches for everyone from the diner for lunch, and Henry gets in some more play time. After that, Chase drives up to the back exit of the hotel, and we pile Mom and Henry inside. I check all the buckles and straps on the car seat.

The local cops watching over us ask questions, but I don't give many details. Protective custody is a mere courtesy, even if Agent Winfrey suggested otherwise. We're not prisoners here. It probably helps that I'm a cop myself. They just shrug when I say my mom and son are relocating.

Chase takes my hand in a warrior's grip. "They'll be fine. But I'm worried about you, man. You'll be careful?"

"What do you mean? I'll be sitting tight in this hotel playing solitaire and eating bad pizza."

He grins sardonically. "Right. Just let me know if you need any help with your solitaire game."

Chase and I both know I'm not staying out of this investigation, no matter what CBI says. But I don't want to get him into trouble by saying more than he needs to know.

Chase gives Jane a hug. "Say hi to Ruby for me," Jane says.

They drive away, and we head back inside. There's an awkward moment where we each pause in the hotel hallway in front of our respective doors.

"Guess I'll...talk to you in a while?" I ask.

"Yep. I have some things to do."

We each go to our rooms. I putter around a bit, trying to gather my thoughts. But my skin crawls until Mom texts me, saying they've safely arrived at the Collins residence. Thank God.

I drink a glass of water. Wash my face. I didn't bother to shave yet, and my chin is dark with stubble. Almost as dark as the rings beneath my eyes.

Jane has left the connecting door between our rooms cracked open. I hear her chatting quietly on her phone. She says the name "Tracey," which means it's her assistant.

I sit at the table in my own room, checking the location for tomorrow's meeting on Google Maps. My informant agreed to a neutral location, away from his place of business. We're supposed to meet up at a food truck in downtown LA.

I still haven't decided if Jane should come with me.

In a way, she's correct. I shouldn't go alone. Every cop knows you stay with your partner. You wait for backup.

But if she figures out his identity, it's a problem. How will I explain that to my former colleagues at LAPD?

Sorry for blowing that CI, guys. I could've called one of you to back me up, but I decided to bring a notorious defense attorney instead. Why? Because…I've got this inexplicable urge to have her near me?

Not good.

And of course, I don't want to put Jane in danger, either.

There's only one solution that makes any sense. I grab my phone and call my ex-partner at Gang and Narcotics.

"Holt! How the hell are you? Bet you're wishing you didn't ditch us for West Oaks."

"You've heard about what went down at the courthouse?"

"Has anyone *not* heard?"

I fill him in on the details, assuring him my family's safe when he asks. "CBI has taken over the investigation, and I'm in protective custody. But I'm looking into things on my own."

"Of course you are."

I walk over to the window, glancing out at the mostly empty parking lot. "I'm planning to talk to a CI tomorrow. Downtown. Was hoping you could take a long lunch break and happen to wander over from headquarters. Back me up?"

There's a long pause. And I already know I'm not going to like what I hear.

"I knew about CBI getting involved," my ex-partner says. "Got a call from Agent Nathan Winfrey about an hour ago, actually."

I close my eyes, cursing under my breath. "What about?"

"Winfrey thought you might use your LAPD contacts to run your own side investigation."

Which is exactly what I'm doing. I squeeze the phone so hard the plastic creaks.

"Winfrey's a control freak," he says. "He wants to know everything that's going on. He's going to make trouble for you if he finds out what you're doing."

"You going to tell him?"

"Of course not. And I'm not gonna tell you what to do. But don't you think you should sit this one out? Enjoy having a few days off. Let somebody else take the heat for once."

"I'll consider it. Thanks for the heads up. Let me know if Winfrey bugs you again."

"Holt, I—"

I end the call. I've heard enough.

I sit on my bed, phone in my hand. I don't even want to *think* about whether Jane could be right—that there's some conspiracy against us. That somebody in the state government could be on Asher Temple's payroll. Maybe even CBI.

So, I'm not sure what to do. I've never dealt with a situation like this before.

Relying on LAPD to back me up? That's out.

I lay down and stare at the ceiling, still puzzling through my options—my *lack* of options—and I doze off.

Half-formed dreams flit through my mind. Streaks of red, the echo of gunshots. Laughter that dissolves into screams.

Then the dream shifts. To a dark sheet of hair falling across my skin. Something warm and yielding underneath me. A sharp gaze pinning me, challenging me, leaving me unable to break away. But I don't want to.

I want to draw her closer. I want to find out what happens if I don't let go.

∼

I GASP, SITTING UP.

Jane is in the doorway, her fist against the frame. Like she was just knocking. "Sorry. I didn't mean to surprise you. I just thought… You were sleeping for a while."

"No. Thanks." I drop my legs off the bed. Rub my eyes. The lights are off, and the window is dark. "I didn't mean to pass out."

Then I realize my dick is straining at my zipper. *Shit*. I'm hard. It must've been those dreams. Sexy dreams about the woman who's standing in this room with me.

And Jane's going for the light.

She flips it on just as I cover my lap with my arm. "You were tired," she says. "I was, too. I napped a bit."

Quickly, I grab my phone from the nightstand and check my messages. And there it is, just what I needed—a text from my mom. Erection thwarted.

I focus on her message. She and Henry are settling in, and Henry spent the afternoon in the park with Chase's two-year-old daughter. I smile and show Jane a picture of the two kids eating popsicles together. They're both covered in chocolate.

"Cute," she says.

"Very." I get lost for a minute in the image. Then I check for any emails or texts from Detective Murphy.

Nothing.

I don't know which is worse. That I might've slept through a crucial email that would blow this investigation open, or that no such message came. What does that mean? Is Murphy too busy to write, or is there nothing to say? Is she bowing to Winfrey's pressure too?

I hate being out of the loop. Especially when this case involves *my fucking life*. And that of my family.

I look up at Jane. "You hungry?"

"Not really."

"Me neither. Might as well be productive." I bend down to grab the lockbox I stowed beneath my bed. It holds my guns.

A Glock 22 and a smaller Ruger that I usually keep in an ankle holster.

"What're you doing?" Jane asks.

I bring the lockbox to the table and open it. Set each gun out. "We need to get ready for tomorrow. If you're my backup, you need to know how to use one of these." *If* being the operative word there. I haven't decided. "Have you fired a gun before?"

"Yes."

"Do you own any?"

"No. But I grew up around guns. My Gran in Arizona had hunting rifles."

My eyebrow ticks. "Arizona? That's where you're from?"

She pauses. I get the sense that she didn't mean to reveal that. "Yep."

Before we got stuck together at the courthouse, I'd assumed she was from Southern California. She doesn't have any particular accent, although that can be misleading. But she tends to have that breezy disdain that I encounter sometimes among LA natives. Well, she had it before. Not so much now.

"Where in Arizona?"

"Here and there."

She definitely doesn't want to discuss it. That's fine. "You don't have to tell me."

"I know I don't."

"Sit down," I say.

She doesn't move.

I add, "Please?" and she takes the seat across from me at the table.

I show her the parts of the guns. Explain safety protocols, how to load the magazines properly with and without the speed loader, and how to chamber a round. Given what we've faced since yesterday, I want us both ready for anything tomorrow. Unfortunately, we don't have a shooting range here for her to practice. But this is better than nothing.

The hotel's quiet. I wonder if the suburban cops got their dinner, if they've had another shift change. They've mostly been leaving us alone.

Jane is replacing the rounds in the Ruger magazine. A bullet slides into place. Another.

I'm surprised when she starts talking.

"My Gran lived in Tucson. But my older sister Pam and I were born southwest of there. Tiny town with nothing but desert around us. That's why I like West Oaks. The green and the water. I'd only seen the ocean in books or online until Gran took us on a road trip here when we were in high school."

"Were your parents around?"

She pauses so long, I think she's not going to answer me. But then she does. "Not my dad. My mother, yes and no. Mostly, Gran raised us." She slides another bullet into the magazine. "Pam and I hitchhiked north on Highway 19 to get to Gran's that first time. We showed up on her doorstep covered in dust and eating Twizzlers some trucker had bought us. God, we were so stupid."

I want to cringe and agree. Sometimes, I'm thankful I don't have daughters. Maybe I will someday, and then I'll have new sources of anxiety. "But you made it okay?"

"Yep. Luckily." Her eyes lift briefly.

I'm curious about Jane. Every small piece I learn about her, I want to know more. She's a mystery to me, and mysteries beg to be solved. Like that picture she took of Henry this morning and sent to me. It was thoughtful of her. As if she'd just wanted to be nice.

A few days ago, I might've thought she had some hidden agenda, but not anymore. When Jane's trying to mess with me, she's upfront about it. I like that about her.

In fact, I like quite a few things about her.

And I want her to like me too, if only to prove I'm not the irredeemable asshole she thought I was.

"What made you become a defense attorney?" I try to ask that as neutrally as possible, but the little twitch in her expression suggests I've offended her. She doesn't answer the question.

She asks me a different one. "Your mom said you're from Houston?"

"The suburbs west of Houston, but yeah. I grew up a Texas boy."

"Did you have a cowboy hat?"

I laugh, shaking my head. "Did *you*, Ms. Arizona? I played football though. I made it through a year at UT Austin, but college wasn't my thing. Joined the Marines. Got sent to Camp Pendleton. That's where I caught the bug for California."

"I never would've thought you were from Texas. You don't have an accent."

"Plenty of Texans don't have much accent. But mine does come out on occasion." I let my vowels lengthen, and my syllables slow. "When I want it to."

Jane gives me a small smile, and I sense she's holding back a bigger one. "I like it. Might work with suspects. Get that charming, *aw, shucks* vibe going."

"D'you think I'm charming?" I'm laying it on a bit thick now.

"Didn't say I did. But a suspect might. I know you cops are always looking for an edge in interrogations."

My accent also comes out when I'm having sex. But Jane will have to figure that out for herself. I mean, she would, if…

Where is my brain going right now? Because a sexy dream

The Six Night Truce

about her is one thing. Trying to get her to act it out? That's another.

"Do your girlfriends like it?" she asks.

"Like what?"

"The accent."

I feel the hairs on my arms raise. Like all my exposed skin is aware of Jane.

"Maybe. Next time I go on a date with someone, I'll ask her. But I haven't dated much since Henry came to live with me."

She nods, her fingers running over the grip of the Ruger. I wonder if her heart's beating even half as hard as mine. And my dick is starting to wake up again and pay attention.

I remember how she felt in my lap earlier in her hotel room, when we were wrestling around. How her skin felt under my hands.

"What about you? Seeing anyone?"

"Why do you ask?"

"I want to get to know you." My voice sounds lower than I'd intended. All husky and suggestive.

She glances at me and inhales slowly, chest lifting. "Careful. It almost sounds like you're flirting with me, detective."

I clear my throat. "Um…"

Jesus, I *am* flirting with her.

I want to get to know you?

I'm showing her my guns and low-key propositioning her like a creeper in a sexual harassment training video. While she's trapped alone with me *in a hotel room*.

I can just imagine explaining this situation to Internal Affairs. Or how about to my mom?

What the fuck, Holt?

I sit back in my chair. "I apologize. Your personal life is not my business."

But she laughs. "I was kidding. I don't date much either. Dating sucks."

I tap my feet on the carpet. I need to watch myself. But do I end this conversation, like I should? Nope. I double down. "Can't be as bad in West Oaks as LA. *Nothing* is worse than dating in LA."

"What's your most horrendous dating story?"

"How about the time my date insisted on a sushi place in Santa Monica, left me with a three-hundred-dollar bill, and disappeared into the bathroom for about half an hour with our waiter?"

She barks a laugh. "You should've taken her to a diner for hot fudge sundaes."

I grin. "You're right. At least *I* would've had fun."

"Any woman with sense would, too." Jane's looking down at the table, eyelashes splayed on her cheeks.

Wait. Is *she* flirting with *me*?

My body is screaming to pull her close. To just say *fuck it* and find out if she's feeling this too.

No. I need to back off. My dick's lonely, and it's responding to the proximity of a beautiful woman. I'm not going to act like the horn dog that I apparently am. Still, I don't want to force her to leave if she'd like to stay.

"Want to watch Netflix?" Yeah, that's my brilliant solution. Watch Netflix. Code everywhere for, *I want to have sex with you.*

"Watch what on Netflix?"

I cough. "A documentary?" That's decidedly unsexy. Maybe a true crime show that we'll argue about. Except arguing seems to end up with Jane and me gravitating towards one another, instead of apart.

"Sure," she says. "Let me wash my hands first."

I lock up the guns and wash my hands next. Then I run down to the lobby for a couple drinks and some chips and pretzels. I get extras for the cops on duty. They grin and thank me.

On the way, I give myself a lecture. I'm going to behave. Jane and I are supposed to be working together, and if anything unprofessional happens between us, it's going to cause problems.

I'm a grown man in my mid-thirties. I'm a father. I can control myself.

Except I haven't felt this attracted to someone in a while. It's weird that it's her, but also not. Even when we "hated" each other, Jane never failed to get my blood pumping. And the thought of getting close to her, feeling her up against me…

This could get complicated.

But has my momma accused me of being a bad influence before? The youngest brother who somehow managed to rope his older siblings into trouble? Yes. Yes, she has.

18

Sean

When I get back to the room, Jane's settled on one of the beds. I hold up the bags of snacks. "Preference?"

She frowns like this is a crucial question. "Chips. Wait, no. Pretzels."

I toss her the bag. "We can trade after a while."

"Good plan."

I hand her a drink, kick off my shoes, and sit on the other bed. Jane already has the remote—sneaky of her—and she switches on the TV. The guide pops up with cable and streaming options, but there's also a preview window showing a live news conference.

It's the governor of California. And standing beside him is Nixon Temple. Asher Temple's father.

"What do we have here?" Jane switches to that channel, and the news conference takes up the screen.

"I want to assure the public," the current governor is saying, "that our judicial buildings are safe. Our institutions are safe. We believe the attack in West Oaks yesterday was a random and cowardly act of terrorism. An attack on all of us. On our collective belief in justice."

"Random?" Jane spits out.

An attack on all of us? Uh, no. Felt pretty targeted to me.

"I'm pleased to announce," the governor continues, "a nonpartisan effort in our state legislature to address security in our courthouses and other public buildings. You all know former Governor Nixon Temple. His own son was at the West Oaks courthouse yesterday when the attack occurred. Nixon is here with me today, representing the other half of our joint effort. It's unacceptable that a single citizen would feel unsafe when—"

Jane switches the TV off. "I can't listen to any more of that."

"Me neither." I clench my jaw so hard it's creaking. "Current and ex-governor, spinning what happened for political gain." Not that surprising, but it still pisses me off. Plus, that news conference ruined any flirtation we might've been having. Mood officially killed.

Jane opens the pretzel bag and shoves one into her mouth. It snaps under her teeth like bones breaking. "David's lying in a hospital bed, and they're pretending it was random? We're in protective custody right now because someone is trying to *kill us*. That is not random!"

"They're trying to act like the shooting had no purpose but to spread fear. Easier to explain it away and turn it all into political theater. But this fits with what Murphy said earlier. Agent Winfrey doesn't see a clear connection between the courthouse shooting and the secondary attacks on you and me afterward. Agent Hartford might be more open-minded, but he's not the one in charge."

Jane turns her incredulous expression on me. "You believe that bullshit?"

"No. Of course I don't."

She gets up from the bed and starts to pace. "This is a cover up. Nixon Temple has his tentacles in the investigation." Then Jane whirls to face me. "How many people know where we are?"

I grip the skin between my eyes. "Very few people are aware of our exact location. And we've been here for twenty-four hours already. Nobody's bothered us."

"But they could."

"We need to stay calm. Does this suck? Yes. But I refuse to believe there's a vast, statewide conspiracy and that everyone's against us."

She tips her head back and groans in frustration.

"It's going to be all right." I get up and walk over to her. I feel that urge again to touch her. I want to brush her hair from her face, run my thumb down her cheek. Make her feel better. But I don't give in.

She'd probably slap me. As she should. I need some *sense* slapped into me.

Even though what I *really* want is to shove her up against the wall and find out how she tastes.

Enough, Holt. Stop it.

"Look, nothing has changed," I say. "We stick with our plan. Tomorrow we're going to keep working on our own investigation, no matter what the CBI thinks."

Jane nods, chewing her lip.

"But tonight, if you want, you can stay over here with me. We'll set all the locks. We could even use chairs to barricade the doors." I'm hoping that doesn't sound like a sleazy come-on. I don't mean it to be. "Unless someone firebombs the entire hotel, we'll be secure."

Her eyes bug. I shouldn't have said that.

"Nobody's firebombing anything," I add. "We're fine."

"I know that. This is just stressful." Jane sits on the end of the bed, head in her hands. "I've never been scared to face down bullies. But I need to know who's coming at me. I have to know who I'm supposed to fight."

"I feel the same. Believe me."

Thank God Mom and Henry are with Chase. I owe Jane for convincing me to move them.

"I'll stay here with you," she says in a small voice. She won't meet my eyes. "Thanks."

"You're welcome."

Jane brings her things over to my room. We lock everything we can and position chairs under doorknobs. My bed is already the one closest to the hallway door. I set my guns just underneath on the floor, within easy reach.

Jane gets ready in the bathroom and then crawls beneath the covers on the other bed. Neither of us mentions Netflix.

She faces away from me. I switch off the lamp. I'm trying to act like this is all normal. But my nerves are on high alert, my body raring to go. To fight and protect.

"Goodnight." *Janie*, I add silently.

"Night," she murmurs.

I'm still awake long after she's fallen asleep.

Whenever I've been on duty, either as a Marine, or a patrol cop, or a detective, I've always known who the good guys were and who were the bad.

What happens when I don't know which side I'm on anymore?

19

Janie

The next morning, Sean is quiet and broody on our way into Los Angeles. He slouches as he drives, one long arm resting on top of the steering wheel.

We're in his Ford F-150, which he brought to the hotel from West Oaks. When we left this morning, our police minders asked where we were going. Sean gave them a vague answer, and though they seemed skeptical about us leaving protective custody, they didn't try to stop us either.

Sean told them we didn't need an escort and that we'd return by the early afternoon.

A baby car seat is in the back, since Chase used his daughter's when he picked up Henry and Liza. I'm not sure if Sean is thinking of his family right now, or if he's worrying over our investigation and what influence Nixon Temple could be exerting on the CBI.

Whatever he's brooding over, I wish he'd share it with me. Because this silence is making me antsy. Especially when you add it to the stop-and-go traffic that greets us on our way.

I tell Sean to just take the 101 and not the 405, but he

argues with me, claiming the 405 is faster at this particular window of time on this particular day. *I know LA better than you*, he says. And, big surprise, it's a parking lot.

Urrrgh.

The most infuriating part? The looks he sometimes casts my way.

When he used to sneer at me at the courthouse or the DA's office or police station, I could usually brush it off. We were on opposite sides. We didn't like each other. It was nice and simple.

Since we've joined forces, though, Sean's been turning up the charm. Last night, I was feeling the chemistry, and I wasn't exactly fighting it. The deep, sexy drawl, the *I-want-to-get-to-know-you* questions. I wasn't going to make a move, but if he did? I might've been into it. But after I agreed to share his room, Sean was totally professional and courteous. This morning, he pretended to be asleep until I was out of bed, showered, and changed.

Which was for the best. I know that.

But now, I swear I see *hunger* when he turns his eyes toward me. Like he's a predator, and his mouth is watering. Then he sighs, as if he's debating something over and over in his mind.

I cannot figure him out. Does he still hate me? Does he want me?

Is it both?

"Why are you looking at me like that?" I ask.

His eyes return to the road. "Like what?"

"Like you have something to say."

"I don't." Then he sighs loudly, once again. "Okay. I'm concerned. This CI we're meeting deals in information. That's why he's been so useful in the past. But the fact that you and I are working together is information in itself. I don't know who he'll decide to share that with."

"He won't risk telling anyone that he works with the police."

Sean's wearing dark jeans, a black T-shirt, and his black windbreaker. He has his gun holster on, and handcuffs hang from his belt. Every inch the cop. Which seems like a problem if he wants to be discreet about this meeting with the CI, but whatever. Not like I know anything about what it's like to be a senior detective.

"But you're an unknown factor," Sean says. "I don't know what the CI will do. What if he tries to double-cross me, and he uses you to do it?"

"You're worried about me?"

"Of course I am." He looks over again. "I don't want anything to happen to you. Especially not because of me."

I break eye contact, bowing my head. I can't remember the last time someone watched out for me. Not because it was his job, but because he…maybe…cared.

Is that what this is about? I realized that I like Sean. But does he like me back?

I sound like a middle-schooler.

You know what? I don't need this. I don't need his smoldering glances, or his pouty full lips, or his sexy muscular body. I don't need the smiles he showed me yesterday that were half wicked, half sweet. I certainly don't need his protective side.

I don't need this confusion.

I can acknowledge he's a good father. But when he's playing big-bad-detective, I can't stand Sean Holt, and that hasn't changed. Doesn't matter how fast my pulse is racing from just sitting next to him and feeling the raw masculinity burning off of him in waves.

I don't want anything to happen to you.

Nope. I don't need it.

I'm done.

"I'm coming with you," I say. "End of story. I'll be fine."

Sean focuses on the traffic ahead of us, shaking his head. But he gives up trying to argue.

I wish I had my red lipstick. Anything to put some distance between me and the rest of the world. I've never felt less like Jane the Panther.

And that's something else that's bugging me. Sean asked if he could call me Janie, and he hasn't. Not once.

On my phone, I send a quick reply to Liza, who's been sending adorable pictures of Henry all morning. I assume Sean gave her my number. I'd thank him for that if he wasn't being so frustrating today.

From the 405, we transition to the 10. We finally make it through the 110 interchange, and our crawl toward downtown enters its final stretch. Sean exits the freeway. We drive along Spring Street into the historic district.

Downtown LA is as varied as the city itself, full of unique little enclaves. Skyscrapers full of fancy offices, down the street from quaint one-story buildings housing hole-in-the-wall restaurants.

Sean pulls the truck into a parking garage. He finds a secluded spot and turns off the engine. Unbuckles his seatbelt. Now, he's staring at the concrete wall through the windshield. All handsome and dour.

"What's the plan?" I ask. He gave me the vague outline last night, but today he's been reluctant to go over specifics.

"The CI said I'll find him at the gyro truck parked near San Pedro and Third. Down the street from the Japanese Garden. We'll use the lunch crowds to keep from being noticed."

"What about me? What do you need me to do?"

"I need…" He's staring through the windshield again, as if he'll read the answer on the concrete.

"What? Spit it out."

"Fuck," he mutters. Sean turns to face me, and I swear his eyes are two pools of dark fire. "I need to say something to you."

He leans over. Reaches for my hand. My heart pounds like it's trying to reach back.

I can't speak. I don't know what this is.

"Janie," he breathes, soft as a prayer, while my lungs just about stop.

"Sean?" I whisper.

Then cold metal snaps onto my wrist.

Um, what?

Before I can react, he fastens the other end to the steering wheel.

"What the *fuck*?" I yank, and the cuffs pull taut.

"You're not coming with me."

I glare at him incredulously. "You cannot be serious. You did not just handcuff me to your car. Unlock me, Sean. This is not funny."

"I have no other choice. You weren't going to listen to me."

Of all the asshole stunts— "This is false imprisonment!"

"It's to keep you safe."

"No, it is not." The realization washes through me. "This is to protect your CI's identity. Because you don't trust me."

"No, it's because I don't trust the CI. I don't want him to know you're with me."

"You could've *asked me* to stay here and wait."

He smirks. "I tried. You already said no."

"You could've asked again!"

"You wouldn't have listened. Would you?"

I open my mouth. Close it.

"Yeah, that's what I thought."

Okay, I wouldn't have listened. Because I don't appreciate anyone, especially Sean, ordering me around. "You're such an asshole. If you didn't want me with you, you could've left me at the hotel."

He presses his mouth into a straight line. "I almost did, but I couldn't leave you alone. I've been debating since yesterday if I should bring you, and believe me, I changed my mind two dozen times. I don't like this any more than you do. If I could've come up with anything else—"

"You don't want to leave me alone, so you're leaving me *locked in your car*? Like a dog?"

"Don't be dramatic. I'm leaving you with your phone and my Ruger. And the key fob. You can drive out of here if you want." He throws up his hands. "Or, hell, I guess you could shoot me. But I do need your help. If I don't come back in thirty minutes, I want you to call my old partner at LAPD and tell him where I went. He won't be happy with me, but he'll help."

"Or I could call 911 right now and say I've been kidnapped."

"You could do that too. I'm not stopping you." Sean bends to pull the Ruger from his ankle holster. He tucks it beneath the front seat. He leaves his key fob in the cup holder beside my phone. "I'll text you my old partner's number. I'm sorry about this, Janie. I am."

The sound of my nickname on his lips makes me see red. "Fuck you, Holt. *Fuck. You.*"

"I'll be back soon." He pushes the driver's side door open. Then he has the nerve to give me a lopsided grin. "Try to stay out of trouble while I'm gone."

"I hate you."

He slams the door closed. I glare as he jogs toward the exit stairs.

I cannot believe he did this.

Sean cuffed me to his steering wheel.

My skin heats with shame. He called me Janie, and I turned into a puddle of goo. This is humiliating.

The asshole played me.

In the past couple days, I was actually starting to think Sean was a nice guy. Not the bossy, arrogant, my-way-or-the-highway alpha male I thought he was. Well, he's proven me wrong.

No wonder he was oozing testosterone on the drive here. He was dreaming up this little ploy. Sean knew he couldn't convince me to agree with him using words, so he just used brute force to get his way.

But that's okay. I'm not so easily defeated.

I dig around on the floorboards, searching for something I can use. In the glove compartment, I find a sturdy paperclip.

Jackpot.

I bend the metal and get to work.

If Sean wants to fight dirty, I'll show him who he's really dealing with.

20

Sean

Damn it, I wish I didn't have to do that. Just when Jane and I were getting along.

I wonder if she knows how much I revealed just now. When I leaned into her, reached for her hand, I didn't want to trick her. That was the last thing I wanted to do. I took no pleasure at all in slapping that cuff on her wrist.

I would much rather have kissed her.

Hard to imagine she'll forgive me for this, no matter how much I apologize. There went my hopes of any more wrestling matches—especially any naked ones. But at least she'll be safe.

I leave the parking garage and head over to San Pedro, walking toward the Japanese Garden. It's a beautiful, cool day. The light is bright yellow, the sky endless blue beyond the skyscrapers. Office workers are heading out for coffee breaks or early lunches.

When I reach Third, I scan the street for the gyro truck.

I spot Carl Proctor sitting on a curb, eating french fries. He's got a Dodgers cap pulled low over his sunburned face, baggy jeans, work boots. He eyes people as they pass.

Especially the women.

Carl Proctor has been an LAPD confidential informant for the last couple of years. He's a scrap metal dealer. Most chop shops are run by particular gangs, but when they're done stripping a stolen vehicle, a lot of them go to Proctor to get rid of the metal. Carl's an unassuming guy, the type who doesn't seem all that smart at first. But he's always listening, and he's good at getting people to talk.

Two years ago, LAPD busted his metal yard. But like many criminals when they're caught, he was eager to share info in exchange for leniency. Now, LAPD lets him run his business, even knowing that he has two sets of books. One for the legit scrap metal he collects, the other for the stolen shit from the chop shops. He knows what he has to do in return.

He's also been busted soliciting prostitutes who are just this side of underage. Each time, he's used his CI status to worm his way out of trouble.

When I was with Gang and Narcotics, I had to work with a lot of informants like Proctor. People who are borderline despicable, but not quite as bad as the others. Thanks to Proctor's input, we busted several car-theft rings. We worked hard to keep his identity under wraps, obfuscating where our information came from. I tried to keep a close eye on him and warn him he didn't have a get-out-of-jail-free card.

But keeping this CI's identity quiet isn't the reason I had to leave Janie behind.

It's exactly what I told her—I don't want Proctor around her. He's always acted like a creep around female officers, so that's part of it. But I don't want him trading in information about Jane. I don't even want that sleaze looking at her and getting ideas.

Proctor knows better than to mess with me. I can manage this meeting on my own.

I walk along a parallel path to where Proctor is sitting. Our eyes meet, and he nods slightly. I bend down to tie my shoe, and when I stand up, he's on the move.

I follow. He turns into an alleyway. We're not far from the crowds on the street, yet this narrow corridor is deserted. Proctor keeps going and stops behind a dumpster. It'll keep us out of sight of anyone passing the mouth of the alley.

The place reeks of rotting food and old grease. Proctor sniffs and rubs his nose. "Holt. I thought you left LA."

I cross my arms, my legs in a wide and dominant stance. "I did. But I'm working a case with LA ties."

"To the Serpents?"

I didn't tell Proctor much on the phone. But I did mention the name of the group I was interested in. "You said you have something for me?"

His eyes are darting around, and his weight shifts from foot to foot. "If you're not an LA cop anymore, why should I help you?"

"Because I still have plenty of friends in LAPD."

Proctor sneers, seeing right through that ploy. "Then why didn't you send them? Or bring them with you?"

"They have their own shit to do. I spared them this lovely visit." I gesture at our surroundings.

He snorts. "At least the fries from the food truck were good, even if I had to pay for them myself."

"I brought an incentive. Because I'm a nice guy." I pull a wad of $20 bills from my pocket. We usually don't pay informants, but it happens on occasion.

Proctor's eyes glitter. "You must really want this."

I put the money away and don't answer. He'll get paid after I'm happy with his info. And he knows it.

Proctor wipes his nose again. "Ask your question. Maybe I've got an answer."

"I want to know what the Serpents are up to. Some of

their members have been getting into mischief in West Oaks. That's not their usual turf, and I want to know why they're branching out."

That sharpness in Proctor's gaze intensifies. He knows exactly what I'm talking about. "West Oaks? The courthouse shooting?"

"I just want to know what you've heard."

He nods and kicks a soda can across the alley. "Yeah. Sure. I hear the Serpents are into something big out of town. Some guy in a car with blacked-out windows has been around. Some kind of Fed. Dressed in shit clothes, like he was trying to blend in, but anybody who knows anything could tell he didn't belong. I hear he was waving around a hell of a lot more money than you just showed me. He offered a deal they were real happy with."

"You're saying this guy was government?"

"I didn't see him. But maybe. Guy's not just paying in money, either. In something even more valuable. That's what one of the Serpents was bragging about."

"A barter of some kind?"

"Who knows? But if this deal is worth as much as people are suggesting, this Fed-type wants a lot for what he's offering."

I doubt the guy Proctor is talking about could be LAPD. There's no way any of them would've been so obvious.

FBI? That seems far-fetched. Why would the FBI want to go after me or Jane?

CBI?

Or maybe it wasn't someone from the government at all. It could've been some businessman who had no real clue what he was doing. Someone like Asher Temple. Or a guy who works for him.

That makes a lot more sense. A rich asshole who didn't even realize how much danger he was walking into. He's

The Six Night Truce

lucky the Serpents let him leave alive. He must've been offering a very sweet deal indeed.

Proctor takes a small step toward me. "You must think I'm pretty stupid. Do you think I can't use the Internet? I know you were at the courthouse when it got shot up. And I heard something about a couple bomb threats? One being at a West Oaks PD cop's house?"

"So?"

He smiles, showing rows of small teeth. "So you showed up here with no partner. Investigating something going down in West Oaks. Your turf. I think the Serpents are after you. And who's paying them? If it's really some G-man, that would be pretty bad for you. Wouldn't it?"

I harden my glare. "Your point?"

He takes another small step. "See, I've put up with cops like you shitting on me for the last two years. You all think I'm so fucking stupid, just there for you to bend me over and use me however. Like I'd never be able to turn you around and use you back."

I don't dare move. I can't show this asshole weakness. But I feel the weight of my gun against my lower back. "Yeah, you're a big man on the streets, Carl. Keep telling yourself that."

It's time to get out of here. This is more backbone than Proctor has ever shown me.

I take out the money and toss it at his feet. "I think we're done. I'm writing up a receipt for that and sending it to LAPD. Just so you know." Casually, I start reaching behind my back for my weapon.

But then there's movement.

Somebody else pops out from behind a stack of wooden crates. He's wearing a red trucker hat, and has the teeth and complexion of a meth head.

And he's pointing a gun at me.

"Don't fucking move, pig. Hands in the air."

Damn. It.

Internally, I'm kicking myself as I raise my hands. How did I manage to walk into this? Did moving to West Oaks make me soft?

Or have I always been this much of a dumbass?

Proctor saunters over to me. He lifts my shirt and grabs my Glock. Backs away, pointing it at me. "Way I see it, somebody wants their hands on you, and would pay dearly for that opportunity. Somebody who's got way deeper pockets than anybody I usually meet, and I want in on that."

"You obviously don't have the balls for this," I say. "Otherwise, there would've been a Serpent waiting to surprise me, instead of a fucking tweaker."

"Hey, we're the ones holding the guns, pig!"

I'm not worried about trucker-hat guy. He's standing yards away, like he's scared of me, and his shot is more likely to ricochet off the brick and hit *him* than find me.

Proctor's closer. He's smarter. But will he actually shoot me?

"I'm going to walk away, and I'll forget about this. But if you keep up with this nonsense? LAPD will turn your life inside out. What's to stop them from letting slip to every group in town that you've been snitching on them?"

Proctor steps over to a door in the brick building beside us. The hinges squeal when he opens it. "Why don't we go inside and wait while I make some calls. I'm going to invite some friends."

I cannot go in that building. Not if I want to get out of here alive.

21

Janie

It takes me less than five minutes to pick the lock on the cuffs. A few more seconds to grab the Ruger and stow it in the pocket of my hoodie.

Then I'm out of the car. I lock it behind me. Sean's key fob, my phone, and his handcuffs go in the back pockets of my jeans. I run toward the stairwell.

When I reach the bottom level, I push out of the door onto the street, scanning left and right.

Where did Sean go?

Right, San Pedro and Third. Which direction is that from here? I don't know downtown LA that well.

I check for directions on my phone and hurry down the sidewalk.

I find the gyro truck pretty easily. But where's Sean? He couldn't be that far ahead of me. It's only been a few minutes since he left me in the parking garage.

Then I spot his black windbreaker and broad shoulders.

There you are.

My anger is like a low flame, licking at the undersides of my skin. Not just anger. Disappointment.

I thought he wanted…

Nope. I'm not going to think about that.

He underestimated me. There's no way Sean could've guessed that I know how to pick locks. I can't remember how many times Mom locked Pam and me out of the trailer before passing out, and I had to get us back in after school.

I'm not following Sean because I'm spying. I couldn't care less about his precious CI's identity.

I'm following because he has no backup without me, and if something happens to him? I'm not going to tell Liza her son is hurt because I wasn't there. I know what it's like to grow up without a parent around. Henry deserves better than that. Even if his dad acts like an arrogant prick.

Sean thinks he doesn't need me, but I'm going to look out for him anyway. When I commit to something, to some*one*, I don't back out. I'm not perfect, but at least I can say *that* for myself. It's more than Sean can claim.

I follow Sean on his path toward the gyro truck. He glances back, and I dip my head, lingering behind a group of office workers and a few panhandlers.

I see him turn down an alley, and I rush to catch up.

I approach slowly, stopping at the edge of the building, and I listen. Sean's voice is a low rumble. Then I hear another man's, thin and nasally. That must be the CI.

I peek my head around, and all I see is a dumpster. But there's a flash of brown hair and a black windbreaker. I feel better knowing where he is.

The Ruger is heavy in my pocket.

I remember what Sean said earlier. That he was worried the informant could try to double-cross him. Was he just saying that because he wanted me to stay behind? He seemed sincere when he claimed to worry about my safety. So maybe it's true. But if I could be at risk from this guy, so could Sean. He's not invincible.

The Six Night Truce

I'm not a cop, and I don't have the training to know how to approach this situation. But it seems to me like I should come around the opposite side of the alley. That way, if the CI does anything shifty, I could step in.

I'm not exactly a special operative or anything. But I'm all the backup Sean's got. I have to think I'm better than nothing.

Quickly, I go around the side of the building, looking for another way into the alley. I find a tiny gap between the old brick structures. It's about two feet wide. I edge down this gap until I'm almost to the alley.

Their voices are louder now. I look and see the back of a man in a flannel shirt. He's talking to Sean.

"You all think I'm so fucking stupid, just there for you to bend me over."

Then I inhale sharply as I spot someone else. There's a guy in a red hat hiding behind a stack of wooden crates. He's watching Sean and the informant.

This can't be good.

Should I get Sean's attention to warn him? Or would that do more harm than good?

I take the Ruger out of my pocket, balancing my weight on the balls of my feet.

While I'm still debating, the guy with the red trucker hat steps out into the open, raising a pistol. "Don't fucking move, pig. Hands in the air."

I cringe. Yeah, this is happening. Shit.

Sean is acting all calm about this development, but I'm sweating and shaking.

What if that guy opens fire before I can do anything?

I try to stay out of sight as I edge toward the guy with the trucker hat. Both he and the informant are focused on Sean. Sean doesn't see me, either. Which is good, because I don't want him to give me away.

"I'm going to walk away, and I'll forget about this. But if you keep up with this nonsense? LAPD will turn your life inside out."

Is Sean trying to provoke these guys? Seriously? That seems like a terrible idea, but what do I know.

The informant opens a door leading into the building beside me. This is it. I know enough to realize Sean will be in trouble if they get him inside.

I step out behind the guy in the red trucker hat. His gun has just drooped, his aim moving slightly away from Sean.

"LAPD," I scream. "Drop the weapon and get on the ground."

Sean, to his credit, doesn't hesitate a single moment. In less than a second, he's elbowed the informant in the face and grabbed his Glock from the guy's hand. Red hat guy is still trying to figure out what's going on.

I chamber a round and shove the muzzle of the Ruger into his neck. "I said, drop it."

He obeys. I grab Sean's handcuffs from my pocket and snap one onto the guy's wrist as I shove him to his knees. I wrench his arms back. Snap the other cuff on. I might not be a cop, but I've seen enough body cam videos. I know how this part works.

Sean has his informant on the ground. He's gawking at me, shaking his head. "You know," Sean says, "impersonating an officer is a serious crime."

"Shut up. Tell me what we're supposed to do with these idiots."

Sean takes out his phone and makes a call. "Hey, it's Holt. I'm downtown. I need someone to come pick up Carl Proctor and his friend. Proctor decided to get cute with me." He rolls his eyes. He's quiet, nodding his head as the person on the line talks in rapid-fire syllables. "Yes, I am a very bad boy. I owe you until the end of time. But can you send someone to pick these two up? I have bigger shit to deal with. When I can explain, I will. But not now."

The person on the line curses loud enough I can hear it, and Sean holds the phone back from his ear.

A few minutes later, two patrol officers show up and take the CI and Red Hat off our hands. Sean flashes his badge and makes excuses, telling them to talk to his former partner in Gang and Narcotics.

Then he puts his palm between my shoulder blades and ushers me down the street. "We need to get out of here before they haul us to LAPD headquarters for questioning. My ex-partner is pissed enough as it is."

∽

We cross the street and jog along the sidewalk, dodging pedestrians on our way to the parking garage.

Once the heavy door closes and we're in the stairwell, Sean stops and turns around. "Are you okay?" He sounds breathless.

"Me? I'm fine. I didn't have any guns pointed at me."

"Yeah, I could've planned better. I'm way outside the lines at this point." His eyes squeeze closed. "But what you just did? That was insanely dangerous."

"You're not even grateful?"

"Of course I'm grateful. But it could've gone a lot differently."

"Yes. You could be dead." I start to mount the stairs, but Sean catches my hand.

"Jane. Thank you. I would've preferred to keep you out of it, but you were pretty badass."

That softens me. Just a little. "You saved my life before. I returned the favor."

"I appreciate it." Now, he looks away, frowning. Like he's not happy about what he needs to say next. "I know that what I did in the truck earlier seemed extreme—"

"Handcuffing me to your steering wheel? False imprisonment? Luckily, I know how to pick locks."

"Lucky for me, you mean." His mouth quirks in a tiny smile. "I wanted to keep you safe. I care about what happens to you, and I won't apologize for that. But I'm sorry about the way I did it."

Suddenly, I'm feeling sheepish. I guess nearly seeing Sean murdered cleared away the bullshit.

"You tried to talk to me beforehand," I say. "You were worried about me, and I wasn't listening. We both should've compromised and come up with a better plan in the first place. So...I'm sorry too."

"Listen to us, being all mature."

I try to smile, but I'm just not feeling it. I start climbing the stairs.

But Sean grabs my hand again. Pulls me back. He's on the step below me. We're eye-to-eye.

"Jane, I want to figure out how to make this partnership work. But I'd be lying if I said you're no different from Detective Murphy or Officer Shelborne. I'm not like this with the female cops I work with."

Not this stubborn? Not this obnoxious? "It's because I'm a defense attorney. I get it."

"That isn't what I mean." Sean's fingers touch my chin, and I rear back.

"What're you doing?" I've whispered these words. Less an accusation than a plea for some clarity. Because I don't know what this man expects from me.

He just stares at me like he doesn't know, either.

Being near him like this, and wanting... Ugh, I don't even

know what I want. Or what I thought. Why I'm even surprised at the way he's acted.

I'm not angry anymore. Just tired. Tired of arguing, tired of this dance between us.

"We're both fine. Let's just go." I start up the stairs. After a moment, he follows.

In a way, I understand his overprotectiveness. That informant was not a nice guy. But I've dealt with troublesome people many times before. We could've avoided most of this mess if Sean had just *trusted me*.

But that was too much to ask, wasn't it?

He is *never* going to trust me.

This isn't a partnership. This isn't even a friendship.

We're just two people who barely tolerate each other. And I feel stupid for imagining—however briefly—that we could be anything more.

22

Sean

We're back on the freeway, getting the hell out of LA.

What a shit show.

Thank goodness Jane knows how to pick locks and didn't listen to me. She's right, we should've figured out a better plan from the start. She could've sneaked around the other side of the alley from the very beginning. We could've worked together. But I didn't imagine she'd be quite so efficient at playing police.

I'm impressed. Really impressed.

This woman…she's got me so tied up inside I don't know which way I'm heading. Well, except out of downtown. That much, I can figure out.

Never would've expected this, but I'm glad she's on my side.

I rest my elbow beneath the driver's side window. "The CI's name is Carl Proctor." Not much point in keeping his name confidential. Now that LAPD knows about Proctor's shenanigans, he won't stay a CI for long. At least, I hope not. It's out of my hands.

"He's a scrap metal dealer," I explain. "A lot of different chop shops use him, different gangs. So he hears rumors. He told me the Serpents have something major in the works. A guy in a car with tinted windows has been negotiating with them. Offering favors and influence, not just money, for a hit. Which I'll bet is against us and David Daily."

Jane hasn't responded. Or even looked at me. But I keep going.

"It's possible they're dealing with someone in law enforcement or the government. Which could mean you were right. This is a bigger deal than I thought. Maybe...conspiracy level. It's hard to say who we can trust."

No response.

"I'm going to check in with Detective Murphy. Discreetly, of course. I want to make sure nobody else is listening in." I'm waiting for Jane to object. To argue that we can't even trust Murphy, though I disagree. Whatever this conspiracy is, there's no way Murphy would be part of it.

"What do you think?" I ask. "Are you good with me contacting Murphy? Telling her what we found out?"

Silence. That's bad enough. But I'm not getting *anything* from her. No anger, no outrage. No simmering annoyance.

When we were talking in the stairwell, I thought we'd resolved our issues. We both said we were sorry, and I told her I wanted to make this partnership work, even if it's difficult. But how can we do that if she won't talk to me?

"Can you answer me? Please?"

She just stares out her window. With some women, I might think this was passive aggressive bullshit. But not her. I don't know if she's gathering her thoughts or trying not to go off on me. But it feels like she's freezing me out. And I hate it.

I squeeze the steering wheel as the miles go by.

Jane clears her throat, and I exhale. Thank God. She's going to say something.

"Don't take the exit for the hotel. I'd like to head back to West Oaks."

"West Oaks? Do you think we should meet with Murphy in person?"

"What you do is your business. *I* am going back to my apartment. The police already checked it out. Nobody broke in there. I'm ready to go home."

I glance rapidly between her and the road. "That's not safe. I guarantee the Serpents know where you live."

She shrugs. She's been speaking calmly, practically in a monotone. Like I'm not even worth fighting anymore. "I'll pack up and go stay somewhere else. I'll figure it out." Jane leaves out the rest, but I hear it.

As long as I'm nowhere near you.

I'd say she's overreacting, except if anything, she's *under*reacting. I want her to yell at me again. Get pissed off and dramatic. Not this. Not shutting me out.

She's not mad. She's acting...fuck, like I hurt her feelings.

I take the very next exit and pull my truck over. The tires crunch on the shoulder. I throw the gear into park. "Don't be like this."

"Like what? Reasonable? I'm just doing what's logical."

"We're safer together. I forgot that earlier, and I was wrong. Obviously. Because I needed you to save my ass."

No reaction. Not even a smug smile.

This is bad.

"Go back to being angry at me," I say. "I can take it. But don't put your life at risk just to spite me."

"I'm not trying to spite you. At all."

"Then why?"

"Sean, you don't trust me. You don't respect me."

"That is not true."

"There's no point to this..." She gestures at me, then herself. "This *whatever* between us."

I unbuckle my seatbelt so I can face her better. "But there *is* something between us. It's more than just the truce. It's the reason my head got so turned around about keeping you safe."

It's what I was trying to explain in the stairwell.

You feel it, I want to shout. *You do.*

"I thought there might be something." Her voice is devoid of emotion. "I...wanted there to be. But it might as well be nothing."

She wanted there to be something? "Jane. *Janie*." I want her to look at me. I want her to say, to my face, that she doesn't feel this wild, unstoppable chemistry. This electromagnetic pull.

I want a fucking reaction.

And I am not just gonna shrug my shoulders and say, *oh well*, and drop her off in West Oaks. I'm worried about what'll happen to her. But even more than that, I'm worried she'll never speak to me again.

This *whatever* between us will be over. Without either of us figuring out what it is. Or what it could become.

So I grab her chin, turn her head, and I press my mouth to hers.

She makes a tiny sound of shock. Her palms land on my chest, but the rest of her goes still. I tilt my head so the bow of her top lip slides into the gap between my lips. I feel my stubble grazing her skin.

She can push me away. Slap me. Curse me out, if that's what she wants to do.

Give me something. Anything.

I press my mouth even harder for a brief moment. Inside me, there's a firestorm. A tornado of *I want* and *I need* and *Janie, Janie, Janie*.

I force myself to break the kiss. I sit back slightly. I wait.

She's breathing deeply. I'm still close enough to feel her exhales. But aside from that, there's no reaction. No anger or disgust. No encouragement either. Nothing.

Then her eyes narrow. "That all you've got?"

That's a challenge if I ever heard one.

I unlatch her seatbelt and push the restraint out of the way. Then my hands are framing her face. I kiss her again. My tongue slides along the seam of her lips. I breathe in her feminine scent. Flowers, a hint of spice and bourbon vanilla. I caress her jaw with my thumb, my touch just on the other side of gentle.

With a sigh, Jane's lips open slightly, and my tongue slips inside. She lets me taste her.

Yes. This.

I didn't realize how desperate I was for this until I started kissing her, and now, I can't stop. Not unless she shoves me away. Maybe she's luring me closer, and she's going to bite down. I'm willing to take the chance. Just to feel her. To know what it's like.

I stroke her tongue with mine. I suck on her lips, and I feel the pliant give of her mouth all the way in my balls, in my hardening cock. She's in all of my senses. I want every inch of Janie, every molecule that she'll let me have.

I want to lay claim to this woman. To protect her from danger, yes. But the real obstacle in my way is Janie herself, all the barriers she constantly throws up in my path. The distance she keeps.

Some of that's my fault. The misunderstandings and misplaced assumptions we've both made.

But I think Janie keeps a certain distance from *everyone*, and I want to cross it. I want *in*.

And holy shit, the way she's letting me kiss her? She's

The Six Night Truce 165

soft and submissive under my hands, under my lips, and I know what a concession this is.

So I'm not surprised at all when she finally breaks the kiss.

In fact, I'm shocked she let it go for that long.

Janie's shivering. "What are we doing?"

I roll my tongue inside my mouth, chasing the lingering taste of her. "I want you." The words rumble out of my chest.

"But you hate me."

"I've never said that." I might've thought it, but I was being an ass. "You're the one who hates me." I smile, showing her I'm okay with it. I don't need her to pet my ego.

The last thing I'd *ever* want her to do is lie to me.

"You can hate me if that's how you feel," I say. "I hope you don't. But either way, I still want you. I can't help it." I think I've wanted her since we met, as much as I tried to tell myself I didn't. I want her passion and her inner fire. The way she pushes me and challenges me.

And then the softness that shows through the cracks in her defenses. God, that sweet softness that's *Janie*. That's what I want the most. The pieces of her I doubt many people get to see.

I glance down at her kiss-swollen lips. My hands are still on her face. Her fingers close over mine.

Janie forces my touch away, shaking her head.

My stomach falls through the floor of my truck.

"That's not…I don't hate you, Sean. I know I said it earlier when I was pissed off, but I didn't mean it." Any trace of bravado or challenge in her expression is gone. She's not hiding from me, but that just makes her vulnerability more obvious. "So if that's what you want from me, a hot and dirty hate-fuck, this needs to stop. That's not me."

Jane faces the window again, looking small and sad.

Like I've hurt her. *Again*.

I'm doing this all wrong.

I grasp her chin and gently coax her to look at me. "Maybe a part of me didn't trust you to handle someone like Carl Proctor and his meth head friend. But when you appeared in that alley and you showed those assholes who was boss? I thought you were incredible. Janie, I do respect you. I trust you. I *like* you."

Her pupils dilate. Her gaze drops to my mouth. "I like you, too." Her words are so quiet, I feel them more than hear them. "I...want you. But..."

I kiss behind her earlobe. The tiny hairs on her skin tickle my mouth. My voice drops to a whisper, and my lips brush against her ear. "Let me show you how I'll take care of you. Let me be sweet to you." Each time I pause, my lips find her skin again, leaving a trail of kisses down her neck. "Let me have you."

"Sean," she breathes.

I can't resist. The tip of my tongue darts out. I trace back up her neck. I suck her earlobe, working it gently between my teeth, and moan. She gasps.

My cock is so hard it's trying to rip through my jeans.

Janie launches herself across the cabin of the truck. We get tangled up for a second, maneuvering between the center console and the door and steering wheel, and I push back the seat to give us more space. She slots into my lap like she belongs there. Her legs straddle me.

My erection presses against her through two sets of denim, and I know she must feel it. Not much point in being shy.

My hands palm her ass, pulling her even closer. Our stomachs touch, our chests. Her breasts are full. The perfect balance between soft and firm. I want to undress her, kiss all her curves, worship her hidden places until she's coming apart. I want that heat between her legs. I just know it'll be wet for me. Quivering.

Fuck, I want that pussy under my tongue, wrapped tight around my dick.

All that wanting gathers in my chest and comes out in a guttural growl.

I need to *slow this down* because I am riled up.

Janie's dark eyes take me in. She ruffles my hair, runs her hand over my cheek. I turn into her touch. Her thumb brushes my lips, and I kiss the tip of it.

I thought I liked when she fought with me, but this is so much better. This is hunger, but it's also affection. A craving for closeness. She's showing me what she wants, and it's what I want too. It's what I want *most*.

We still don't know each other that well, but I understand this need she's conveying. To show kindness and regard for another person. To show care.

I truly care about Janie, improbable as that would've seemed a few days ago, and she must care, at least a little, about me. We have a connection, and we both feel it. We want to express it. Simple as that. There's no way this can be wrong.

I don't think Janie's ever been this quiet around me, and I wonder if her thoughts match up with mine.

This time, I wait for her to kiss me. If there's any doubt in her mind, we won't do this. I won't keep pushing. Maybe I've already pushed too much, but at least I've put myself out there. If my words and my kisses left any room for interpretation, my hard-on filled in the gaps. So to speak.

Janie pushes my windbreaker off my shoulders. She helps me take it off, which is good because we have very little room to move right now. She tosses it into the rear seat.

Her hands move over my T-shirt, then along my arms. She

laces our fingers together. I want to take off her hoodie, but I've been demanding enough.

With aching slowness, Janie leans into me, and our lips brush again. Her tongue barely licks into my mouth. Her kiss is like an invitation. A tease, hinting at how much more she wants to give, but telling me I'll have to take it.

And *oh*, do I want to take it. I want it all.

Not here, though. This isn't nearly enough space for everything I want to do to her. And we're in broad daylight just off a public highway. A couple cars have driven by already.

Yet I can't stop touching her. I deepen the kiss, my tongue surging. Janie's honest-to-goodness kissing me back now, meeting my enthusiasm with her own. My toes curl in my shoes.

This need is so overpowering that I'm doing geometry in my head, wondering if we can move to the back seat—if maybe—

I must be crowding her, because Janie's back hits the steering wheel with a shrill *honk*. We both jump and gasp.

And then we collapse into each other, giggling. Her arms are around my neck, her forehead touching mine.

The heat between us still simmers, but this is nice too. I run a hand along her spine, cradling her to me. I kiss her hair. "Do you still want to head back to West Oaks?"

"No." Janie separates from me and gives my lips another soft kiss. "Take me to the hotel. You're right. We're safer together."

I nod. "I won't forget that again."

"Neither will I. And maybe..." She bites her lip. "We can be sweet to each other some more when we get there."

"I like being sweet to you."

"But sweet and spice are a good combination," she whispers.

"Very good." My cock twitches. I was starting to soften, and now I'm getting excited again. But I can wait.

She crawls back into her seat. We latch our seatbelts, and as I drive to get on the freeway again, I reach for her hand.

Janie smiles at me. I've had glimpses of this side of her before, especially when she was around my mom and Henry. But she's never turned that sunshine so fully toward me until now. I like it. A lot. It feels like a gift.

Yesterday, Jane pointed out that nobody is just one thing. I like and admire the fiery part of her. The fierce opponent who keeps me on my toes. Who picked the lock on my handcuffs and chased after me to save my ass, when she could've just bailed.

But I want to know all the different shades of her. I think she might actually let me.

I want Janie to know me, too. She's opening up, and I'd like to do the same. That's something I haven't felt in a while. But I'm going to be cool from now on. I'm going to follow her lead.

Even if this closeness only lasts a few more days, until the end of our truce, I'm pretty sure it'll be worth it.

23

Janie

I can hardly believe this is happening. Sean kissed me. And it was definitely in my top five kisses ever. Okay, top two.

Who am I kidding? He wins the blue ribbon.

It was…wow.

I'm usually the one who kisses first. Who makes the opening move. I think it's because men find me intimidating, and that's no accident. If a guy sticks around, then I'll show my softer side. If he doesn't seem into it, I'm out. I refuse to be someone who gets stepped on or left behind.

Yet with Sean, I keep showing those inner parts of me I reserve for my closest friends. I don't know if it's the stress I'm under or missing Gran or what. Maybe it's something about Sean, his family, the small details I've learned of his history. With him, I feel like I can reveal more of myself.

That's why I didn't want a hate-fuck with him. I love hot and dirty sex, but if we're going to do this, I want…more.

Don't get me wrong, fighting with Sean is a major turn on. But I've had angry sex before, and it always leaves me feeling a bit empty. A little used.

The Six Night Truce

I've seen how kind Sean can be. *That's* what I want from him. That conscientiousness and that regard. As well as that very sexy body, those strong hands, that dextrous tongue... Mmmm.

I *do* want to be someone he takes care of. Even if it's just for the next few days.

So long as he doesn't lock me away when I'm inconvenient. That was not okay. But he's apologized, and I've put the handcuff incident behind us. I'm leaving it in LA. I'm not a fan of the city anyway.

As we drive, Sean lifts my hand and kisses my knuckles. My insides are fluttering like I'm every stereotypical girl in a romantic movie.

"Such a gentleman when you want to be. I bet all the girls back in Texas swooned for that act."

"Not just in Texas." He winks. "But it's not an act. I'll admit, I'm not always this well behaved. But I don't fake it."

He's using my words from—jeez, was it just yesterday?

Spending nearly every moment together the past couple days has done strange things to my sense of time. It feels like much longer since we got to the hotel. And the shooting at the courthouse feels like a lifetime ago.

Two nights down, four to go.

A lot can happen in four nights.

I want to get back to the hotel. I want to unwrap that gift in Sean's pants that was pressing into my ass a little while ago. I want to explore him and see just how sweet he can be.

And how hot and dirty he can get.

But right now, my stomach is rumbling and it's ruining the mood. Pretzels for dinner and yogurt at breakfast wasn't enough.

He must hear it, because he laughs. "Let's get some food. Fighting bad guys is hungry work."

"So is kissing." And it seems this truce includes both. Not a bad deal, really.

∼

WE STOP AT A GAS STATION. SEAN FILLS THE TANK, while I go inside for a pitstop and to peruse the packaged sandwiches. He meets me by the refrigerators, and we stare into the rows of cold, ready-made meals.

"I was hoping to take you somewhere better," he says. "Pre-made tuna salad isn't how I usually roll with a girl I like."

There's another cascade of flutters in my center. Sean's way too charming when he wants to be.

I open the glass door and grab a chicken wrap. "We could go back to the diner later."

He grabs a sandwich of his own and some drinks. Our hips brush together. "Want to share a hot fudge sundae with me?"

"When you plan it ahead, it starts to sound like a real date."

"I do want to get to know you better," he says. "That wasn't just a line."

"Good, because I can't imagine it works that well for picking up."

"Maybe that explains why I'm single." His mischievous grin lights up his face.

I can't believe I've been missing out on the real Sean all this time. I thought he was nothing but scowls and grumpy attitude. I still find that side of him sexy, but if I had to choose, I'd take him like this. Because he actually looks happy.

We pile our purchases onto the counter and race to see who can get a credit card to the clerk faster. Sean wins.

But outside, his buoyant expression vanishes. He's looking down at his phone.

"What is it?" I ask.

"Missed call from Agent Winfrey. And a voicemail. I might get to that next week."

"Do you think that's wise?"

"Probably not. But after what happened today, I think caution is out the window." The phone buzzes in his hand. "Crap. Now Murphy's after me."

We're standing over by the side of the gas station store, out of the way of the foot traffic. Sean's thumb hits the screen, then he lifts his phone to his ear.

"Murphy? It's Holt." He frowns, listening.

After we left LA, he said he still trusts Murphy. I don't know her well enough to say if that's a good idea. But we're running low on allies. I hope she's one.

"No, we didn't think we needed an escort. We had errands to run. No. Just…out."

Sounds like Murphy already knew we left the hotel. But has she heard from LAPD about our little adventure with Carl Proctor?

"What's this about?" Sean asks. His eyes dart to mine. Whatever Murphy's saying, he doesn't like it. "I'll consider that. I'll get back to you." He lowers the phone.

"What's going on?"

"Murphy wants us to come back to the West Oaks station. At least, that's what she said. But she sounded off. I think Agent Winfrey was in the room with her."

"What does that mean? Why do they want us to go back to the station?"

"That's what seemed weird. She wouldn't say."

I bite my lip. "Whatever Agent Winfrey wants, my instinct is to do the opposite." We still had more questions than answers, but from everything we'd learned, I wasn't about to turn myself over to the CBI. Not until we knew exactly who'd hired the Serpents to go after us.

"I agree. Fuck them. I don't jump when Agent Winfrey says. He already dismissed me from the investigation, so I'm basically on paid leave. They wanted me in protective custody, so that's where I'm going to stay. With you. But I want to speak to Murphy without Winfrey listening in."

We go back inside the store, and Sean buys a burner phone from behind the counter. He pulls it out of its clamshell packaging and activates it. "I hope this is just a precaution. But if it's not…"

"If we think there could be some conspiracy going on, we might as well act like it."

"Exactly." Sean transfers numbers from his regular phone onto the burner. "I just sent Murphy a text, and I'll see what I get back. This is turning into one of those action movies where everybody's against the main characters."

I lean against the side of Sean's truck. "But apparently, it's also the kind of story where the protagonists get to kiss. Which doesn't seem that bad."

Sean sticks both his phones in his back pocket. He crowds me against the passenger door. "Can I kiss you right now?"

"You didn't ask my permission before."

"I know. I was very naughty. I'm trying to be good." Sean's standing with his legs apart, his hands on the door on either side of me, and I feel surrounded as I look up at him.

"I like a little naughty," I say.

"Do you?"

His lips nibble at mine. Sparklers are shooting off inside me. His hands move to my hips as his kiss deepens.

I want to laugh at how ridiculous this is. I'm kissing Sean Holt. What is this world coming to?

What's stranger: that I'm kissing him, or that I *really* don't want to stop?

The Six Night Truce

Earlier, I let him take charge, but now I clasp my fingers behind his neck and lick his tongue. My whole body is somehow lighting up and relaxing at the same time. This feels *good*. I didn't even realize how strung out I was until that fear and tension ebbed away. I can only imagine what it'll be like when we're alone in the hotel room, able to release all our pent-up anxiety.

Maybe the stress of this situation has turned a small spark of attraction into a wildfire. It's possible we never would've kissed if the courthouse shooting hadn't led us here. Does it matter?

What would be the point of fighting it, if it feels this nice?

Sean nuzzles my neck. I tip my head back against the truck. I know people are staring, but I can't bring myself to care.

"What else do you like?" he whispers.

"A little rough."

He hums. I feel the rumble in his chest. "Salty *and* sweet."

We both laugh. "Anything from Murphy yet?" I ask.

I see the reluctance on his face as he takes a step back. He pulls out both his devices. "Nope. But my mom wrote."

He holds up the screen on his regular phone. It's a picture of Henry picking a flower in a garden. I assume it's near Chase's apartment building.

Sean flips through more photos of Henry on his phone while we wait for Murphy's response. We open our packaged food and eat on the tailgate of the truck, smiling at Henry on a zoo carousel. Henry at the beach. Sean's shirtless in that photo, looking extremely sexy, but I keep that comment to myself. The man's got enough ego already.

I notice the photos only go back a few months. He doesn't show me any of Henry crawling or as a newborn. I'm not sure why, but it feels too personal to ask.

This is so new, this thing between us. This kissing instead

of fighting. It might be a fragile, rainbow-edged bubble, and it's about to pop. I want it to keep floating along for as long as it'll last.

After about ten minutes, we give up waiting for Murphy to respond. "Maybe she can't get privacy to write back or call," Sean says. "Winfrey might be lurking."

We get back in the truck and head toward the hotel. My eyes keep moving across the cabin and landing on him. Sean is more rugged than movie-star handsome. His brown eyes have flecks of amber in them. He has a thin scar on his neck, just below the tapering of his hairline, and his hands look weathered and calloused. I wonder about each of these clues to him, what they mean.

"I like your tattoos," I say.

"I got most of them when I was in the military."

"The patterns fit so well. Was there a grand plan?"

He glances down at the ink. "Nah, just came together I guess."

I run my fingers across his forearm, which is holding loosely onto the gear shift. His skin's warm, softer than it looks. "Why do you always cover them? I mean at work. You wear long sleeves."

"Chief Liu doesn't think tattoos are professional."

"What's his deal?" Liu has been chief for about three years, I think. It's not an elected position in West Oaks, but it's still political. He was appointed by the current governor.

"He's a little uptight. But he lets us run our cases as we see fit. I don't mind him. Usually."

"But?"

"The chief cares a lot about the opinions of West Oaks elites. The billionaire types who live in the hills."

"Like Asher Temple?"

"Exactly. Public opinion is pretty divided on whether Asher's guilty or not, so I think Liu is treading carefully. He's probably happy to let CBI take over because it decreases the pressure on West Oaks PD."

And we don't know CBI's true motivations. This is why I like working for myself. No office politics. Around my law practice, I'm the benevolent dictator. Just ask Tracey. Clients can fire me, but I don't have a boss. Sean does. He has different problems to navigate than I do.

Could he get fired over disobeying Agent Winfrey?

Could he get fired for going out of his way to protect *me*?

As we near the hotel, I'm thinking about the danger. The threats we haven't seen coming. "Do you think the hotel's still safe?" I ask.

Sean rubs his jaw. "I've been considering that. We did okay last night with the doors barricaded. We can do that again. There's a risk to remaining in one place, but there's also a risk to moving."

If we do decide to move, we'll have to get our belongings. Our clothes are in our hotel rooms. But a bigger question—where would we go?

Where would we be completely off the radar?

Sean exits the freeway. But when we near the turn for the parking lot, his fist tightens on the steering wheel. "Fuck. Do you see that?"

There are three unfamiliar police SUVs parked in front of the hotel's main entrance. And they're all marked, *California Bureau of Investigation*.

"Did Winfrey send them? To force you back to West Oaks?"

"Seems likely."

"But why?"

Sean's shaking his head. He stops the truck, right there in the road, and the car behind us honks.

"What do we do?" I ask. "Find out what they want? Or…" Or do we go all-in on this conspiracy theory?

Do we *run*?

Sean taps his fingers on the steering wheel. "You call it. Stay or go."

If we do this, run from the CBI, there might be no turning back. I'm sure Sean knows that.

But if someone in the state government actually hired the Serpents to kill us?

More cars honk. Someone's going to notice us sitting here, blocking the road.

"Get us out of here," I say.

The tires squeal as Sean makes a U-turn. "Looks like we're moving out of the hotel after all."

And our stuff's still there. "Where are we going? Back to the freeway?"

"Freeway's too exposed." Sean doesn't speed. But his knuckles are white. We turn onto a boulevard that runs parallel with the freeway.

Then a police cruiser pulls onto the road a few lengths behind us. Followed by another.

Sean curses. "Hold on."

I grab onto the door. "What are you—" He accelerates at the next intersection, jerking the truck to the left. I push my hand against my chest, trying to get my lungs to work again.

I've always thrived on a certain amount of stress, but this is a lot. Even for me.

We race down the next street. There's a gas station, and Sean steers into the lot. He drives straight through a self-serve car wash kiosk. Another vehicle honks. We swerve and narrowly miss it.

I'm clenching my jaw, trying not to shriek.

Sean turns into a narrow alley behind a grocery store. I don't see the police cars, but now I hear sirens.

I'm fairly cool under pressure, but this is getting to me. My entire body is a clenched knot of tension.

We reach the grocery store parking lot. It's packed. Sean skids into a space between a station wagon and a Tesla.

"Come on." He fits his guns into his holsters, grabs his windbreaker, and pushes out of the car. My phone is already in my pocket. I hurry to follow him.

We walk briskly toward a row of flowering hedges. Nope, nothing to see here folks. Just out for a stroll. As soon as we're hidden by the hedges, Sean pulls me behind a palm tree.

A police car crawls through the parking lot. It's from the local force, not CBI, which makes me wonder how many people are searching for us right now.

My heart is thumping against my ribcage.

"We have to keep going," I say. "It won't take them long to find your license plate."

"Yeah." He casts another agonized glance at the cop car.

Has Sean ever run from the police? I can't imagine. I haven't either, but I know many people who have. If this is as bad as we think it could be, then we can't afford to get caught.

I take his hand, tugging him behind me. We stick to the shadows and try to disappear.

24

Sean

Janie and I are running, and I'm not even sure what we're running from.

Is this a mistake? Have we gotten this completely wrong? The idea that my fellow officers could be plotting against me somehow—it just seems ludicrous.

But after everything we've learned, we have to take the threat seriously. Even if it's just a possibility.

"Our phones," Janie says. "Should we dump them?"

"Airplane mode. That'll be plenty." We both change our phone settings. This is my personal device, not owned by West Oaks PD, but we both know how easy it is to track the location of an active cell number. Assuming you have a warrant.

Janie and I haven't committed any crimes, and far as I know, we haven't even been accused of any. But if someone's tracking our cell numbers *without* a warrant...

That would mean we're definitely in conspiracy territory. Big time.

After a little while, we leave the shadows and have to walk down the day-lit street. It would be foolish to run.

Unless someone's wearing athletic gear, running attracts attention, especially a cop's attention.

I've tied my windbreaker around my waist to conceal my holster. Janie does the same with her hoodie, and we hold hands like this is a casual lovers' stroll.

We're blocks away from where we started. This is still the suburbs, but it's a nice area. Flowers in planting beds, restaurants with shady patios. It's the LA metro, though, and pedestrians stick out.

"We need to get out of the open," I say.

We turn onto a side street, and Janie points at a diner. "How about there?"

We push inside. It's a greasy spoon, complete with red leather stools at the counter and formica tables. A few elderly couples are having an early dinner. Last time I looked at my phone, it said it was just after four o'clock.

"Take any seat." The woman behind the counter has the scratchy voice of a smoker. She grabs two giant, laminated menus and brings them over.

I don't hear sirens anymore, thank God. But my mind is spinning like a strobing emergency light.

If I were alone, I'd probably go back to West Oaks and take my chances. I desperately want to believe that my world hasn't turned upside down. The truth is, I hate uncertainty. I've dealt with bad guys and violence since my first deployment way back in my early twenties, but I was surrounded by fellow Marines I believed in. I hate feeling isolated and unsure of myself.

But I'm not alone. Janie's with me. I can't take the risk of bringing her back to West Oaks, not when we have no idea who's really targeting us.

I'm already way beyond normal protocols and regulations. Might as well keep going and try to fix it later. If I still can.

I think of my mom and Henry. There's no way for them to

reach me. But I've left my burner connected to the cell network, still hoping to hear back from Murphy.

Janie and I slide into a booth. There's a TV behind the counter tuned to a local news broadcast. They show an image of the West Oaks County Courthouse, which means they're still talking about the attack. An image of the governor's press conference with Nixon Temple appears next.

The chyron says, *Ex-Governor's Son Among Witnesses to Shooting.*

Will CBI put out a BOLO with our pictures? Why in the hell were they at our hotel in the first place? Why would the local cops have been chasing after my truck? Could this have something to do with my run-in with Carl Proctor?

I was outside West Oaks jurisdiction, but I can't imagine LAPD went tattling on me. Certainly not in a way that would get me in *this* much trouble, this fast. I glare at my burner, willing it to ring. Murphy is my only tie to normalcy right now, and I need her to provide some answers.

The server comes over, and Janie says, "Two coffees, please. Black. And some fries and a hot fudge sundae."

"You got it."

"Thanks." I want to go back to an hour ago, when Janie and I were kissing. When we had nicer things to think about than the people chasing us.

I shouldn't have let myself get distracted.

My burner rings, and I bang my thighs on the table trying to jump up. "That's Murphy. I'm going to step outside."

"Should I come?"

I debate. "No. I'll see what she says, and I'll be right back."

Janie's expression is guarded, but she nods.

"Don't eat all the hot fudge," I say, which earns me a small smile.

I hurry outside as I answer the phone. "Murphy?"

She exhales into the phone. "Good Lord, Holt, this is a fucking nightmare."

I sit on the bench in front of the diner, keeping an eye on the cars passing by. "What's going on?"

"I take it you're not coming in."

"*No*, I'm—" I lower my voice. "I'm not coming in until I know what's really happening. Why was CBI at my hotel?"

"There was a break-in. Your hotel rooms got tossed."

"*What?*"

"That's why it took me so long to call you back. When I spoke to you earlier, Winfrey was breathing down my neck, saying he wanted to question you and Jane again. In person."

"Why?"

"Winfrey wouldn't explain it to me. But I spoke quietly with Hartford. Apparently, Winfrey heard you'd left protective custody, and he was pissed. He wanted answers about what you were doing. Then, we got word about the incident at your hotel."

Fuck. Does that mean the local guys were reporting to CBI the whole time? I can't stop the questions from multiplying.

Winfrey contacted my old partner, too. Why's he so obsessed with what I'm doing? What is he hoping to learn?

"Are the local officers okay? The ones who were assigned to the hotel to protect us?"

"Yes, I don't think there were any injuries. They caught the guy who broke into your rooms. Another Serpent gang member. Snake tattoos. Apparently, he'd already gone through your belongings and was trying to set another of those lovely pipe bombs for when you got back."

Jesus. "What about the two Serpents already in custody? Have you gotten anything from them?"

"Not much. Their fingerprints were all over your house and Jane's office. Like you expected. They're refusing to talk. Winfrey's the one who questioned them, but I watched on video. I got the sense they didn't know enough to tell. These are foot soldiers. They're not privy to the real plan."

"But how'd the Serpents find out the location of our hotel? Almost nobody knows that." *Except CBI. And the locals.*

"No clue. It concerns me."

"And why the hell did a couple of black-and-whites follow my truck?"

"Like Hartford said, Winfrey wants you to come in. Now he's claiming you have info he wants *and* that you're not safe. Winfrey's been in Chief Liu's office with the door closed, and I feel like I'm only getting glimpses. I don't like it, Sean. I don't like this at all."

"Do *you* think I should come in?"

She pauses. "I think…we should wait until I know more. You and Jane should stay out of trouble. That means staying away from anyone who's LAPD. Or its informants."

Yikes. She *did* hear about that. Guess my ex-partner couldn't keep it quiet. Or chose not to.

"Sounds like you don't trust Winfrey or CBI," I say. "Any particular reason you feel that way?"

"At this point, just a bunch of creepy feelings."

"You don't even know all of it." I fill her in on what Carl Proctor told me about someone hiring the Serpents for a big job.

"My intuition is clanging the alarm bells," Murphy says. "Winfrey wants to keep things 'moving,' according to Hartford, and you know me. I'd rather dig in my heels and slow down. I want to see exactly where I'm going."

"Yeah. I get it."

"And with people like Nixon and Asher Temple? They have a lot of friends. An unfair number of friends, I'd say."

"My thoughts exactly."

Neither of us wants to voice our suspicions in explicit

terms. That CBI could actually be working against us. Even targeting me and Jane. Trying to kill us.

But Murphy is considering the possibility. She's taking it seriously. If anything, she's usually more cynical than I am.

"Do you have someplace to keep your head down?" she asks.

"We'll figure it out."

"We?"

"Me and...Jane." I almost said *Janie*. "Murphy—we've still got people protecting David Daily at the hospital, right?"

"Yes."

"He still unconscious?"

"Yep. But stable."

"Make sure we can trust the people watching him."

Murphy pauses again, but I know her silences. They tend to speak, and this one says she understands what I mean. "Officer Shelborne is at the hospital. Not 24-7, of course, but she's outside Daily's room a good chunk of the day. I'll be sure to check on whoever else is there."

I'm relieved to hear that. "Sounds good. Use this number if anything else comes up."

"Will do. Everything's...going well with Ms. Simon? You're getting along?"

"We're managing."

"And avoiding complications, I hope?"

"Don't know what you mean, Murphy."

"Sure, Holt." I swear, I can hear her rolling her eyes. "It might be smarter if you and Simon split up. I don't know why you two seem to be the center of this, but more targets are better than one."

"We'll consider it." No. No, we won't.

"Would've thought you'd be eager for an excuse to part ways with her."

I glance back at the diner. "Yeah, would've thought."

I head back inside. Jane is swirling her spoon in the whipped cream on her sundae. She perks up when I slide into the booth, and this time, I sit beside her.

"Food just came." She holds out the spoon to me. I press my leg to hers and take a bite.

We're safer together, I remind myself. In my mind, she's Janie now. The woman I've come to know the last few days. Doesn't matter if Murphy or anybody else understands or agrees.

We share ice cream and french fries while I catch her up on everything Murphy said. I don't leave anything out, not even Murphy's skepticism about me and Janie sticking together. At least Murphy's on our side.

I'm constantly casting glances at the TV, which has moved on to weather. Our pictures aren't splashed across the screen. Yet.

"So we need a place to lie low," Janie says. "I've always wanted to say that."

"I highly doubt you've wanted to say that."

She shrugs one shoulder, which happens to be pressed against me. "Okay, maybe not. It's lazy dialogue. But I do have an idea for a place. Or at least, a resource. Someone we can call."

"Yes?"

"Mutual friends of ours. They're helpful in a jam. And definitely neutral when it comes to the government."

The answer appears in my head. I can't believe I didn't come up with this first.

"Bennett Security," I say.

She smiles and pops the last fry into her mouth.

25

Janie

When our ride arrives, we leave the diner and jump into the waiting Jeep. Sean gestures for me to take shotgun. He gets into the back, then grabs the hand of the man driving.

"Thank you for doing this, Tanner. You have no idea. This is Jane Simon."

Tanner Reed grins at me, offering his hand. "Of course. I've heard a lot about you, Jane. Let's get you both to the safe house." He puts the Jeep in drive. "I saw a dozen cruisers on my way here from West Oaks. Those weren't all for you, were they?"

Sean and I both groan, but neither of us has an answer.

We drive off.

Tanner is a huge beast of a man. His shoulders are twice as broad as mine. He's wearing a tight T-shirt, but I'm guessing it's not tight on purpose. He's got full sleeves of tattoos on both arms, which are thick as my thighs.

Tanner's a bodyguard with Bennett Security. They provide personal protection services to the wealthiest of West Oaks. Before I worked with them myself, the company had always struck me as a bit elitist. Not the kind of service that I or my typical clients can afford. But Max Bennett also volunteers his company's resources to help law enforcement with difficult investigations.

They'd never helped out the defense side until one of my cases.

Now, I'm friends with Max and his wife, who happens to be the West Oaks Assistant DA. I even went to their wedding. Bennett Security still makes its money from the West Oaks rich, but Max pays back his good fortune by working pro bono, sometimes for police and prosecutors, sometimes for the defense. I'm beyond grateful that they're helping Sean and me. I intend to pay them for their aid, but I have the feeling Max Bennett—when he returns from his honeymoon—will refuse.

Tanner and Sean fall into an easy banter. They're clearly good friends. "Did you meet each other working on a case when Sean was with the LAPD?" I ask.

"Nah, I've known this guy for a lot longer than that." Tanner hooks his thumb at the back seat. "Since our military days. Makes me feel old."

Sean huffs, shaking his head.

"Were you a Marine too?"

"He wasn't that cool," Sean says. "Just the Navy."

Tanner barks a laugh. "I was a SEAL."

"*Oh.*" I make a show of being impressed—and I am—but mostly I'm just playing along. I'm pretty sure Tanner's sharp eyes caught Sean and me holding hands as we left the diner. "Well, then."

"Yep, what can I say? Sorry Ms. Simon, I'm taken."

Sean grumbles, but he's hiding a smile. "What is the obsession with Navy SEALs? The ones I know are annoying."

"Yeah, so annoying when we swoop in to rescue your ass."

"I think Sean's still smarting from the first time he needed rescue today," I point out. "But this morning, it was me doing the swooping."

"Figures," Tanner says, grinning. "What kind of mess has got both Jane Simon and Sean Holt in need of a safe house? This about the courthouse shooting?"

"Have you guys heard much about it?" Sean asks.

"Just that you two were there. But I'm guessing if you're still running, it's a lot bigger than a random terrorist attack."

I nod. "Exactly. But we're still trying to figure that part out."

We reach a vast neighborhood of tract houses. It seems to stretch forever, with brown hills in the distance. Each house has an attached garage, a short driveway, a small stoop. Horizontal siding in different earth tones. Reminds me of Gran's neighborhood in Tucson. To Pam and me growing up, it was like a tiny corner of heaven all our own.

Tanner pulls into one of the driveways. "This is it. I'd offer to carry your luggage, but it looks like you packed light."

"It was a sudden departure," Sean says.

"No worries. The house is stocked with clothing in various sizes. Nothing fancy, but it'll be enough for a few days. There's laundry machines if you need." We all get out. Tanner goes around to the back of the Jeep. "I brought along some groceries for you. Just whatever I had on hand at my house, so it's random. Sorry. But there's some blueberry muffins Faith made yesterday. Those are really good."

Sean and I gawk at the boxes of food in the back of the Jeep. "Faith is in for a surprise when she gets home today," Sean says.

"Nah, this was her idea. Better than wasting time at the grocery store."

I want to say thank you, but the words feel stuck in my throat. If I force them out, I'm worried tears will follow.

We each grab a box from the Jeep. Tanner enters a code in the electronic keypad, and we file into the house. It's just as nondescript inside, but it's comforting. This is a place someone could blend in and get lost.

We set the boxes in the kitchen, then spend a few quiet minutes stocking the fridge. After we're done, Sean turns to his friend.

"Tanner, if you wouldn't mind doing me another favor, could you text my mom? I'll give you her number. But I'd rather she not have my burner. I'm trying to use it as little as possible."

"Yeah, no problem at all. There should be an iPad here somewhere, set up with a secure VPN. You're free to use it whenever. But I'll text your mom right now. What should I say?"

"Just that Janie and I are safe. Ask her to give Henry a kiss for me." Sean grimaces. "And you could tell her you're one of the SEALs I got to know in Afghanistan. She'll get a kick out of it. But if she asks you for a shirtless selfie, don't fall for it."

Tanner laughs. "You sure you don't want a bodyguard team to sit outside here? I can make it happen. Say the word."

Sean shakes his head. "I don't want to draw attention. Or get you guys involved any more than you already are. If you can keep this quiet…"

Tanner nods. "I made a note in the logs that we've got someone in this safe house, but nobody but me and Faith knows it's you. I'll tell Max when he's back in town. This house has a Bennett Security alarm system, and you can use the perimeter alarms and cameras as you choose. And I'll arrange a car for you and drop it off nearby tomorrow. I can have Faith caravan with me."

"Thank you. My truck's probably been impounded by now. You've gone above and beyond."

I hug Tanner. "Tell Faith thanks as well." I've never met his girlfriend, but I already like her.

Sean gets a hug next. The men slap each other's backs, and I feel the affection between them.

"Take care, man," Tanner says. "Stay safe. Don't do anything I wouldn't."

Sean laughs. "I think I'll be a little more cautious than that."

As Tanner leaves, Sean locks the door. He goes to the alarm panel, activates the system, and punches through the various menus to disable the interior cameras. He leaves the exterior ones running.

We're alone, and the house is so quiet.

He turns around and faces me. Hooks his thumbs into his jeans pockets. "Hey."

I close my hands over my elbows. I'm starting to shiver.

Too. Much. This day—the last several days—has just been too much. "I think I'm crashing."

Sean walks over to me. "Me too. This has been…a lot." He runs his hands down my arms, then hesitates. "Is it still okay? Touching you like this?"

"That's maybe the only thing in my life right now that's okay." We wrap our arms around one another. I rest my forehead by his collarbone. It's still light outside, but my eyes are trying to close. "Could we lie down for a little bit?" I ask. "I know we need to talk and figure out what we're going to do, but…"

"That sounds really nice. I could use a rest too."

He takes my hand and leads me to the nearest bedroom. There's a dresser, two nightstands, a floor lamp. A thick quilt and ample throw pillows. A room designed to comfort people who are overwhelmed.

The curtains are already drawn. We toe off our shoes.

Sean crawls beneath the covers, then holds up the quilt for me to get underneath. I cuddle up against his side, my head on his chest.

I feel his fingers running through my hair as the world falls away.

26

Janie

When I wake, it's dark.

I blink, letting my eyes adjust. There's a light on in another room, and it's bleeding into this one. I'm snuggled against something warm and solid. I wiggle closer.

There's a steady rhythm against my cheek. A heartbeat.

All at once, I remember where I am. What's happened.

I'm with Sean.

I lift my head. His brown eyes are darker than usual, watching me as he lies against the pillow.

He doesn't say anything. Instead, his hand lifts and his fingers slowly trail along my hairline. My eyes fall closed.

His fingers go to my cheekbone next. My chin. I don't want to move because I want him to keep touching me like this.

With the mood lighting and the quiet, I'd think I was dreaming if it wasn't for the intensity of these sensations. Shivers of pleasure run down my spine and arms and legs. It's not even sexual, exactly. It just feels so nice. So relaxing and kind and *good*, when we've been dealing with so much that's bad.

I want to return the favor.

At the risk of breaking this spell, I scoot upward until my head is on the pillow next to Sean's. We're lying on our sides, facing one another.

I drag my fingertip down his cheek, the way he was just doing to me. It's his turn to close his eyes, and his whole body *shudders*. Seeing his response is almost better than being on the receiving end.

I curve my hand at his neck. His pulse thrums against my palm. His fingers trace the shell of my ear.

Even if I knew what to say right now, I don't think I'd be able to speak. His eyes glimmer, fixed on mine.

Plenty of men have looked at me like they're terrified. It's a running joke with my girlfriends. *Frighten any men lately, Janie?* Like I'm so scary, just because I'm an assertive, professional woman. But not Sean. I've seen him annoyed at me, frustrated, pissed off. Never once has he seemed intimidated by me.

This is something different. Very different. Sean's watching me with a kind of reverence. Almost like he's in awe.

We're staring into one another's eyes and caressing each other and it's *really freaking intense*.

My gaze moves to his lips. I know how soft they are. How they feel against mine. I want to kiss him, but even more, I want him to kiss *me*.

Sean's touch disappears from my face. His fingers close around mine, and he lifts my hand away from his cheek. I'm wondering if I did something wrong.

Then he presses his mouth to the center of my palm, his eyes never leaving mine.

My body is a live wire, nothing but craving. Every cell in my body is calling his name.

"Sean," I whisper.

He shifts. Suddenly I'm on my back, and Sean is above me, propping himself up on one elbow. His thick thigh nudges between mine.

His lips brush my cheek.

He's kissing my face with the same reverence, but now his fingers trail down my body. When they reach my thigh, they squeeze. That sudden roughness to his touch does something to me.

I need all of his skin pressed against me with nothing between.

I shove my hand under his shirt, pushing it up. I'm not being subtle or elegant right now. But Sean smiles knowingly at me. He sits up to tug off his shirt.

I try to wiggle out of mine. He helps me when the fabric gets stuck around my head.

We're both giggling, so I figure, what the hell? I pop the button on my jeans and reach for the button on his. His smile disappears, eyes flaring with heat.

"Please," I murmur.

Then it's a race to see who can get their jeans off fastest. Lying down, it's awkward and kind of ridiculous. But it's worth it when we're down to our underwear, and Sean's leaning into me, and his thick, hard cock pushes against my stomach through his boxers.

I make the most desperate-sounding whimper.

He groans. His strong hands pull me against him. Sean's lips finally land on mine, his tongue eagerly sweeping into my mouth because I've instantly opened to him.

I'm feeling very pliant and just a touch slutty. Or I would, if he wasn't being so careful with me.

When I'm in the courtroom, I love confrontation. I love to dominate and to win. Ethics are important to me, of course, and I won't cheat or break rules to get ahead, no matter how much the other side might accuse me of being ruthless.

But I don't want to be in charge right now. I don't even want to think—about what I should or shouldn't do, about what this means.

I want Sean to take me, *have* me, just like he asked. And he seems more than willing. His tongue explores my mouth, and he's holding my head in his firm grip. His fingers are at the back of my neck, his thumb just on the underside of my chin.

His tongue retreats. I take over, kissing him gently for a while. Showing him how much I want him. His thumb runs up and down the delicate, sensitive skin of my throat. One of my arms is trapped by the way we're lying, but I use the other to touch the rounded muscles of his pecs, my fingers dragging through his dark chest hair. My fingertip brushes his nipple, and it hardens. I flick the nub with my thumbnail. Teasing it.

Sean growls and pulls away.

His knees straddle me, and he looms above me, sitting up. His erection tents his boxers so much it's somehow dirtier than if he was naked. There's a wet spot on the fabric where his tip is leaking.

My eyes take in the rest of him. The tattoos on his forearms, the veins in his biceps, his chest hair and the way the low light hits his abs and his big thighs. I can't get over how sexy he is.

Sean plays with one of my bra straps. "Can I?" His voice is deeper, ragged with lust.

I nod. He slides a hand underneath me and unhooks my bra. The moment my breasts are uncovered, he bends forward and starts kissing and nuzzling. He tongues the bottom edge where the rounded swell meets my ribcage, and wow—I had no idea that spot was so sensitive.

He's paying attention to everything but my nipples. They're so beaded it's almost painful.

Finally, Sean lashes his tongue over the left bud. He sucks the nipple into his mouth, and my back arches off the mattress. His hands rest on my stomach, easing me back down. He forces me to lie still as he teases and worships each hardened bud. Sucking. Tugging with his teeth. Then kissing gently.

"*Oh.* Fuck. Sean."

I would've thought it was impossible to come from nipple play alone, but now it seems at least plausible. I cannot believe what Sean is doing to me. I have no idea how much time has passed. He's certainly not rushing, like we have all the time in the universe and this night is endless, like we have no purpose except to give each other pleasure.

I *really* want to make him feel this good. But when I try to touch him again, he takes my hands and holds them to the bed.

Well okay, if he just wants to feast on my body, am I going to argue? Hell. No.

Then, after a long while, his mouth leaves my breasts and makes a trail of kisses, moving downward.

Oh, Sean. Yes. Please. I need it. I feel my lips form the words, though I manage to keep my begging silent. I do have a little bit of pride.

But when he pauses at my belly button, his tongue dipping inside, he looks up at me. His lips curve into a wicked smile. I'm not fooling anybody. I guess my heavy breathing and the way my thighs are rubbing together is giving me away.

He kisses each of my hip bones, which are sticking out just above the waistband of my panties. "Okay?" he asks. If anything, his voice has gotten even deeper. Thicker.

"Yes. Yes yes yes." I can't stop saying it.

He tugs my panties past my hips. They're not even down

my thighs yet, and he's dipping his nose into my crotch like he can't wait.

Suddenly it's all way too intense. But also nowhere near enough. I grab the sheets in my fists. Tip my head back, already moaning in anticipation. I know I'm soaking wet. My clit is throbbing.

If he takes his sweet time with my inner thighs the way he did with my breasts before getting to the good stuff, I am going to lose my mind.

He gets my panties off the rest of the way, then lays his cheek against one of my legs, stroking the knee of the other. I'd think he was trying to provoke me, except for the way he's closed his eyes. The gentleness of his touch. How can I be angry at a man who seems to be enjoying my body so much?

I'm in a suspended state of heightened arousal. My whole being is vibrating.

Then, at last, he parts my legs and tastes my inner folds.

My gasp is loud enough to wake the neighbors.

His tongue moves with aching slowness, and somehow that makes the experience all the more powerful. He's alternating between sucking my clit and sliding his tongue deep inside my pussy.

I'm panting and moaning and keening. My hips try to rock against his face. I've lost all control of myself.

I didn't know I could feel so much at one time. I might not survive this.

Then my orgasm is just *there*, this white light exploding through me. And it's like Sean can't hold back anymore. His tongue and his lips work feverishly, pushing the pleasure to a higher level, keeping me at the edge of that wave, not letting me come down. I feel like I'm breaking apart.

When it's over, Sean sits upright, kneeling at the edge of the bed, watching me. Licking his lips.

I'm wrecked.

I watch as he stands and pulls down his boxers. I'm paralyzed. It's a little embarrassing, how drugged I feel. He could do absolutely anything he wanted to me right now, and I couldn't possibly stop him.

Maybe this is some weird cocktail of pleasure and adrenaline and being chased and attacked, combined with the absolute certainty that I'm safe in Sean's arms.

Or it could be the incredible release that comes from giving in to him. Not fighting Sean or what I need anymore.

He grabs his jeans from the floor and fishes something out of his pocket. A small box of condoms. I would ask when and where he got those—is he always this prepared?—if I could manage speech.

He opens the box and pulls one out. "Yes?" He holds it up.

I nod vigorously. Yep. No subtlety over here. My pride, my inhibitions. They're all scattered on the floor with our clothes and the condom wrapper he's just dropped.

He crawls back onto the mattress. Grabs hold of my thighs and pulls me closer.

"Janie," he moans. "So beautiful."

Sean watches his cock slide into me, tongue at the corner of his mouth. His eyes are wild with lust.

He could give me a pounding right now, and I'd be down with that. But instead Sean drapes himself over me. He strokes my face again with his fingers. Reverently, just like earlier.

Let me show you how I'll take care of you, he said. *Let me be sweet to you.*

I get my arms to work enough to circle them around his neck, scraping my nails into the short hair at his nape.

Once again, he starts slow. Letting the moment build. We're kissing and swallowing each other's moans.

His hips begin to thrust. Each delicious slide of his shaft in and out makes my nerve endings hum. My whole body is a symphony.

Sean lifts up onto his hands and keeps his eyes locked on mine. Our breathing is in sync. His muscles flex and sweat beads at his temples, between his pecs.

"So good," I whisper. "Sean, your cock feels so fucking good."

After a while, he drops to his elbows, his rough cheek scratching against my smooth one. He pumps his hips faster. He makes a guttural, animal cry. His cock pulses, and I wrap my legs around his waist, chasing every hint his body's giving of how good his orgasm feels.

He looks at me again as he catches his breath. Checking on me.

I know my expression is betraying *everything*. My gratitude and affection for him, and the shock that it's *Sean Holt* doing this to me. Taking me so completely apart.

I've had kinkier, more scandalous encounters. But for me, this is more daring than any other sex I've had.

My eyes are showing him how much I need him. I need Sean right here, beside me. I cannot fathom going through the past few days, much less tomorrow, alone.

And for someone like me, who's relied on my own strength for almost my entire life, that realization is just as exhilarating as it is terrifying.

27

Sean

Janie's lying naked in my arms. It's around two in the morning, and I should try to get back to sleep. But it's going to take me a while to come down from this high.

It's been a while since I felt a connection like we just shared. The last person who came close was Alexis, and she was nowhere near as into me as I thought. Our relationship gave me Henry, but my mistakes with Alexis were totally separate from him.

I'm not good at casual relationships. I tend to get attached. With Alexis, I fooled myself into believing we had a future.

This thing with Janie is so surprising that it's no wonder it's blowing my mind. I know she's not like Alexis. She's nothing like Alexis. But beyond that, there's still so much I need to learn about Janie. That I want the *chance* to learn. I'm not sure how she'll feel about that.

I saw the freaked-out look on her face just now, after the orgasms were done. I almost asked if anything was wrong, but I guess I was afraid to hear. But if she didn't like what we just did, Janie would've told me. She's not the type to lie to spare my ego. That's something I respect about her.

I don't know if we're both just reacting to the pressure we've been under. Isn't it natural for two people to feel bonded when they've been forced into a crucible together? We've had no one else to turn to. I shouldn't overthink what's happening between us.

But my heart and my head are both telling me that Janie is special. Even if what we're sharing lasts only a few more days, it's going to mean something to me.

I think maybe she's asleep. But then she pops up and sits at the edge of the bed. My heart surges into my throat. Shit. She's upset. She's going to say that getting naked was a mistake.

But when Janie looks over her shoulder at me, she's smiling sheepishly. "I know it's the middle of the night, but I am dying of hunger. What about you?"

I sit up. "I'm hungry, yeah. I was trying to ignore it."

She sighs. "I'm not as disciplined as you ex-military types."

"Hardly. I just didn't want to get out of bed."

Janie stands. I get up and grab my boxers from the floor. Before Janie can get dressed in her own clothes, I snag my T-shirt from where I dropped it. "Lift your arms."

She rolls her eyes at me, but she obeys. I put my shirt on her. It hits partway down her thighs, and she looks so sexy in it, I want to take it right back off.

I step in close, one hand on her hip, the other in her hair. "You are one gorgeous woman." My Texan drawl's coming out. Just can't help myself.

She beams at me. She's basking in this attention, and I love giving it. I kiss her slowly, taking my time.

But she puts her hands on my bare chest and pushes me

toward the door. "Food, Holt. We skipped dinner. I'm going to get hangry."

"Uh oh, Jane Simon's getting grumpy? Look out."

"I can only stay nice for so long."

"Hurricane Jane, coming through."

"You did *not* just call me that."

"Pretty proud of myself, actually. Just came up with it."

"Really? That's not my nickname down at the station?"

"Oh, it will be. Once I tell everybody. I'd better text Murphy to let her know."

"Aaand…I'm back to hating you."

I laugh and lace our fingers together for the short walk to the kitchen.

"I wonder if Tanner sent your mom a selfie," she says.

I don't want to talk about Tanner or any other man with Janie, but if she needs small talk, I can deal. "If he did, I know what Mom's new lock screen will be on her phone. Forget me and Henry."

Janie digs into the fridge. "Let's see what our favorite Navy SEAL left us." She pulls out eggs, spinach, cherry tomatoes. "I'm going to make you a frittata. Much healthier than what we've been eating. Sit down." She nods at the island, which has a couple of stools.

"Really? You're cooking for me?"

"You were awfully nice to me, so I think you earned it."

I want to argue that going down on her was the best kind of foreplay for me. Getting up close and personal with her gorgeous body, that rush of sweetness on my tongue when she came.

My dick's thickening up again as I remember it. I smell her all over me. And the sight of Janie in my T-shirt isn't hurting, either. I want my hands on her again. She did tell me to sit, but I'm bad at following directions.

I walk around the island, circling an arm around her waist

from behind. She's facing the counter and breaking eggs into a bowl.

"Are you here to help, or just get in the way?" she asks.

"Probably both."

She complains more, but she snuggles back against me while she cooks. Janie pours the eggs into a heated, buttered skillet, then sprinkles on the spinach and chopped tomatoes, followed by some shredded cheese. I'm glad she knows how to cook, because I would've been clueless about how to put together the random stuff Tanner brought us.

Then Janie puts the whole skillet under the broiler in the oven.

"You're very affectionate," she says, once the oven door is closed.

"Is that okay? I can back off if you need me to." I say this matter-of-factly. I'm into her, not gonna lie, but I don't want to be pushy. This is the third night of this truce of ours, not our third date. Unless...well, there was the diner the first night. And sleeping in the same room the second.

Does handcuffing her to my steering wheel count as a date? Maybe the tuna sandwiches at the gas station?

She smiles at me over her shoulder. "I like being affectionate."

I kiss the back of her neck. "Good. Me too."

Stop overthinking it, Holt. Just enjoy this.

She spins around in my arms so she's facing me. "Do you always have a box of condoms in your jeans pocket?"

"I bought those at the gas station. When we stopped."

"A few minutes after we first kissed? That was presumptuous of you."

"Hey, good Marines are always prepared."

We kiss some more until Janie scrambles for the oven, cursing. "Shit, I hope I didn't let it burn."

The cheese is golden and bubbly. Looks amazing to me,

and it tastes even better. We sit at the island, eating off of one plate, knees pressed together.

After that, I check the burner phone. Murphy hasn't written. Neither has Tanner. I have to assume everything's fine. Or at least that there's no news, and maybe that's the best we can hope for at the moment.

"We should go back to bed," I say.

"Should we?" Janie's eyes rake over me. I'm still just wearing my boxers, and it's obvious how quickly my body responds to her.

We should probably rest so we can focus on the investigation tomorrow. But...maybe we need this more.

We go back to the bedroom. Then she's on me, stripping off the T-shirt that she's wearing, pushing me down on the bed. I let myself fall back against the mattress. Janie tugs down my boxers and goes right for my half-hard dick.

She licks a stripe up the underside of my shaft. By the time she reaches the tip, I'm so stiff I'm lightheaded. "Oh, fuck." My fingers wind into her hair.

I love when a woman knows exactly what she wants.

She's nowhere near as patient as I was with her. Janie goes right for the swollen head of my cock. Her tongue swirls around my tip, probes my slit.

Then she pays some attention to the spot on the underside of my cockhead, where I'm extra sensitive. "Right there, Janie. God, yes. Right there."

She kisses and licks that spot until I'm shivering and panting.

Finally, her lush mouth closes around me and sucks. "Ahhh." My hips jerk off the bed. My shaft slides further past her lips, but she just hums and takes down more of me. Her hands are kneading my thigh muscles. She's bent over, her gorgeous tits swaying.

My fingers are still in her soft cascade of hair. She reaches up, her hand touching mine on her head, and she curls her fingers into a fist, forcing mine to do the same.

I'm confused until, all at once, I get it.

I fist her hair and pull. Gently. Then harder. Her eyes sink closed and she moans. I feel the vibration all over my dick. Precome flows out of me onto her tongue.

Hot, molten arousal is shooting up and down my spine, pooling in my belly and in my balls.

I really don't know how I ended up here. Naked with Jane Simon, with her lips wrapped around my cock. After all we've been through since the shooting at the courthouse, the biggest shock isn't so much that it's *us* together. The thing that truly amazes me is that I didn't see it before. I didn't see *her*. What else have I messed up? What else have I missed?

All right, this isn't the time for philosophical questions. But I'm trying not to come down her throat. I want this session to last, and I'm not sure I'll have another in me before I need to sleep.

I let go of her hair. "Janie, that feels incredible, but I want to come inside of you." I've done that once tonight, and I'm raring to feel it again.

She slowly pulls off of me, suckling at my tip a little more, tonguing the underside and the slit again. I'm clenching my jaw and my ass cheeks trying to keep from losing it.

Janie crawls up my body. My palms frame her face and I kiss her, slowing things down.

I think of her hand, showing me how she wanted me to pull her hair. "You want it rougher this time?" I ask.

Her teeth nip at my mouth, my chin. "Make me feel you."

My cock leaps like it's saying, *Reporting for duty*. I grab hold of her and flip her over, so she's on her back and I'm above her. "Do you need a safe word? How about, *Objection, Your Honor?*"

The Six Night Truce

She tips her head back and belly-laughs. "And I used to think you had no sense of humor."

"Hey, I can have fun. On occasion."

"You going to have fun with me?"

I kiss her jaw. "I *have* been. Now I want more." So much more.

I take her hands and shove her arms over her head. I hope it's not hurting her wounded shoulder, but I trust Janie to use her safe words if she needs them. Or just tell me.

My mouth crashes onto hers. My tongue is forceful and demanding, pushing deep like my cock was a moment ago.

I've fantasized about this. Shutting Jane up with a kiss. The reality is much hotter because she wants me to do this. Maybe even needs it.

I'm a simple guy in many ways. I like to be useful.

I flip her so she's on her stomach. I'm straddling her thighs, and her ass is right in front of my cock.

I keep hold of her wrists in one hand and use the other to touch her. Earlier, I explored her body like she was some priceless treasure, a museum piece, but this time I want to leave my mark. My fingertips dig into the thick curve where her hip meets her thigh.

I shamelessly rub my hard dick against her. Precome smears on her ass cheeks. This isn't that rough, but it *is* dirty.

Excitement blooms in my center and spreads outward. My chest feels tight, my balls heavy and full.

"Keep your arms right there," I say. "Above your head."

I rake my short nails down her back. She shudders. My hands work their way down, and I spread her thighs open, pinning her like that as I kneel behind.

Janie's arching her pelvis, baring herself to me. Nothing shy about this woman. My mouth waters as I stare at the most private parts of her. I smell her arousal, see it glistening at her opening.

I had some ideas about teasing her, spanking her, really getting her begging for my cock. But I can't wait that long.

I'm supposed to be in control here, but I'm fucking desperate for her.

I frantically search for the small box I tossed on the corner of the bed earlier. It had three condoms inside, so there's only two left. Nowhere near enough with a woman like Janie in my reach.

I sheath my erection as quickly as I can. Jeez, my hands are shaking. I want inside her so badly. What is she doing to me?

I pull her hips up until she's on her knees. Her upper body is still relaxed against the mattress, and I put a hand between her shoulder blades to keep her there. My tip lines up with her pussy, teasing her opening.

"Sean," she gasps.

I'm embarrassed by the needy groan I make as my cock sinks inside her. She's just as tight as she was earlier, a perfect, snug fit. I caress her thighs, her hips, her ass that's pressed into my crotch.

I lean forward and gather her in my arms, lifting her up. Now we're both upright, her back to my chest. I brush my lips at her neck, behind her ear.

My fist closes in her hair, and I pull her head back. She cries out. My other hand cups her throat, then carves a path down her body. Squeezing her breasts, pinching her nipples.

My teeth scrape the firm, smooth skin where her neck meets her shoulder. My fist is still tight in her hair. Her whole body is quaking as she moans my name, again and again.

And my cock is buried inside of her, pleading with me to move.

I've never felt this possessive. Is it the battles we've waged in the last months since we met, which now seem like extended foreplay? Is it because I've protected her from danger, and she's protected me? The way it feels like we only have each other right now? It's us against the world?

Janie, my heart says. *Janie, Janie.*

I can't take it anymore.

I push her shoulders forward, bending her at the waist. I won't let her fall, but she catches herself against the headboard, as I expected she would.

I lean into her and brace a hand on the headboard beside hers. We're both on our knees. I grab her hip, my thumb and fingers digging in enough to bruise.

My cock pulls almost all the way out, then slams into her again.

No more being gentle.

I set a fast, punishing pace. With every thrust, I pull her hips back against mine. Our bodies slap together. The bed trembles, the headboard knocking into the wall.

Over and over and over.

The room fills with the scent of sex and sweat, a haze of heat. Of grunting and moaning and pleasure that makes my vision cloud. I fist her hair again and hold on that way.

My balls swing into her until they draw up tight, achingly full. But I can't let go yet. Not yet.

"How do I get you there?" I ask, chest heaving. "What do you need?"

She drops her hands from the headboard. Lowers her head and shoulders to the mattress. Her hips are still propped up in the air, and I get it. This angle is better for her. I love this small piece of knowledge about her body, how to make her feel good. I want to learn everything, unlock every secret she's holding.

"Hard, Sean. Please."

I drive my swollen cock into her, thrusting as hard and fast as I can, and then she's screaming and clenching around me.

Everything goes bright and hot and blinding. Like I'm staring at the sun. Pleasure rockets through me and out of me with each pulse of my cock. It takes me over completely. All I can do is hold on.

Yes. Yes. More.

I collapse onto her. We're both gasping for breath. Janie's shivering like she's cold. I turn us so we're on our sides and I'm spooning her.

I should deal with the condom, but first I just need to hold her. I wrap her up, trying to cover as much of her as I can. Sheltering her.

Finally, she stops shivering, and our chests rise and fall in sync as we breathe.

28

Sean

"Henry's mom was a blind date," I say. "A friend of a friend set us up."

We're lying in bed, limbs tangled together. All the lights in the house are off now, and I have no idea what time it is. Janie and I should be asleep. My eyes are burning with exhaustion. But although I dozed a bit after that last earth-shaking orgasm, my mind wouldn't let me pass out for long.

I want to talk to Janie, look at her profile in the dark, feel her against me. Her fingertips make languid circles on my chest.

"Alexis works in public relations. Seemed like an odd match with a cop, but we hit it off." My voice is near a whisper. "She took me to art gallery openings and dinners at clients' houses in Venice Beach. I think she liked showing me off. Her Marine, blue-collar boyfriend. Her friends loved hearing my gruesome stories about murder scenes and gang drive-bys."

"And what did you get out of that?" Janie's skeptical tone says she already knows. I can't get anything past her, not that I'm trying.

"Attention, maybe?" I remember that I accused *her* of craving attention. I'm sure Janie remembers that too. "A little ego-stroking."

And the sex was pretty hot, though I'm not going to share that fact. Besides, it was a flickering candle compared to the bonfire between Janie and me.

But from that first date, I was caught up in Alexis's flattery and interest.

I couldn't stand her friends, how they talked about art and real estate like it was life or death. When I actually deal in life and death for a living, and it's *ugly*. Brutal.

But they asked me probing questions at their parties, hung on my every word, and it felt good to be desired. Especially in LA, in certain circles anyway, where being wanted is a valuable commodity and hard to come by.

I assumed that Alexis really wanted me, too. That I was more to her than just exciting sex and a conversation starter for her to parade around. I liked that her life was so different from mine. I thought I could fall in love.

She told me the same thing. *Sean, you're amazing. I'm falling so hard for you.*

But when you're a gimmick, you get old fast.

"Turned out, she was seeing someone else. An executive at her PR agency. Guy was married. I don't know if she was using me as a cover, or if she genuinely liked me for a while. It doesn't matter. She completely fooled me. I had no clue. One of her friends took pity on me, pulled me aside, and told me the truth."

Janie's fingers trace my happy trail. "That's shitty." I'm glad she doesn't say she's sorry for me. "When did you find out Alexis was pregnant?"

"I didn't."

Janie lifts her head to look at me.

"She called me when Henry was a few months old. She

said I had a kid, and she needed money. She'd left her job after the whole dating-the-boss thing. I think what she *really* needed was an employment lawyer, but that wasn't my business. I asked for a paternity test."

"Makes sense."

"I was stupid with Alexis, but not that stupid."

I was in a daze in that time in between, while I waited for the results. I'd been trying to get over Alexis's betrayal, the humiliation, and there she was again exploding the parts of my life she hadn't already damaged. She'd sent me a picture of the baby, and I could barely even look. The hurt was too much.

My son. I'd lost all those months with my son. Hadn't even known he existed.

"I didn't meet Henry until after I got the test results, but from that first moment I held him, I loved him. I loved him enough to offer to marry his mother. Thank God she said no. That would've been a bigger mess."

"You moved to West Oaks after that?"

"Yep." Alexis had been mad about the commute to drop Henry off, but she quieted when I started paying her rent as well as mine. "I was lucky West Oaks PD hired me so fast. I do have a lot of experience, so maybe they felt lucky too. I already told you the rest."

How Alexis decided joint custody was too burdensome. How my mom left her life in Houston and relocated to help me. Didn't have to twist her arm, though. She adores Henry.

"That must've been hard to go through," Janie says.

"I'm not saying it wasn't worth it. For my son, it's all worth it. I just want to be enough for him."

I've never been able to say these things so plainly to anyone. My mom only knows parts of this story. Even my best friends, like Tanner, don't know Alexis cheated. It's embarrassing how clueless I was.

I don't want to make those mistakes again. Trusting someone who's going to lie to me and only tell me what I want to hear. Who'll choose what's easy and convenient, with no regard for anyone else.

A week ago, I would've said Jane Simon fit into that category.

Scary how a few days can turn everything you knew, everything you believed, inside-out.

All of my instincts are saying Janie's not who I thought she was. She's genuine. A genuine pain in the ass sometimes, but also fiercely loyal to those she cares for.

It means a lot to have someone like Janie in my corner. For however long this can last.

29

Janie

I snuggle against Sean's side. "You are definitely enough for Henry. I can tell you're a great dad."

It was brave of Sean to tell me that story. He showed me something meaningful, another sliver of who he is.

And what the hell is up with this Alexis chick? I normally wouldn't judge some woman I've never met. But after what she did to both Henry *and* to Sean? She'd better pray she never meets me in a dark alley, especially if I'm wearing my stilettos.

I can't believe Sean offered to marry her. And that she said no. But I'm glad.

It must be nearly sunrise. I've stayed up all night working before, but never like this. Making love and talking. And eating frittatas.

This has been the longest night I've ever spent, and also the best.

My skin heats as I think of what we were doing a few minutes ago. The sheets are still a mess around us. The way Sean fucks is so raw, so shameless. I was on board for every moment of it. He gave me everything I needed.

I'm going to be replaying those memories long after this is over.

His chest moves as he sighs. "I don't even know what a 'great dad' is. I loved my dad, and I think he did well by us, but there are things I'd change. You know?"

I'm not sure I do know. I never knew my father, and I barely know my mother.

"And Mom was there too," Sean adds. "When we were growing up. Filling in the gaps."

"From middle school on, it was just Gran for me and my sister, but that was enough. She was tough. And not very maternal. But we knew she loved us. She took us in and always made us feel like we belonged with her."

"Sounds like she's gone?" Sean asks gently.

I nod.

"How long?"

"Um…" Without warning, my eyes sting. Tears form a solid mass in my throat. "A few days. It was the night before the shooting at the courthouse. That's when she passed."

Sean props himself on his elbow. "Your grandmother died the night before the hearing? Your grandmother, who was basically your only parent? And you still showed up that morning?"

"I had to be there for David. I—" I almost say I wanted to convince him to change his mind about not testifying. David's decision to violate his plea deal surprised everyone, including me. But that's confidential. I've told Sean about the threats against David, but I can't reveal more.

"I had to be there," I finish.

"And I was awful to you."

"You caught me when I almost slipped on the steps. Very chivalrous."

"Then made my smart-ass comments."

"When you said I'm an attention whore and love chaos? And I have big balls?"

He groans and drags the pillow over his face. "Don't remind me." His voice is muffled.

"I ogled your butt on the way into the courthouse. I blatantly objectified you, and my thoughts were very inappropriate. If that makes you feel better."

"It does. A little." Sean puts the pillow under his head. His strong arms hug me close. "I'm sorry about your Gran. She sounds like an amazing lady."

"She was." I know she had regrets about her relationship with her daughter—my mom—and she tried to fix it with Pam and me. "But she would've wanted me to be strong and keep going forward. She would've been pissed if I didn't show for that hearing, or if I tried to reschedule."

"When's her funeral? You're not missing it, are you?"

"Memorial service. It's…" I try to remember what day it is today. What night. "It's in three days in Tucson. I won't miss it, not if I can help it. My sister needs me to be there."

"You think a lot about other people," Sean says.

I close my eyes. The tears are receding, and that's good. Tonight's been too enjoyable for tears. "I try to. I mean, not everyone, because some people only want to take and tear others down. But I'd never want to fail my friends or family or my clients."

"But who takes care of you?"

I think of Tracey, but she's my employee. I know that's not what he means.

I say, "There's someone. He took excellent care of me tonight." My eyes are so heavy now, I couldn't open them if I tried.

I'm half asleep when he responds. I can't make sense of the words. But I feel myself smiling.

∽

WE SLEEP UNTIL THE EARLY AFTERNOON. I WAKE briefly a few times when Sean gets out of bed, but he always comes back.

I like curling into him with my head on his chest. I also like when he's behind me, and all that warm skin is against mine.

Eventually, I don't go back to sleep. The room is bright with sunlight, despite the curtain, and Sean's eyes are closed. His chest lifts and falls rhythmically. His lips are slightly open and pouty and look very kissable.

He's also got an erection. The thin sheet over us is doing nothing to hide it. I drape my leg over him so his dick presses into my thigh.

He blinks his eyes open, inhaling. His hips are already thrusting his hard-on at my leg. Must be instinct.

"Hi."

"Hello, detective." I shift and lay on top of him. He palms my ass, and then we're kissing and rocking against each other.

"Only one condom left," he says. "You want to use it now? Or…"

I grumble. "Later." There's probably a grocery store or pharmacy around, but I don't want to leave the safe house unless we have to. "Let's do other stuff."

"I like other stuff."

"In the shower." That way we're getting out of bed. We both have crazy sex hair and could stand to wash up.

There's more making out under the spray of the water. Sean makes me come with his fingers—taking some suggestions from me, which he's excellent at—and I give him a hand job. I pay extra attention to the notch on the underside of his tip. He's so sensitive there.

We wash each other's hair and bodies, which naturally turns to a tickling contest. I win. Of course I win. But I get a little overzealous, and Sean grabs me by the waist so I don't slip and crack my head on the tile.

When we get out, Sean finds a first aid kit and takes the old, wet bandage off my arm. He carefully inspects the stitches and announces that the wound looks good. He might not have a clue what he's talking about, but I like how attentive he is. He puts a new bandage on and kisses my shoulder above the injury.

I make us ham and brie sandwiches on bagels, and Sean checks the burner phone. "Nothing new. But I texted with Murphy this morning while you were asleep. She said CBI has cut her off from their investigation. So she doesn't know what they're doing. She hasn't seen Hartford today at all, and he's not returning her calls."

Not ideal. Murphy was our one source on the inside. "Is Officer Shelborne still at the hospital?"

"Yes. Murphy confirmed that."

"Is CBI still looking for us?"

"Murphy said they've put out a statewide BOLO calling us witnesses to an 'incident.' She asked Agent Winfrey about it, and he put on a song and dance about how we're in danger and need protection. He demanded to know if she's aware of our location."

I bring our lunch plates to the island and sit on the stool next to his. "She doesn't know where we are, right?"

"No. But if she turns over my burner number, they can find us real easy using cell tower data."

"True. If they get a warrant."

"Or not." Sean takes a bite of his sandwich.

"So you've joined my conspiracy theory?"

"Don't think it's a theory anymore. Someone hired the Serpents to target us and David Daily, and that someone likely has ties to the state government. Enough to find out the details of our protective custody and try to set a pipe bomb in our hotel rooms."

"And they're probably working for Asher and Nixon Temple."

"Probably."

We go quiet as we eat. I know Sean's mind is trying to put the pieces together, just like mine.

"When I get stuck on an investigation," he says, "I like to brainstorm. Make lists of what I know, what I don't know. What I need to do."

"That's what I do with my cases. I write down possible leads. Witnesses I need to interview."

"It's sexy when you talk like a detective."

"Hey, I run my own investigations for my clients' defense. I'm damn good at it, too."

"I've never had any doubts about that." Sean drums his fingers against his knee. "What about the break-ins? My house. Your office. And now the hotel, too. What's the reason for it?"

"They're trying to find something." We already know that.

"Exactly. But what?"

"Some piece of evidence that could be used against Asher Temple," I suggest.

"That would make sense. But why those locations? Why didn't they break into your apartment? Or my office at the station? Unless..." He grabs the burner phone from the counter. His thumbs move over the screen. "I'm texting Murphy to see if she can check the cameras in the hallways at West Oaks PD. If somebody went in my office when they shouldn't have, the cameras will show it."

That would be enlightening. "David said he had an insurance policy..." I remember what David said to me shortly before the shooting at the courthouse. *I'm hoping you never have to know anything about it.*

I drop the rest of my sandwich on the plate. "Oh my God. What if David tried to send this evidence to you and me? *That* was his insurance policy." I've blurted this straight from my subconscious without really stopping to consider it.

Sean stares at me. "How would that work?"

"Let's say David was scared. Temple had been threatening him. So David sent us this evidence right before the hearing. Just in case. Maybe it was a computer file, password-protected or something. Or a physical document, but in code. So David could control when and if we had access to it." It seems like the kind of thing David might do. He was all about details. Records.

"But to justify murder, this secret evidence would have to be more earth-shattering than anything David had already told us. Your conspiracy just keeps getting wilder."

"I'm trying here!" I say. "We're brainstorming."

Sean gives me a lopsided grin. "All right. David had secret evidence, kept as an insurance policy, and he sent it to us. To your office and to my house. And Asher Temple somehow found out."

"Then Asher hired the Serpents to kill the three of us and find and destroy the secret evidence. The threat would be neutralized." I hold out my hands, like I'm saying, *Ta-da*.

Sean chews his lip, considering. "I think you could be right. Or, maybe your crazy is rubbing off on me." He winks.

I flip him off.

Then Sean grabs me and kisses me. "It's a solid theory. Now, we need to prove it. If David sent us this evidence, did it arrive? And where is it now?"

I'm imagining an envelope with papers inside, maybe a thumb drive. Something physical that the Serpents would've been searching for.

"Who opens the mail or gets deliveries at your house? Your mom?"

"Usually. What about at your office?"

"Tracey. We should talk to Tracey and your mother. See if they can remember receiving anything unusual. A package or envelope or something."

"Good plan, counselor."

I go in for another kiss, this one celebratory. We work well together, Sean and I. It finally feels like we might be going in the right direction.

30

Sean

We set up the Bennett Security iPad with its secure, untraceable connection. Janie suggests I call my mom first.

Even aside from asking our questions, I just want to see my family. I'm missing them both like crazy.

Mom answers with Henry in her arms. "Look, it's your Daddy!"

Henry points at the phone and says something unintelligible. I feel a grin splitting my face. "Hey, buddy, I miss you."

People often say that Henry resembles me. I see my mom in his features, and maybe my older brothers. Not sure yet about me. But I'm always looking.

I pull the stool closer to the island. "How are things going, Mom?"

We chat a little, and Mom seems to be studying me as closely as she's able through the camera. "Where's Janie? Is she all right?"

I check. She's sitting on the couch, flipping through a magazine somebody left on the coffee table.

"Hey," I say, "come over here. Mom wants to say hi."

My mother clucks her tongue. "That's no way to ask."

"Please?" I add.

Smiling, Janie walks over to sit beside me. I'm trying not to show on my face how into her I am. "Hi, Liza. I'm fine."

"I hope you haven't had too difficult a time, dealing with my son?"

I press my leg against hers below the line of the counter. Janie looks thoughtful. "It's been manageable. Sean handcuffed me to his steering wheel so I couldn't leave the truck yesterday. But I can pick locks, so it was no big deal."

I'm sputtering. I can't believe she just told on me to my mom.

"So you *did* leave the hotel?" Mom's tone is stern, but I can tell she's trying not to laugh. "I got the text from your handsome Navy SEAL friend, but he didn't share many details."

"How do you know he's handsome?"

Mom just smiles smugly.

"Don't send Tanner any emojis, Mom. Please."

Janie takes over, thank goodness. "We had a few complications yesterday, but we're in a secure location. We've been working on the investigation, and we have a question for you. Do you recall if you or Sean received any unusual envelopes or packages in the last week or so? It would've been mailed locally, or maybe delivered in person or by a courier?"

"Aside from my usual online purchases and junk flyers, no. Nothing at all."

I quiz Mom, hoping to jog something from her memory, but she's certain. Up until she left the house the morning of the shooting, nothing had arrived.

"Thanks, Mom. Henry, be good to your grandma, okay? And to Chase and his family for hosting you."

Mom kisses Henry's forehead. He's reaching for something he sees on the floor, trying to wriggle out of her arms. "He's been a perfectly angelic wrecking ball, as usual. Both of you be careful. Stay in your safe house and don't get hurt. Or strain anything." Mom adds a wink, and I'm afraid to consider what she means by it.

When the window closes on the iPad, Janie turns to me. "I see where you get your winking from. And your innuendos."

I am not going to touch that one.

∼

Tracey answers Janie's call with a whispered, "Hello?"

"Everything okay?" Janie asks.

"I'm hiding in the upstairs bathroom. Ralph and my cousin are arguing about which TV channel to watch again. It's History Channel versus Bravo, and you'll never believe who wants which."

Ralph must be Tracey's husband. Jane told me that Tracey's staying with her cousin and not loving it.

"How are you?" Tracey asks. "I've been so worried. I tried calling yesterday and you didn't answer."

"I'm sorry. We had to relocate. But we're safe now."

Tracey is staring at me warily. "Hello, Detective Holt."

I wave. "Call me Sean."

Tracey pauses, a comical look of shock on her face. She's glancing between Janie and me and the absence of space between us. "Alright, detective."

Janie doesn't waste much time. "Sean and I have been working on our investigation." She asks Tracey about receiving any unusual envelopes or packages. After my mom didn't remember any, I'm not expecting much.

But Tracey's eyes widen with recognition. "There was

something. It arrived with David's check for his latest invoice. I thought the paper check was odd enough, because he'd never paid that way before. Who uses paper checks these days? But there was another, smaller envelope inside that had your name on it."

Janie groans. "The check. You mean the one David was asking about the day of the hearing? He was so concerned about whether we'd received it?"

"I suppose so, yes. I'm not sure what was in the envelope, but it felt like a small rectangle, maybe plastic. I left it on your desk."

"What're the chances it could still be there?"

Tracey grimaces. "I went by the office yesterday to salvage what I could. The back areas are hardly touched, but your desk had been ransacked. I didn't see David's envelope anywhere."

Janie covers her eyes with her hands.

"I'm so sorry, Janie. If it was important, I should've kept it safer."

Janie lifts her head. "No, it's not your fault. I should've gone into the office the morning of the hearing. I would've seen it."

Tracey gives her an admonishing look, just like something my mom would use. "That was a tough morning. You were distracted and..." Tracey eyes me again. "You were having a bad day."

Because her grandmother had died the night before. I put my hand on Janie's knee and gently squeeze.

Then I get up to let Janie talk to her friend without me hovering at her shoulder. I go into the bedroom to gather my thoughts, and I hear Janie and Tracey murmuring in the kitchen.

There's a message on the burner phone from Murphy. She says she's checking the camera footage from the hallway outside my office, but hasn't seen anyone going inside yet except cleaning staff.

I spend some time checking email and puzzling over our investigation, trying to come up with new insights. When that doesn't work, I toss our dirty clothes and the bedsheets into the laundry machine. The extra clothes that came with the safe house are functional, but I miss my worn-in jeans.

I'm also hoping I'll get lucky again tonight, and some fresh sheets will be a nice touch.

Eventually, the sun is setting on another day. I go back out to the great room. Janie's still sitting at the island. The iPad is dark, and she's staring into space.

"The evidence was there. Right on my desk. David sent it to me, and I had no idea."

I brace my hands on the kitchen island. "Because he didn't tell you. Not your fault."

"He wanted to make sure I'd received his payment, and now I know why. He said he didn't want to tell me what was really going on. Why didn't he trust me?"

"He was afraid you'd get hurt." I guess David Daily isn't such a bad guy.

"But it was my job to help him. My duty. And I was too busy being…sad."

"Nobody would blame you for that, not even David. You can't do everything and be everywhere."

But I'm starting to understand Janie better. She *wants* to do everything for the people who count on her.

She's hinted at a difficult childhood, especially before she and her sister went to live with their grandma. I wonder if that's why Janie is always fighting. Not just to protect herself, but those she cares about.

She basically knows my life story now. Texas, Marines, LAPD, and now Henry.

That's it. That's me.

So much about Janie is mysterious to me. I hope, at some point, that she'll trust me enough to share it.

I think I know what'll make her feel better—if we keep working. We can't end this day without feeling we've done something more. I want to see triumph on her face instead of defeat.

"I've been thinking," I say. "We've been so focused the past few days on Asher Temple and the Serpents. But really, this all comes back to David. To the evidence he wanted to send us as his insurance policy. Right?"

"Right. Which I should've realized from the beginning."

"But that's in the past. No use beating yourself up over it." It's a reminder I need sometimes, too.

But *understanding* the past? That's what's useful.

Investigations are really about the people, and all I know about David is that he worked for Asher. But who is Daily outside of that? How can I get inside his head and understand him?

I have the best possible resource right in front of me.

"Tell me about David," I say.

"What about him?"

I round the island and open the fridge, but I keep talking as I poke through the contents. "Nothing that's too confidential. But I want to understand him. He can't tell us what he was thinking, so we have to figure it out ourselves."

I look over my shoulder. Janie's got her thoughtful face on. While she's considering, I pull things out of the fridge to make us dinner. I have a couple blueberry muffins, half a gallon of milk, half a bagel, an apple, a carrot, and plain yogurt. Also ketchup and mustard.

This is like one of those scary cooking shows my mom watches.

But then I remember Tanner also brought some dry goods. There's cereal and a few other things in the cupboard.

The Six Night Truce

I can work with this.

While I'm chopping the apple, Janie starts talking. "David's very intelligent. Especially with numbers. But when it comes to people, he can be naive. Asher was the governor's son when he and David met in college. David was there on scholarship."

"What's his family like?"

Janie rests her elbows on the granite. "He's not close to them. And it only got worse after he was arrested. He only had Gabriela, his fiancée, and they grew apart after the arrest too. Though I'm not sure why. I could tell by the way he looked at her, spoke about her that he was head over heels." She grips the bridge of her nose. "Which I shouldn't have mentioned. This is all…private."

"But we're trying to help him, right? Let's go back to Asher. How'd he fool David into doing his bidding?"

"Asher can be very charming. He was everything David wished to be. Confident, rich, dynamic. David thought he'd found a business partner. A friend."

"He would've done anything Asher asked? Without looking too closely?"

Janie stiffens. "Your words. Not mine."

"I'll leave the lawyering to you." I pour cereal into two bowls and try to come up with better questions. Less loaded ones. "From our investigation into Asher's fraud scheme, it looked like David had kept very thorough records."

"Yes. And Asher took advantage of that. Asher doctored their duplicate business records and said it was David who'd stolen the investors' money. The documents seemed to support him."

"I remember what David claimed about it, yeah."

"It's true."

"Not arguing. I'm no fan of Asher Temple. You're the one who went out with him."

She snorts. "Jealous, Holt?"

"Doesn't sound like there's anything to be jealous of." But there's a twinge of something in my chest. Annoyance that a douche like Asher got to take Janie on a real date—two in fact—and I haven't managed one.

"I met him at some charity event, he asked me out, and I guess I was hoodwinked for a minute by his charm. And the Temple name, like David was. I'm just more cynical than David. I saw through Temple faster than he did." She peers at the ingredients I have out. "What are you making?"

"You'll see." I spoon yogurt over the cereal, then sprinkle on the chopped apples. "The idea to have duplicate accounting records. Was that Asher all along? Or did that start with David?"

"Well, David had admitted that it was his idea to keep duplicates. He cares about details."

"That's what I thought, but I only came in toward the end. You know this case a lot better than I do."

"Quit trying to flatter me." She says that, but it's working. She's totally preening right now.

"So David always kept duplicate records?" I ask.

"I don't know if I'd say—" Her eyes widen. "Oh. *Oh.* Of course. He would've kept an extra copy of this super-secret evidence somewhere!"

"I was thinking it could be possible."

"And you're brilliant."

Now I'm preening, but it doesn't last too long.

"I mean, it's obvious," Janie says, "but you saw it before I did. I hate how you keep doing that."

I laugh and hand over her bowl and a jar of honey.

"What's this?"

"Yogurt with cereal and apples. Choose how much honey you want. Also there's blueberry muffins on the side." I get the muffins from the oven, where I was warming them up.

"Yogurt and cereal?"

"My mom eats it for breakfast. Don't look at me like that. Breakfast for dinner is a thing. This is the best I could do."

"I'm just looking at you like you're cute. Because you are." She drizzles honey over the apples, then takes a bite. "Yummy. I like it."

"Sure you don't want some yellow mustard and carrots with it? We've got those too."

"Ew. Gross." She elbows me when I sit down to eat with her. "David would've kept an extra copy of the secret evidence. You said David's apartment was broken into. Probably by the Serpents?"

"Yeah." I dip my spoon into the bowl. "Maybe they found the extra copy there. But maybe not. Who else did David trust?"

Janie takes another bite. "Just his fiancée. Tracey's been trying to get in touch with her since the courthouse shooting, but Gabriela hasn't answered."

"Then we'd better find her."

31

Janie

The next morning, we take the car Tanner left for us. It's a risk leaving the safe house, but a manageable one. Nobody but Tanner knows our exact location, and nobody will be looking for this car. Sean and I are wearing hats and sunglasses, fresh clothes, and we're going to be careful.

Besides, we need to buy more food or we're going to starve.

And we need more condoms.

We made love again last night. I can't stop visualizing Sean above me, his muscles flexing, that sexy snarl on his mouth. The way he manhandles me, lifting and placing me however he wants.

Listen to me, calling it "making love" instead of just fucking. But Sean is some kind of sex sorcerer. He's the perfect combination of rough and dominant, sweet and gentle. And he listens to what I'm saying in bed, giving me exactly what I need.

I could easily get addicted to this.

We've spent the morning searching for info about David's

fiancée, Gabriela Torres. I've met her a few times, early on, when she came into the office with David for meetings. But after that, the media attention and the stress got to be too much for her. David said she'd moved out of their apartment.

He was heartbroken after that. He withdrew from me too, getting more and more depressed. Delaying his testimony to the special grand jury. I wonder if Asher was threatening him, even back then.

Now Gabriela seems to have vanished. The police haven't found any sign—that we know of—that Gabriela's hurt or in danger. But what if she knows something about the secret evidence David was hiding? What if he gave a duplicate copy to *her*?

After the shooting at the courthouse, of course she'd want to stay hidden.

Sean drives, while I navigate. "Take the next right."

We enter a neighborhood of older homes. The trees are mature, casting shade on the houses. I see bikes in driveways. Swings in yards.

Tracey's the one who found this lead. Gabriela's mother Isabel lives in Thousand Oaks. She didn't answer her phone, maybe because I was using the secure iPad and the number would come up as blocked. So we're taking the risk of driving out.

I certainly don't want to bring any danger to her door. But if we find Gabriela and she gives Sean and me what she has, then we can get that evidence to the special grand jury before it's too late. Asher Temple will be charged for what he's done. Even if we can't prove Asher sent the Serpents after us, at least he won't skate for his fraud.

Sean parks at the curb. "Should I come to the door with you?"

"Yes. But let me ring the bell. I don't want the first thing she sees to be a big, scary man." I take off my hat and sunglasses.

"Scary? If anyone's scary here, it's you."

"That's when I'm Jane the Panther. Janie the Kitty Cat isn't scary at all. She's great at getting people to talk." I start to get out, but Sean stops me.

"Whoa. Wait a sec. Janie the *Kitty Cat?*"

Oh, God. I hadn't even thought before I spoke. Why did I let that slip out?

"You're blushing. I don't think I've ever seen you blush, not even when we're…you know."

"And we're never gonna *you know* again if you don't shut up."

We go to the front door. Sean's still chuckling behind me. But he looks like a sweetheart when he's smiling, so that's good. Maybe he won't intimidate Isabel with his alpha cop vibes.

I ring the bell. I hear noise inside, and then a small woman opens the door. She's got warm but cautious eyes.

"Isabel Torres?" I ask.

"Yes?"

"My name's Jane Simon. I know your daughter, Gabriela. I'm her fiancé's lawyer. I was hoping I could speak to you for a minute or two. About David."

Her expression shifts to fear. "I heard about the shooting. Is there bad news? From the hospital?"

"No, no. Nothing like that. It's about David's legal case."

Isabel nods at Sean. "Who's he?"

"My…associate." He's off the clock right now. It's true enough.

"All right. I have a few minutes. You can come in." Isabel widens the door. Sean and I both step inside. I notice the shoes organized neatly by the entrance, so I slip mine off. Sean does the same.

We follow Isabel into the living room. It's a bright, airy space, with Scandinavian furniture and lots of throw pillows. She clears a couple of hand-painted mugs and plates from the table, then returns.

"Is anyone else here?" I ask.

"No. I live alone. I wasn't expecting visitors, so things are a bit messy. Sorry."

I glance around again. The place doesn't look messy at all. Just lived in. Welcoming. Watercolors hang on the walls, and I wonder if Isabel is the artist.

We sit. "How did you find me?" she asks.

That question surprises me. "You're Gabriela's mother. My assistant Tracey looked up your contact info for me."

Isabel shifts on the couch, looking uncomfortable. "Gabriela and I have been…estranged. For many years. Her father and I divorced when she was younger, and it wasn't amicable."

"I'm sorry to hear that. But we've been trying to find Gabriela, and haven't had any luck. Were you aware that she's missing?"

Isabel's brows shoot up. "What? I'd only heard about David on the news. I follow Gabriela on social media, and she hasn't posted, but I didn't think…"

"I don't want to worry you unnecessarily. But I want to make sure she's well, and I also needed to speak with her."

"About David?"

"We think he might've given Gabriela something for safe-keeping. Something important to his case."

"Like what?"

"I can't give out too much information."

I ask more questions, and Sean does as well. But Isabel has turned cagey. I don't know if she's hiding anything, or if she's just upset by this conversation.

Finally, she stands up. "I have another appointment." She walks us to the door, where we put on our shoes.

There's a creak upstairs.

Maybe the house is settling. Or maybe not.

"If you do hear from Gabriela, or see her," I say, "could you pass on our message and call my assistant?" I take a card from my wallet. "If Gabriela has something relevant to David's case, it's urgent that we get it. *Extremely* urgent."

Isabel stares at my business card. For a moment, I'm sure she's going to say something more.

But then she nods slightly and closes the door.

As we leave, Sean glances back at the house. "You noticed the two sets of mugs and plates?"

"Yep. And there was a noise upstairs."

"And two sizes of shoes by the front door. I wonder if Isabel and Gabriela aren't as estranged as she claimed."

"Or if Gabriela was hoping to disappear and went to a place she didn't expect anyone to look."

"She didn't count on Jane the Panther and her expert investigative skills."

I shove his shoulder as we walk toward the car. "More like Tracey's expert research skills."

We get in, and Sean starts the engine, but we don't drive off yet. "There's a good chance Gabriela is inside right now," he says. "Or that Isabel knows where to find her. We could stake out the house and find out for sure."

"And if we see Gabriela but she won't speak to us, what then? We can't force her. Better to back off and let her come to us."

Sean's frowning. "But do you think she'll get in touch?"

I watch the house. The curtains are all closed. "I really hope so."

We need David's evidence to prove that the courthouse shooting and the break-ins are connected. And, of course, the prosecutors will be able to use that evidence against Asher.

If we can't find it, I don't know what else we can do.

Sean reaches for my hand. "We have two more days until the special grand jury expires. And until you need to leave for Arizona. I won't give up if you don't."

I smile at him and run my thumb over his palm.

∽

WE STOP AT A GROCERY ON THE WAY BACK. SEAN and I pool the cash in our wallets so we can avoid using credit cards. We're also wearing our hats and sunglasses. But even though there's a BOLO to law enforcement about us, we're not exactly on the most-wanted list. TV news isn't flashing our images. There's no reason to think average grocery clerks will recognize us.

I hope.

We try to shop quickly, choosing to divide and conquer. I grab bagged salad and some rolls. Sean gets a rotisserie chicken. We're going to have a real dinner tonight.

I find him in the condom aisle. He's frowning at all the choices. I tip my sunglasses down and look over them. "That difficult?"

"Just trying to decide how many to buy. A few, or…a lot."

Another man walks past us and grabs a box, avoiding eye contact. Sean and I both start giggling like middle-schoolers.

"He went for the value pack," I point out.

"It is a good deal, price-wise. But I mean, how many can we use in two days? Unless…"

"Unless?"

He shrugs, all casual, with his grocery basket of chicken in one hand. "Unless it's more than two days."

I think I know what he's asking. And my heart is running

some kind of race, like it's trying to outrun this conversation. More days with Sean... It sounds nice. But also complicated.

I push my sunglasses up. "Buy the jumbo pack. Let's see how many we can use."

"You know I'm up for a challenge." He drops the box into his shopping basket. Then he leans in, close enough his breath is hot on my neck. "I want to hear Janie the Kitty Cat purring all night."

I try to tickle him, and he dances out of the way. But he puts his hand on the back of my neck and keeps it there until we leave the store. Like he's telling the world I'm taken. I'm *his*.

For right now, I am.

When we get back to the safe house, there's a message from Murphy waiting on the burner phone. Out of an excess of paranoia, we left it behind on our outing. If someone— such as CBI—figured out the number and tracked our location, we didn't want them to know we'd been to see Isabel.

I load the groceries in the fridge as Sean reads the message. "What did Murphy say?" I ask.

"She found something on the camera footage from the station. Somebody went into my office in the middle of the night. The day *after* the shooting at the courthouse."

"Shit." I look at the still image that Murphy sent. There's a man in a baseball cap and hoodie, his face hidden from the camera.

"Do you recognize him?" I ask.

"No. Murphy didn't either. Medium height, medium build. Arms covered, so we can't see if there's tattoos."

"But a Serpent gang member wouldn't be walking freely around the station."

"Not unless somebody gave him access." Sean sets down the phone, wiping a hand over his face. "More likely, it was somebody with every right to be at the station. And he waited until the hall was deserted, put on his hat, went right into my office. No clue what he was doing in there, but we can guess."

"Looking for David's evidence." I've been saying from the beginning that someone inside the government or law enforcement was involved. But it's still a shock to see the proof. "Can you find out who was at the station at that time? Do your key cards log who goes in and out?"

"Our key cards aren't coded to individual users that way. People don't like to be tracked and watched."

I roll my eyes. "No kidding." *I will not rant about the irony. I will not.* "Could it be Agent Winfrey?"

"Sure. But it could also be someone else. Murphy says she's working on it, and I have no doubt she is. She's every bit as pissed as we are, and she's not the type to let things go."

We keep brainstorming and picking apart every clue, looking for new leads. But the hours tick by, a minute at a time, and pretty soon we're making dinner. I throw together the salad. Sean heats up the rotisserie chicken and rolls. It's a simple, mostly pre-made meal, but it's hearty and comforting.

The past couple of days, I've been tracking time by meals instead of hours. The ones we share, the ones we skip. The ones Sean makes for me, and I make for him. It's such a regular, everyday thing, eating together, keeping us going. No matter how difficult and disruptive this week has been, our basic needs haven't disappeared.

I want to think that our physical connection is more than that, though. More than just a need for stress relief.

Could this actually last?

We eat at the island with our stools way too close, legs and shoulders crowded together. Sean has his arm around me half the time. It's not the most efficient way to eat dinner, but it's fun.

After we're done and the dishes are washed, we end up on the couch, making out.

My responsibilities are always in the back of my mind. But for moments here and there, while I'm kissing Sean, those problems fade and it's just him and me. Two people who like each other. And nothing else matters.

I'm in his lap, and he's running his hands down my back to my ass. "You're not purring yet."

He's not going to let me live that down, is he? "Guess you have to do more."

Sean picks me up. My legs wrap around his waist, my hands at his neck. He carries me to the bedroom and lays me down on the bed. His fingers pop the button on my jeans and tug the zipper down.

I reach for his fly, but he stops my hand. "Nope, not until you're purring for me. Just for me."

Only for you. I'm not shy in bed, but I'm not daring enough to say those words out loud.

Sean undresses me. When I'm down to my panties, he trails open-mouthed kisses all over my body. He pays special attention to the small bruises he's left the past two nights on my hips and thighs. It's nothing that hurts, but he was rough enough for the signs to linger on my skin.

I can tell from the way his breath hitches that those reminders turn him on. They turn me on too. Sean kisses and licks every mark he's made.

I want him to make so many more.

For ages, his knuckle runs from the hollow of my throat down to the valley between my breasts, and back up again along my sternum. Just there. Over and over. Nothing has ever felt so relaxing.

He's taking his time, cherishing me like the whole world

is just the two of us. Like we have no deadlines. Nobody looking for us, no worries. Like we'll never have to stop.

Where did this man even come from?

How am I going to let him go?

I sigh and moan. "I'm definitely purring now."

"Mmm. I hear it."

I love how his voice gets all dark and deep and rumbly when he's aroused. His bulge is huge in his jeans.

Just for me.

"Now *I* get to do what I want." I sit up, pushing him by the shoulder to get him to lie down. He doesn't go easily. Sean is strong and solid, and even when I try to take control, it's only because he lets me. "Please," I say, kissing below his ear. "I want to be as good to you as you are to me."

He helps me take off his shirt and his jeans. I strip off his boxers too and straddle his thighs, just admiring him. His erection lays against his stomach, long and thick and tempting. I can't help licking my lips.

But Sean was patient enough to caress and kiss every inch of my skin. *Almost* every inch. I'm still wearing my panties, and they're soaking from how much I want him. He hasn't touched me there yet.

I want to do the same to him. It's not so much making him wait as making him feel appreciated. Seen. Desired.

I'm worried about how attached I'm getting to Sean. I don't want to get hurt, and he often seems to realize things before I do. What if he realizes this can't work when we're back to our regular lives? Back to being on opposite sides, if not exactly enemies.

He could let me down. He could leave me behind.

But I can't think about that right now. Sean showed me so much sweetness, and I'm going to do the same for him.

I start at his neck. Kissing and nipping. Sucking at his

pulsepoint. The throb of his blood under my lips is intoxicating. How it speeds up to a breakneck pace.

I lick his Adam's apple. Every sign of Sean's masculinity drives me wild.

I move down to his collarbones and his pecs. I dig my fingers into his chest hair. Suck his hardened nipples. *"Janie."* He tries to grab hold of me, but I brush his hands away.

"Wait," I say. "Let me give this to you."

I get lost in his warm skin. The dark ink of his tattoos and the smooth spot where his hip meets his thigh. His fingers tangle in my hair. His cock keeps twitching. It's leaking like a fountain onto his stomach. I want to lap up that moisture, but I'm forcing myself to be patient too.

When I can't possibly wait any longer, I lick just under his tip. His moan is guttural. His hands tighten in my hair, and his thigh muscles clench tight. I can tell he's barely able to keep himself still.

I nuzzle his balls and kiss each one. Then rub my cheek against the velvet skin of his shaft.

My mouth closes around the head and sucks, and that's all he can take.

Sean sits up, pulling away. In a moment, he has me flipped onto my back, and he's towering over me.

"You want my cock? I'll give it to you."

He grabs my hands. Pins my arms over my head as he kneels to either side of me.

He pushes the leaking tip of his cock to my lips, the pressure light. Teasing. "Yes," I moan against him, and his whole body shivers. I slide my tongue up and down his slit. Salt and musk spread over my tastebuds.

Sean nudges the head of his cock past my lips, and I gladly take him in. I hollow my cheeks, sucking him. My eyes flick up to meet his gaze. His mouth is partway open, his eyes hazy and dark with primal lust.

He gently fucks my mouth. My hands clench into fists, release, clench again.

"Janie. Watching you like this. God, you don't know what it's like."

I can barely stand it, I'm so turned on. My clit throbs with each thrust of his hips. I want him inside all of me, everywhere.

I am going to combust.

I love his cock in my mouth, but it's a relief when he lets me go and backs off. He left the box of condoms on the nightstand earlier, and I watch him tear one open. Roll it onto his swollen shaft. His movements are jerky, stilted, like he can't move fast enough.

Sean grabs my thighs and yanks me across the bed, closer to him. With one swift motion, his cock plunges inside me, and we both cry out. He's got a foot on the ground, his other leg bent to kneel on the mattress. His upper body falls forward, and he catches himself on his elbows.

His mouth captures mine in a smoldering kiss.

For a few minutes, we're nothing but heat and gasps and wild movements. I buck against him. His tongue lashes against mine. My nails claw into his shoulders.

That initial frenzy passes, and we slow down, finding a rhythm. Staring into each other's eyes.

Sean rolls us both. I straddle him. He holds my hips. I rock and slide and grind against him, our stomachs pressed together.

"Come for me, Janie. I need to feel you come on my cock. Need it so bad."

He keeps whispering dirty things. I feel the orgasm building, a small hum in my clit that gets louder and stronger until I can't hold it back.

Pleasure sears through me, a starburst exploding from my core and shooting outward. "Oh. *Sean.*"

He rolls us again so I'm on my back and thrusts wildly into me. I'm still coming. I feel my body squeezing around him. Hot jolts spread through my belly and down my thighs.

Then Sean's losing control, too, his cock pulsing inside me, his thrusts turning staccato. He pushes his face into my hair, groaning against my ear.

We're still rocking against one another even after it's over. Chasing that incredible high.

Eventually, we lie there, a mess of sweat and tangled limbs. He slides off of me, but cuddles against my side.

He lays his hand above my heart as I catch my breath.

"It's never been…with anyone. Like this." He smiles and closes his eyes. "That didn't make sense. I think half my brain just shot out of my dick."

"I know what you mean. It's the same for me."

It's never been like this with anyone. Except you.

32

Sean

I take care of the condom and get a glass of water for us to share. When I return to the bed, Janie's got one arm slung over her head, her expression dreamy and happy.

She is gorgeous. There aren't even words. I have to stop and look at her.

"What?" she asks.

"I've never seen anything so beautiful."

Her eyes widen like she's surprised I said that. I shrug. "Just being honest." I get back into bed and pull the sheet over us. I love that Janie's not self-conscious about being naked, and neither am I, but I want us to be warm and cozy. I gather her in my arms and kiss her forehead. She caresses my cheek.

"When this is over," I say, "I'd like to take you out."

Her head moves back by an inch. She's scrutinizing me. "Out? Like...a date?"

"Yes. Will you go on a date with me?" An old-fashioned one, because that's the kind of guy I am. I want to pick her up, pay for her meal or movie ticket, kiss her on her porch. Assuming she's got one.

"What kind of date?"

"Any kind you like."

"No, you asked *me*. You can't expect me to plan it."

I grin and shake my head. Always busting my balls, this one. "I would take you out to dinner."

"Somewhere fancy?"

Ha, I see that test coming a mile away. "Nope. Somewhere lively and fun. With music playing. Maybe burgers. Or Mexican. Then we'd go dancing."

"Like, ballroom dancing? Or dancing at a club?"

"None of the above. We'd go slow-dancing. At a bar." I turn toward her, lowering my voice and giving her my best sultry stare. "With sexy dark lighting splashed with neon. And I'd kiss you until we were ready to rip each other's clothes off, right there on the dance floor."

"Yes," she whispers. "Take me there."

I can't help it. I smile so wide, it feels like it starts in my chest and might burst out of me. "When this is over," I say again.

She grimaces comically. "Assuming we can still tolerate each other by then."

"Hey, don't do that. Don't push me away before we even get started."

She opens her mouth, eyes stunned, and doesn't say anything.

I've never had this kind of chemistry with someone. Janie and I have a good time together, even when we're fighting. My mom likes her. She's kind to Henry.

Even with all the madness surrounding us, Janie and I have been having *fun*. And melt-your-face-hot sex. I'd be a real dumbass if I didn't want to keep that going. And I don't see why we can't.

"I understand that you want to protect yourself and your feelings," I say. "You don't let people in very easily. But—"

Her jaw tightens.

"Just saying what I see. I'm not criticizing."

"Please, Sean. Tell me what else I'm feeling. Since you seem to know me so well."

"I don't yet. But I *want* to know you."

She looks away, chewing the inside of her cheek. Ouch. That can't be comfortable.

She's annoyed at me, but I also think she's scared of this. So am I. But I'm more scared of losing whatever we could become.

"Just go on a date with me," I say softly. "And have an open mind. That's all I'm asking." I lift her hand and kiss her knuckles. Then I turn it over and kiss her palm. "I made the kitty cat purr. Bet I can tame the panther, too."

She snorts a laugh. "One date. Then we'll see."

Oh, yes. Victory is sweet.

∽

WHEN I'M WORKING AN INVESTIGATION, THERE'S A lot to my job that's not glamorous or exciting. I spend hours doing paperwork, making phone calls, interviewing witnesses who know nothing, and listening to wire taps that are brain numbingly dull. All in the hopes of finding those small nuggets of value that will build to a solution. And every once in a while, there's a revelation that completely changes the picture.

After all the progress Janie and I made yesterday, today it feels like we're standing still. Maybe even going backward.

We spend the morning on the iPad. Janie calls Isabel, Gabriela's mother, again, but there's no answer. She leaves a voicemail just in case.

Then we video chat with my mom and Henry for a while. Chase's mother-in-law, Megan, is spending time with them today. Henry and Chase's daughter run around, making us laugh. It seems like my mom has found a new friend in Megan, and I'm glad to see that. Megan already knows Janie well, and the affection between them is obvious through the screen.

I also check in with Detective Murphy, who says she's busy following up on a hunch. Something related to David Daily. But she's not ready to discuss it yet. I haven't told her about Daily's secret evidence, probably because that's our ace in the hole. As much as I trust Murphy, this information is dangerous. I want to be careful about who we give it to.

Time is running out, and any false move could mean disaster.

At the end of business tomorrow, the special grand jury expires. Already, it'll be difficult to assemble the jury members in time even if we *do* find David's new evidence.

And before that—tomorrow morning—Janie is supposed to leave for Arizona.

When this all began, we agreed to a six-night truce. But when that time is over, that doesn't mean we're out of danger. I have no idea if the Serpents are still going to come after us. And I have no clue what CBI will do when I return to West Oaks. Will I be punished? Accused of something? Or worse?

All of those are unknowns.

But what I do know is that I don't want this closeness with Janie to end. The deadline for this truce means nothing to me anymore. I don't think it's important to Janie either, from the way she keeps sneaking kisses and touches, seeking me out anytime I wander away. That thought is keeping me going, despite the frustration.

Tonight is our sixth night since this started. I know it won't be the last.

∼

After lunch, we get the call we've been waiting for. But it's not Gabriela Torres.

"I found something." Murphy's voice is breathless. She's on speaker on the burner phone. "It's a small memory card."

Janie gasps, hand flying to her mouth. I reach for her hand.

"Where?" I ask.

"David Daily's belongings. The things he had with him when he was admitted to the hospital. They were checked in as evidence, but there was an envelope in Daily's shoe, taped to the inside. The patrol officer who went through everything obviously missed it. It was addressed to you."

"To Janie?" I ask. "Or to me?"

Murphy pauses, and I wonder if she's stuck on the name "Janie." But she doesn't remark on the nickname.

"To you, Sean. To your home address."

I blow out a breath. So David had meant to send the evidence to me, but failed to get it done. Either because he didn't have a chance or because he had second thoughts.

"And you opened the envelope?" Janie asks.

"Yes. It was just the memory card. No writing, no papers, nothing. I haven't tried to see what's on it. Figured I should call you first thing. Any clue what this could be?"

I nod at Janie. She's the one who figured out that David had new evidence.

"We think it's something David was holding back," she says. "New evidence against Asher Temple. We think this is the reason Daily was shot at the courthouse. And the reason someone's been trying to kill Sean and me. Whatever this evidence is, it's important enough to kill for. But we haven't been able to find a copy of it, or even prove that it exists for sure, until now."

Murphy whistles. "Well, you can thank me later."

"Don't tell anyone or go anywhere," I say. "We can't take any chances with this. Janie and I are pretty sure CBI is working with Temple."

"*What*? Is that a joke?"

"I wish it was."

"I've had my suspicions about Agent Winfrey, but you're serious? You have proof of this?"

"No, no proof. That's why I was hesitant to make accusations. But now, with this memory card, we have to be extremely careful. Wait until Janie and I get to you. We'll look at what's on it and decide what to do from there. Together."

If it's really the evidence we think it is, then all three of us will take it physically to the DA's office. I'm not sure what we'll do if the contents of the memory card are encrypted or coded. But we'll figure that out once it becomes an issue.

This is David's insurance policy. He must've planned a way for us to use it.

"Where are you?" I ask.

"My house. Like I told you, I've been suspicious of Winfrey. I thought he was being more of a dickhead than actively undermining the investigation. But he's been shutting me out, so I didn't want him to know I'd taken Daily's belongings out of evidence."

"What about Hartford?"

"I haven't seen him. Do you have concerns about him too?"

"Not specifically, but let's keep this to ourselves. I'll see you soon."

I know where Murphy lives. On the southern edge of

West Oaks. She had a barbecue there about a month back and invited most of the department.

Murphy offers to let us stay with her overnight. Janie and I grab our few belongings, close up the house as quickly as possible, and get in the car. We hit the usual afternoon traffic, but it's never been so frustrating. I keep honking the horn, hitting my hands against the steering wheel. Janie taps her fingers against the dashboard and the window glass.

We're both crawling out of our skins.

Finally, we reach Murphy's neighborhood. This is a fairly new development, with a lot of houses still under construction. Murphy lives at the end of a cul-de-sac, right up against a dried-up riverbed with trails running through it. The riverbed is an expanse of brown dirt and rocks sprinkled with lines of green, where tangled brush and black walnut trees grow.

I park in the driveway. Janie's opening the door before I've even turned off the engine. I'm right behind her.

The moment we're outside, a scream rends the air.

"Around back!" I yell, drawing my weapon.

Then there's a loud pop. The noise echoes across the riverbed. A gunshot.

"Janie, stay behind me!"

I don't wait to see if she's listening. I just run. I race into Murphy's backyard and find my friend sprawled on the grass.

Her eyes are panicked. Her hands claw at the blood pumping from a wound in her chest.

And I see a man dressed in black, running for the trail along the riverbed.

Janie dives forward, pressing her hands to Murphy's chest. "Go!" she screams at me. "Stop him."

I sprint after the shooter, my feet pounding into the brown grass.

I reach the trail. The shooter is up ahead, wearing a

hoodie. He could be the same person who broke into my office. Our shoes slam into the concrete, and my pulse rushes in my ears.

The guy aims a gun behind him. Squeezes off a few shots. I zag out of the way. It's not likely he'll hit me from that far while we're both running. Yet adrenaline makes me raise my weapon and fire in response. I miss.

"Shit!" I stumble slightly on some broken concrete, and that's all he needs.

The shooter dashes off the path and disappears into a thick snarl of brush. It's the beginning of a scrubby wilderness of trees and bushes stretching along the old riverbed.

I shout curses into the air, my words boomeranging across the landscape.

No matter how hard I try to pick up the guy's trail, I can't find him.

33

Janie

"Murphy, look at me, okay? Stay with me."

I yank off my sweatshirt and press it to the wound in Murphy's upper chest. It's bad, but I'm praying it's not so bad that it's hopeless. I spot Murphy's phone on the ground, about a foot away, and grab it. I rapidly press the side button to activate emergency calling.

The operator answers.

"Police officer down! Detective Angela Murphy has been shot." I rattle off the street address, which I somehow pluck from my memory of navigating here.

Murphy is trying to speak. Her eyes are frightened but determined.

"They're on their way," I say to her. "Just hold on. Don't try to talk."

But she continues to whisper. I can't hear. I lean closer.

"Card."

"Card?" I repeat.

She nods her head once.

Her fingers are outstretched, like she's trying to reach something. Her hands are near her pockets. I gently check her jeans, but there's nothing. "Do you mean the memory card? It's not here. Not in your jeans pockets. Could it be somewhere else?"

But the despair on her face is answer enough.

I hear footsteps. Sean appears, racing back toward us from the running trail. "I fucking lost him." He holsters his gun. Kneels beside Murphy. "How's she doing?"

Murphy shakes her head, her mouth a thin line.

"She's just as stubborn as you or me," I say. "Murphy's going to be fine." *Please.* I hold one of her hands. Sean takes the other. I keep pressure on the wound.

In another minute, sirens cut through the quiet.

The EMTs swarm around Murphy, shouting and giving directions as they render aid. Within moments, she's on a stretcher and headed for the ambulance.

My T-shirt and jeans are streaked with blood.

"I think the shooter got the memory card," I say to Sean. "Murphy was trying to show me where it was, but it was gone."

Sean digs his fingers into his hair. "How could this have happened? How could they have known? If she didn't tell anyone…"

"Unless she did. Or maybe someone was listening." Murphy's phone is locked, so for now, we can't check her call log. All we can do is head to the hospital. We have to do whatever we can. Whether that's donating blood, or reporting what we saw. Or just being there.

Whatever's on that memory card, whatever David was hiding, it's left a trail of bloodshed in its wake.

"Should we follow the ambulance?" I ask.

"I need to stay to secure the scene." He's rubbing his forehead. Like he's struggling to keep his thoughts on track. "I need to call the on-duty detective. And the sergeant. We need dogs here for a manhunt. Fuck."

"Then can we head to the hospital?"

Sean nods, his eyes glassy.

∼

WE STORM INTO THE EMERGENCY ROOM. West Oaks PD officers are already crowding the waiting area. The word is out—one of their own has been shot. The worst news any of them can hear.

Sean looks haggard. He's been on the phone since the moment we got back into the car. I drove. He's been using his real phone, which he switched off of airplane mode. I did the same to mine, though I ignored the buzzing of dozens of messages that I've missed in the last few days.

We're done hiding. That's not an option anymore.

I sit in the waiting room while Sean talks to his fellow officers and makes more calls. Several people eye the bloodstains on my clothes and frown, whispering my name to each other.

They want to know what I'm doing here. What part I've played in this. I'm not even sure what to tell *myself*.

Then Agent Winfrey arrives, with Hartford right behind him.

I see the moment that he and Sean make eye contact. Tension crackles through the room.

Winfrey and Sean stride toward the other, meeting in the center of the space. Sean's in jeans and a T-shirt, his hair a mess from sticking his fingers into it. Winfrey's wearing a suit, his hair slicked back.

The rest of the waiting room has gone quiet.

"This is your fucking fault," Sean growls.

"I don't see how that's possible, when you were there at the scene. You've been missing for days, and now you turn up when Murphy gets shot? Tell me why I shouldn't have you arrested right now."

"For what? Murphy and I are the only ones who've actually been investigating. CBI hasn't done shit."

Winfrey pokes his finger into Sean's chest. "You're going down to the station, and you're going to answer all of our questions."

Neither man is keeping his voice down. I see shock in the eyes of everyone around me.

"You've pushed us out, tried to shut us down at every turn," Sean says. "Are you getting paid by the Temple family? Or are you just doing this as a personal favor to them?"

"How do I know who *you're* really working for?"

Sean shoves Agent Winfrey, and Agent Hartford steps forward like he might intervene. Several patrol officers jump out of their seats. I'm not sure whose side they're on, if they want to stop Sean from doing something stupid, or if they're actually going to arrest him.

I stand up slowly, knowing there isn't much I can do. But I'll back Sean up. If he needs me, there's no question.

"Get back to the station, Holt." Agent Winfrey is practically spitting the words. "Or I will charge you with obstruction and assault on a law enforcement officer. And anything else we can think of. You're welcome to try me."

"I'm not a fucking kid on my first day of patrol. You're not doing shit."

"You're suspended," Winfrey barks. "Without pay."

"You can't do that."

"I just fucking did. And if I have my way, I'll see that Chief Liu fires your ass. You're done, Holt. Get out of my face."

Sean stalks toward me. He looks unhinged.

"Sean—"

"I need a few minutes. I'll be right back."

I start to go after him, but he storms down the hall and pushes into a men's restroom.

The door slams into the wall.

I wouldn't presume to know how he's feeling right now. Detective Murphy is important to him, a friend, someone he likes and respects. I almost never pray with any earnestness, but I say a quick prayer to whoever's listening that Murphy gets through this okay.

Sean must be racked with guilt. Tortured by all the questions we still can't answer.

But whenever my anger gets the best of me, I need time to cool down. Time without anyone bothering me, even if they're trying to help. I'm going to let Sean be.

I decide to do something useful instead of waiting around here, getting stared at by West Oaks PD officers. I'll text Sean where I'm going.

I need to find David's hospital room. I owe him a visit, even if he's unconscious. I want to check on his security arrangements, too. Especially with what's happened to Murphy.

I head upstairs and see Officer Madison Shelborne walking down the hall.

"Madison!" I'm relieved to see her. But her expression tightens when she sees me.

"You heard? I thought you were still in a safe house."

"Sean and I came here as soon as we could. We were there with Murphy right after it happened."

"Murphy?"

"Yes, just about an hour ago, when..."

I trail off when I see how confused Madison looks. She hasn't heard about Detective Murphy yet.

"Murphy was shot. She's in the emergency room right now."

Madison curses. "My phone was buzzing, but with everything else going on, I didn't have a chance to check. God." She wipes her hands over her face, shifting her weight. She doesn't know whether to stay here or go.

"Everything else?" I ask.

Madison pulls me aside, holding me by the shoulders. "Jane, David didn't make it."

The words don't make sense. "What?"

"David died. He's gone."

Every part of me goes cold. "*No*. That's..."

"I'm so sorry. He was stable the last few days, but then he started crashing."

I still can't get what she's saying through my head. I'm looking around for the police response. The outrage. A witness has just been murdered in the middle of the hospital.

"But I thought you were here. He was supposed to be protected."

"We've been here. Me and the other patrol officers Murphy assigned. We haven't let anybody through. But David just didn't make it, Jane. They said it was the head wound, there was too much pressure and he just... You can talk to the doctors. I am really sorry, again. He never regained consciousness. He wasn't able to talk to us. But I doubt he was in pain."

I'm stunned. Slowly, my mind starts to process. David is dead. And I still haven't heard from Gabriela. She probably doesn't know. Didn't even have a chance to say goodbye to her fiancé.

I need to call Tracey. I need to figure out what I'm supposed to do. If David's next of kin or emergency contact isn't here...

Madison walks with me to the nearest waiting room, but I know she must be eager to find out how Murphy is doing. I promise her I'm fine alone.

Alone. That's where I always end up.

My voice shakes on the phone when I tell Tracey the news. She can't believe it either. I ask her to call Isabel's number and leave a voicemail, as well as trying Gabriela's numbers again. I don't think I can do it. Not until I have a few minutes to gather myself.

I sit in the waiting room, staring at the wall.

I'm in a daze.

I think of the last time I saw Gran. She was in her hospice room, slipping in and out of consciousness. She'd had a stroke, and the doctors knew she didn't have long. It was just a matter of days. Of saying goodbye.

She wasn't aware of much. Yet I was sure there were times she recognized my voice. Smiled when I held her hand.

But I wasn't there on the last day. Because I had to come back to West Oaks.

And I wasn't here for David, either. He died in his hospital room with no one beside him. No one here that he loved.

I'm not sure how long I sit there. But suddenly, Sean is kneeling in front of me, holding my elbows. Pulling me up.

"Hey. I'm so sorry, Janie. Let's get you home."

34

Sean

I ask Janie for the directions to her apartment. She recites her address in a monotone. Her skin's too pale, and there are dots of blood at her temple. On her neck.

It might be a bad idea to take Janie home. After all, we've been in hiding for almost a week. The Serpents have tried more than once to kill us.

But wasn't this really about David's evidence? The evidence that they now have? They must've found the memory card sent to Janie's office that first day, right after the courthouse shooting. They took the other copy from Murphy today.

If Gabriela has a miraculous duplicate, she's hiding it well.

So, what reason would anyone have to continue targeting me or Janie? If we knew the substance of this mysterious evidence, we would've told someone by now.

And if I'm wrong, I've got my guns. They can fuckin' come at me.

I guess these are all rationalizations. The truth is, I'm

numb. We've been running for days. We've done everything we could to unravel the mysteries of who and what and why. And fuck all that's done.

Murphy's in the hospital, the evidence is gone, and David is dead.

The most important thing to me now is Janie. I'm taking her home so she'll be comfortable, surrounded by the familiar. Whatever I can do for her, I'll do it.

Janie lost her keys somewhere in the chaos of the last few days, but one of her neighbors keeps a spare for her. We head upstairs and I unlock the door, careful to check out the apartment before letting her inside. The place looks untouched.

I also unscrew a few light fixtures, checking for hidden cameras. Just out of paranoia. But there's nothing.

I find her bedroom and take her into the en suite bath. First thing she needs is to get cleaned up.

"Lift your arms," I say. She obeys without a word. I slide off her shirt and then her jeans. I wet a washcloth and rub away the spots of blood.

The focus of her eyes start to clear. She manages a weak smile. "Thanks," she whispers. "Your turn."

Janie takes the washcloth from me. She replaces it with a fresh one and proceeds to dab gently at my face and neck and hands.

She claims there's dirt. I don't know. I didn't see any in the mirror.

But she undresses me carefully and runs us both a bath in her oversized jet tub.

"I thought I was taking care of you," I say.

"We can take care of each other."

We sink into the hot water. Janie sits between my legs and leans back against my chest.

I start to let myself really feel the shittiness of what

happened today. I was so angry earlier, and that was all I could see. Just fury at Murphy getting hurt, the evidence being stolen. Agent Winfrey's cocky disregard. And rage at myself for letting the shooter get away.

The anger wears thin, and disappointment is left. Frustration. Agony that I failed Detective Murphy and the DA's office and that the people responsible for these travesties will probably get away scot free.

Janie must be feeling something similar. We don't talk about it. I suspect she's like me, and the most bitter things she feels in life don't ever leave her lips.

But we're here together. We're sharing this moment. And it helps. I needed this as much as her. Maybe even more.

Janie's nestled between my bent legs, her cheek against my chest. Like she's trying to curl up as small as possible and disappear into me. I hold her. My hands spread on her back, trying to cover as much of her skin as I can.

We stay there until the water's gone cold.

Janie climbs out and hands me a thick towel. I drain the water, and we dry each other, fluffing each other's heads.

I don't have a change of clothes, so I just put my boxers back on. Janie slips into a soft tank top and matching sleep shorts.

The light on her nightstand is on. There's a golden glow in the room, though it's dark outside. We both sit on the edge of her bed, holding hands.

"Any word on Murphy?" she asks.

I check my phone. There's a huge text chain going, full of West Oaks PD officers and admins. I scroll through. "Sounds like she's in surgery, but she's doing well. They're saying she got to the hospital just in time."

Janie exhales. "Thank goodness we were there."

"Yeah." I pull her against me, hugging her close.

We've already reported everything we saw at the scene. I

gave a description of the shooter. But I assume CBI and Agent Winfrey are in charge of this investigation, and it sucks. If I could, I'd be out there hunting down Murphy's attacker myself. But I'm not welcome, and Janie and I haven't had much luck with going rogue.

I haven't heard any confirmation from Chief Liu of my suspension. But I'd be shocked if he sticks his neck out for me and defies Winfrey.

"I really am sorry about David," I say.

She shrugs. "There was nothing anyone could do. The doctors tried. Madison was there. But his injuries… I just wish I'd been able to help him before this all got so messed up. I wish I'd known."

"He kept his secrets." If David had shared whatever's on that memory card before, this might've been avoided. I don't know what motivated him. If it was pure fear, or strategy, or what. But I hope he's at peace.

We haven't had any dinner. I'm not hungry, and Janie doesn't say anything about food. We get into her bed and snuggle together beneath the covers. Janie drags her fingers in circles and patterns on my chest. I massage her scalp.

"Are you still heading to Arizona in the morning?" That's been the plan, but with the latest developments, I don't know if her plans have changed.

"I have to. My sister…"

"It's okay. I get it."

There's so much I want to say. How much the last few days with her have meant. How I don't want it to end this way, feeling like all we've done is for nothing. Like we've failed.

It's our sixth night. Six nights since this all started. Five of those, we'll have spent in the same room. Four in each other's arms. It's so little time in some ways, yet it feels like *everything* when so much can change in a single moment.

I don't want to give up. Not on Janie, not on the case against Asher Temple. But I'm not sure where to go from here.

I wish we could have a seventh night together, and an eighth, and… I don't even know. All the nights, if they're anything like the others. Not just the sex but the affection and laughter, the chemistry, the push and pull. When I'm with Janie, I'm energized. Like my blood is fizzy. Even when I thought I didn't like her, I felt that intensity between us.

I told her last night that I want more with her. She knows. She agreed to go on a date with me at some vague point in the future. But when we separate tomorrow and we go back to our lives, who knows what she'll feel? She might decide it's easier to forget about this week. There are definitely parts of today I'd rather forget.

I can't force her to open up to me. I can't push her into letting me in. Janie has to make that choice.

So I'm quiet when she gets out of bed to pack. She throws items into a small bag. "Could you give me a ride to the courthouse in the morning?" she asks. "I have a spare key fob here, but my car's still over there in the parking lot. At least, I hope it is. Guess I'll find out."

"Yeah. Of course."

"I'm sure you're excited to see your mom and Henry."

"I am." I do want to see them, though I'm still cautious about making sure the danger's past.

We'll need to get my house cleaned up. That, I'm not looking forward to. But hugging my kid? Seeing his smiling face? I can't wait. For the past several months, he's been the brightest spot in my life.

Until Janie.

As a father, I love my son in a bigger way than I thought was possible. He makes me feel infinite, like I'd move heaven and earth for him. Like I could be a superhero.

But Janie makes me feel human again. I'd be a superhero for her too, but I don't have to be. Because she's incredible all on her own. Picking up the slack when I screw up. I could rely on her. I could...fuck, I think I could fall in love with her, given the chance. And to have her love me would be like winning the lottery. A long shot, but it would change my life.

I get out of bed and follow her around as she bustles through her apartment, preparing for her trip. "Need help?" I ask.

"No. Just trying to catch up on things around here." She waters houseplants that look droopy. Tosses junk mail and expired food from the fridge.

I get the feeling she's avoiding me. Or maybe I'm being arrogant, assuming anything she does is about me, just because of the things I'm feeling.

But then she drops her bag by her front door and turns to me. She seems unsure of herself, in a way I've never seen before.

"Sean." Her voice is breaking. I want to touch her, but she's crossed her arms over her middle.

"What is it?" I'm bracing myself.

She's going to say it would be easier if we say goodbye now. If we make a clean break. She wants me to leave, and this time, I can't be the asshole who refuses. I can't force her to want me back.

I'd rather know what she truly feels for me than fool myself, even if it's not what I'd like to hear. But damn, this is going to sting.

"Would you come with me?" Janie asks.

"I..." I turn the words over in my head. Like artifacts that I hope will reveal something essential. Something true. "Come with you?"

"To Arizona. I know you want to see Henry, and it's a

really long drive to Tucson, and a memorial service is a *horrible* venue for a date, but—"

I can't rein in my smile. "This would be a date?"

She cringes. "Yes? Nowhere near as good as your date idea. But it's what I've got. I need to be there for my sister and for Gran. But I…"

"Janie." I cross the space between us and touch her chin, waiting until her eyes come back to me. There's that spark of defiance I like so much. Even when she's uncertain, even at the hardest moments, she refuses to stay down for long.

"But?" I prompt.

"I don't want this to end. I really like you. *Really*, really like you. I want the chance to find out where this goes. And…I don't want to hold my secrets so close that I shut other people out. Shut *you* out."

She's thinking of David being alone at the hospital. Whatever she's holding inside, I can't imagine Janie's situation is anything like his. But I hate to think of her being alone. Janie is far too giving and clever and wonderful not to be loved.

"I'd be honored to go with you. I miss my mom and Henry, but they're doing fine. I can't imagine a few more days is a big deal. I'll check with Chase about his plans."

"Yeah?" Her face lights up. I smile down at her.

"Yeah."

Janie runs her fingers through my hair, and her touch is so tender it makes me ache.

"You said you want to know me," she says. "This is how I can show you. I'd *like* to show you."

"I do want that." My arms circle her waist. I want her closer. Thighs, stomachs, chests, our bodies lining up asymmetrically—since I'm taller, longer limbed—yet fitting perfectly.

I touch our noses together, then press my forehead to hers. "When do you think we'll be back?"

"A couple days? I wasn't planning to stay long, but I want to help my sister Pam with some things. She and Gran have so many friends there. A lot of support. I just want to make sure Pam has what she needs."

"I look forward to meeting Pam. And hearing more about your Gran."

"You're sure it's okay? Leaving your mom and Henry?"

"Mom will understand. She'd probably tell me I was an idiot if I didn't go."

We kiss and run our fingers over each other. I want to show her how happy she's making me, how much she already means to me. It feels more natural to do that with my hands than with words.

I walk backward with her toward her bedroom, still kissing. Good thing her apartment's small, because this is not an efficient way to move. We finally end up back in her bed beneath the covers.

I could go for some sexual healing, but Janie doesn't escalate things. Seems like she just needs affection right now, and I have no problem with that. I've got plenty.

We make out and cuddle. I try to keep my erection from poking her. Around Janie, my dick's greedy, but he can wait. This isn't our last night, and I am ecstatic about that.

"I'll set an alarm to wake us up extra early." The room's dark, and Janie's whispering, though it's not like we're disturbing anyone. Maybe because we're lying so close, with our noses and even our lips brushing, that there's no need to speak louder.

"It's about eight hours to Tucson, right?"

"Little longer. But I wanted to stop somewhere else first. If that's okay? It's on the way, but it'll add some time to the trip."

I can tell from the tightness in her voice that this is a big deal. "Sure. Whatever you need."

You want to know me, she said. *This is how I can show you.*

"Be ready, though." She's back to teasing. "Almost nine hours driving through the desert is really boring."

I've driven the I-10 plenty of times before. But that's not the point. I tangle my fingers through hers. "You and I are a lot of things, Ms. Simon, but when we're together, we're never boring."

35

Janie

We set out just as the sun is rising.

God, it feels good to be leaving California. I love this state, but I need some space.

I look over at Sean sitting beside me, and my fingers relax on the steering wheel.

We're in my car, and I insisted on being in the driver's seat. We left the Bennett Security vehicle in the courthouse lot, and Sean already called Tanner to let him know. He and I said thanks to Tanner for all his help. I've never been so grateful for friends. Certainly doesn't hurt that they're well-connected.

We pass through Los Angeles and the hills beyond, and the horizon opens up around us. The green diminishes fast, giving way to endless miles of desert.

It's still early morning, and we sip coffee that we buy at a drive-through kiosk. Near the state border, we stop for a hearty breakfast at a restaurant I like. I'm always glad to see that it's still here when I pass through. I don't go back to Arizona all that often, and half the time I just fly. But it's nice that some things don't change, even when I expect them to.

Since I was a kid, I've had trouble believing that anything is forever. As I've grown, life has only confirmed that truth.

But with Sean here beside me, I want to hope. I want to imagine things could be different this time.

I did a lot of thinking yesterday. I've been in touch with Tracey, and she's looking once again for David's family to let them know he's passed. Still nothing from Gabriela. If I need to, I'll arrange and pay for his funeral. I'm not going to leave him there without anybody to claim him.

But I'm not his family. At some point, my role as his lawyer has to end. I wish I could fix everything for my clients, but I never can. That's hard to live with.

Yesterday, I realized Sean was right. Okay, I knew before that he was right, but I could finally admit it. I try to protect people who need it, but I protect *myself* most of all. I thought caring for others was enough for me, but it's not. I'll never stop giving my all, but it's a lonely place to be if I hold myself separate.

I want someone to care for me, too. I want to be my whole self with someone who gets me. I want to be brave enough for that.

I almost kept all that inside yesterday. I could've kept making the same damned mistakes, refusing to change. I could've let Sean walk away not knowing how I feel. I'm not sure where that courage came from—was it you, Gran?—but I'm so grateful that I got my act together.

Sean is amazing. He deserves someone who'll give him everything, and I think…maybe…that could be me.

When we have cell service, he FaceTimes with Henry and Liza. I know he's already checked in with Chase, but Liza assures us again that they're doing great. Liza's enjoying her new friendship with Chase's mother-in-law, and Henry loves having a playmate. Chase's little girl talks up a storm, giving Henry all kinds of advice and instructions.

After we lose the connection, Sean tells me more about the joys and struggles of becoming a dad. Then he tells me about growing up in Houston with his two older brothers, both of whom still live there. Then about his tours in Afghanistan as a Marine.

We laugh a lot, and I wish I didn't have to keep my eyes on the road, because all I want to do is stare at Sean. At the way his eyes shine as he talks. The flirty smiles he sends my way. The way the morning sun hits his hair and skin.

If we hadn't gotten stuck together after the courthouse shooting, would I have ever known him like this?

I'm not going to thank Asher Temple or the Serpents for the opportunity, but I will thank the universe. Mysterious ways…etc., etc.

He asks me questions here and there about how I grew up, but he doesn't push. I think he knows I'm working up to that.

The big *thing* that I've been dancing around. My secret.

It's not that much of a secret, really. It's public record, if anyone cared to look. But it's not something I share readily. Even Tracey doesn't know this about me. I wouldn't say I'm ashamed. Not exactly. But this truth is a window into my soul.

I regularly listen to my clients' life stories, worst secrets, deepest traumas and fears. I just don't like anyone looking that closely back at me.

As the miles disappear under the tires, my chest gets tighter. I feel the urge to turn around or keep on driving straight ahead. Anything but taking the detour I *have* to make.

Being the one in the spotlight is uncomfortable for me, but I need to do this. And he needs this from me, too.

Let me have you, he said.

If we're going to be…*more*, Sean deserves all of me.

Finally, I exit the 10 freeway and turn south. We drive for another twenty minutes, and Sean still hasn't asked where we're going. But he must see the signs. His eyebrows raise.

Arizona State Prison Complex.

Baked red mountains stretch in the distance beneath a stonewashed blue-jean sky. We get close enough to see the barbed wire and drab buildings. There's a visitation office, but I don't actually want to go inside. It's not a visit day, and even if it was, there's no point to me going inside anyway. I learned that years ago.

But I need to sit here with Sean. So he can see it in person. So it's physical and real.

I shift the car into park. Instantly, the sun starts warming the car. "You asked a few days ago why I became a defense attorney. This is why."

He takes my hand, his face open and curious. No judgment. He doesn't rush me.

It's a couple more minutes before I can go on.

"My mother's been in prison since I was in middle school. Life sentence, no parole."

Agnes Simon is somewhere in that building, right now. I haven't seen her face in over twenty years.

Sean's a cop. He knows how this works. But I still need to say it. "She's in for first-degree murder."

I tell him the story in fits and starts. Mom worked at a bar, but she turned tricks on the side.

I can't sugarcoat this story. I have to give him the truth, ugly as it is.

My mother took her customers to a motel across the street from the bar. One night, a customer beat her up really bad. I know she'd had rough encounters before, because I'd seen her come home with bruises. But that time, she'd been hurt so severely she could hardly walk. While the guy was asleep in the bed—clearly not bothered by what he'd done—she found a gun in his jeans.

She shot him with it.

"She confessed?" Sean asks.

"No. But the evidence was clear. She did it. There's no doubt." I'm not sure if he expects me to protest her innocence, to say it was a great miscarriage of justice. But I can't. This isn't that kind of story.

"It turned out the dead guy was a private investigator and had a lot of cops and lawyers as friends."

My mother was convicted. I have no idea if she might've gotten a lesser sentence if she'd had better representation. If maybe the judge or jury would've seen some mitigating factors in what had happened.

But I think it's possible. Sometimes, that possibility haunts me.

"Pam and I were sent to foster care right after she was arrested. They separated us. I wasn't having that, so I took the bus to get her, and we hitchhiked to Tucson to find Gran. I told you about that already."

He nods, expression solemn. He's still holding tight to my hand.

"Before that, Gran didn't realize how things were with my mom. Gran and my mom didn't get along at all. But Gran... she was wonderful. Just accepted us and took care of us. Don't get me wrong, she was tough on us too. Especially me, because I was always talking back, never did what she said. But that toughness is what I needed. She taught me how to fend for myself because I couldn't count on anyone else to do it."

"I see why you wanted to defend people," Sean says.

I don't want to make too big a deal about the symbolism. But this is what I meant about this truth being a window into my soul. Anyone could probably connect the dots.

"Did you not want to tell me because I'm a cop?"

"That's not really it. I just don't like talking about it. Not even with my friends." I've never shared this with a man I was dating before. Never even considered it.

"Do you still see her? Your mother?"

I sniff and wipe my nose, though no tears have fallen. "She only wrote once and said we were better off without her. When I was eighteen, I got on the prison visitor's list and took the bus from Tucson a few times, but Mom refused to see me. She gave up hope. Completely. I'm surprised she's still alive, honestly. I send her care packages a few times a year, especially holidays, and I hope that…" I clear my throat, unable to finish.

"Janie," Sean whispers. "Come here."

I lean across the center console toward him. He envelopes me in his arms, and I bury my face against his chest. And it's like a heavy door opens inside me. Sean's here, and he's holding me and murmuring soothing words.

His shirt soaks up my tears.

Good thing I'm not wearing makeup, because this would be a mess.

After a while, I feel like all the stuff I've been holding in has poured out of me. I'm sure my face and eyes are puffy. I must look awful. But when I kiss Sean, he kisses me back. His lips are gentle, nibbling at mine. His tongue moves sweetly into my mouth. My breath hitches.

Even at a moment like this, he makes me feel sexy and beautiful. And cared for. That's the best of all.

We keep kissing, and Sean keeps holding me, until the car gets unbearably hot, thanks to the Arizona sun.

I turn on the engine and blast the AC on our way back to the 10.

I feel like a weight that's been strapped to my back for

twenty fucking years has been lightened. Not lifted altogether. But it's easier to bear.

"Thank you for sharing that with me," Sean says.

"Thanks for listening." The stifling air in the cabin is starting to cool. Saguaros stand sentinel along the highway. "Well, that's it. Now you know everything about me."

"I doubt that."

"You think I'm hiding more?"

"Nope. Not hiding." His hand rests on my thigh, and his crooked grin turns wicked. "But I'm sure there's more to learn about you. I'm going to enjoy finding out. I think you will, too."

"Promises, promises."

36

Sean

We skip lunch and keep driving. Janie gets us to Tucson with barely any time to spare, and we head straight to the church where the memorial service is being held.

When we get inside, the room is already buzzing with people. There are flowers everywhere. Roses, carnations, lilies, in tall standing arrangements, in vases on tables.

There's a portrait at the front of the room that must be Janie's grandmother. She has a closed-mouth smile, but her eyes are glittering. She looks a lot like Janie. Large, dark eyes, delicate cheekbones.

We're standing at the back, and Janie's holding my hand. For a moment, she seems hesitant. But then she lets go of me with a smile and a squeeze, and strides over to another woman who looks like her, but closer in age than her grandmother.

"Pam," Janie says. "How are you, sweetie?" The two hug. Pam was composed before, but the moment her chin lands on Janie's shoulder, her face crumples. She's already holding a handkerchief, like this isn't the first bout of tears today.

They talk a little, and Janie leads her over to me. "Pam, this is Sean."

Pam blows her nose and wipes her eyes. But she manages a smile. "This is a surprise. I'm sorry, I wasn't expecting you. Otherwise—"

"Don't worry about it," I say. "It was a last minute decision. I'm sorry for your loss."

She nods and thanks me, a hand going to her chest as if she truly means it. Janie is obviously different from her sister, but I think the two are equally genuine.

In the minute or two we're standing there, several more people come over to talk to Janie and embrace her. I don't catch all the names. She said her Gran had friends, but there's got to be over a hundred people packed into this room. And they obviously care about Janie, too. She means something to them. I'll bet she's important to a lot of people, even if she doesn't let them very close.

I wasn't really shocked by what Janie shared with me. Her mom being in prison. It's not her fault, and it's not anything for her to feel ashamed of. It's just life. But I was surprised she took me there and told me. It meant a lot to me, and I have a sense of what it meant to her.

She's been through hard times in her life, and she's trying to make other people's lives better as a result. If anyone should be ashamed, it's me. For my shitty opinion of her and the way I treated her. I'm the luckiest asshole in the world that I get this chance with her.

But my life seems to be made of second chances. With Henry, with Janie. I might mess up at first, but I'm smart enough to recognize an opportunity to start fresh when I see one. It's never too late. I really believe that.

The service begins, and we all take a seat. I sit next to Janie in the front row, holding her hand again. Pam and her husband are on my other side.

I listen to the minister's words and wonder about the strangeness of the world.

If things were perfect, my mom and Henry would be meeting up with us afterward. I do miss them. And I bet Henry could cheer Janie up. But right now, based on the way she's gripping my hand, I think Janie needs me more than they do. It's maybe the greatest compliment I've ever received. Her trust. Her willingness to invite me into her life this way.

It's Janie's turn to speak. She steps up to the podium, pausing to gaze at her grandmother's photo.

I know she's a great speaker because I've seen her in the courtroom. But still, as she begins, I'm drawn in immediately. She doesn't try to be commanding. Instead she's quiet, and everyone in the audience is leaning in. There is an honesty in the way she speaks. In the inflection she uses, the moments that she subtly wipes her eyes or smiles. I hear people crying around me, especially Pam, but these aren't despairing tears. Janie's lifting up the spirits of everyone here. Even me, though I never had the honor of meeting her grandmother.

It's like there's a collective sigh, a condensing of emotion in the air. She's giving everyone in this room the best parts of her grandmother's life, and it's exactly what they all need to hear.

Or maybe I'm just that smitten. I think she's pretty damned incredible.

While she's lifting everyone up, her eyes keep finding mine, like she's looking to me to keep herself steady. At least, I hope that's what it means. She's comforting her friends and family with her words, but I'd like to think—I hope—that my presence comforts her.

~

The Six Night Truce

WHEN THE SERVICE ENDS, WE HEAD TO PAM'S house. Janie drives. She's quiet and thoughtful on the way. But when we join the long line of cars parked along the curb on Pam's street, she leans over to kiss me.

"Is this okay?" she asks. "The memorial service. And now this get-together with my family. It's a lot, isn't it?"

"Seems like it was exactly right. Everyone enjoyed hearing you speak."

She rolls her eyes, but I think it's more at herself than me. "I mean, is this okay *for you*. If you want to skip this part and grab a beer at a pub instead, I will not be offended. In any way."

I run my thumb over her cheek. "Janie, I came here for you."

"But…"

"I wouldn't be here unless I wanted to." I shrug. "Besides, I have an ulterior motive. If I stay, I get to be near the girl I'm crushin' on."

"Bringing out the accent, are we? You're really working hard to win me over."

"If it works, it works."

She leans in for another kiss. "Oh, it works."

We head inside. Many of the same people are here, and I say hello. Immediately Janie gets cornered by some older ladies.

I go to the kitchen and help Pam's husband set out food on the counters. "So are you Janie's boyfriend?" he asks.

The question flusters me for half a second. "Not yet. I'm…someone who'd like to be her boyfriend."

He grunts. "She's never brought anyone around before. But it's nice to see her happy."

I stop, halfway done unwrapping a tray of mini quiche. "She seems happy?"

"More than the last time she was here."

Janie comes to find me, but she's pulled away by someone else. I don't mind. I look around for more things to help with, and then park myself on a chair, eat a couple sandwiches and more than one slice of pie, and sip a Coors Light.

I check my phone and scroll through the West Oaks PD text chain. There's finally word—Murphy's doing well. The gunshot missed her vital organs. There's minor damage to a lung, a broken collarbone, but she's expected to make a full recovery.

The investigation has remained in the back of my mind since last night. There's maybe another hour left of the special grand jury. So that's finished. It's gone. In some ways, it feels like I gave up and ran away in the face of defeat.

But I'd say I'm regrouping.

I told Janie I'm here for her, and that's true. But this distance from West Oaks is good for me as well. It'll give me some perspective. And when we head back, I'll be ready.

I'm going to figure out who shot Murphy, who came after Jane. Who trashed my belongings and drove my mom and son from their home. Agent Winfrey and the Serpents and the entire damn state will just have to deal with that. I'll take them all down if I have to. Even better if they don't see me coming.

"Another beer?"

The voice of Janie's sister breaks me from these vengeful thoughts. Pam holds out a fresh Coors Light. My longneck has been empty for a while.

I accept the replacement. "Thanks."

Pam sits in the chair beside me. "Nice of you to come along with Janie. I think it's been helping, having you here."

I smile into my beer. "I'm glad to do it."

"It's been hard on her, saying goodbye to our grandmother. Especially because Janie's been mostly absent since she moved to California. I don't blame her. She doesn't make it out here as much as she'd like, but she also hates to leave her clients. She's always worrying about other people."

"I've noticed that, yeah."

"Gran was the same way. She did not suffer fools, and I used to be terrified if I brought home a bad report card or got caught smoking. But she had the biggest heart. Just like Janie. Janie's my little sister, but she's the one who looked out for me. From the start, she was tougher than I was. She stood up to bullies for me. Janie was fearless. Or, I guess she did a good job of convincing everyone she was."

I can imagine her as a spitfire teenager. Never backing down. I was the same way, but I know I didn't have to face down the same things.

Pam's gaze is scrutinizing. "So, what's your story?"

"I'm a major crimes detective with West Oaks PD."

Pam's mouth hangs open. A long beat goes by.

"I'm sorry. A detective? Janie's dating a cop?"

"I didn't see it coming either."

She shakes her head like she's shaking off the surprise. "Okay. What else?"

I give her the abridged version, but I hit all the highlights. Marines. LAPD. Single dad. I explain that we've been in danger the last few days, placed into protective custody together.

"Unbelievable. Janie didn't even tell me that stuff was going on! I mean, I heard something on the news about West Oaks, but I didn't know she was in the middle of it."

"I'm sure she didn't want you to worry."

Pam grumbles. "All right. I'll bug her about that later. But you and Janie, it's a new thing? I mean, I guess that's why she hasn't mentioned you. It must not be that serious. No offense."

I guess it's a fair question. Janie doesn't have a father or brother to interrogate me, so good on her sister for stepping up. "At the moment, I think we're taking it a day at a time. But I like her. A lot. I think she's really special."

"She is. Are you looking for her to be a mother to your son?"

It's my turn to be speechless.

Janie's not the only sister who can conduct a cross-examination.

"I mean…" I try to find words. Any words. "I…it's pretty soon to consider something like that."

Pam crosses her arms, doing an excellent impersonation of a dad questioning his daughter's prom date. "A friend of mine got swept right off her feet by a divorced guy with a kid. Whirlwind romance. Now she's saddled with the kiddo, which she doesn't mind 'cause she loves that child, but her new husband's always off on business trips and late nights with the boys. He wanted someone to play housekeeper and nanny for no pay."

Jeez, that sucks. "That's definitely not me." And it's not because my mom moved to California to help me. I'm beyond grateful to her, and I know how fortunate I am. My mom's my best friend. If she ever felt taken advantage of, I'd be the first one to hear it.

None of that's what I want from Janie. Or anything I'd expect.

But do I see her folding into my life on that kind of level? Becoming part of my family? Part of *Henry's* family?

My rational mind is beating a hasty retreat. This is getting heavy. I'm not ready for it. Too much too soon.

But my heart's kind of into it.

I remember those couple of mornings at the hotel. Waking up to my little guy smiling, and seeing Janie with her messy bed-head, holding Henry and laughing at how cute he is. Having breakfast together. Giving my mom extra time to sleep, and then all of us hanging out.

It would make a nice Sunday morning. Especially without the danger and protective custody part.

And *especially* if Janie and I got to sneak in some private sexy times before everyone else woke up.

I settle on a wishy-washy response, but it's the best I've got. "I'm not sure where this is going. I think Janie and I could make each other happy. That's all I want from her. If it gets more serious someday, that's great too."

Pam seems satisfied, if undecided. "I just don't want her to get jerked around."

"I don't either. I don't intend to."

The gathering winds down. The sun sets. Pam's husband and I put plastic wrap and foil over the leftovers and stack them up in the fridge. I'm looking out the window at a moonlit cactus garden when Janie's arms wrap around my waist from behind. She tucks her cheek between my shoulder blades.

"Want to get out of here?" she asks.

"You don't need to stay?"

"Pam doesn't have much extra room. I usually stay in Gran's guestroom when I'm visiting, but it doesn't feel right without her there."

I spin around so I can return the hug. "Hotel, then?"

She nods. "There's a bed-and-breakfast pretty close. It's small, but less corporate."

"Sounds good to me."

We finish with the clean-up and say goodnight to Pam and her family. In the car, I say, "Your sister gave me the third degree."

"*Really?* Pam? Usually she avoids confrontation. What did she ask you about?"

That conversation was a bit much to recount to Janie. "She was just checking up on my intentions toward you. Not sure you realize it, but she's got your back. I bet a lot of people do. It's obvious that plenty of folks around here love you."

"Maybe." Janie steers the car away from the curb with a small smile. "I wish Gran could've met you. She would've liked you. And her third degree would've been so much worse than Pam's."

I laugh. "I'm sorry I missed out."

37

Janie

By the time we get checked in and step into the hotel room, I'm wrung out.

The room is on the top floor of a stone building. It's full of brightly colored southwestern decor. Native American blankets and rugs make the space warm and cozy. I drop onto the loveseat by the window and close my eyes.

"I just need a few minutes," I say.

"Take your time. I'll check my messages."

It's been another draining day, full of a lot more emotion than I'm typically confronted with. Taking Sean to the prison where my mom will spend the rest of her life. Then sharing grief and memories of my Gran with everyone I know here.

When I spoke at the memorial service, I tried to focus on the best parts of the past. But the difficult moments kept popping up in my mind. I think it's because Gran knew how to navigate the tough times so well. I wish I'd had more time with her, but I wouldn't substitute anything that we shared. Not even the worst of it.

And somehow, by the end of it, I wasn't even feeling sad

anymore. She made me stronger. I sure hope I made her proud.

Thinking about endings today naturally made me wonder about what I'm beginning with Sean. When we were sitting together at the memorial service, I asked Gran for her advice. How can I make this work with him? How do I not mess this up? Because I really do want it to work.

With Sean, I don't have to be my fiercest self all the time, always strategizing. I can just be me and feel whatever I'm feeling. It's liberating. And it's such a relief.

"How's Murphy?" I haven't had a chance to ask for an update.

Sean sits down beside me. "I've been following the department text thread. Murphy's awake now, and they've moved her out of the ICU. She doesn't remember anything, though. Nothing about what she was doing before the shooting, what the guy looked like, how it went down."

"So she hasn't mentioned why you and I were there? Or the memory card?"

"Not that I know of. I guess CBI could be keeping that quiet from the rank and file. But my partner and the other detectives don't know either."

Yesterday, when I was interviewed by one of the patrol officers at the scene, I just said Sean and I had been on our way to see Murphy. I'd chosen not to give further details. I assume Sean didn't either. We might not always be on the same side, but we both know full well that witness interviews are voluntary. They can't force me to say more.

"I'm texting with Shelby separately," Sean says, "and she's been trying to get in to speak with Murphy. No luck yet."

"Do you think it was a Serpent gang member who shot her?"

"That's the most obvious answer, and that's what I've said to anyone in the department who's willing to listen. I assume they're following up on it, but CBI's not about to share that with me."

Without any proof that David's secret evidence exists, there's no possible link to Asher Temple. Unless the Serpents spill who hired them.

But there's nothing that Sean or I can do. Not tonight, not here.

What I *can* do? Cheer him up.

"We could still get that date in," I say.

"What do you mean? This whole day's been a date."

"A very unsexy date. To a prison and a memorial service."

"It's okay if you don't feel sexy."

"Hey, who says I don't?" I swing my leg over him and straddle his lap. His hands go right to my hips, like they belong there. "I'd take you out for Mexican, but I ate five different casseroles at Pam's house." Gran's church friends brought obscene amounts of food.

Sean barks a laugh. "Who doesn't love a hearty casserole that somebody's momma made?"

I lightly massage his shoulders. "What about dancing, then?"

"I'm down. Know any good bars around here?"

"We could stay in and dance." I lean in for a kiss. It's teasing, a brush of my lips over his. "My phone has music."

"So does mine. I know just the thing."

I move so Sean can get up. He's already holding his phone, but he takes it over to the dresser and calls up a playlist. A guitar and drums start up a slow rhythm, and Sean turns to me.

"What's this?"

"Chris Stapleton." He shakes his hips a little, making me laugh, even though it's also very sexy.

He tilts his head. Holds out his hand.

What girl could possibly resist?

I take his hand, and he brings me to the center of the rug. I put my arms around his neck. His eyes rake over me, heating my skin.

We start to sway, cheek to cheek. I get lost in the music and in the man in my arms. The room fills with sultry guitar riffs, smokey vocals, the hint of country twang. It's Sean, distilled into musical form. Hard-edged masculinity and aching tenderness.

He sings along to a few lyrics here and there, his voice breathy yet also rich and deep. Chills race through me.

"I didn't scare you off today?" I ask quietly.

"Pam almost did."

I playfully punch his bicep. "Come on."

"You know, you make my heart beat like crazy." He takes my hand and puts it to his chest, and God—it really is beating a mile a minute. Just like mine. "And you make it hard to breathe. But nothing about you scares me."

My chest squeezes in response.

We hold each other as close as possible, yet with every sway, we fit ourselves even tighter together. Our lips meet and stay there, sharing one another's air.

This is the slowest of slow dances, the sweetest of endless kisses. We're trying to smother every last millimeter of distance between us. Trying to get past the boundaries of each other to what's beneath.

And we're inching closer and closer to the bed. I'm not even sure which one of us is doing it. But our kisses are getting deeper, more heated. Our tongues stroke each other, lazily at first, then with more purpose. I feel the pressure of Sean's hard length against my belly through our clothes.

Suddenly, all I want in the world is my mouth wrapped around him, making him lose every ounce of control. I want to make Sean forget about the problems still waiting for us back in West Oaks. I want to appreciate him for everything he is.

Reluctantly, I break the kiss, and Sean's got the sweetest look of confusion. I slide my hands in between us and cup his face, pulling him down for one more taste of his lips.

Then I drop to my knees.

"Janie…"

"Let me suck you?" I nuzzle his erection through the denim. "Please?"

"Like I'm gonna say no." He lets me unbutton his jeans and work his zipper down. I slide his jeans and boxers down to his thighs, and Sean's cock springs up, all pink and veiny.

I like that we're still in the middle of the room where we were just dancing. I'm completely dressed. Makes this feel just a little scandalous.

I run my hands up and down his thighs. My cheek brushes his shaft, and Sean groans, his hands resting on my shoulders. His fingers massage me, searching out the tension I've worked up over the course of the day.

My fist circles the base of his cock. I stroke him at a leisurely pace, and then add some kisses to the velvety skin. I haven't touched the head yet, and I can tell from the way he's breathing and groaning that it's frustrating him. But I loved the way he slow-danced with me. The music continues to play, and I'm still feeling that drawn-out, aching rhythm.

I lift my gaze to meet his. Sean's brown eyes are molten, pure dark fire. I hold his stare as the flat of my tongue licks over his tip.

"*Ughn.*"

Precome wells from his slit, and I lap it up on my next pass.

My mouth closes around his cockhead, tongue rubbing the underside. Sean's hands dig into my hair. He tugs on the strands. I close my eyes and enjoy the feeling. His firm grip on me, his steely length in my mouth.

I take him deeper. My hands find his hips and hold on. I'm still moving slowly, drawing this out as long as I can. When Sean's hips make little snaps, trying to fuck my mouth, I pull back and smile up at him.

There's so much in his expression. Lust and wonder and tension. His nostrils flare. "Either you're gonna need to speed things up," he says, "or I'm gonna have to strip you and fuck you. One or the other."

"I think we have plenty of time for both." I squeeze the base of his cock and tease him with another lick over his slit.

"*Janie,*" he growls.

I take mercy on him. My mouth works him over, my hand stroking, giving him the tight friction and momentum he needs. His thighs are shaking, and his cock gets even harder under my tongue. He's cursing and muttering and his fingers are tangled in my hair.

Sean comes with a shout. His cock jerks, filling my mouth and my throat with salty warmth. I greedily swallow down his release.

I give him one more good suck, then pop off of him.

Sean sits heavily onto the bed. "Holy…wow. That was…" He looks come-drunk and satisfied. But that languid expression goes back to wicked in an instant. He tears off his clothes, then lunges for me.

"Get over here, woman. Can't dish out something like that and not expect to get it right back."

I'm laughing when Sean dumps me onto the mattress. I don't even know why I'm cracking up. Probably the silly smile he's trying to hide.

It doesn't take long for Sean to pry my jeans off, then the rest of my clothes. He drops open-mouthed kisses on my stomach, kneading my thighs with his big, strong hands. I'm not laughing now.

I'm already extremely turned on from feeling him come in my mouth, tasting it on my tongue.

He doesn't make me wait nearly as long as I did to him. Sean nudges my legs open and drags his tongue over my center. I gasp and sigh.

Sean's tongue traces around my opening, up and down my folds, my clit. Like he wants to taste and savor everything.

I'm panting, barely holding myself together. I prop onto my elbows to watch this muscular alpha male on his knees for me, pure ecstasy on his face as he drinks me in.

This man is completely undoing me. I've never been this defenseless. I'm falling, but I've never been so sure of where I'll land.

38

Sean

Janie's right on the edge. I hear it in the way she's moaning my name. In the sweet taste of her that's coating my tongue. *That's it, baby*, I think. *Let me hear you.*

I love that I'm getting to know her body. Learning the clues and secrets about what takes her apart.

There's an openness between us tonight, nothing hidden. No barriers. We're just two people who care about each other, want to make each other feel incredible. No games or facades or bullshit. Not that there was with me and Janie before, but I know without a doubt how much she trusts me. I don't have to worry about anything with her, and she's on the same page about me.

She's writhing under my tongue. Calling my name like a prayer.

I stroke my hands over her belly and down her inner thighs. Then I repeat the same path, this time letting my nails drag along her skin. She makes a choked, desperate sound.

"Your fingers. Please," she begs. "Inside me."

I love it when she tells me how to get her off. I push two digits into her wet heat, twisting and pumping into her. My lips suck her clit.

Her legs kick, and I hold her still with my free hand as she shakes and bucks against my mouth. Janie's vocal when she comes. Shouting and cursing and chanting my name. I want to draw out every shudder, every gasp.

When she's done, I lick my lips and just look at her. She's sprawled flat on the mattress. Head back, mouth open. Glossy, dark hair spreads over the comforter. Her nipples are stiff, rosy peaks.

My dick is achingly hard again. More than ready for round two. I give it a few pumps with my fist while I find my jeans and dig into the pocket, where I tucked a couple of condoms from that jumbo pack. We left the rest of it at the safe house, not knowing we wouldn't return.

Janie opens her eyes when she hears the foil ripping. She frowns slightly.

"Okay?" I ask.

"Well...I'm on the pill. I get tested regularly."

"Me too. After Alexis—yeah, I got checked out, and I tested clean again after my last partner. You want?"

She smiles and nods, Guess we didn't need that jumbo pack after all.

Janie scoots higher on the bed and pushes the comforter out of the way. Music still plays from my phone, though it's moved onto some other artist. It's still sultry and smooth, a mix between country and blues and rock.

I drop the half-opened condom on the floor. My knees fall to the mattress, and I knee-crawl toward her, stroking my dick lightly again. I'm not in a rush now. Janie helped me take the edge off, and this round I'll be able to go a nice, long time even without the condom.

I want to make love to her just like we're slow-dancing.

I lower myself over her. She reaches for me, arms circling my neck. I groan as my stiff cock slides into her heat. No resistance. No barriers. Nothing but Janie and me. Her legs tighten at my waist.

Our chests and stomachs are pressed together. Our sweat-damp skin, our hot, heavy breaths. We kiss and touch and rock our hips to the rhythm of the music.

I feel her heart beating like it's inside me. I suck her tongue all the way into my mouth.

This is as close as our bodies can get. It's gentle and passionate and I'm living for it.

But eventually, I want more. I want Janie begging again. I want to shoot everything I've got inside of her, claiming every part of her that I can.

I grab hold of her and roll us both over. Janie's legs are spread over me. She sits upright. It's a hell of a view.

"Looking good up there," I say.

She's enjoying herself too much to respond. Her tits jiggle as she rides me. I roll and pinch and tug her nipples. She keens like she's trying for the high note in a solo. Janie holds my wrists and undulates her hips, taking exactly what she needs from me.

We're on a wooden sleigh bed that might be an antique, and we're definitely putting it to the test. I hope these walls are thick or the other guests are going to get a free concert. I put my fingers in her mouth to keep her from shouting more. Of course, if our neighbors haven't guessed what we're up to already, I'd be shocked.

Janie bites my fingers. Her body tightens everywhere. She's like a taut bowstring. I'm glad all the lights are on so I don't miss any of it—the curve of her throat as she throws her head back, the quivering of her breasts and belly.

I feel her shuddering around my cock. Her muffled moans as she comes are the sweetest music.

She collapses forward onto me, her mouth searching out mine in a messy kiss. It was not easy to restrain my enthusiasm while she rode me. My balls are tingling and ready to unleash. And she's still moaning, rubbing her cheek against my face as if she wants my scent on every part of her.

I prop my upper body on one elbow, circle her hips with my other arm, and I fuck into her hard and fast and deep. She grasps my shoulders and tries to hold on like I'm a bucking bronco.

It's possible I'll have to explain to the B&B's owners how this bed got destroyed. And get out my credit card to spring for a new one. But Janie makes me wild. I couldn't hold myself back at this point if I tried.

The orgasm starts in my balls and rockets up my shaft. It's like careening headlong off a cliff. And now I'm thrusting and spurting inside her and just riding that wave.

I'm drowning. I'm being taken over completely. And God, it's so, so good.

I fall back against the mattress, Janie on top of me, our spent bodies still connected. We just lie there, a puddle of tangled, twitching, sweaty limbs.

Janie slides to one side of me and turns her head. Our mouths are perfectly aligned. We trade lazy, relaxed kisses.

I wish I could split myself into pieces, so at least one part of me would never have to leave this bed. Never have to leave her side.

But even better? If I do this right, maybe Janie will stay next to me through whatever comes next. I can be a dad to Henry, and a good son to my mom, and do my job for West Oaks PD. And Janie will be there through it all. Not physically, of course, that would be weird. But her spirit, soul, whatever you wanna call it. Her heart. Beating with mine.

That's what I want with her. I want it all.

She makes me believe that I can have it.

~

I WAKE UP SPOONING JANIE FROM BEHIND. SHE'S still asleep, her cheeks slightly flushed, eyelashes splayed prettily. I admire her for a few breaths in the soft morning light.

Then I reach for my device on the nightstand. If Janie were awake, I could probably resist the siren call of texts and emails for longer, especially if she wanted to make use of the morning wood I'm sporting. But I'm a human with a phone, and it's what we all do.

I unlock the screen.

Five missed calls. Shit. This can't be good. I had it on silent during the night, but I'm surprised the vibrations didn't wake us.

All from my ex-partner at LAPD.

I jump out of bed and pull on my jeans. It's not like we're going to video chat, but it would feel awkward to talk to my friend while I'm naked and covered in the physical evidence of my night with Janie.

She stretches and yawns. I bend down to kiss her head.

"Where are you going?"

"Just need to return a call. I was going to step out. Didn't mean to wake you."

"That's okay. But are you going outside the room like that? You're a bit underdressed."

"I was going to put on a shirt." I go to grab mine from the floor.

Janie props up against the pillows. "Wait, can I just look at you for a second? Because...*damn*, Holt."

I hold out my arms and look down at myself, tee hanging from my hand. "What?"

I haven't closed the fly on my jeans yet, and I'm shirtless. I'm going commando, so my happy trail leads straight into dark curls of pubic hair. There's just a hint of dick on display. A glance in the mirror over the dresser shows me a guy with messy sex-hair who's in dire need of a shave.

"Can I move now?" I ask.

"Nope. Not yet. I need to get you imprinted on my retinas real quick."

I cock one hip. "This is all yours if you want it. Anytime, anywhere." My stomach swirls, even though I said those words as casually as possible. "But later. I need to make this phone call."

"I'm awake now. Just make your call here. That way, I can keep ogling you."

I sit on the bed beside her and hit the call button. My former LAPD partner answers.

"Holt?"

"Hey, did I wake you?"

He sighs. "I wish."

Janie's drawing circles on my stomach with her thumb. I'm trying not to get distracted, but I don't want to get up either.

"Saw your calls. What's going on?" I ask.

My ex-partner answers with another question. "Where are you? In West Oaks?"

There's something about his voice. This feels heavy. "No, I'm out of town."

"Where were you last night?"

"*Excuse* me?"

Janie sits up straighter, looking concerned.

"Just answer the question, Sean."

This is definitely serious if he's using my first name. "Same place I am right now. In a hotel room in Tucson. Not alone, in case you need corroboration."

Another heavy sigh. "Good. That's good. I hope you were having more fun last night than I was."

"You want to tell me what this is about?"

"Well, you remember how you sent me Carl Proctor and his meth-head friend wrapped up in a nice little bow?"

"Trust me, I didn't forget."

"Proctor had interesting things to say about the Serpents being hired to go after you and some defense attorney."

"Yes," I say stiffly. "I'm aware of that."

"Once he realized just how much trouble he was in, assault with a deadly weapon on a police officer and all that, he wouldn't shut up. Gave us plenty about the Serpents' current business endeavors. Drugs, guns, the usual. It was specific enough that we decided to go ahead and move on it. Got a warrant for a house they usually frequent. But when we got there, the place was a bloodbath. Freaking massacre. Twelve dead, shot execution style."

I need him to repeat that. *"Twelve?"*

And he thought I could've done that? My old partner is seriously overestimating my warrior skills. Three or four, sure. But twelve all by myself?

"Mostly rank and file, but some shot-callers too. Since you were already wrapped up in whatever they've got going on, I was worried for a few minutes there. Glad to hear you've got an alibi. You don't happen to know anything about this, do you?"

"Nothing that you don't, assuming you heard about Detective Murphy taking a bullet in West Oaks."

He grunts affirmatively. As I expected, because a cop getting shot is not the kind of thing to slide under the radar. He asks how Murphy's doing, and I share the latest.

"I thought it was possible a Serpent went after her," I say. "That it might be related to the courthouse shooting and everything else that's been going on."

"You'll have to fill me in on how it all fits together. But

my best guess is this was a power struggle. Some of the Serpents turned on the others and took them by surprise."

I decide not to tell him about the CBI angle. Or how this relates to Asher or Nixon Temple. If it's really the state government involved, I'd rather my ex-partner stays out of it. Especially after what happened to Murphy.

But this massacre at the Serpents' headquarters? Sounds to me like someone is cleaning house. Trying to wipe away the evidence. I might not have much time before any trace vanishes forever.

And I still have no idea where to look next for answers.

When I get off the phone, I explain my concerns to Janie.

"What do you want to do?" she asks. "Do we need to head back to West Oaks?"

"What about your sister?"

"I told her I'd stick around today, but she'll understand."

I think for a moment.

"No," I decide. "Let's stay in Tucson. I'm not sure what I can do in West Oaks except get in the way. But I'm going to keep rattling doors on the phone. Would that be okay? While you're at your sister's? I can meet up with you later."

"No problem."

I glance down at her. Janie's buck-ass naked beside me. Long legs, smooth skin. And she made a big deal about how *I* looked?

Suddenly, my cock's trying to pop out of my open fly.

I lean in to kiss her, wondering if we have time for some more stress relief before she needs to head to her sister's.

But a ringtone interrupts us. Not mine, but hers.

"Busy morning," she murmurs, still kissing me even as she climbs over me. She hops onto the floor, and I study her curves as she answers the call.

"Hey, Tracey."

Janie turns around to face me, and her eyes are wide. I

know right away something's up. "When? What did she say? Yes. I will. Yeah. I'd better go."

"What is it?" I ask when she lowers her phone.

"Tracey said Gabriela Torres called her and left a voicemail last night. David Daily's fiancée. She's finally ready to talk, but she wants to do it in person as soon as possible. She has something she needs to give us."

Hope leaps inside me. "A memory card?"

Janie nods. "Exactly."

"Then we'd better get cleaned up and get the hell out of here."

"Yeah. I'll let my sister know."

No time for quickies. Sounds like we're headed back to California this morning after all.

39

Janie

In a gap between Southern California's tallest mountains, near Palm Springs, lies the San Gorgonio Pass. Acres of white windmills stretch out across the open expanse on either side of the freeway. The giant turbines rotate against the cloudy sky.

"Next mile marker," I say.

Sean pulls us over to the righthand side. Cars continue to fly past. He switches off the engine, and the roar of the wind fills in the quiet. I watch the blades spin for a moment.

We're alone on the shoulder. Gabriela hasn't arrived yet.

Pam was understanding on the phone when I explained. *Do what you need to do,* she said. *I'm good here. I promise.* I still feel guilty about leaving her—again. I wanted to stay longer in Tucson, reminiscing about Gran. And sharing those memories with Sean. I've never opened up to any man the way I have to him. It's addictive, this feeling. Wanting to be seen. Known.

I brush my fingers over his knuckles. We've both been tense and quiet on the drive, but Sean smiles at me. It's reassuring. A promise that this will be over soon. At least, that's what we're both hoping.

A few minutes later, a hatchback pulls onto the shoulder behind us. I see Gabriela's dark hair through the windshield. She's the only one in the car. It was her idea to meet here, and she must've driven up from the LA area and then made a U-turn to be on the westbound side of the freeway.

I get out of the car and wait for her to do the same. She moves slowly, her expression dazed, movements halting, like she's sleepwalking. Her eyes are red-rimmed.

"Gabriela," I say. "I'm so sorry about David."

She walks into my arms. We've only met a few times in the past, but she clings to me like we're old friends reunited by tragedy.

"I'm so sorry," I murmur again.

"No, I'm the one who's sorry. I should've been there for him. I loved him, and I don't think he knew."

Sean is standing a few yards away, his short hair buffeted by the wind. I meet his gaze and hold it over Gabriela's shoulder.

I've never been in love. But I think I might be heading that way with Sean.

This morning, we showered quickly so we could get out the door, but I still feel his touch all over me, inside me. The memories of our last several nights together have weight to them, like a physical change in my body. I'm not the same person I was before this. No matter what happens between Sean and me, I can't go back. I would never want to.

Gabriela might've had that exact experience with David, felt that shift in her world from *alone* to *together*, and now he's gone forever.

"David knew you loved him. And he loved you, too. So much." This isn't something David spoke about with me, yet I know deep down that it's true.

She wipes her eyes and sniffles, taking long breaths and blowing them out again. "Sorry. I came here to talk, not to cry on your shoulder."

"I don't mind."

She nods and turns around. "You're Detective Holt, aren't you?"

Sean comes closer. The wind gusts over the three of us, making us squint. "Yes. I am."

"David talked about you."

His brows raise in a question.

Gabriela shrugs. "David wasn't a fan of the people prosecuting him, but he didn't mind you as much as the others."

"Really?" Sean and I both ask. He's probably thinking of the day of the proffer, like I am. When Sean was such an asshole because he was having a terrible day.

"He thought maybe he could trust you," Gabriela said. "That's what he told me."

"With the memory card?" I ask.

She nods. "I don't know everything, but I'll do my best to explain what I can."

The three of us sit against the hood of Gabriela's car. It's warm, and I hear the engine ticking as it cools.

"David and I met in an intro American Lit class, and God, he was lost. Got an F on his first essay. I sat next to him and saw how upset he was, and offered to help with his writing." She smiles sadly at the memory. "He was really quiet and shy, and I was too. It was easy for us to talk to one another. We just clicked, you know? It felt right. We graduated, and I started teaching high school English. David joined an accounting firm. Almost all our money went toward rent in Culver City, and the rest went toward our student loans. We ate lentils and rice and instant cups of noodles most of the time. But I didn't care. I loved our life. I was happy."

Gabriela looks out over the fields of windmills. "Then

David heard from Asher Temple. Asher had gone to our school as well, and he'd moved in completely different circles. I guess David had shared some business classes with him. Asher wanted David to come work with his start-up. The big tidal-power plant investment. David was so ecstatic. So proud that a guy like Asher, the son of Nixon Temple, would see something worthwhile in him. I was nervous because it all seemed too good to be true, but David wouldn't hear it. He wanted to believe the fantasy."

As the investors had as well. Asher had fooled plenty of people.

"When the money vanished and the lawyers came asking questions, I was furious with David. I...I blamed him for being naive. My anger at David went away pretty quick, but by then, he was pulling away from me. There were those couple of meetings I attended with you and your assistant, Tracey, but after that, David stopped inviting me. We fought, and I went to stay with friends. Then I heard David had agreed to plead guilty. He refused to talk about the case."

"He was trying to protect you by keeping you out of it," I say.

"But I should've fought to stay involved. I should've told him I still loved him, and nothing would change that. I should've done *more*." Her eyes squeeze closed. "David had so many secrets, so much to deal with, and he was all on his own."

"We both could've done more. But it's hard to help someone who doesn't want it." Guilt gnaws at me again, though of course my pain is nothing to hers. "David's gone, but it's not too late for us to do whatever we can."

Gabriela slowly sticks her fingers into her jeans pocket. She comes out with a small, folded envelope. "I received this a few days ago. David enclosed a note with it, asking me to keep it safe and not tell anyone. He didn't even explain what it was. I used a computer to try reading the memory card, but it was password protected. Then, yesterday, I got an email. David had sent it. It had some details about our relationship that nobody else would've known. And it also had the password for the memory card."

"He sent it yesterday?" I ask. "But he'd already…"

"He'd died the night before," Gabriela finishes for me. "And he'd been unconscious for days. I think he set up that message to me to email automatically if he didn't reset the delivery date. Obviously, after the shooting at the courthouse, he wasn't resetting anything. It must've been on a delay."

"A dead-man's switch," Sean says. I give him an exasperated look, and he cringes. "Sorry. Poor word choice."

But Gabriela barely reacts. "In the email, David asked me to get in touch with you, Jane. And if I couldn't reach you, then Detective Holt. I was supposed to share the password with you. My copy of the memory card was a backup for safekeeping. He knew that if I was reading that email, then something terrible must've happened to him." She pauses, wiping at her eyes. A gust of wind yanks at the collar of her jacket. "And it did. It did."

I rest a hand on her shoulder. "Were you at Isabel's house when Sean and I visited?"

"Yes. But I was scared. That's why I hadn't gone to the hospital, why I was hiding. I didn't know what was going on or who to trust. And I hadn't gotten the email from David yet."

"Have you used the password on the memory card? Have you seen the contents?"

She shakes her head. "I was too freaked out by then. I got in touch with your assistant instead. I can't deal with this, you know? I still have no clue what it's really all about. Asher

Temple has powerful friends. Compared to that? I'm nobody."

Sean leans forward. "Did David's email mention who was threatening him? Did he say anything about someone inside the government working with Asher?" He asks this gently, his demeanor far softer than the intensity he displays at times.

Gabriela is trembling, and I wonder how much longer she can hold together. "He didn't give me the specifics. Why couldn't he have just *told me*? Instead of all this secretive nonsense? Now David's gone, and it's too late. I can't go back and fix it. I...I can't..."

That's what it's like when something like this happens. Endless questions, running circles around your mind. I've been there before.

She holds out the envelope to me. The paper bends in the wind. "Will you take it? Will you try to make this mean something? *Please?*"

I gather her hands in mine, the envelope in both of our grasps. "Sean and I are going to do everything we can to punish whoever's behind this."

"Do you have a safe place to go?" Sean asks.

"Isabel—my mom—is waiting for me in Palm Springs, and from there, I don't know. We're just going to get away." She sniffs. "I hadn't spoken to my mother in years before this. But I didn't know where else to turn. Maybe it's one good thing that can come out of this. If nothing else."

I want to promise Gabriela that we'll get justice for David. But I can't do that. I can never promise results.

But I can promise that I'll fight like hell.

40

Sean

I follow Gabriela's car as we turn around to the eastbound side of I-10, then head into Palm Springs. I want to make sure she gets there safely.

Isabel is already waiting in the parking lot of a fast-food joint, and we wave goodbye as we head back toward the freeway.

"I hope she's okay," Janie says.

"You're doing all you can."

Janie and Gabriela spoke briefly about funeral arrangements for David. Tracey is going to take care of as much as possible, including her continued efforts to get in touch with David's estranged family. But funeral or no, Gabriela won't be able to return to West Oaks until we know it's safe. If David's enemies find out she had a memory card and the password, they'll assume she knows all their secrets.

"I just wish…" Janie trails off, her weary eyes focused on the mountains in the distance.

"I know." She's always trying to do more. My hand searches out hers, and she laces our fingers together, then leans over the cabin to rest her head on my arm. "Our job now is to get this evidence to the West Oaks DA's Office."

Janie nods against my shoulder.

It's about three and a half hours to reach West Oaks from here. Maybe more, depending on how traffic decides to treat us.

More than enough time to make phone calls to pave our way.

While Janie was talking to Gabriela, I was busy strategizing our next moves. I don't want to take the risk of stopping anywhere before this evidence is in the hands of a prosecutor. The special grand jury has already expired, but I'm sure there are other options, especially with whatever must be on this memory card. The prosecutors will know what to do.

But I have to make sure we're not intercepted by anyone from CBI or the state government. I'm only trusting West Oaks police and prosecutors with this.

I unlock my phone and hold it out to Janie. "We need to talk to Nicolas Dominguez."

She makes a face. "Is he really the best you can do? He was always in over his head."

I'm inclined to agree. Nicolas is the most junior deputy DA. But for that same reason, it's a lot less likely that anyone from the state would bother to tap his phone. I'm still operating in paranoid conspiracy mode. I'd be a fool to do anything else.

"Nic is what we've got," I say. "Until we can get this in front of either the district attorney himself, or Lana Marchetti when she gets back to town." The assistant district attorney would be the ideal person to handle this. But until Lana's back, we just have to do the best we can. "And he'll follow my directions, which is probably most important."

I can tell from Janie's face that she agrees.

She pulls up Nicolas's contact and hits the call button. I hear ringing. She's got it on speaker.

"Holt? Is that you?"

The kid's voice wavers. I pray he can hold his backbone together long enough to see us through today. "Yeah, it's me."

"Dude, it's been nuts around here. I heard about your fight with Winfrey at the hospital."

So much has happened since then. "That's not important. Where are you?"

"At the office. Why? Where are you?"

"On the road. Long story. Is this a good time to talk? It's sensitive. I'd rather keep the CBI and the state out of it."

"Um, hold on." I hear shuffling, and then a door closing. His voice has dropped to a whisper. "The attorney general's office prosecutors are in the conference room down the hall. What's this about?"

"David Daily. And Asher Temple."

I can hear the click when Nicolas swallows. "Aren't you suspended?"

"As far as CBI is concerned, I am. That's part of why I'd like to keep this quiet."

"Okay. But what's up? You're being all mysterious."

"I have something for you. Can we meet? In private?"

I tell him I'll text the location, and I ask him to bring a laptop. Last, I warn him not to tell anyone. He seems freaked out, but he promises to do as I say.

"Where do you want to meet him?" Janie asks.

I come up with a few options, then dismiss them. We don't want to be noticed, and we don't want to be out in the public, either.

Then I realize the obvious solution.

"My house. As far as I know, it's still a mess from the break-in. But it's been released as a crime scene. CBI won't have any more interest. It will be a good place for a private chat."

I have Janie use the burner to send my home address to Nicolas. After that, I drive five over the limit but no more. I doubt there's a BOLO out on Janie's car, but we can't risk getting pulled over.

There's a triumphant feeling growing inside me. Whatever evidence is on Gabriela's memory card, Asher Temple has been doing everything possible to keep it hidden. And we're about to bring it into the open.

I'm trying not to get overly confident. We haven't had the chance to confirm what the evidence is, or even if we can access it with the password Gabriela gave us. But Janie is smiling too, like she's battling the same feeling.

"The bastard's going down," I say.

Her lips twist viciously. "I can't wait to watch."

There are other logistics we'll have to address. Authenticating the evidence, for one. Establishing the proper chain of custody. Getting an affidavit from Gabriela about how she obtained it, how she handed it over to us. But Nicolas is the lawyer, and he can figure out that part.

There's something else I plan to do, whether he likes it or not. I'm going to make copies of the evidence on this card myself, and I'll send it to as many people as I can think of. To Detective Murphy, to my ex-partner at LAPD. Maybe to news outlets as well, though I'm less sure about that. I don't want to compromise a future trial. But after today, and after everything we've had to do to secure this evidence, I'm not going to let it disappear again.

If we're lucky, this whole conspiracy will unravel, and Asher's friends will abandon him. Whoever's helping him might turn on him. Or better yet, Asher will turn on his friends in the state government, and they'll be pointing fingers at each other all the way to prison.

I'll have to sort out my issues at work with Chief Liu. This stupid suspension. But I'm confident I'll be forgiven once this new evidence comes to light.

"I want you there at the meeting," I say to Janie. "This is our victory, you and me, and I don't intend to take the credit."

"Oh, trust me, I won't let you. But you and Nicolas will be talking prosecutor stuff. He won't want a defense attorney there. You can catch me up afterward."

"Technically, you're a witness."

"True, but that doesn't mean Nicolas wants me sitting in on your meeting."

I don't love the thought of leaving her out of this. And I don't really give a fuck what Nicolas thinks. But I see her point. "As soon as I'm done, I'll tell you everything."

I'm already imagining how the rest of today might go. I tap my fingers on the steering wheel, suddenly feeling nervous. "Would you come with me to pick up Mom and Henry afterward? I was thinking I'd take them to another hotel, since my house still needs some TLC. You could hang out with us. If you want."

For a moment, she doesn't say anything. And I figure I'm pushing. I'm asking for too much, too soon. She probably wants space after so much togetherness, and I don't blame her.

But then her eyes crinkle as her smile returns. "I'd love to see Liza and Henry, but we've all had enough hotel rooms, don't you think? Let's go back to your house. I can help with cleaning up. Let's get your mom and Henry back home."

"Really? You're up for that?"

"Why not? We can borrow tools from Chase to fix things that're broken. And we can stop by a store for cleaning supplies and whatever else you might need."

Some clothes would be good, since I've been wearing the

same ones for a couple days now, though they ran through the laundry at Janie's apartment. And maybe the Serpents left some of my stuff at the house intact.

I love this idea. Home sounds perfect. The more we talk about it, the more it feels right. My mom will love it, too.

"Let's do it," I say. "We can order some dinner. And you could stay the night, if you like. No pressure either way. We'd have to behave ourselves with my mom's bedroom next door."

She giggles. "Sure you can keep your hands off me, Holt? Are you that civilized?"

"Never mind. I'm definitely not." I wink. "Mom will just have to plug her ears."

Janie swats my chest playfully. But it sounds like she's up for staying over. She hasn't said no. I'm optimistic.

We descend into the LA basin, and I feel our world opening up along with the skyline. The future is full of possibility. I can't wait to find out what's in store for us. I'm holding a lot of wishes and hopes in my chest.

I guess moving out of West Oaks drove the cynic out of me after all. Thanks to Mom and Henry, in part, but also Janie. Her honesty and her kind heart and her unfailing loyalty.

We hold hands and talk for the rest of the drive. Half an hour from my house, Janie sends a text to Nicolas using the burner phone, and he confirms. As we near the coast, the sky turns pale gray. It's like the day of the courthouse shooting, rainy and dour. But nothing can bring down my mood.

This started over a week ago. Incredible how much has happened in the days—and nights—since.

Now, I'm holding the evidence against Asher Temple in my pocket, and this is almost, *almost*, finally over.

I park down the street from my house, not wanting Nicolas to see that Janie's here with me. I don't want him getting antsy and asking annoying questions or making comments. And he probably would. Nicolas is terrified of her. It's funny to me now that I know her. But not funny enough that I'd enjoy sitting through his complaints.

She's mine, and that makes me even more protective of her.

I switch off Janie's car. "You'll be okay here?"

She looks around. "I can't get into *that* much mischief. I'm just going to call Tracey."

"You'll wait for me?"

Janie rolls her eyes. "Hurry up already. We didn't stop for lunch, and I'm hungry."

"Hurricane Jane," I whisper, leaning in for a kiss.

She tilts her head, grabbing my shirt in her fist. I meant this to be a quick peck, but Janie takes it deeper. Her tongue teases mine. She sucks my lower lip, rolling it in her teeth. My toes are curling and my dick is starting to take notice.

Then she pushes me away. I growl, leaning in again, but her hands press firmly against my chest. "Hurry back," she says.

Evil. She's pure evil. And I hate to miss a single moment of it.

"See you soon." I get out and jog toward my house.

41

Janie

I watch Sean's ass in his jeans as he jogs down the street. Then I slump against the passenger seat of my car and sigh.

Sean still needs to confirm what's on that memory card. We don't know for sure that Gabriela's password will work. Will all our questions be answered? Is this David reaching out from the grave to take down the people who wronged him? I don't know. But we're so close.

It's as if the first rays of the sunrise are breaking over the horizon. All we have to do is be patient. Keep going, as if the rest is inevitable.

Sean unlocks the front door of his house and goes inside. It's a one-story bungalow, white wooden siding. Pale blue shutters on the windows. Flowers grow in window boxes beneath. An adorable house that I never would've expected Sean Holt to live in, yet it feels perfect for the family I've come to care for this past week.

Since leaving Tucson, I haven't been a part of something like that. Something...*precious*. I've had friends and I've had

Tracey. My clients. But it's not the same thing. Now I feel that craving under my skin. I don't even know what to call it yet, but it's a longing for something I didn't know I could have until now. Until Sean.

Ugh, I'm getting so mushy.

I take out my phone and call Tracey's number. She answers right away. "Hey, have you met with Gabriela?"

"We did. It was what we were hoping for." I'm still being cautious, not giving specifics over the phone. Tracey knows enough. "It's progress," I say. "Now I'm waiting while Sean handles the next part."

"Yeah? And how is Detective Holt?" Tracey's voice is teasing. "I was surprised you two were still hanging around together."

I look over at his house, settling back against the upholstery. Tiny raindrops are dotting the windshield. As I watch, Nicolas Dominguez gets out of a car and mounts the steps to Sean's front door. He's got a computer bag slung over his shoulder. He knocks. Goes inside.

"Sean went to Tucson with me. To Gran's memorial service."

"Did he? Well… That's…"

I can't help myself. I burst out laughing. "We were stuck under the same roof for almost a week. Things…happened."

"I guessed earlier, after video calling with you two. I have been dying for the details. But if he went to Tucson, it sounds like more than just a, you know, walk on the wild side."

We're both laughing. "It was definitely wild. And it still is. But it's a lot more than that. Sean's…" Amazing. Wonderful. Everything.

"Oh, Janie." Tracey's gone all melty. She's speaking in hushed tones. "You sound so happy. Like I've just delivered a whole box of neon glitter cookies to your door."

"He's much better than that. And all natural."

She snorts. "Be still my heart. You'd better give me some details, missy. I want to make sure Mr. Holt is good enough for you."

I spend a while sharing the story of how we got together. Not too much, of course, but I tell her all about Liza and Henry and what a great father Sean is. How I couldn't help but warm up to him after seeing him with Henry.

Then I talk about the memorial service and Gran. My heart squeezes, but the hurt isn't so raw.

"I'm glad Sean was there with you," Tracey says.

"So am I." I wonder if he and Nicolas are looking at the contents of the memory card yet. "Does Sean get your seal of approval?"

"It's looking that way. Are you back in West Oaks? I'd love to see you. And the minute you're ready to head into the office, I'll be there. I've been keeping things going from here, but it'll be a few weeks until we can dig ourselves out on all the matters I've had to push for your other clients."

I sigh. I've been expecting this. Thank goodness for Tracey, because I'd be in dire straits without her. "Maybe tomorrow. Maybe in a day or two. I know you're anxious to get back to normal, and I am too. Believe me. But I need to make sure things are settled. Sean got news this morning from his ex-partner at the LAPD. Apparently, there's been a purge inside the Serpents gang."

I explain what Sean learned—how someone murdered a dozen Serpents in LA, and Sean believes it's connected to the plot against us.

"I've been looking into the Serpents more as well," Tracey says. "Just because I was bored and wanted to feel like I was doing something."

"Oh? Find anything?"

"Maybe. That Serpent you did a consultation for? Jacob

Ritter? I did some research. Found out a little more about him. Remember I told you he's serving a sentence in California City?"

"Right." Ritter's the guy I rejected as a client. The one who left me those obnoxious voicemails for a while. "Anything interesting?"

"He ended up making a plea deal. That's why he only got four years, instead of all the enhancers the prosecutors could've gone for."

It makes sense. "Did you get a look at the transcript of his sentencing? Did the judge mention if Ritter gave information on the Serpents in exchange?"

"I haven't gotten the transcript, no. I could put in a request, but you know how that goes. Thirty days at least."

True. There's the bureaucracy to deal with.

"But here's what I thought could be interesting. The prosecutor who handled Ritter's case? It was Dominguez. Same deputy DA who was on David's case. I mean, I don't know what that means, but I just thought…"

Tracey's still talking, but I feel like a bomb has gone off inside my head.

Nicolas was the prosecutor on Ritter's case.

He would've spoken to Ritter. Would've known he was a Serpent.

Suddenly, *everything* looks different.

"Tracey," I say, interrupting her. "I'm sorry. I need to go."

"You do? Why? Is something wrong?"

"Maybe. I'm outside Sean's house. He's inside meeting with Nicolas Dominguez right now."

"Is that bad?"

"I don't know, I…" I can't even get my thoughts together, they're spinning so fast through possibilities. But I don't like what I'm seeing. Not at all. "Maybe this is nothing. But I need to call Sean."

"Wait, what's Sean's address? Janie, I want to know where you are."

I recite the address for her, then end the call without saying goodbye. Immediately, I try Sean's number.

No answer.

42

Sean

My house is cold and lifeless when I step inside. It's pretty much as I left it the last time I was here. Broken shit everywhere. The spilled food is really starting to stink.

I wish I could've dealt with this before now. I don't want Janie to have to do it. But I'm also incredibly grateful for her offer. Now that I'm back here, all I want to do is fix it. Erase the smears on the walls and throw away every last trace of the break-in. I want to put this house back together for my mom and Henry, make them feel safe and whole again.

But I won't be doing that alone. Janie will be here beside me.

There's a knock at my door, tearing me from the fog of conflicted feelings in my brain. There's no conflict about Janie, though. I wish she was here right now. She should be.

I go to open the door, and Nicolas steps inside. "Hey. Thanks for coming. Got the computer?"

He holds up his bag. "Yeah. Nobody saw me leave, not like they'd care anyway. You really sounded worried about the state prosecutors on the phone."

"There's a lot going on that you don't know."

I clear off the dining table. While Nicolas sets up his laptop, I try to explain what's been happening. His eyes keep getting larger, and he chokes out a cough.

"CBI? Really? Agent Winfrey's an asshole, but trying to *kill* you?"

"I didn't want to believe it either. But somebody's been working against me and Jane. Somebody sent the Serpents after us. And after Detective Murphy."

"Why, exactly? I get that you think this ties back to Asher Temple, but what were they trying to accomplish by killing you and Jane Simon and Murphy?"

I take the envelope from my pocket and hold it open, showing the tiny rectangle of plastic inside. "This. I'm about ninety percent certain this contains new evidence against Asher Temple. Something bad enough he was willing to kill to keep it secret."

Nicolas exhales, shoulders tightening. "Man, if you say so. I can see why you wanted to keep this under wraps. That's what the computer's for? To see what's on that memory card?"

"You got it." The kid's following along. I'm proud of him. "You got a card reader on your laptop?" If not, I've got an external adapter in a junk drawer somewhere in my house, assuming the Serpents haven't destroyed it.

But as I expected, Nicolas points to the side of his laptop. "Here. You can plug it right in."

I hold my breath as he opens a folder showing the contents of the tiny storage device. A window pops up.

"Password?" he asks.

I take out the paper Gabriela stowed inside the envelope. Nicolas enters the code, and the folder opens.

It's a single file. A video. Anti-climatic after all this. How could a single video be worth so much death and destruction? What's Asher Temple been so desperate to keep hidden?

I grab a chair, set it in front of the table, and sit down. Nicolas stands to my side, one hand braced against the back of my chair.

I double-click on the video. It starts to play. And at first, I just don't understand it. There's a sinking inside of me. Dread. Denial.

"What is this?"

Behind me, Nicolas says nothing.

But he's in front of me, too. On the screen. The Nicolas on the video speaks.

"Mr. Temple, I think we can come to an agreement that would be advantageous to us both."

On the video, Nicolas is sitting on the other side of a conference table, facing the camera. Another man speaks.

"I'm listening."

That's Asher Temple's voice. It looks like Asher is wearing the camera. Recording this interaction. But where's Asher's lawyer? It seems like it's only Asher and Nicolas in the room.

Behind me, there's a creak as Nicolas's hand tightens on the back of my chair. But I can't tear my eyes from the screen.

"The District Attorney has decided to convene a special grand jury to consider charges against you," Nicolas says in the video. *"And David Daily is now in talks with us to testify for the People's case. If I were you, I'd be very concerned."*

"What is it that you're proposing?" Temple asks.

"A deal. But not one that we'd file with the court."

"What the *fuck*?" My fists tighten, every part of me vibrating with fury. I rise in the chair and spin around to confront Nicolas.

But he's already grabbed my Glock from the holster at my lower back. He points it at me, backing slowly away.

The Nicolas on the screen continues talking. *"I could*

provide information. Steer things from within the DA's office. Make certain problematic evidence…cease being problematic."

"And in exchange?"

My guts are churning, and I might be sick.

With his free hand, Nicolas takes a smaller pistol from his pocket, aiming that one as well. "Don't, Sean. Don't you dare move."

Behind me, his voice continues to drone from the video. Making his demands for money.

"You sold out the DA's office?" I can't stop my hands from shaking. "You're the leak within the government. It was *you*." I take a step toward him, and Nicolas raises both weapons, aiming at my face.

This is the second time in days that I've had my own gun pointed at me. But with Proctor, I already knew he wasn't to be trusted. It was my own arrogance that got me into danger in that downtown LA alley.

This? This is betrayal. Like the way Alexis betrayed me, but so much worse. And I never saw it coming.

"Are you working with Agent Winfrey?" I demand. "Nixon Temple?"

"Shut up," Nicolas snaps. "Show me your ankles. If you try anything stupid, I'll shoot."

He wants to know if I have another weapon. I carefully lift the cuffs of my jeans, then straighten, raising my hands. I left the Ruger in the car with Janie.

Janie. I'm thankful she's not here. I don't want her anywhere near this place.

"I don't know how all of this went down," I grind out, "or what led you to join Temple's side. But this whole time, it's been the Serpents doing the dirty work. You're not going to shoot me."

Nicolas's eyes harden in a way I've never seen. "I'm standing here with a gun, and you're mocking me. You think

I'm a joke. Just like everyone else at the DA's office and at West Oaks PD. No goddamn respect."

"So you decided to sell us out in exchange for money? That's the kind of respect you wanted?"

"This entire system is rigged, anyway. It's all about who you know, how much money you have. Asher Temple was always going to walk, just because of who he is. Son of the governor. Silver spoon up his ass. What's the point of playing by the rules? Why shouldn't *I* get something?"

The justifications of criminals everywhere. I'm struggling to keep calm, even though I want to lash out. My vision feathers at the edges with barely contained rage. "But Asher must've hired the Serpents. Gangsters like that wouldn't have listened to someone like you." *A coward*, I want to say.

"I was the prosecutor on a case against a Serpent. Jacob Ritter. For the past year, I've been making side deals with defendants, and nobody knew. *I* had an in with the Serpents. Asher didn't do a thing for me. Neither did Nixon Temple. I did it all myself."

And he's so proud of it. The little shit. Nicolas wants to revel in beating me. Shove my nose in it.

"So you sent the Serpents to the courthouse. And here, to my home. They destroyed my son's things. My mother's things."

"I didn't tell them to do that. The Serpents have their own issues with you, Holt. I mean, look at this place. They had some resentment to work out."

"Was it their idea to kill me, too?"

"Nah, that was a mutual decision. I knew David sent copies of that video to you and Jane Simon. I couldn't be sure what exactly David had told you."

"But how did you know David had sent the evidence here to my house? And to Jane's office?" He doesn't answer, but the connection dawns on me. "The camera at David's apartment. Inside the light fixture. Was that yours?" That has to be it. He must've seen David making the memory cards and addressing the envelopes.

"I don't see the point of explaining it all to you."

"Because you're going to kill me?"

"I just don't know if your brain's big enough to understand."

"Yeah, you're the genius here, Nic. But you let yourself get caught on tape. You let Daily get his hands on that video. How was that smart?"

His hand is wobbling on the Glock, he's so pissed at me. "Because of Asher! All of this is his fault! He's the one who recorded our meeting, and the idiot stored that file on an online storage website. A storage site that *David Daily still had access to*. That's how much of a criminal mastermind Asher Temple is!"

I shift my weight. Broken porcelain and splintered furniture crunch beneath my shoes.

Does he have a plan? Is he trying to figure out what to do with me?

Nicolas is sweating. Nervous. I don't know if he's waiting for something to happen, or just waiting for his courage to appear.

I think I'm right. He *doesn't* want to shoot me. It's one thing to order someone's death, another to carry it out yourself. But that doesn't mean he won't.

I need an advantage. An opening.

"I don't get it," I say. "I thought Temple was threatening Daily. That's why Daily pulled his testimony."

Nicolas looks at me like I'm the idiot. "I was the one handling Daily. From almost the minute Daily agreed to his plea deal and offered to testify, I told him what would happen if he went through with it. I told him to keep delaying. We had to run out the clock on the special grand jury. I warned Daily that if he told anyone, if he opened his mouth about any of it, he and his fiancée were dead. He was always supposed to pull out of his plea deal at the last minute. But then? He found that video Asher Temple had saved."

"I'm sure that was a shock. To all of you."

"Daily said he'd keep the video secret, so long as everybody left him and his fiancée alone. It all should've worked out fine. But then I saw him on the camera I'd planted in his apartment. Making copies of the video onto memory cards. Addressing them to you and Jane Simon."

He wouldn't have known that Nicolas had password-protected those memory cards and set up a dead-man's switch. "And you panicked?"

"No, I figured out how to deal with it," Nicolas spits out.

"Which is when you recruited the Serpents. Through your connection to that one you'd met. Jacob Ritter."

"Good for you, Holt. You're getting the hang of it."

The real irony? If Nicolas hadn't arranged that shooting at the courthouse, David Daily would probably never have revealed that video. He would've served a prison sentence instead of testifying against Asher—because that would've kept Gabriela safe.

But instead? Nicolas's attack guaranteed that Daily's insurance policy, his dead-man's switch, would go into effect.

The day of the courthouse shooting, Nicolas intended to take out all the threats in one swoop. Kill Daily, Jane, and me. Find every copy of that video. But he didn't find the copy Daily had addressed to me, probably because Daily got cold feet—didn't know for sure if he could trust me.

Nicolas must've used his access to find out where Jane and I were staying under protective custody. He sent a Serpent to search our hotel rooms, hoping the extra copy of the video would turn up.

"It was you on the cameras at the station," I say. "You went into my office. You were looking for the evidence."

"I was the on-call DA that night. Got pulled in for a vehicular homicide, and I decided to take advantage of being there to check out your office." He shrugs. "Didn't find the second memory card, but I was trying to be thorough."

"And Detective Murphy? How did you know she'd found it?"

"She called me. Asked for my help getting the special grand jurors in place to hear new evidence. I went to meet her. I was trying to convince her to hand over the card when I heard your car pull up. I had no choice but to shoot."

Rage surges again. Murphy trusted him. I could've caught him that day, chasing him along the riverbed trail, and I failed.

Nicolas uses his forearm to wipe the sweat from his brow. "I packed my bags after. I was ready to run. But she didn't remember any of it."

I trusted Nicolas too. I never suspected. I thought it was CBI and Agent Winfrey working against us.

An idiot. A fool.

But I can't let anger—at Nicolas or at myself—cloud my judgment. I have to focus. Find his weakness, watch for my moment. That's when I'll strike.

"Enough questions," Nicolas says. "Where's Jane Simon?"

Anxiety crashes through me, turning my mind briefly to static. "Why?"

"Because she must know you're here."

"I haven't seen her in days. I don't have a clue where—"

"Don't lie to me," he roars. "You were in a hotel with her for days. When CBI showed up there, you both ran. *Together.* She was with you at Detective Murphy's. You've been working with her. Is she letting you fuck her, too?"

I take an involuntary step toward him, my fists clenching again.

His gaze is scrutinizing. Smug. "You *are* fucking her. Is she as ice-cold on the inside as she is outside? Surprised your dick didn't get frostbite."

"Shut your mouth."

A moment ago, Nicolas was furious at my dismissal of him. He was desperate for acknowledgment, approval.

But now, it's me who's barely holding onto control. Nicolas is manipulating me, and I'm letting him do it. But I can't calm this fire in my blood. I can't listen to him talk about Janie that way.

"For a senior detective, you have a terrible poker face," Nicolas says. "You're giving it all away. I'll bet she's the one who found the extra memory card that David stashed. He was her client, and she knew him a hell of a lot better than you did. And, no offense, she's smarter than you. So, where is she?"

I clamp my mouth shut. He watches me. I swear I don't move. I don't even flinch. I don't give a single thing away.

Then my phone buzzes in my pocket.

"Take it out," Nicolas says. "Slowly."

Heart racing, I dip into my pocket. Take out my phone. It's still vibrating, and the caller ID is on the screen.

"*Janie?*" He glances down at the phone, eyes flicking back up before I can move. "She's got her claws all the way into you, doesn't she?"

I want to smack her name out of his mouth. That doesn't belong to him.

I remember when she texted me that photo of Henry. That was before I'd called her Janie out loud, but my mother had. Ages ago. Now, it feels wrong to call her Jane. Like that's a formal name for people who don't truly know her.

Nicolas's eyes move from the screen and back to my face. "Is she waiting for you? Close by?"

"She doesn't know anything. She has no idea what's on that memory card. Just leave her out of it."

"But she must know I'm meeting with you. She'll figure out what must've happened when you don't leave this building. Besides, after all the shit she's pulled in the courtroom, she deserves what's coming."

My thumb hovers over the screen. Do I answer? Do I warn her?

Nicolas has both guns raised again. "Drop the phone."

The call ends, and I toss the device to the carpet in disgust.

Don't just stand here, I scream at myself. *Do something.*

"You're just going to kill us?" I sputter. "Here?"

"No, one of the Serpents is going to do it." He lifts his pistol, waving it. "They've been trying to kill you for days, and they're finally going to succeed. CBI will be happy to take the easy explanation. Especially since you've been complaining about the Serpents to anyone who will listen. I'll be the distraught colleague who finds you after it's already too late. Now call her back. Tell her to come inside."

"I won't. Go ahead and shoot me."

The black muzzle of my Glock stares me down, unblinking.

"Call Jane and tell her to come in. If you don't, I'll call your mother and have her come here instead, along with your son. It's your choice. You have two seconds to decide."

43

Janie

I run toward Sean's house. It's raining harder now, cold droplets landing on my cheeks and hair. I've got my phone in one hand, and the Ruger Sean left under the car seat is in my waistband.

Why didn't he answer his phone?

What's going on inside that house?

I can't really be thinking this. That Nicolas would turn on Sean, that he could be working for Asher Temple. But the more I consider, the more the puzzle pieces slot into place.

As a prosecutor with the DA's office, Nicolas would have access to a huge amount of information. He could manipulate the cases against both Asher and David Daily. He works closely with West Oaks PD every day, and he could've found out which hotel Sean and I were staying at.

He could've shot Murphy if she made the mistake of trusting him. And why wouldn't she? Sean trusted Nicolas too.

I never would've thought Nicolas capable of something like this. He's quiet, shy, the kind of weak-willed person who caves at adversity. Maybe he's working with CBI and Nixon Temple. Maybe Nicolas is just one cog in a vaster conspiracy.

But he's inside with Sean *right now*. If Sean's in trouble, I can't wait around. What if Nicolas has called for help, and his friends are on the way?

I can't let anything happen to Sean. I'm supposed to have his back.

It's only been a minute since my call to Sean's phone didn't go through. I've made it along the side of the house, and I peer into a window.

That's when I see them, and all my worst fears are confirmed.

Nicolas is holding two guns on Sean in the living room. Sean's face is murderous. His entire body is taut, a live wire of fury. He wants to tear Nicolas limb from limb. But he's standing there, stock-still, because he's cornered.

I need to get inside.

I remember downtown LA—how I flanked Carl Proctor and came around from the other direction. That's exactly what I need to do now. To catch him by surprise.

But as I look toward the rear of the house, I realize the back door is probably locked. Or even nailed shut, since that's where the Serpents broke in before. Sean and Nicolas both went through the front door.

That's my only way in. Head on. No sneaking around this time.

I glance again at the window. Nicolas has his back to the front entrance. I hurry to the front and quietly mount the steps. My hand finds the Ruger in my waistband. Holds it ready.

I press the latch on the door and throw it open. Nicolas starts to turn.

We both aim our guns at the same moment.

Nicolas has a gun on Sean, another on me. Sean's on one

side of him, hands empty. I'm in the doorway, raindrops slanting in behind me, my knuckles white as I hold the Ruger.

Sean's furious eyes dart from me to Nicolas's guns and back again. He does not look happy to see me.

"Jane," Nicolas says. "We were just talking about you."

Sean feints toward Nicolas, who takes two steps back, still aiming at us. Nicolas's shoe slides against broken ceramic shards on the carpet. He adjusts his balance.

"I guess we know who's been helping Asher Temple from within the state government," I say.

"I'm not helping anyone but myself." Nicolas keeps his profile to me as he tries to watch us at the same time. "I don't need the Temples. Asher needed *me*."

I see something in Sean's glare. He's blinking, glancing down. A message he's trying to beam into my brain. But what? I don't have a clue.

So I'll just have to do this my way.

"You were the prosecutor on Jacob Ritter's case," I say. "The Serpent? That's how you met?"

"Congratulations, *Janie*. Your boyfriend didn't know that part until I told him."

Sean flinches when Nicolas uses my nickname.

"Actually, Tracey found that bit of info. My assistant. I can guess how you got wrapped up in all this. You couldn't win your cases on your own, so you decided to cheat? I knew you were a shitty attorney, but I didn't realize you were *that* pathetic. How many tries did it take you to pass the bar exam, anyway?"

Nicolas's face screws up in a scowl. "You're a bitch, Simon. A conniving bitch."

Sean's eyes blaze at me, and this message is plenty clear. *What the hell are you doing?*

"And such original insults. I've never heard that one

before." My hands and my voice want to shake, but I keep them steady. "But I wouldn't expect much creativity from you. I know someone else planned this whole thing. Nixon Temple, right? I want to talk to the former governor or whoever's really in charge. It's clearly not you."

"I'm in charge! And you're going to—" Nicolas turns his head fully toward me, and that's when Sean lunges.

Sean crashes into Nicolas, grabbing for both weapons. A gunshot rings out. I scream and dive for the floor.

I look up to see Sean head-butt Nicolas in the face.

Both men land in a heap on the debris-strewn carpet beside me. In a blink, Sean is kneeling on Nicolas's back, wrenching the guns away. Nicolas keeps kicking his legs and fighting until he feels the muzzle of Sean's Glock against his neck. He's moaning. Blood pours from his nose onto the carpet beneath him.

Gasping, my ears ringing, I take my phone from my back pocket and call 911.

Then I realize the shrill sound in my ears isn't just from the gunshot.

Sirens blare, climbing in pitch.

In minutes, West Oaks PD officers burst into the room. Their shouts are muffled to me, but their lips move furiously. I drop the Ruger, put my hands up. One of the officers pushes me down.

There's momentary confusion as Sean sets down his weapons, offers his badge. Recognition when the patrol officers realize who he is.

I must have Tracey to thank for this police response. She must've called for help after I hung up with her. That could've turned out badly, but she did the right thing. Once again. I owe that woman a raise.

Soon, Sean's back on his feet and hauling me up against him. "Janie, you okay? Are you hurt?" His gaze moves over me like he's searching for injuries. The roar in my ears has faded to a whine.

"I'm good. What about you?"

"Okay, now." His lips pull into a frown. "Do you have any idea…"

"How dangerous that was? Yeah. I do."

"You decided to provoke a guy holding a gun."

"Where would I have ever learned something like that?"

"That doesn't matter. You shouldn't have done it." Shaking his head, Sean pulls me into a kiss. His tongue sweeps into my mouth, possessive and demanding. Like our argument is officially over, simply because he's had the last word.

But when he kisses me like that, I'm happy to give up and let him win.

∼

It's not long before rain is lashing the windows and Sean's house is swarming with law enforcement. Agent Winfrey from the CBI struts in through the front door.

"Holt. You'd better start explaining yourself."

Sean shares a long look with me. "Sure. We can spare a few minutes."

Winfrey eyes me, and then where our hands are clasped. "Ms. Simon, someone from patrol will take you to the station. You can speak with us there."

I'm about to protest, but Sean gets there first. "No, she stays with me. Most of what you want to know is on that laptop, thanks to her." Sean nods toward the table, where Nicolas's computer still sits. "If Janie goes, I go."

I shrug. I think we've both finally learned that lesson. We're safer together. Stronger together.

Nicolas has already been placed under arrest and taken away. Officers have been asking questions, taking photos, marking items as evidence. The usual scene processing.

Police Chief Liu and Agent Hartford come in, traipsing more wet footprints over Sean's ruined carpet, and we all gather around Nicolas's laptop.

Following Sean's instructions, an officer wearing gloves uses the laptop's track pad to mouse over to the video file.

Everyone in the room watches in silence as Nicolas makes his offer to Asher Temple. Agent Winfrey's face turns nearly purple. "Where did you get this?" he demands.

Sean opens his hand, gesturing toward me.

"David Daily found it," I say. "And he gave a copy to his fiancée, Gabriela Torres. She turned that copy over to us. Nicolas was behind everything. He hired the Serpents, he set up the courthouse shooting. He shot Murphy. All because of this video file."

"And why didn't you bring it to me?" Winfrey demands. He's turned back to Holt, like I'm irrelevant.

I cross my arms. We both know Winfrey isn't actually part of a conspiracy against us, but he's still an asshole. "Because you suspended Sean and your investigation is worthless. You've messed this up from day one. You should be groveling at Sean's feet for handing you Nicolas and all the answers."

Sean drapes his arm around my shoulders. "Jane's being modest. She did some of the work. Almost half of it."

"*Hey*." I poke him in the side, and he smirks down at me before dropping a kiss onto my nose.

There's some uncomfortable foot shuffling and throat clearing among the others. And I figure, what the hell?

I pull Sean down for a real kiss. Tongues and lips connecting, tangling. I feel him smiling against my mouth.

"Alright, alright." Chief Liu has a hint of amusement in his tone, which might be a first. "We've got the idea. Let's get the rest of this evidence bagged up and head back to the station. I want to know everything. The where, what, when, who and why. And Holt—you're not suspended. As far as I'm concerned, you never were."

"Is that an apology?" I snap. "He deserves one." So do I, but I'm realistic.

Sean leans in, his smile brushing my ear. "Ease off, Hurricane Jane. I love it when you defend me, but I can take it from here."

∽

THAT NIGHT, AFTER FAR TOO MANY HOURS WITH MY new besties at West Oaks PD, Sean and I head to Chase Collins's house. We stay for dinner, explaining everything that's happened. Liza remains stoic through the story, but when I describe how Nicolas almost shot Sean and me, she pales.

"But Janie was there to save the day." Sean's bouncing Henry on his knee. The joy on his face when he held his son again was priceless. And Henry's smile at his dad could've lit up the sky. I don't think I could ever get tired of seeing that effortless love.

"I hardly saved the day. I just pissed off Nicolas enough to distract him."

Sean nods. "It's one of your greatest talents."

Liza shoots a warning look at her son. "Unfortunately, it sounds like our house is a crime scene. Yet again. Just when Chase and Ruby thought they might be rid of us."

Our hosts start to argue that they're happy for everyone to stay as long as they like, but I have a better idea. There's not enough room here at the Collins residence for Sean and me anyway. And I know that Sean wants to be with his family. They've been apart for long enough.

"Why don't you three stay with me at my apartment?" I ask. "It's not huge, but I have a guestroom."

"You sure?" Sean asks softly.

"I wouldn't ask if I wasn't." I squeeze Sean's knee beneath the table, and Henry reaches over to grasp my ear.

After lots of hugs and thank-yous to Chase and Ruby, we head to my place. Liza and Sean set up the pack-and-play crib in one corner of the living room, and I set out some fresh towels for Liza in the guestroom. Henry resists going to bed, wanting to play with his dad instead. But eventually, Henry's down, and all the lights in my apartment are low.

Liza excuses herself next, heading for the guestroom. "I just downloaded a new romance, and I can't wait to start. I'll see y'all in the morning." She gives me a kiss on the cheek, hugs Sean, and shuts the door with a wink.

Sean turns to me, hands in his jeans pockets. "Should I sleep out here on the sofa?" he whispers.

I glance at the little sleeping form in the portable crib. "Do you need to? For Henry?"

"I'd hear him if he yells for me. Trust me, that kid has lungs. I meant..." He tilts his head. "Can I share your bed?"

"I was hoping you would." I tug him into my room and close the door. "We're better together. Or have you already forgotten?"

We shower first, washing away everything that's happened today. The long drive back to California, the worry and turmoil. I've already checked in with Tracey by phone to update her, and I've called Gabriela Torres too.

Sean and I have been going nonstop for hours upon hours. Hard to believe we spent last night making love and woke up happy this morning. I want to get back to that. This miraculous connection that we've made in the last week. Sean and me, together.

It's not us against the world anymore. We're out the other side, past the danger and the mysteries and the fear.

Just us. That's what I want right now. What I need.

In the shower, we kiss and run our hands over each other. We wash each other's hair and skin. Then Sean pushes me up against the tile wall. He goes to his knees, drapes my thigh over his shoulder, and tongues between my legs. The spray of the water runs down his back. Droplets sit like tiny jewels on his eyelashes. He licks and sucks my sensitive folds, his fingers working in and out of me until I'm arching against the shower wall and barely holding back my shouts. My body is alive with electricity. Pleasure shoots along my thighs and my stomach.

My orgasm shakes me to my core and leaves me breathless. Almost unable to stand. He shuts off the water and lifts me up into his arms. Sean doesn't even bother drying us off.

He carries me to the bed, pushing down the blankets before he lays me down. Water rolls from my hair and face, and he kisses the drops as they slide down my skin. He grabs the blankets. Pulls them over us.

I chase his mouth with mine, wrapping my legs around him to bring him close. Sean tastes like rain water and summer sun. His erection is hard and hot against my stomach.

"Want you in me," I murmur. "I can't get enough."

His thick cock pushes inside of me, spreading me open. I whimper at how good he feels.

Earlier, we joked about the awkwardness of having his family nearby for this. But we're both quiet, caressing each other with gentle reverence. We sigh into each other's mouths.

This lovemaking doesn't feel like something illicit that we're hiding. It's sweet and soft and beautiful.

His hips thrust faster. The blankets fall away. His shaft is slicked in my wetness, every part of him so warm he's radiant. He dives forward and sucks my nipples between his lips, one then the other. I bite down on my lower lip. Sean's fingers dig into my hip.

"Janie." His voice is rough and dark and rumbly. "Tell me you're mine."

There's something so raw about him. No pretensions, no facade. Sean wants to have me exactly as he chooses, and nothing—except me—will hold him back.

"I'm yours," I whisper, breathless, panting. "Just yours. Only yours."

When he comes, he makes that sexy growl I love and presses his face into my neck. I feel the hot pulse of his cock, the spill of his release. Filling me.

Groaning, he lies down next to me and rolls me on top of him. Sean drags his fingertips up and down my back.

"I mean it," he says. "I want you to be mine. Exclusively."

"Good." I snuggle against him. "That's what I want, too." For me, it's not even a question.

44

Janie

Quietly, I tip-toe out of my bedroom, closing the door so I won't wake Sean. Henry's delighted giggles ripple through the living room. Sunlight dances through the gaps in the curtains.

"Hey, cutie pie." I lift him out of his pack-and-play, stopping to change his diaper before we head into the kitchen. "Hungry for some breakfast?"

I pick up a ripe avocado from the counter, and he reaches for it. "Hold on, let's wash hands."

A couple of minutes later, Henry's in the portable high chair Liza brought to my apartment. He squishes avocado cubes in his fist on the way to his mouth. The coffeemaker gurgles on the counter.

It's our third morning waking up at my place. Sean and his family have been staying with me, and we've got a bit of a routine going. Henry and I wake up first. I get breakfast cooking, while Sean and Liza sleep in. Then it's work for Sean and me. Back here after, for dinner and conversation and laughter.

For the first time, my apartment's filled with life when I get home.

We've just been drawing out the inevitable, easing back toward normalcy after the chaos of running for our lives. It's been fun, though. Every moment of it.

Henry's on the second half of the avocado when Sean emerges. He's wearing sweatpants and nothing else. He packed up some of his clothes from his house when we were there last—the day all the truth came out, and Nicolas was arrested.

He rubs his face, padding over to the kitchen. "Morning, counselor."

"Morning, detective."

He winks at me. Sean's shared my bed each night they've been here, and Liza absolutely knows. Her frequent smirks and teasing have made that clear. But we've avoided kissing in front of Sean's mother or Henry. I'm not sure why. Maybe that would be a little too...official. We've agreed not to see anyone else, but that's not the same as naming this thing between us.

I'm happy enough to figure it out day-by-day. We've both got plenty to stress about as it is.

On his way to the coffeemaker, Sean's fingers brush my leg and squeeze. My whole body lights up with affection. Anticipation. Memories of the nights we've shared make my skin flush with heat.

It's too soon to be falling this hard for Sean. I know that. But I'm well on my way. I see what's coming. The goal line is downhill, and I'm careening straight toward it. No way to stop this momentum, even if I wanted to.

"Don't forget," I say. "We're supposed to meet everyone at your house at nine."

Sean pours a cup of coffee. "Yeah, I'd better rouse my

mother. It takes her a solid half hour to get out the door sometimes. She's worse than Henry."

Later today, all of our mutual friends are meeting at Sean's to get his house cleaned up and repaired. Sean will finally move his family back into their home. I'm sure he's looking forward to it. I'm excited for him, though it means my apartment will go back to being empty tonight.

My bed will be lonely, too.

Sean pinches my butt beneath the line of the counter. "Maybe we could sneak in a shower for two before we have to leave?"

I like that idea, but there's a twinge of bitterness in my chest at the same time. "Hoping to get one more for the road?"

"What does that mean?"

I roll my eyes at myself. "I don't know. Ignore me. I'm being weird." I turn toward the fridge, but Sean stops me, hand on my waist. Henry's watching us and eating avocado.

"Are you okay?"

"Yeah. I'm having a great morning." I squeeze him back, going for his meaty thigh. "And if we make that shower happen, it'll get even better."

He smiles, but there's something in his eyes. Hesitation? Worry?

I don't want to spoil today. This is happy news, getting back to our lives. Getting Henry and Liza—and Sean—back into their home where they belong.

I'm just not sure this apartment will feel like *home* anymore after they've left it. Now that I know what I've been missing out on.

Someone to come home to. Someone to wake up with. Giggles and shared quiet moments and goofy smiles.

Family.

I pop some bread in the toaster, feeling Sean studying me.

At five past nine, we pull up on Sean's street. Tracey's already there, waiting on his front stoop with a bucket full of cleaning supplies. I give her a big hug. Chase and Madison Shelborne are here too, joking and slapping Sean on the back. Tanner—the former Navy SEAL who works for Bennett Security—and his girlfriend Faith arrive next.

We all bundle into Sean's house, everyone commiserating about the mess, and we get to work.

The last three days have been busy with the aftermath of Nicolas's arrest. Tracey and I have been digging our way out at my office—both literally and figuratively—and I'm well on my way to fighting back the chaos. It's been client meetings, strategy sessions, and court filings nonstop.

I've been in touch with Gabriela Torres, who agreed to return to West Oaks and tell the police everything she knows. I've been helping her make funeral arrangements for David, and the service will be held next week.

Sean's been keeping me updated about the goings-on at West Oaks PD. CBI has packed up and left with little fanfare. No apologies from Winfrey, but no further accusations either. Chief Liu grilled Sean one afternoon over our rogue investigation. But we solved the case, caught the bad guy, and delivered the evidence. Can anyone honestly complain?

The LAPD has also made arrests in the massacre at the Serpents' headquarters. Two members, both with ties to Jacob Ritter, have been charged with the killings. Camera footage confirms they're the same two Serpents who shot up the courthouse. Who murdered David.

Sean figures that Nicolas wanted to get rid of anyone who knew about his deal with the Serpents. Ritter decided to take advantage, recruiting his allies in the gang to take out the other leaders. Ritter was probably hoping to seize power

The Six Night Truce

once he finished his current prison sentence. But now, with the new conspiracy charges the West Oaks DA will file any day, Ritter won't get out of prison for a long time.

It would be harder to prove that Asher Temple had a role in Nicolas's murderous plans. But with that video showing he agreed to a bribery scheme, Temple's lawyers are begging for a plea deal. I doubt he'll see much prison time, but the West Oaks DA's Office needs some good press after this. I'm sure they'll drive a hard bargain with Asher's lawyers, including millions of dollars in restitution for the victims of Asher's fraud.

As for Nixon Temple, the ex-governor has been quietly contributing to victim advocacy groups and compensation funds. We have no proof that he had any involvement in any bribery or in Nicolas's scheme. We'll probably never know.

"Need some help?"

I look up from sweeping the kitchen floor and see Detective Murphy. She's got her arm in a sling, a colorful scarf tied over her hair.

"Murphy!" I say. "You're back on your feet."

"Heck, yeah. About time." She rolls her eyes. "I thought the doctors would never let me out of there."

Sean and I have been to see Murphy in her hospital room. We delivered dinner and cupcakes, and also all the news she'd missed. Murphy still doesn't remember Nicolas shooting her, and doesn't even remember contacting him that day. But the call log for a cubicle near her desk showed a call to the DA's office the day she was shot.

"Where's Holt?" she asks. "Shouldn't he be present and accounted for? Or is he planning to let the rest of us do all the work?"

I glance down the hall. "I think he's in Henry's room. But you should be relaxing and enjoying your leave. Not doing Sean's chores."

"Don't worry, I'm just here to supervise. Besides, someone stopped by the station, and I knew she'd want to be here, too."

Murphy steps aside, and Lana Marchetti—the West Oaks Assistant District Attorney—waves at me. I laugh and pull her into a hug, dropping the broom on the floor.

"Lana! I thought you weren't due back until next week."

"That was the plan. Then I went and checked my email and found out what's been going on." She pulls back from me, a wry smile on her lips. "This is why Max and I waited so long to take our honeymoon in the first place. This town can't last a week without things going haywire."

She helps me tidy the kitchen while we catch up. Lana's going to take over the prosecution of Nicolas and the Serpent members who took part in the plot. Thank goodness, because I know Lana will do an incredible job. She and I might be on opposite sides much of the time, but we're good friends.

And because of her ties to Bennett Security, it seems she's already heard some rumors floating around about Sean and me.

"So," she says, "what's this about you and Detective Holt cozying up when you were in protective custody?"

I tell her the short version, and I feel myself blushing. Lana and I have our heads bent together, giggling, when Sean and Detective Murphy wander through the kitchen. Sean's questioning look sets off another wave of breathless laughter. The top prosecutor and the top defense attorney in West Oaks, gossiping like a couple of schoolgirls.

"You've been together every night since?" Lana whispers. "That seems big. Right?"

"We've agreed to be exclusive. Beyond that? I don't know. I just know I've never felt this way before." I wipe off the counters, needing something to keep my hands busy. "How did you know Max was the one?"

Lana tilts her head thoughtfully. "I fell in love with him at nineteen. Fell hard. It took us ages to figure it all out, but deep down, I always knew. I don't think time has anything to do with it. It's this ache, you know? This emptiness that opens up inside you, and you realize the other person was always meant to fill it."

"The hard-nosed assistant DA is a romantic? Stop the presses."

She bumps my shoulder. "Don't hate. Pretty sure Jane Simon is a secret romantic, too."

"You know, you really should call me Janie."

∼

It's late in the afternoon when I catch up with Sean again. He's in his bedroom, putting a fresh set of sheets on his mattress. The house is finally looking tidy, more like a normal living space and less like the scene of a crime spree.

"Want to order pizza?" I ask. "No pineapple, obviously."

"Obviously. But yeah, good idea. I should feed all these people who're helping me."

I shake my head, leaning against the doorway. "You shouldn't make messes for other people to clean up."

"Rude of me, isn't it?"

"Very. But you do like attention."

Laughing, Sean pulls me into the bedroom, shutting the door. The voices in the other rooms are muffled. He presses me against the closed door, his body fitting against mine. Thighs, stomachs, chests, not exactly aligned, yet fitting just right together. Last, our lips, lingering in a soft kiss.

"You heading back to your place tonight?" he asks.

I play with the collar of his T-shirt. "That was the plan. I mean, I should. Right?"

"Probably."

"We can't keep living together. We've barely been dating a week. That would be fast."

"It would. I've got my place, you've got yours."

"Exactly. Yeah."

He runs his hands down my arms. "But…spending the night isn't the same as moving in. It doesn't have to be a whole thing. You could stay over tonight. I mean, why not?"

I look up at him. Excitement is doing funny things to my chest. "Would Liza be okay with that? If I stay over?"

"She'd love it. Mom loves having you around."

"I like being around too. Around Liza and Henry. And you."

"I *really* like being around you." Sean's gaze paralyzes me, stealing my breath. It's tender and smoldering and irresistible. "Stay. But tomorrow, we might want to sleep at your place instead, just to give my mom a break. You can get noisy. When we're…you know."

"*Me?*"

"Yep, you." He kisses me. "Spend the night with me, Janie," he whispers. Another kiss. "Spend every night with me."

What can I do but say yes? I enjoy battling with Sean, but it's even more fun to give in.

EPILOGUE

Sean

"Okay, buddy." I hand Henry the bouquet of tulips. "You got this?"

He nods. "'Kay, Daddy." I beam at him. At two, Henry is still a man of few words, but he's got that one down.

He holds the bouquet aloft in both hands, his little face drawing up with seriousness. I don't think he fully gets what's going on, but he knows this is a big deal. He probably sees that I've been sweating it and working up to it.

I grab the tray. It has a plate of chocolate-chip french toast, berries, and a cup of black coffee. Janie's favorite breakfast. I woke extra early to make it, and miraculously, she's not up yet.

Here goes nothing.

I push into our bedroom. I have to pause a moment in the doorway to admire her. Janie's dark hair is spread over the pillow, her lips in a pout as she sleeps. She's wearing one of my West Oaks PD T-shirts. I happen to know she's got nothing underneath.

"Hi!" Henry shouts.

Janie blinks. "Hi, Henry," she says blearily. "You two are up early."

I slide the tray onto the bed beside her. "We had a project." Henry's jumping up and down with the flowers, though he's still holding them carefully in front of him.

Janie sits up, yawning. "Breakfast in bed? This is so sweet. What's this for?"

"It's Mother's Day."

She drags in a breath, hand covering her mouth, eyes going wide. "For me?"

"Yeah, why not?"

I'm trying to be all cool and casual, though inside I'm a swirl of nerves.

It's been almost a full year since the shooting at the West Oaks County Courthouse threw us together. I know David's death is still a tough subject for Janie. But since then, every day with her has only gotten better. Every night especially.

For the past year, we've spent only a handful of nights apart.

At first, we switched between my house and Janie's apartment. We folded our lives together into something new and unexpected, and I'd never imagined I could be that happy. Janie, to her credit, threw herself completely into our new family unit. My world suddenly went from three to four. And just like when Henry first came into my life, Janie's presence felt natural. Like we were always meant to be together.

I would come home from a late night at work to find her and my mom drinking wine and laughing. Or, God forbid, sharing those Navy SEAL romance novels. I'd wake up some mornings and find Janie cuddling and giggling with Henry, reading him books, playing games.

About six months ago, my mom moved out of the house that she and I shared. She'd met a man at her YMCA fitness class and fell head-over-heels in love. He's a retired Navy lieutenant commander, a great guy, though I'll admit I let him sweat a little before giving my approval.

Right after that, I asked Janie to move in officially with me and Henry. We'd already shared I-love-yous by then, already knew we were in it for the long term. But even then, I wasn't sure exactly where we'd end up.

We've traveled to Houston to see my brothers and their families. We've made several trips to Tucson, including spending Christmas there with Janie's sister Pam. We've gone camping in Yosemite and the Grand Canyon and watched the stars together.

Janie and I have had long conversations about what we both want out of life. I never wanted to push her into being a "mom" if she wasn't comfortable with that role or ready for it. One night, Janie told me that she'd always doubted that she'd be a good mom. I think it's because of her history with her own mother. *But I want that*, she whispered. We were curled in bed together after making love. *I want to have kids. And Henry...that's how much I care about him.*

I think she was nervous, telling me that. She wasn't sure how I'd react. But it was the best thing I'd ever heard. Janie's got the biggest heart of anyone I've met. How could I not be ecstatic about her loving my son?

She even tracked down the contact info for Alexis, my ex, and persuaded Alexis to visit Henry again. Janie asked for my permission first, of course. But that's how incredible and big-hearted my Janie is. She's already the best mom Henry could ever hope for. The best girlfriend to me.

She's a damn good lawyer, usually giving the West Oaks DA's Office—or West Oaks PD—hell. She tries to avoid cases where I'm the lead detective because it's a possible conflict of interest. Not that she'd ever take it easy on me during cross-examination. Holiday parties were interesting. But most of my colleagues are used to it now. Slowly, they're saying "Holt and Simon" instead of "Holt and that defense attorney."

At home, we have lively debates about the justice system that sometimes veer into arguments. But they always end up in the same place—hot make-up sex. I'm not above kissing her to end the discussion.

Janie and I don't always agree, but I'm always proud to call her mine.

But is that enough for me? Nah. I want more.

Henry dumps the tulip bouquet unceremoniously into her lap. Then he tries to climb up next to her, and I grab him around the middle before he can jump on the mattress and spill Janie's coffee. "Hey, careful."

She smiles and smells the flowers. "Thank you both. This is a wonderful surprise."

Then I realize that Henry has a surprise for us too, but it's not so wonderful or sweet-smelling. "Uh, hold that thought. Diaper change needed. Stat." I dash to Henry's room and change him. "Just couldn't wait, could you?"

We're on our way back to the master bedroom when Janie gasps. "*Sean?*" Her voice is sharp. Almost panicked.

With my son under my arm, I run into our room.

Janie's holding the flower bouquet in her shaking hands, fingering the red ribbon tied around the stems. "What is this?"

There's a diamond ring threaded on the ribbon.

"I had this all planned out, I swear. I didn't account for diaper emergencies." I stand by the edge of the bed. Henry stops squirming in my arms, watching me and Janie like he's realized this is it. This is the moment.

Please let this be good news. Please let her be happy.

I clear my throat. "I love you. We both love you. You're already part of our family."

The Six Night Truce

Janie's covering her face with her hands. Tears streak between her fingers.

"I want you as my partner in life. The person I wake up to every morning. I want you to be Henry's mom, and hopefully we can give him some siblings. I just…I want everything with you. The debates and the battles and the making up after. All the happiness and all the love."

I go down on my knee, sitting Henry on the lifted one. My heart spins and races out of control, ready to burst. Whatever she says, I'm not sure I can take it.

"Janie, will you marry me?"

She wipes her face on the collar of my shirt she's wearing. "Yes. Of course it's yes. I love you. I love you both so much."

My chest heaves, and I make a sound that's part laughter, part relieved moan. Henry and I climb into bed with her, and she kisses Henry's forehead, and then my lips. I untie the diamond ring and slide it onto her finger, almost knocking over her coffee cup with my foot before I right it just in time.

We spend the morning there, feeding each other french toast. Henry ends up eating most of it. Janie and I keep kissing gently and staring into each other's eyes.

I'm a simple guy. I could be happy with just this for the rest of my days—my son grabbing my ear to get my attention, the woman I love cuddled close beside me. The woman who loves us both.

But eventually, we have to get up and get dressed. I send Mom a quick text. It's just two characters. A diamond ring emoji, and a check mark. She texts back the "mind blown" emoji, which is perfect.

Janie is going to be my wife. She's already Henry's mom in every way that counts. Mind blown indeed.

In a bit, we're meeting Mom and her boyfriend for a Mother's Day lunch at a trendy new spot on Ocean Lane. My mom's choice. I'd prefer a diner or burger joint, but that's okay. What matters is that we're all together, even if the food's overpriced and has ingredients I've never heard of. I'm happy to share it with the people I love.

That's what I want with Janie and Henry. All the moments. All the nights. Everything. Together.

The End.

~

Next from Hannah Shield—Madison gets her happily-ever-after in THE FIVE MINUTE MISTAKE.

He's my instructor. He's way out of my league.
And he's the twist I never saw coming.
One kiss will put everything—even our lives—at risk.

ALSO BY HANNAH SHIELD

LAST REFUGE PROTECTORS

Hard Knock Hero (Aiden & Jessi)
Bent Winged Angel (Trace & Scarlett)
Home Town Knight (Owen & Genevieve)
Second Chance Savior (River & Charlotte)
Iron Willed Warrior (Cole & Brynn)

- And more coming soon -

∼

WEST OAKS HEROES

The Six Night Truce (Janie & Sean)
The Five Minute Mistake (Madison & Nash)
The Four Day Fakeout (Jake & Harper)
The Three Week Deal (Matteo & Angela)
The Two Last Moments (Danny & Lark)
The One for Forever (Rex & Quinn)

∼

BENNETT SECURITY

Hands Off (Aurora & Devon)
Head First (Lana & Max)
Hard Wired (Sylvie & Dominic)
Hold Tight (Faith & Tanner)
Hung Up (Danica & Noah)
Have Mercy (Ruby & Chase)

∼

ABOUT THE AUTHOR

Hannah Shield once worked as an attorney. Now, she loves thrilling readers on the page—in every possible way.

She writes steamy, suspenseful romance with feisty heroines, brooding heroes, and heart-pounding action. Visit her website at www.hannahshield.com.